BREATHLESS ECSTASY

Chingue's hands had grown bolder with his passion, and now, gently caressing her, he began pressing her body lightly against his.

"Without you, Amanda, there is no life within me. I wish to bind you to me forever, to make my body part of yours, as you are part of me. Do not refuse me," he pleaded with a sudden depth of passion that touched Amanda's heart.

His hands moved sensuously up her back until they cradled her neck, and he bent his head to run his mouth slowly along the slender whiteness of her throat. Amanda felt unaccustomed shivers of delight as his mouth slowly descended, tracing the line of her collarbone with his tongue, then on to her shoulder. In an ever-descending motion, his mouth followed the curve of her firm young breasts, and she gasped at the sudden surge of emotion she felt inside her.

"Chingue," she cried in a desperate voice, clutching his head tightly to her breast. "Please stop. My heart is pounding so hard I'm sure it will burst."

"No, Amanda." A tremor of passion was obvious in his breathless reply. "It will not burst, but expand to take me in...."

ELAINE BARBIERI

CAPTIVE ECSTASY

LOVE SPELL BOOKS NEW YORK CITY

LOVE SPELL®

October 1997

Published by

Dorchester Publishing Co., Inc.
276 Fifth Avenue
New York, NY 10001

ISBN 0-505-52224-1

The name "Love Spell" and its logo are trademarks of Dorchester Publishing Co., Inc.

Printed in the United States of America.

One

August 8, 1757—*The battered lady was still standing, but only barely. Heavy cannon smoke clinging to the humid summer air shrouded her in a floating diaphanous curtain, almost obscuring the late afternoon sun. Its acrid odor permeated even her dankest reaches. Despite her staunch supporters and valiant stand, the horrendous toll taken in five days of siege and shelling from French cannon had left her northwest bastion devastated, most of her artillery useless, and had reduced her brave defenders from a meager 500 to an ever dwindling 200 in number. Her casement rooms sheltered, however inadequately, an overflowing number of wounded and dying. The men of Speakman's Company of Rangers, at the first sign of attack, had fled their nearby camp and brought their women and children behind her walls for protection, bringing the total within to 1700.*

Outside her weakened and crumbling walls, the Marquis de Montcalm's attacking force of 6000 French and Canadian regulars and 1700 Indians awaited with growing impatience her demise. Sadly, they were not to be kept from their victory much longer, for Fort William Henry, Britain's gallant lady, proud mud-and-log sentinel of strategic Lake George, was soon to succumb.

The monotonous din of the French cannon was steady and devastating, reverberating in her head like the beat of a huge, monstrous drum. Its deadly music was accompanied by the sickening sounds of splintering and falling wood and the crackle of occasional flames. The combined odors of gunsmoke, charred wood and death caused a momentary heaving sensation in her stomach. Taking quick, surreptitious breaths, the petite young colonial swallowed hard, willing herself back to normalcy as she struggled to regain her composure. Guiltily glancing around the room, she quickly brushed away the tears that had so easily filled her eyes. She was immensely relieved to see in the tense, solemn faces around her that each was engrossed in her own private thoughts; her own temporary weakness had gone unnoticed. She turned again to her task of making bandages for the wounded, her mind rebelling at what was proving to be an endless task. What was the use in pretending? The bandages would be used up as quickly as they would be delivered to the casement rooms housing the wounded, and were so pathetically inadequate in the face of the need she had seen there earlier in the day, that they would be almost useless.

She couldn't seem to shake the picture of the wounded from her mind, or the room's breathtaking stench of sweating, unwashed bodies, blood, rotting flesh and human excrement from her nostrils. Their agony and despair had filled her with horror, and she had fled ashamed and disgusted with herself as she had retched uncontrollably. Now, only a few hours later, her stomach was again beginning to prove her master.

"Blast!" she whispered under her breath, "It won't happen again!" She couldn't face Robert if she again allowed fear to assume control of her emotions. He had come upon her immediately after she had fled the casement rooms. The heartrending moans of the wounded were still echoing in her ears, and she had been hardly coherent as she had sobbed, "Don't look at me, Robert. I'm so ashamed of myself. But it was so ghastly. They were all so sick, just lingering in misery and dying. One of the militiamen from New Jersey—he was really only a boy—wanted me to hold his hand. Robert, his whole arm was gone and he didn't know it! I ran out, and then I was sick. I didn't even help him. What's the matter with me, Robert? Why didn't I help him?"

"There's nothing wrong with you, Amanda. Just try to forget what you've seen. Don't think about it anymore. It won't do you any good to torment yourself. It's all over now and even if you had stayed, there wasn't much you could've done for that poor boy."

"But I could've comforted him."

"You shouldn't have gone down there in the first place." His voice was angry. "It was no place for you. You're too young to be faced with that nightmare."

"That boy wasn't too young. He was close to my age."

"I told you, forget everything that happened!"

7

Robert's voice became sharper. He couldn't bear to see her torment herself. "Do you think you're the first one who ever panicked? We've all reacted the same way at one time or another. You have no reason to hate yourself."

"I was a coward, Robert!" All the self-hatred she felt for her impotency at that moment was evident in the words she spat out so venomously.

Robert looked momentarily startled at her vehemence and then spoke more softly, attempting to ease her pain. "You're wrong, Amanda. Everyone in the fort is afraid right now. Only a fool isn't afraid when there is something to be frightened of."

Giving him a quick upward glance, she said unbelievingly, "Do you mean you're afraid too, Robert?"

A brief smile flicked across his lips as he saw the first trace of her returning spirit. "Well, since I don't consider myself a fool, I guess I'm a little afraid, too, Amanda. There's a small spot of fear down deep inside all of us, but it's something you learn to live with after a while. The only difference is that this is your first experience. It's always harder the first time."

Amanda was silent for a short while, using the time to regain control of her emotions and angrily wipe her face clean of the tears that had so shamed her. She still could not completely forgive herself, but he was right. It was past, and she wasn't doing any good the way she was acting. Finally, her eyes still averted from his, she said softly, "I'm a fool, Robert. Are you very disappointed in me?"

Very deliberately he raised her chin with his hand

until their eyes met, so she might fully realize the sincerity of his words. He held her gaze firmly with his own. "No, Amanda, you've done nothing to disappoint me."

At that moment she was grateful beyond words for his understanding. Her voice choked again despite her resolve as she answered with determination, "I won't, either, I promise you."

Now, remembering the statement she had made only a few hours before with such resolution, she was filled with self-contempt. She had almost fallen prey to the same demons again, but she had not realized that fear would be so constant a companion, and so jealously reluctant to relinquish its hold.

Deliberately avoiding the view of the interior yard of the fort, now littered with spent cannon balls and debris, where the frantic movement of their depleted forces only inflamed her anxieties, Amanda kept her eyes on her work. In an effort to maintain her calm, she forced her mind out of the present to the time just a year and a half before when she had arrived at the ranger camp. Now, looking back with her new, hard-won maturity, she was bitterly amused with the child she had been. She had been so elated when she had finally been able to convince her parents that at fifteen years of age she was old enough to be an asset in the village springing up across the creek from the fort. Inspired with a deep sense of purpose, she had immediately volunteered her services at the establishment set up by some of the women to do the rangers' laundry, and was thrilled at being accepted as a small part of a great effort being expended by her country. She had idealistically

9

entertained no other outcome for their efforts but victory and could still remember what now seemed to be wild, childish dreams of glory.

Covering her eyes in a revealing, weary gesture, she struggled to raise spirits still sinking from the weight of grim reality. What a far cry from glory was the endless agony of siege, the slow, relentless pounding of the French cannon that was gradually and steadily reducing the fort to rubble under which they would soon all be buried. And to complete her humiliation, now, when it was obvious to all that Fort William Henry was in its final death throes, her courage was fast deserting her.

Suddenly realizing how dependent she had become on Robert's warm encouragement and unfailing humor to relieve her fears, she whispered to herself, "But I won't be an anchor, dragging him down with my childish fears. Never again!"

Her resolve strengthened by her mental battle, Amanda looked again and again to the doorway of the casement room where she was assigned, along with some of the other women and children during the hours of bombardment. Surely Robert would be relieved of duty soon. She wanted him to know she had mastered her fears. She did not question that he would immediately seek her out; she never wondered why he always appeared to prefer her company to that of any of the young women in the camp who gazed so soulfully in his direction. She simply felt her heart leap when his tall, broad figure filled the doorway. His face was smudged with gun powder and dirt, the two-day growth of beard and dark circles beneath his eyes revealing the strain of siege.

But even so, he is still the handsomest man in the fort, she thought absentmindedly, noting the thick shock of reddish-brown hair tied to the back of his neck, his strong profile, and the soft brown eyes beneath heavy dark brows, that flicked over the crowded room in search of her.

Within a few minutes he was at her side. He took her hand with an urgent, sober expression.

"Amanda, I don't have much time, but we must talk."

Not waiting for her reply, he pulled her gently but firmly across to the doorway. His eyes searched out a safe spot that afforded a little privacy while his mind reviewed again his thoughts of that afternoon.

From the first moment of attack, Robert's thoughts had centered on Amanda, and each successive day had only increased his anxieties for her until she was almost never fully out of his mind. That afternoon he had realistically faced the fact that a tomorrow for him and everyone within the fort was really questionable, and his greatest sense of loss was that he had never openly declared his true feelings for her. How long had he loved her? He could not really recall the exact moment his feelings had turned into love, but he could remember with the utmost clarity the first time he had seen her.

With a touching sense of dedication she had been laboring over a tub of hot, soapy water, her silver-blond hair tied carelessly into a knot on the top of her head. The intense heat of the day, as well as her vigorous scrubbing had caused several wisps of hair to fall and stick to her neck with perspiration, while

11

others curled in little tendrils along her hairline. Her slightly faded blue dress was spotted with water, and her concentration was deep as she worked at removing a spot from a uniform that was, in fact, his own. Her creamy complexion was heightened by two red spots of color on her cheeks, no doubt due to her frantic scrubbing, and the failure to remove the spot caused her to bite her bottom lip in an expression of complete determination. As she lifted her eyes in momentary exasperation, Robert caught a flash of brilliant blue that caused a gasp of amazement to pass his lips. With renewed vigor she had returned to that stubborn spot, and looking at the fragile, disheveled young beauty, Robert could not help but liken her appearance to that of an overworked angel.

From that moment on, Amanda haunted his thoughts until he became secretly embarrassed that at twenty-five years of age he was obsessed with a girl who was hardly more than a child! How clever he had thought himself as he hid his warring emotions, playing the friend, while his visits to the Starkweather hut became more and more frequent. But Jon Starkweather had not been deceived for a moment. The memory of the older man's expression of feigned innocence, so incongruous on his sun-darkened, lined face, when he had broached the subject for the first time, even now caused him a reminiscent chuckle.

"It seems you've become almighty fond of my company lately, Robert. Tell me, is it my keen military mind you admire, or my wife's cooking?"

Taken completely by surprise, he had begun to sputter a few incomprehensible sentences until a slow flush began to transfuse his face. Continuing to direct his piercing gaze directly into his eyes, Jon had asked pointedly, "Or is it something both my wife and me had a hand in making together that draws you here night after night?"

"Damn you, Jon," he had finally laughed, "you know well enough the reason I'm hanging around. I can't keep my eyes off her, and I guess I haven't fooled anybody but myself. But right now I feel like a love-struck cradle-robber!"

His obvious frustration had seemed to tickle Jon's funny bone, and while he had done some uncomfortable squirming in the realization that his predicament was so obvious, Jon's deep laughter had boomed across the room. Finally, wiping his eyes, Jon had said reassuringly, "Well, it's nothing a little time won't cure, Robert, but I'm glad you're showing some sense and not rushing her before she's ready, even if you're more than ready." Jon's smile had broadened again at that last remark, but he had added consolingly, "Girls grow up fast these days, and Amanda's going to make some man a real good wife. I'd have no objection to that man being you, Robert, just as long as you give her a little time to finish her growing up."

Unaccountably, there had come a thickness in his throat, and he realized he had made the commitment to himself long before it had been forced out into the open. He had answered soberly, "I guess I can hold out a while, Jon." And then, as his eyes moved to Amanda, who was entering the room, his heart quickened, and he had added almost inaudibly, "A little while, anyway."

With those words, the two men had shaken hands, and the matter had not been discussed again. The months had become a year, bringing with it many changes. In Amanda, change was reflected in her increasing beauty and maturity, and in himself in the deepening of his already overwhelming love for her. At the end of a year and a half, Robert had secured a place for himself in her life, and had only to bridge the gap between intimate friend and lover. Suddenly he had run out of time.

Pulling her behind him into the shelter of one of the walls, Robert turned around to face her. Amanda looked up questioningly, to see him gazing wordlessly down into her face.

Lord, she's beautiful! was his unconscious reaction to the face turned up to his. He had never truly become accustomed to her beauty, and was still dazzled by it each time he looked into her face. His eyes traced for a moment the soft, almost silver hair now cascading over her shoulders; the soft white skin of her high forehead, where fine, little curls of hair escaped at her hairline and enchantingly framed her face; those incredible, luminous blue eyes that never failed to thrill him; the amazingly thick fringe of dark lashes bordering them; her fine, straight nose; and lastly, her mouth. As he looked at those warm pink lips, now formed in an inquisitive half-smile, the small dimple at its corner winking appealingly, he began to tremble with desire.

She has no idea how lovely she is, he thought, or how much I want her. Cautiously he began to speak. "Amanda, I have something very important to say, something I've wanted to say for a long time." He

14

stood very close to her, his broad shoulders completely hiding her small figure from view. "You know how desperate our position here is. If Colonel Monro's courier to Fort Edward doesn't bring reinforcements, our fight is hopeless. Then it's anyone's guess what will happen."

Amanda tensed at the voicing of all her silent, innermost fears, but Robert drew her closer, and caressing with unbelievable gentleness the silky white skin of her cheek with his huge, calloused hand, he continued softly, his voice husky with emotion, "I had promised your parents I wouldn't speak to you about this for a while, but we may be running out of time, and I want you to know how I feel. I want you to know I love you, and want you for my wife."

Robert waited expectantly for words that did not come. Instead, her face incredulous, Amanda stared up at him, rendered speechless by his sudden declaration. A short wry laugh escaped Robert's lips as he said softly, pulling her against his chest and burying his face for a moment in her soft fair hair. "If you're surprised, Amanda, then you're the only one. I think I must be the joke of the camp. A fully grown man of twenty-six mooning around calf-eyed after a pocket-sized sixteen-year-old." But then, as if refuting the impossibility of their love, he drew her even tighter against him, sorely testing the strength of her ribs. And then suddenly he released her and stared inquiringly into her face. She still had not responded with word or action, and he could feel his apprehension building. Maybe it was too soon, after all, to speak to her. But, damn it, tomorrow could be too late!

15

Spurred on by his anxiety, Robert pressed for an answer.

"What is it, darling? Are you really so surprised? Is it the difference in our ages? Couldn't you at least grow to love me, Amanda? Amanda," his voice pleaded, "please answer me."

To her amazement, Robert's eyes filled with emotion, in expectation of her refusal. Again he pleaded, his voice growing hoarse with the depth of his feelings, the trembling in his body increasing.

For a few endless minutes Amanda was frozen with surprise. She had always sensed a special feeling between her and Robert, but she had not yet reached the point of a serious consideration of those feelings. Not realizing the heartlessness of her delay, Amanda's eyes slowly perused Robert's face. The earnest plea shining in his eyes softened something inside her, and the trembling of his strong, masculine body as he waited for her to speak was an appeal she could not ignore. After all, her mind argued, I've always loved Robert. I certainly can't imagine my life without him. Maybe this is love after all, this warm feeling when he touches me. Whatever it was she felt for Robert, she knew when she saw his tortured expression as he awaited her reply that he desperately needed her acceptance for his peace of mind.

Her voice was an incredulous whisper as she responded, "It's just that I never expected—" And then, seeing the look of pain in his eyes, she continued hesitantly, "But if you're sure you really want me, Robert, yes, I'll be your wife."

A look of incredible joy swept over Robert's face, and with a groan that seemed to release something

16

deep inside, he swept her petite form against him and crushed her lips in a deep, lingering, long-awaited kiss.

Amanda was totally unprepared for the arousal she experienced as Robert's mouth claimed hers, insistently pressing her lips apart until his tongue probed the wetness of her mouth. And still his kiss deepened, searching and stirring her senses, until her mouth lay open under his, completely conquered by the invasion of his lips and tongue. As he pulled her even tighter in embrace, the full length of her body welded to his by the intensity of his passion, Amanda felt herself drawn into the current of an emotion with which she was completely unfamiliar. Suddenly, Robert pulled himself away, this time visibly shaking, his breathing deep and ragged.

"Amanda," he whispered hoarsely as he held her slightly apart from him, "We'll be married as soon as this battle is over. It will work out for us. That courier must come through." His voice was desperate as he pulled her into his arms again, but this time his kiss was short and controlled. "Come on, let's tell your parents." His arm slipped around her waist, and he pulled her against his side as they walked toward the hall with the happy news.

Sleep was elusive as Amanda lay that night on her pallet in the area in which the refugees from the ranger camp were housed, and her mind whirled in confusion. The silence of the night seemed unnatural, so accustomed had she become to the constant thunder of the French cannon. Time and time again she had closed her eyes in search of sleep, but it would

17

not come; it was defeated by the thoughts that crowded her mind. Her parents had not been surprised or displeased by Robert's proposal, but the dire circumstances of the fort and the uncertainty of their futures had taken much of the joy from their announcement. What would happen to all of them? It was common knowledge Fort William Henry could not stand another day against the French attack, and what then? Amanda swallowed hard to control the sob rising in her throat, when she suddenly saw movement in the doorway, and a tall figure began picking its way across the sleeping forms scattered across the floor. When it reached her side, it crouched down and she heard Robert's voice whisper, "Amanda, are you awake?" His hand reached out to stroke the long hair that glowed like molten silver in the moonlight streaming through the doorway.

"Yes, Robert, I can't seem to sleep tonight."

"Then come outside for a while. I have to report back for duty in an hour, but I'd rather spend the time with you than sleeping."

In the faint light she could see the flash of his smile, and hastily pulling back the blanket, careful not to wake the others, she picked her way to the door. The darkness of the night afforded them the privacy that had been hard to attain in the brightness of the day, and before they had gone a few feet, Robert swept her into his arms in a tight, passionate embrace, his lips hungrily seeking hers. But he was not long satisfied with just the taste of her lips. Slowly he moved to cover her face with soft, searching kisses, daring to kiss her at last as he had desired for so long. He pressed kisses on her eyelids, on her long, silky lashes, on the bridge and tip of her small, straight nose, the hollows of her cheeks, and on that dimple that had always tempted him so flirtatiously. Pulling her even tighter in his arms, he wound her hair around his hand and bent to kiss the soft, white nape of her neck, from there following a trail to her ear, where he paused briefly before moving to the hollow of her throat.

Amanda's heart began pounding in unison with Robert's as an unknown emotion overwhelmed her senses. She, also, began to tremble as a feeling of languor stole over her. Robert's kisses proceeded steadily downward, pressing warmly against her firm, young breasts through the softness of her night-gown.

She spoke softly in a trembling voice. "You'll have to help me, Robert. You'll have to tell me what I should do. I want to make you happy, but I don't really know what's expected of me." The innocence in her voice tore at him.

"Don't trust me too much, darling," Robert whispered. "I can't even trust myself right now." He laughed wryly as his mouth sought hers again and he wrapped her breathlessly tight in his arms.

"I think you'd better leave and get some sleep before your next watch, Robert." The deep voice sounded from the doorway, and, startled, they raised their heads to seek its origin.

"Not yet, Jon, please," Robert pleaded. "Just a little while longer. I just want to hold her a little while longer."

"Now, Robert." Jonathan's voice was mercilessly

firm. Reluctantly Robert released her. "Maybe you'd better go in now, darling," he said softly. "I'll see you tomorrow as soon as I'm relieved again from duty."

Turning slowly to do Robert's bidding, she suddenly felt herself pulled back into his arms as his mouth hungrily sought hers once again. After a long, deep kiss that left Amanda trembling, he released her suddenly. "That's to make sure you dream of nothing but me, darling." And with a short salute to her father, he walked briskly away.

August 9, 1757—Another brilliant summer day, its serenity marred at the first light of morning by the resumption of the seemingly ceaseless shelling of the French cannon. The parallels of the cannon had once again been moved forward during the night, and the damage being done the battered fort was relentless. All within knew the final hours had come at last, and as the valiant men continued their futile efforts in defense of the doomed fort, the women and children huddled in silent expectation of their fates. Suddenly the firing ceased. The unnatural silence seemed deafening as the inhabitants of the fort, knowing they were at the mercy of the French, awaited their enemy's next move.

Robert sought Amanda quickly within the crowd forming in the yard, and came to her side, taking her hand reassuringly. Within a few minutes an observer on the wall shouted, "A rider is approaching bearing a white flag!"

Struggling hard to hide her trepidation, Amanda stood beside Robert in the crowd of the two hundred or so surviving members of the garrison and some rangers and their families, anxious to hear the demands of the French.

The sober-faced young Frenchman was admitted to the fort and advanced toward Colonel Monro with an air of confidence that was betrayed only by the thin veil of perspiration covering his face. Saluting smartly, he handed him a paper and retained a second batch in his hand.

Within a few minutes the crowd was buzzing, and Amanda heard a gruff voice in front of her growl, "By God, Jeremy, it's the colonel's own letter to Fort Edward they've brought him to read, the bastards! Poor Jake probably didn't get any further than a mile or two from this fort."

"You're crazy, Bart. It can't be!" The reply was unbelieving.

"It is, I tell you! I recognize the seal. Just look at his face! You can tell by looking at him that it's all over."

Amanda's eyes moved immediately to Colonel Monro, and seeing the truth confirmed in the rugged Scotsman's blanched countenance, she turned sad eyes to Robert. Managing a tight smile, he whispered encouragingly, "Don't worry, darling. Everything will be all right." But his voice lacked the optimism of his words.

The dispirited crowd was in total silence when the young courier handed Colonel Monro the second set of papers. His face still and unnatural, the colonel accepted them without a word and adjourned with his officers to the south barracks to consider what they all knew to be the Marquis de Montcalm's articles of capitulation.

21

Amanda stood clutching Robert's hand amid the anxious crowd keeping silent vigil in the fort yard. Before the hour was up Colonel Monro and his aides emerged from the barracks. There was no hesitation as they marched toward the Frenchman, who had remained standing at attention for the duration of their conference, saluted and returned the papers to him. Surrender was now a mere formality, and before the courier cleared the gates, Lieutenant Foster began reading the terms of surrender to those waiting so solemnly.

ARTICLE 1st

The garrison of Fort William Henry and the Troops in the entrenched camp adjoining shall march out with arms and other honors of war; the baggage of the officers and of the soldiers only.

They shall proceed to Fort Edward escorted by a detachment of French troops and some officers and interpreters attached to the Indians, and at an early hour tomorrow morning.

ARTICLE 2nd

The gate of the Fort shall be delivered up to the troops of his Most Christian Majesty after the signing of the capitulation and the entrenched camp, on the departure of his Britannic Majesty's troops.

ARTICLE 3rd

All the artillery, warlike stores, provisions and in general everything except the effects of the officers and soldiers specified in the first article, shall upon honor, be delivered up to the troops of his Most Christian Majesty, and with that view an exact inventory of the property herein mentioned shall be delivered after the capitulation, observing that this Article includes the fort, entrenchment and dependencies.

ARTICLE 4th

The garrison of the fort, entrenched camp and dependencies shall not be at liberty to serve for eighteen months, reckoning from this date, against his Most Christian Majesty, nor against his allies; and with the capitulation shall furnish an exact return of his troops, wherein shall be set forth the names of the officers, majors, other officers, engineers, artillery officers, commissaries and employees.

ARTICLE 5th

All the officers, soldiers, Canadians, women and Indians, taken on land since the commencement of this war in North America, shall be delivered at Carillon within the space of three months, on the receipts of the French commandants, to whom they shall be delivered; and equal number of the garrison of Fort George shall be at liberty to serve, according to the return which shall be given in thereof by the English officer, who will have charge of the prisoners.

ARTICLE 6th

An officer shall be given as a hostage until the return of the detachment which will be furnished as an escort for his Britannic Majesty's troops.

ARTICLE 7th

All the sick and wounded who are not in condition to be removed to Fort Edward, shall remain under the protection of the Marquis de Montcalm, who will take proper care of them and return them immediately after they are cured.

ARTICLE 8th

Provisions for the subsistence of said troops shall be issued for this day and tomorrow only.

ARTICLE 9th

The Marquis de Montcalm being willing to show Lieutenant-Colonel Monro and his garrison some token of his esteem on account of their honorable defense, grants them one piece of cannon—a six-pounder.

Done at noon, in the trenches before Fort William Henry, the Ninth of August, One thousand seven hundred and fifty-seven.

The six days of siege were over, and a white flag was raised. Fort William Henry had capitulated. The first step in France's attempt to gain control over the waterways in the New World had been successful.

Robert breathed a deep sigh of relief. it was all over, and if they had not won the battle, at least the terms of surrender were fair and honorable. One

24

point in the long list of conditions stood out in his mind. According to the terms of surrender, he would be honor bound not to fight again for eighteen months. He smiled. It would be a long, generous honeymoon granted by his enemy, the French.

Amanda looked up at Robert, awaiting his reaction to the reading of the conditions of surrender, and to her amazement, he was smiling widely. Noting her surprised glance, he slid his arm around her waist and said almost lightheartedly as he urged her forward, "We had better find your parents and start putting our things together."

But Robert's feelings of well being did not last long. When they entered the civilian quarters, they found it already frantic with activity, and Amanda was shocked to see on the faces of the women, for the first time, the fear they had hidden so well.

"Amanda! Robert!" Jon's voice summoned them from the corner of the room. "Hurry, we won't have much time." And as they drew nearer, he added more softly, "Those Indians have been waiting a long time and won't understand this kind of victory. They haven't gotten their quota of scalps from this battle, and the French won't be able to hold them back much longer." As if in verification of his statement, the Indian activity outside the gates increased suddenly and wild yells and chants filled the air.

Jon turned to Robert and a silent look of mutual understanding passed between them as Jon placed his hand heavily on the younger man's shoulder. "I can't tell you how relieved I am knowing I can depend on you to look out for Amanda, Robert. I have a feeling the women are going to need as much protection as they can get during the next few days, and I know I can turn her over into your keeping with complete confidence."

"You have my word, Jon. Amanda will be safe as long as I'm alive," Robert answered solemnly, and with a silent nod, they turned to join Amanda and her mother, who had already begun packing.

Within a few minutes a young corporal, obviously harried and anxious to get on to the next room with his message, shouted officially from the doorway, "Colonel Monro has requested that all chests and trunks be left behind, securely locked, and that all liquor be destroyed. He feels that it will be to your advantage in delaying the looting and keeping the Indians busy while our column makes its way to the entrenched camp." His message delivered, he turned immediately on his heel and left.

Despite the attention they had given the courier, the moment he left the area the message was all but ignored. The women, already having lost so much, refused to part with any more of their precious belongings, and resumed packing. However, as early evening approached, even the most determined were forced to abandon those things they could not easily transport, and all joined the remains of the British force and began their march out the eastern gateway toward the entrenched camp to spend the night. They left the sick and badly wounded behind with great apprehension, despite Montcalm's assurance of fair treatment. Even as the rear guard of the column cleared the gateway, Indians began to swarm over the western embrasures. Amanda, walking silently beside Robert, her parents in line directly in front of her, felt

26

fear climb her spine as the wild war whoops and scalp yells inside the fort rent the anxious silence. Robert clutched her hand reassuringly.

"Just be sure to keep as close as possible to me at all times, Amanda. Remember, where I go, you follow immediately." And at her anxious glance, he managed a meager smile. "Don't worry, darling. Montcalm has guaranteed our safe conduct to Fort Edward."

But their silent suspicion of Montcalm's guarantee was mutual. Each realized that the guards they had been provided were vastly insufficient to protect their column, which numbered approximately 1000 defenseless men, women and children, against what was reckoned to be 1700 armed Indians, wild with scalp lust.

Fear and uncertainty seemed to lengthen the short distance to the entrenched camp endlessly as the weary column moved forward. Finally, their uncertain haven reached, the evacuees attempted to rest, only to hear again and again screams from within the fort shattering the silence. They heard the wild shrieking and yells of the Indians as they drank themselves into complete intoxication and then scalped the helpless wounded in their beds. The camp listened in helpless despair, some crying, others dropping to their knees in silent prayer, and others, too tired to do any more, just closing their eyes, hoping for the oblivion of sleep.

After a few hours, Amanda finally managed to fall asleep, only to be awakened by Robert's deep voice as he whispered, "It's four o'clock. We're going to move out now. Hurry, Amanda!" Helping her to her feet, he snatched up her bundles and urged her into the column.

Montcalm, at that very moment supervising his regulars in the removal of stores from the fort to Fort Carillon, was unaware of the line of Indians that began to gather alongside the frightened column of prisoners as they stumbled forward to begin their sixteen-mile walk to Fort Edward. Robert's hand held Amanda's in a crushing grip as they walked silently past the muttering Indians who crowded closer and closer. Suddenly, an Abnaki scalp yell pierced the uneasy silence and an Indian leaped into the column and brought his war axe down on the head of a wounded soldier. In the space of a few seconds, and before anyone could react to the horror, the Indian had scalped his lifeless body and was proceeding to tear off his coat. As if by prearranged signal, a dozen more Abnakis leaped on the prisoners, swinging their axes, and within a few terrifying seconds the sober procession became a barbarous, screaming melee.

At the first yell, Robert, fearful for Amanda's safety and realizing the value her bright silver-and-golden hair would have on a scalp pole, jerked her roughly to the ground to remove her from immediate danger. He stood in front of her as an Indian, yelling and swinging his tomahawk wildly, attacked him. He fought skillfully while Amanda, crouched on the ground, watched in horrified fascination as one after another of her friends fell around her, their eyes staring sightlessly upward and their blood gushing from their wounds and mingling in the dirt on the rough path.

28

Suddenly a particular scream pierced her shocked daze, and she jumped to her feet to see her mother's terrified face as an Indian axe descended with pitiless force into her head. Amanda's mind froze at the stunned expression her mother wore the second before a stream of blood spurted from the savage gash. Then, before her eyes, the grinning Indian proceeded to remove a strip of graying auburn hair from her mother's head.

With an anguished cry that tore her throat, Amanda rushed forward screaming her father's name, only to see as she reached her mother's side the blood-covered body of her father lying a few feet away. She stood still, too shocked at the gory spectacle to think coherently, when a sudden vicious jerk on her hair threw her to the ground. Fighting fiercely to be free of the maniacal hold on her hair, she turned her head to see a blood-spattered Indian standing above her, his axe raised and swiftly descending. Abruptly the descending arm was jerked backwards as Robert's voice shouted, "Run, Amanda, run!"

Amanda struggled to her feet as Robert wrestled with the kill-crazed Indian, then ran off the trail into the bushes. One backward glance showed her Robert had been struck to the ground and the Indian, wild with rage, was following her in hot pursuit.

Her breath coming in deep sobbing gulps, Amanda raced on through the forest, her streaming hair catching on the outstretched lower limbs of trees, the underbrush tearing at the skin on her arms and legs. Stumbling, falling, and getting up to run again, she could hear the pursuing footsteps behind her coming ever closer. Suddenly, above the almost deafening pounding of her own heartbeat in her ears, she could hear the labored breathing of her pursuer, and she realized with a jolt of horror that he was directly behind her! Amanda turned, her eyes wide with fright, to behold in an instant of hopeless terror the fearsome, painted face of death as a war axe savagely descended and a sharp, brilliant explosion of pain put an end to the gruesome reality of consciousness!

Two

The sun filtered through the high, graceful
umbrella of trees, weaving a lacy pattern on the forest
floor, allowing just enough warmth to easily dry the
last remaining drops of water on Adam Carstairs'
broad, tanned chest. Squinting slightly against the
glare of the shimmering water, his cool, green eyes
leisurely skimmed the lush forest foliage that was
just beginning to edge with color in the second week
of August. A few minutes before he had finished
bathing in the small, nameless lake, one of the many
that eventually fed into Lake George, and had felt
alive and refreshed for the first time since leaving
Fort Carillon. But he had slipped back into his buckskin britches and moccasins, finding his depression
slipping back as well, and did not have the heart to
finish dressing and continue on his trek to Fort
William Henry to see the destruction he was sure
awaited him. He lay on his back, his arms pillowing
his head, the sun warm against his skin, his relaxed
position a direct contrast to the turmoil raging inside
him. For the first time the forest did not restore his
sense of peace, too much had happened there for him

31

to be deceived by its tranquil beauty. Instead, count-less abstract memories flooded his mind.

His parents—a fleeting smile crossed his face. He had grown up in these woods. Those happy times were gone now, gone with a few swift strokes of a war axe. Suddenly he was chuckling to himself, remembering when he was sixteen, eager, surprisingly innocent, and on his own for a day in town. And Dolly, who was older, and not so innocent. Dolly who smelled warm and sweet like a meadow full of clover, and who opened up a whole new world for him. He chuckled again. "Thank you, Dolly."

And Pa's slightly uncomfortable expression when he had called him aside to speak to him that night. He could still remember his stomach twisting into knots as his father had mumbled gruffly, "Adam, about Dolly. . . ."

"How did you know, Pa? I mean, who told—" Suddenly he had run out of words to say because nothing was coming out right, and he had just sputtered to a stop and sat, nervously swallowing, awaiting his father's next words.

"It doesn't matter how I found out, I just did. I guess you figure you're a man now that Dolly has shown you a thing or two, but I just want to make sure you understand a few things." He had run his wide, calloused hand through his shaggy, gray hair and continued hesitantly. "Knowing Dolly, Adam, I expect she was the one to do the seducing, not you, and I guess there's no harm when both people are willing, but—" his father's face had suddenly become intense, and he could still remember his embarrassment when his father had stared directly into his eyes and continued— "there is a certain amount of responsibility that goes along with becoming a man. There is one thing I want you to understand here and now. I will not stand for any bastard children from your pleasures, and if you should get any innocent girl in trouble, you'll answer directly to me!"

He hadn't doubted for a minute the sincerity of those words, and he had a long-standing respect for his father's ability to enforce them. Gulping, he merely nodded silently into his father's flushed face. His father's smile, when it came a few seconds later, had given him such a tremendous sense of relief that he got to his feet on legs that were shaking. He knew he would never forget the way his father threw his arm companionably around his shoulders then as he said, "Come on inside now and eat, Adam. Your mother has supper waiting."

He hadn't forgotten his father's warning, but he had to admit to himself it hadn't inhibited him to any great degree either. He had found that there were always plenty of willing ladies, especially for a man with a full pocket after a winter spent trapping, and it didn't take an abnormal amount of vanity to realize that the tall, blond, good looks he had inherited from his father hadn't hurt him either. Whatever the reason, he knew he had developed quite a reputation with women, which he felt he didn't completely deserve, but which he nevertheless enjoyed.

His mother, though, had been a different matter. She seldom missed the opportunity as he grew old to remind him that he was her only child, and it was up to him to provide her with a daughter and grand-children. She observed the envious glances of the other men, the knowing winks and hearty slaps on the back he received after a night on the town with an exasperation that was only secretly tinged with pride. His visits home usually ended with his father's smiling sheepishly while his mother took the opportunity to plead her cause.

"Adam, I'm beginning to believe you're never going to settle down and raise a family. Have some pity on your poor old mother, dear. I want to see my grandchildren before I die."

Even now Adam winced inwardly at the recollection of her womanly intuition, but then he had only picked her up and, swinging her around, answered laughingly, "I promise you, Ma, I'll think on it."

If memory could only stop there, Adam thought, and the pain returned again as he began to remember the last time he had approached his parents' cabin a year ago. He had spent the winter months trapping, and had gotten heartily sick of his own company and anxious for some of his mother's cooking and his father's special brand of humor. As he had neared his parents' cabin the odor of charred wood and the familiar sickening odor of decay reached his nostrils, startling him for a moment before fear took over. He had begun running, running wildly until his lungs were near to bursting, but he had been too late, months too late. In the yard, beside the charred remains of their cabin, he had found their partially decomposed bodies, their heads mutilated and bare where their scalps had been stripped away.

Even now his stomach revolted at the memory of

his parents' lonesome burial, and he renewed again with passion the vow he had made over their graves. He would see that the French were paid back for the encouragement they had given the Indians to burn out and slaughter British subjects in order to regain the land for France. How much had they paid the Indians for those two graying scalps? The pain of their deaths had not faded with the passing year, and his desire for revenge had become a burning knot in his chest that only seemed to tighten as time wore on.

A chill passed over his muscular frame at the memory of his failure to warn Fort William Henry at the time of the impending French attack. Captain Moreau's jealousy had been his undoing. Realizing his wife's interest, he had declared Adam a suspicious character, and had put him into the stockade until after the commencement of the attack, and it had been only due to Marie's pleading that he had been released and had been able to make a fast exit from the fort. Now, just two days trek from Fort William Henry, he couldn't bring himself to hurry, to see the results of his failure.

A sudden movement in the bushes a short distance away brought him back sharply to the present. Slowly and quietly he reached for his gun, his mind reasoning that no Indian would be approaching with all that thrashing about, and that by now the French would either be headed back to Fort Carillon or on to take Fort Edward. Then who?

His senses were alert, his finger on the trigger, awaiting the emergence of the noisy intruder when Adam heard a short scream, followed by a shrieking female voice saying, "It bit me! It bit me!" as a small blond figure stumbled into the partial clearing.

A child! he thought as he jumped forward. A child here? He caught her as she fell almost into his arms, crying softly and repeating, "My leg, my leg."

Lowering her to the ground and tossing her skirts aside, Adam looked at the slender scratched legs to see two small puncture wounds just above one ankle, where blood still oozed, and where already an angry red swelling had started to rise. Leaving her for a moment, Adam returned seconds later with a knife, and without hesitation cut a cross between the two points of puncture. The pain seemed to bring the girl around, and she began to struggle weakly, crying and pulling at his short-cropped hair in an effort to stop him as he bent to place his mouth over the wound and draw out the poison. Adam could feel the girl's weak, hysterical pounding at his back and head, as the bitter taste of blood and venom filled his mouth and he spat it out again and again. The pounding slowed and finally came to a stop as the girl slipped into unconsciousness—whether from shock or the poison, he was not certain—and he continued to draw the poison from the wound.

When Adam had satisfied himself he had done all he could, he ripped a piece from the girl's ragged petticoat, and pushing her skirt up higher, tied a tourniquet on her leg to prevent the passage of any possible remaining poison into her body. Then, scooping up the unconscious form in his arms, he carried her to the edge of the water.

Acting purely by instinct, Adam ripped another piece from her fast diminishing petticoat, and dipping it in the cold water, began to swab her face.

The young girl's features were all but indiscernible beneath the layer of dirt and dried blood. The cold water aroused her just enough for huge blue eyes to flicker open for a moment and stare fearfully into his. She then twisted her head to the side in a feeble effort to avoid his graze, revealing to him for the first time a deep and bloody wound on her scalp, before she slipped back into unconsciousness. It was obvious she had been struck from behind by an instrument that from the shape of the wound had a sharp, wide edge, similar to a war axe. Adam was incredulous! This girl could not possibly be from—no, the fort was almost two days trek away. But he had no more time for conjecture as he began cleaning the matted hair and caked blood from the wound.

To Adam's relief, the girl remained unconscious during the painstaking procedure, as he retreived a small ball of soap from his pack, worked up a lather with a piece of torn petticoat, and gently and slowly cleansed the wound. When he was done, he sprinkled a small measure of Indian herbs he found effective in aiding healing on the wound. Rinsing out the cloth, Adam then attempted again to remove the layer of dirt and dried blood from her face. With a gentleness previously unknown to him, he worked the soapy lather into her face and rinsed it clean again, to reveal a young, delicate face of unmistakable beauty! He stared in awe at the soft white skin, miraculously unmarked by her flight through the forest, at the long, dark lashes that lay curled from the dampness against her cheek. While he stared in utter fascination, her eyes flickered open and a magnificent smile curved her lips, causing a small dimple to wink in

37

and out beside her mouth as she said softly, "Robert, I knew you'd come to help me. Thank the Lord you are here." And reaching up, she gently touched his cheek before unconsciousness again overtook her.

Adam felt a deep, unreasonable tenderness at the girl's light caress, and berating himself for the pleasure he experienced from the touch meant for another, he lifted her skirt again to check her wound and remove the tourniquet. Realizing his relaxation was now at an end, he started to prepare for what he suspected would be an ordeal ahead of him. No doubt there would be some fever and weakness as a result of the snakebite, the head wound, or both; and when it was over, if the girl survived, she would need some nourishing food to regain her strength. He knew now he would not be resuming his journey toward Fort William Henry for many days.

The expected reaction was not long in setting in, and as Adam continued applying cool compresses on her ankle in an attempt to take the fever from the wound, the girl's temperature steadily mounted. Bent over her as he checked her leg, he sensed eyes on him, and looking up, he experienced for the first time the full force of the child's azure gaze. Rendered momentarily speechless in the presence of such true, overwhelming beauty, he remained silent, waiting for her to speak.

"What are you doing?" The girl's weak voice did not quite meet the intensity of her stare.

"You were bitten by a snake, and I had to draw out the poison. Don't you remember? I was checking to see how it was coming along," he answered, trying to strike as casual a note as possible, and hoping the heavy thudding of his heart was not obvious in his voice. "My name is Adam Carstairs. What's your name, and what happened to you? How did you get that head wound?"

The young girl pushed back a lock of hair that had fallen forward and looked suddenly puzzled and uncertain, completely flustered by his rash of questions. "My name is Amanda Starkweather," she stated hesitantly, "and I live at the Ranger camp outside Fort William Henry with my parents." She began to falter as she continued in a shaky voice, "But I can't seem to remember how I got here." Her huge, bewildered blue eyes filled with tears, and Adam, overcome with tenderness, succumbed to the urge to comfort her. Drawing her warmly against his chest, he was startled by the heat of fever emanating from her small body.

He heard her muffled voice from the comfort of his arms, as she lay her head against him. "I would be afraid if it wasn't for you, but I know I needn't worry now that you're here, Robert." Snuggling her head against his chest, she passed once more into unconsciousness, leaving Adam unreasonably annoyed at being mistaken for Robert a second time.

The late afternoon drifted into evening and then night, and Adam continued in vain his efforts to reduce Amanda's fever. She had drifted off into a restless sleep, and as her fever burned hotter, her delirium continued to mount. Adam began to feel the rise of panic. He had seen young children and even grown men, when fever raged unchecked, go into wild convulsions that eventually killed them or left their brains marked forever. I can't let that

39

happen to her, his mind insisted as his eyes took in Amanda's small, shuddering form, sweet, beautiful, and innocent even as the fever gained greater control. His frantic efforts to force the delirious young girl to drink were all but useless, and his attempts to cool her fevered body by sponging her face and neck were to no avail.

In her delirium Amanda related piece by ragged piece, the story of the surrender of Fort William Henry, and the horror of the massacre of the civilians as they started on their way to Fort Edward. Adam's blood ran cold as Amanda shrieked, "Stop it! Don't do that! She's bleeding. Mother! Oh, Lord, her head! Father, help us. No, he's dead!" she had sobbed. "So much blood. So much blood. Robert, help me, please." Her eyes suddenly jerked open, and she screamed, staring upward at the memory of a descending war axe, "He's going to kill me, Robert!"

Abruptly Amanda's wild, delirious thrashing stopped short, and she appeared to lapse into a deeper sleep. Just one touch to her body told Adam she was, if possible, even hotter than before, and he realized in that instant, if he could not reduce the fever quickly it would be too late.

With shaking hands, Adam turned Amanda on her side and began to undo the buttons on the back of her dress, and when he was finished, quickly drew it off over her head. He then proceeded to remove her undergarments and shoes, until she lay naked on the blanket he had provided. Quickly removing his shirt, he scooped up her small burning body, and walked into the lake with her in his arms. The cool water was shocking against Amanda's fevered skin, and she started violently, opening her eyes and struggling to be free of him. Adam walked steadily into the lake until Amanda was submerged to her neck, all the time talking soothingly in a calming voice.

"Amanda, don't be afraid. You have a fever, and this is the only way to get it down. See, don't you feel cooler already?" Her struggles continued, but somewhat more weakly as his voice began to penetrate the fogginess of her fevered brain.

"Amanda, dear, I'm going to help you feel better. Relax, let the water relax you. That's right, you'll be better soon."

Within the quarter hour, the fresh cool water had accomplished its work and Adam was certain he could feel a drop in her body temperature when she suddenly began to shudder convulsively. Once again Adam felt panic begin to overcome his senses.

"Oh, Lord," he thought, now more frightened than he had ever been in his life, "I hope I haven't made her worse." .

Quickly he carried his small, precious, and shaking bundle out of the water, and laying her back on the blanket. Then he started to rub her naked body dry with her dress. When she was as dry as he could manage with the makeshift toweling, he laid out the one remaining dry blanket he carried in his pack and putting her gently on it, proceeded to wrap her like a child.

Amanda's shaking continued increasing in intensity. Adam realized that while her body temperature had cooled considerably, he now was afraid she had taken a chill which would cause her to lapse into a lung congestion of some sort. Her long hair lay dripping wet around her, and Adam began to rub it vigorously with her dress, feeling that perhaps her wet hair in the coolness of the forest night was causing her chill. But her shaking continued, her teeth chattering violently, her lips a frightening blue color that sent Adam almost over the edge of panic.

He rose, still looking at the helpless girl who lay wrapped in the blanket at his feet, and absentmindedly spread her dress over a nearby branch to dry. Then, stepping out of his wet buckskin britches, he spread them, too, over the same branch, and bending down, began to unwrap Amanda from the blanket. He stopped short for a second in sudden realization as Amanda's naked body lay before his eyes. This girl was no child. How could he have been so mistaken? Her body, although slight in stature, was beautifully and femininely mature. His eyes flew back again to her lovely young face, slid down the slender column of her throat, across her petite, narrow shoulders, and came to rest on the round, white globes of her breasts, so perfectly shaped, the tips two inviting pink rosebuds. His gaze continued to her incredibly small waist (surely, his two hands could circle it with room to spare), past the slender curve of her hips, and rested momentarily on the curls, only slightly darker in color than her glorious halo, nestling so appealingly between her long, slender legs. Adam felt a tightening in the pit of his stomach. No, this girl was no child.

Then, as her naked body gave a deep shudder, Adam quickly lay down next to her, and drawing her into his arms, he pulled her tightly against him, her soft smooth flesh against his hard, muscular nakedness, and wrapped them both tightly together in the blanket. Slowly the natural heat of Adam's body began to do its work, and Amanda's convulsive shivering continued to lessen until, finally, she rested peacefully against him. Adam did not loosen his hold on the lovely girl, his mind reasoning that even the slightest change might start her to shivering again. He closed his eyes and rested his cheek against her still damp hair. How good, how right she felt in his arms. He drew his face slightly away to look down on her sleeping countenance, and was rewarded with the expression of peaceful contentment Amanda wore in slumber, her head resting against the golden hairs on his chest. She mumbled something unintelligible in her sleep, and smiled briefly. Her smile caused an unfamiliar warmth to sweep over him. She mumbled again, but Adam closed his mind to her quiet utterances, not really wanting to know what she said, for he knew he could not bear to hear her call the man Robert again, not right now.

Amanda slept the remainder of the night in his arms, the natural sleep of complete exhaustion. Adam's own sleep was sporadic. The tenderness he felt for the lovely young girl who slept naked in his embrace was a new emotion for him, and although his body was reacting predictably to the stimulus of the warm, naked, feminine form pressed so closely to his, he was amazed by the strength of this emotion. He pressed a light kiss against her hair and caressed her gently, stopping to press his lips softly against her temple.

"Poor, sweet little innocent," he whispered, pulling her even tighter in his arms until she moved restlessly in her sleep. Seeing her discomfort, Adam slackened his embrace and slowly lowered his head to press a light kiss against those pink, inviting lips. At the touch of his lips to hers Amanda's eyes flickered open momentarily to look up into his. Catching his breath at the warmth generated by that one, brief glance, Adam closed his eyes and, forcing all further thought out of his mind, held her close against him until he finally slept.

The animated chirping of birds awoke Adam from his restless sleep as the first silver light of dawn creased the morning sky. In the manner of a man accustomed to sleeping with a portion of his mind still alert to danger, he was instantly awake and acutely aware of the petite naked form pressed so tightly against him in sleep, straining for his warmth. He could not repress a small smile as he looked down at the angelic face burrowed against his chest and he gently pushed back the silver-blond hair that lay against her cheek to feel her forehead for signs of fever. There was still some heat there, but very little compared to the raging blaze of the night before. Her body was soft and relaxed against his, and he was satisfied that Amanda was on her way to recovery.

Adam's eyes wandered aimlessly over her face for a few minutes, until they came to rest on her mouth, her lips slightly parted in sleep, showing the trace of perfect white teeth beneath. Slowly, without realizing his own intent, Adam lowered his head to cover for an instant those soft pink lips with his own. At the first sweet taste of her mouth, a low groan escaped him. His body's reaction was immediate and painfully difficult to resist. It would be so easy, his mind tempted him. She is here in my arms, her flesh pressed against mine, lovely, sweet, young, desirable, and innocent. He couldn't doubt the innocence that had radiated from that beautiful face in the short time they had been able to talk together.

He shook his head slightly, as if to deny his body's craving, and thought, "I'd better get up and dressed before she wakes up. It'll be hard enough to explain to her what happened last night, even fully clothed."

Gently he slid his arm out from beneath her head, and drew himself away, pausing slightly as he did to take one last look at the glorious creature he was denying himself. In the few seconds he gazed at her unbelievable perfection, he again felt a tight sensation in his stomach and wished fervently his father had not instilled in him such a deep respect for innocence and virginity. A small shudder passed over her body as the cool morning air touched her skin, and Adam, quickly and guiltily tucking the blanket around her, rose to slip on his still damp buckskins. Then, satisfied that Amanda was still sleeping, he started to collect kindling for a small fire. This morning he would use some of his precious store of tea, laced with rum, to give Amanda strength. His supplies were meager, only those he had been able to carry on his back when he had made a hurried exit from Fort Carillon. A small amount of tea, some biscuits, some strips of dried venison, and the ever present bottle of rum. After all, he had not contemplated a lengthy stay. But he was not worried. Game was abundant, and even if he could not risk a shot, he would set some snares this morning that were bound

45

to bring results. After stealing another covetous glance at his sleeping patient, Adam prepared to make a fire.

Within minutes a small blaze was burning, but a sense of watchful eyes interrupted Adam's concentration and he glanced up quickly to see Amanda's wide, puzzled gaze fastened on him, the blanket held securely up to her chin. The picture she presented, her eyes wide with bafflement, her hair in wild disarray as she clutched the blanket tightly around her, brought a broad smile to his lips. Turning, he said with exaggerated courtesy, "Well, good morning, my sleeping beauty. How are you today?"

Amanda had awakened slowly, her mind foggy, her memory blurred. The first thing she saw as she opened her eyes were trees overhead, moving gently in the soft morning breeze. She strained her mind, but could not seem to remember where she was. Fear began to take hold as her vagueness failed to clear, and looking to each side of her, she realized she lay on the ground, securely wrapped in a strange blanket. And I am naked! her mind shouted. Oh, why can't I think?

Suddenly the light sound of snapping twigs caught her attention, and she twisted to see a huge, sandy-haired man a few feet from her, feeding a small fire and tending a small pan that rested on it. He was not immediately aware of her gaze, and she silently studied the profile that was turned to her. His short-clipped, wavy blond hair combed back from a wide forehead curled gently at the nape of his neck, and his skin was deeply tanned. Sensing her perusal, he turned quickly to stare in her direction. Light, curious green eyes beneath heavy brown brows regarded her steadily and seemed to smile, as did his wide, generous mouth, which revealed a row of even white teeth. His nose was long and straight, and his strong, square chin bore a deep cleft. Surveying him further, she noted the incredible width of his shoulders, and as he stood and began to walk toward her, she was amazed by what seemed to her his unbelievable height. Noting the massive muscular structure tone of his body, obvious even through the buckskins he wore, she thought he appeared to be a giant of a man, a handsome, friendly giant. He came to her side, crouched down, and looked searchingly into her eyes as he reached out with the huge palm of his hand to touch her forehead.

"You haven't answered me, Amanda. How do you feel today? Your fever seems to be gone."

"You know my name?" she gasped, her puzzlement growing by leaps and bounds at his obvious familiarity with her and her complete ignorance of his identity.

"Of course I know your name. Don't you remember anything about yesterday? My name is Adam Carstairs."

Memory began to stir at the mention of his name, and fragments of pictures flashed across her mind: cool water against her skin, cooling the fire that was consuming her; and those same green eyes looking down at her, a deep voice repeating over and over, "Amanda, I'm going to help you feel better, feel better."

Amanda began to relax as she linked this face now looking down into hers with the man in her fragments of memory. She wasn't quite certain of the reason, but, no, she wasn't afraid of him.

As she continued searching her confused mind, he reached down beneath her blanket to her small foot, and holding it gently in his hand, he examined a small wound above her ankle that was still tender to the touch. Wincing slightly, she regarded it with a puzzled expression and Adam spoke slowly, his rich deep voice soothing and reassuring her with its warmth.

"You were bitten by a snake and stumbled out of the bushes almost into my arms. Do you remember, Amanda? You have a head wound, too, and had a very high fever last night. I had to carry you into the lake during the night to bring it down."

Inadvertently, Amanda glanced at her dress where it hung over the limb, and noting her glance, Adam continued, "Your dress is still damp. I'll bring it to you as soon as it dries completely. I don't want you to get a chill."

Nodding solemnly, her face flushed with embarrassment, Amanda accepted completely Adam's explanation, realizing he had done his best to eliminate some painful inquiries she might feel pressed to make.

"It seems I owe you a great deal, Mr. Carstairs."

"My name is Adam, Amanda." Adam corrected a bit more sharply than he had intended, feeling more annoyed than he cared to admit at her formal tone. Despite himself, Adam already felt extremely strong ties to her and was irritated beyond sensible proportion at her formality.

Blushing slightly at his unanticipated rebuke,

48

Amanda continued, "It looks like you've saved my life, Adam." She added his name hesitantly, and when its use brought the broad smile back to his face, she attempted to continue, only to be interrupted once again.

"I'm sure you would've done the same for me, wouldn't you?" Adam's gaze continued to hold hers.

"Probably so, but I am glad it happened the way it did. Otherwise," she added, shooting him a brief assessing glance, "I think I would've had a terrible time carrying you into the lake."

Adam gave a short hoot of laughter at her remark and, leaning forward, impulsively kissed her cheek, his green eyes dancing with merriment. Getting up he said, the laughter still at the edges of his voice, "Your tea should be ready now." And within minutes he held out a cup of tea and a biscuit for her to eat.

Propping herself on her elbow, Amanda took the cup and sipped it slowly, savoring the delicious brew as it slid down her throat, spreading its warmth throughout her. But within a few minutes her strength had drained away, and she was suddenly unable to support herself any longer.

Adam immediately moved to her side and sat, his arm supporting her as she drank. "The tea is laced with a little rum to give you strength, Amanda. Drink all of it, now, and eat your biscuit."

He smiled as Amanda docilely followed his directions, alternately sipping the tea and taking bites of the hard biscuit. His eyes stayed trained on her until the cup was emptied, and then he lowered her to the ground and tucked the blanket carefully around her.

"The rum will make you tired," he said, noticing the droop of her eyelids. "You'll sleep easily. Don't worry. I'll watch over you."

True to his predictions, within moments she was asleep.

Amanda's short term of wakefulness had not left her much time to dwell on the horrifying sequence of events during the past week, but in her subconscious, released in sleep, she relived again the death march. She saw savage war axes rending their victims, heard the agonized screams of the dying as the blood-curdling scalp yells echoed again and again. She saw her father's blood-drenched body, her mother's face as the last spark of life drained away, and Robert falling to the ground as the Indian started hotly in her pursuit. The sound of his ragged breathing behind her once again filled her ears; the descending war axe glinted brightly in the sun; and Amanda awoke screaming to feel herself being drawn into a warm, comforting embrace. She rested her tear-stained face against a now familiar chest.

Adam's voice was soft and reassuring. "Don't cry, Amanda, it's only a dream. You're awake now and you're safe with me."

"No, no," Amanda cried softly between deep, gulping sobs. "It wasn't a dream. It was a nightmare, a true, living nightmare. I'm awake now, but they're still dead, murdered. Mother and Father. . . ." She still couldn't bring herself to think of Robert. "I hate them all: the French, the Abnakis. . . ."

Adam held her until her heartbroken sobs diminished and finally stopped, all the while stroking her

50

hair lightly. After a few minutes of silence, Amanda related in a soft, hoarse voice the story of the devastation of the British fort, ending with heated intensity, "They're murderers, all of them, animals, killing without reason or mercy."

Adam stared down into her tormented face, sharing her anguish. "I don't know how to comfort you, Amanda. You're right, but there's been senseless killing on both sides. Sometimes I think we're all just pawns in a war started by France and England's excessive greed. Fort William Henry just had the misfortune to be situated at the head of Lake George, blocking the French passage southward from Canada. With the waterways being the only easy means of travel, it either had to be taken or destroyed or both. Unfortunately the French have been a little wiser in their treatment of the Indians than the British. They managed to convince the Indian leaders that Louis XV is their Great White Father. They consider themselves his children and expect his protection and generosity if they help in his war against us.

"You know, Amanda, before this war started, my parents and I lived in these woods in peace with the Indians. Most of them were honest and good neighbors. It was only after the tribes were incited to travel with the French and help drive out the British that I returned to find my home burned and my parents murdered and scalped like yours."

Adam's deep voice dropped off into silence after his last statement while Amanda's gaze studied his face, her sympathy evident in her sober expression. Giving her hand a reassuring squeeze, he continued.

"It's a poor reason for all this death and destruction, isn't it, Amanda? That's why I avoided the conflict for so long; but when my parents were killed I knew I had to make a decision. My own personal thought is that if this country has to be governed by any nation in Europe, although I can't understand why we can't govern ourselves, then I would prefer to be a British subject."

When he finished speaking, Adam smoothed back the silver wisps clinging to Amanda's damp face and gently brushed the last traces of tears from her cheeks with his calloused hand. She rested back heavily against his arm. Her head was aching, and she was confused and fatigued by the violent, unfamiliar emotions raging within her. Seeing her emotional exhaustion, Adam changed the subject lightly.

"I think your dress is dry now, Amanda. Would you like to get dressed?"

For a moment she was startled. In her befuddled state of mind, she had almost forgotten her state of undress; she blushed furiously. "Yes, Adam, I would like that."

Rising quickly, he retrieved her dress and, after handing it to her, turned his back to afford her some privacy. After a few moments, a sudden gasp from behind caused him to turn quickly back in her direction to see Amanda slipping to the ground. Her face was ghostly white, and small beads of perspiration shone on her forehead and delicate upper lip, disclosing how dearly the small effort of attempting to dress herself had taxed her limited strength.

"I'm a fool," Adam berated himself under his breath as he scooped her up to place her back on the blanket. "I should've helped you." Slowly, while

Adam watched her intently, chafing her cold hands, the color began to return to her face, and the dazed look left Amanda's eyes.

"Adam," Amanda's voice held a slightly shame-faced note. "I can't button my dress." Her face, so white only minutes before, suddenly colored hotly, and she lowered her eyes as she added quietly, "Would you help me, please?"

Without a word, Adam pulled her to a sitting position and, crouching down beside her, pulled her as if into an embrace, swept her hair over her shoulder and proceeded with his arms encircling her to button her dress. His fingers touched the smooth, white skin of her back exposed in her open dress, and, the desire to feel its silky texture under the palms of his hands was almost overpowering. Realizing his feelings were beginning to rise out of control, Adam, with trembling hands, finished the job quickly and just as quickly held her out an arm's length from him, his pulse racing. The paleness of her face, far from detracting from her beauty, only added to Amanda's fragile air, the light shadows emphasizing the blueness of her eyes until, as he looked at her, he felt himself almost lost in their depths. Silently cursing her sweet innocence, he dropped his eyes before her quizzical glance and lowered her again to the blanket.

"You'd better rest," he said gruffly, avoiding her eyes again. "I'll be close by. I'm going to check the snares."

With that statement, he rose and strode away, leaving Amanda completely puzzled by his abruptness. But she didn't ponder his illogical behavior long, and within minutes fell into a fast sleep.

Amanda awoke a short time later from a gentle dream to the delicious aroma of roasting meat. She sat up cautiously and, at the sound of her movement, Adam, who was crouched by the fire, turned sharply in her direction. Amanda was glad to see his earlier gruff mood had disappeared and a generous smile once again covered his face. Her bright answering smile caused Adam's heart to jump a beat as he watched the small dimple dart in and out beside her mouth. This little minx could wrap me around her little finger with just the slightest effort, he admitted to himself as he rose and walked toward her.

"What is that delicious smell, Adam?"

"We are going to have pheasant for supper tonight, my lady," he said laughingly as he scooped her up into his arms as easily as he would a child. Refusing to admit to himself he was holding her unnecessarily close, he brought her nearer the fire. He sat her down on a log which served as a seat, ripped two legs off the golden bird, and handing her one, supported her with his arm as they ate.

The meat was juicy and delicious and Amanda ate with unexpected relish. While she ate, she sneaked a look at the handsome giant seated beside her, so considerately supporting her back with his strong arm. Catching her glance, Adam looked down into her face inquiringly. She answered quietly his unasked question.

"I've been lucky in one thing, at least." And in answer to his speculative look, she continued, "That you were the one to find me."

Adam turned back toward the fire, a small voice in

54

the back of his mind whispering, I'm the lucky one.

The bright light of afternoon quickly slipped into evening, taking with it the warmth of the sun and bringing a chill to the damp forest air. Amanda shivered slightly as she lay on the bed Adam had so carefully arranged. Noticing her chill and fearing a recurrence of her fever, Adam quickly touched her forehead. It was blessedly cool under his hand.

"I'm not sick again, Adam. It's just getting a little cool, that's all."

Adam quickly poured some tea into their solitary cup and adding a healthy portion of rum, put it in her hand. "Here, drink this. It will warm you."

As she drank, Adam took the other blanket and tucked it around her. Unaccustomed to strong spirits, Amanda almost immediately felt the effects of the rum and began to doze drowsily. As her eyes fluttered open, she noticed Adam had moved the log closer to the fire and lay propped against it, trying to warm himself by its heat. Looking down, she realized that she lay wrapped in both his blankets, and embarrassed by her thoughtlessness, she called out, "Adam, it's cool tonight. Please take one of these blankets for yourself. I'm really quite warm now."

"You need them more than I do, Amanda. I'm used to sleeping outdoors. I really don't feel the dampness at all."

Realizing he was merely making excuses for his generosity, Amanda started to pull at the top blanket, at which Adam rose angrily and walked toward her. He bent down and tucked the blanket firmly back around her. "I told you I don't need a blanket, Amanda. Go back to sleep."

"I will not sleep with two blankets when you have none!" Amanda's voice was weak, but her determination was evident.

"And I will not take one of these blankets from you!" Adam's voice was just as adamant as he stared into her stubborn blue eyes.

Realizing as she looked into his determined face that neither was willing to budge from his resolve, she hesitated a moment and then said matter-of-factly, "Then you'll have to share these with me. Come on. Get under," she said, lifting the corner. "Then we'll both be warm."

At his dumbstruck expression, Amanda laughed shyly. "I know it's not conventional, Adam, but I know I can trust you, and I no longer have anything to hide." Her face flushed with embarrassment, she determinedly continued, "So if you have no objection to sharing these blankets with me, I'll be happy to share them with you."

Then, as she saw stubbornness replace the incredulous look on his face, she added quietly, "As a matter of fact, Adam, I'll only use both blankets under those conditions."

Adam stared at her for a few minutes, realizing she would not budge from her stand, and then a slow smile started across his face. His deep voice tinged with laughter, he bowed his head, saying with mock formality, "Whatever you say, my lady."

He then lowered himself to the ground and slipped under the blankets, pulling her snugly against him to tuck the blankets around them both. Looking down into the face that was pressed so sleepily against his chest, he said, "Now will you go to sleep?"

"Whatever you say, my lord," was her soft reply as she gave him a quick wink and just as quickly closed her eyes, a small smile dimpling her face.

His answering smile was unseen by Amanda as she drifted off into slumber, and he lay awake for the better part of an hour, more disturbed than he cared to admit by the sensation of holding her so close in his arms.

Amanda had fallen asleep quickly. The rum added so generously to her tea had the effect of a sedative, but she found herself wakeful as the night progressed. Several times she had awakened startled by the huge figure holding her so close, even as he slept. After a few moments her foggy mind had set the facts to right, and once she had recalled her suggestion that Adam share her blankets, the only question that remained was why she had suggested it! Surely Mother and Father would be scandalized if they found out. But they were both dead, and there was no longer fear of any of her behavior upsetting them. But Robert, he would be angry if he knew that she had spent the night sleeping in another man's arms! But as far as she knew, Robert could no longer hold her to account for her actions because she had also seen him fall. Well then, certainly her present arrangement was strictly against all the codes of conduct she had been taught. As a decent, well-brought-up young lady she should not be sleeping under these conditions, much less be the instigator of the situation! Holding herself completely and solely at fault, Amanda pulled herself back a bit to steal a look in the bright moonlight at Adam's face as he slept.

He's very handsome, she thought as she slowly perused his sleeping countenance. His thick, unruly hair had fallen boyishly forward on his forehead, and his heavy, dark lashes lay against his tanned cheeks, hiding those bright, intense green eyes that she had been unable to forget even in her delirium. Her eyes traveled Adam's face, resting for a moment on his straight, perhaps a bit sharp nose. But certainly it was in perfect proportion with his face, and with his wide, generous mouth, whose smile she could still remember warming her with its openness and sincerity. And that cleft in his chin. She had never known anyone with a cleft before. Without thinking, she reached up a finger to touch it lightly as he slept. Adam stirred slightly at her touch and Amanda guiltily snapped her eyes shut for fear she had awakened him and would incur his displeasure. Within a few minutes, realizing he had not stirred any further, Amanda peeked out behind partially closed lids to see he still slept, and then boldly continued her perusal of him as he lay on his side facing her. Her eyes went down the strong, wide column of his neck, across his phenomenal expanse of shoulders, and came to rest on his chest, where the open lacing of his shirt exposed a light covering of golden brown hairs. Amanda giggled as she recalled how those same hairs had tickled her nose when she had lain with her face pressed against his chest only minutes before. She then remembered clearly. What had been her alternative to inviting him to share her blankets? Since he selflessly refused to take one for himself, he would have had to shiver out the night trying to keep warm by a fire that had already burned low. This sympathetic, generous man had saved her life not once, but perhaps twice in the past twenty-four hours. No, she had not been foolish or immoral in insisting he share her blankets, and no matter how unusual the appearances seemed, she knew she didn't have to fear him. He had had all the opportunity he needed to do his worst to her, but had only treated her with sympathetic concern. Amanda knew her parents, had they been able to see the situation, would understand, and she could only hope that Robert would understand also.

Looking up again at Adam's face, his dark brows knit together in a frown, no doubt the result of a disagreeable dream, Amanda smiled, completely at peace with her conscience. Moving slightly, she pressed a light kiss against his chin and whispered softly, "Thank you, Adam."

Snuggling back against his chest, she then fell into an easy sleep.

Amanda finally awoke the next morning and looked around, judging it to be midmorning by the brightness of the day and the position of the sun that within a few hours would be directly overhead in the brilliantly blue sky. She was alone and Adam was not visible within the camp. She called his name and waited a few minutes, but no response broke the silence that seemed to her to grow more oppressive with every minute. She called again, her voice seeming to echo in the stillness, but heard no response. A fierce stab of fear pierced her stomach, and she started to tremble as unreasonable panic overtook her. The memory of glinting black eyes and a descending war axe returned to her mind and rationality deserted her.

"Where is he? I must find him."

She hurriedly began to rise from her blankets when the sudden sound of a footstep in the bush behind her caused her to freeze with fright. Then she turned expectantly, only to see Adam step into the clearing, holding a rabbit in his hand.

"It looks like we'll eat well today, Amanda," he stated with a satisfied smile. Then Amanda's panicked expression met his gaze, and dropping the game he rushed to crouch at her side. "What is it, Amanda? What's wrong?" he asked, touching her forehead with his palm, testing for fever. She was cool to his touch, but was still shaking violently and unable to speak. Adam was bewildered. Glancing around cautiously, he pressed, "Did you see something that frightened you? Did something hurt you?"

When she did not respond to his questions, Adam, grasping her shoulders in a firm grip, gave her a light shake, as if to shake loose the answer she was withholding. Her eyes still wide with panic, she swallowed convulsively several times and finally regaining her voice, murmured haltingly, "I woke up and you weren't here. I thought you had left me."

Amanda's eyes fell before Adam's unbelieving stare as he said incredulously, "You thought I had what?"

For a few moments there was silence and then a small, wry laugh escaped his lips as Adam pulled her comfortingly into his large, brawny arms. "Amanda, you little fool, how could you believe that for even a minute? Don't you realize that I care about you?" His voice halted strangely in midsentence as he whispered softly against her hair.

Amanda rested weakly in his embrace, those few short minutes of panic having depleted much of her small reservoir of strength. Rising, Adam drew her up with him and then carried her in his arms to a seat near their small fire where he announced solemnly, "It's time for breakfast, my lady."

Amanda spent the remainder of that morning either dozing or watching Adam as he prepared the rabbit he had caught for supper. As midafternoon approached, the golden summer sun glinting on the placid surface of the lake seemed to beckon her, and she began to rise. At her first sign of movement, Adam turned sharply.

"What are you doing? If you need something, just ask me. I'll get it for you. I don't want you wasting your strength. There'll be time enough for walking when we start out for Fort Edward."

For a moment Amanda flushed with anger at his unwarranted attack, and then his words registered with startling impact. Back to Fort Edward! He was right, they would have to go back. She hadn't considered that yet; but what would she go back to? Her parents and all their possessions were gone. And Robert! She couldn't bear to think of him because in her heart she was certain he, too, had been killed. What then? Perhaps Aunt Margaret. But her large brood was difficult enough to provide for. She didn't need an extra mouth to feed. No, she just wouldn't think of it yet.

Looking up, Amanda realized Adam had paused in his work, still awaiting her reply. Why was he so angry?

"I'd like to go to the edge of the lake and bathe, Adam."

Adam frowned. He had been unnecessarily sharp. Why did he resent her first independent move? The answer was only too clear in his mind. He was enjoying her dependence on him and wanted to keep her tied to him with that dependence. One part of him rejoiced at the health he could see returning to her hour by hour in the clarity of her eyes and in her returning color, but another part of him despaired at her fast progress toward good health and out of his care.

"Do you think you'll be able to handle that so soon, Amanda? You haven't even walked alone yet. I wouldn't want you to fall or risk getting a chill."

"I'm not as fragile as you think, Adam. I can make it." There was a trace of rebellion in her tone.

Before he realized, he had moved to her side and helped her to her feet. He stood watchfully as she wavered hesitantly for a few seconds and began walking to the lake. After a few steps, Amanda seemed to sway as a pain struck the wounds in her leg and head simultaneously, almost causing her to fall, but Adam's strong arm was immediately around her waist, supporting her. With his help she walked to the edge of the lake and sat abruptly.

Mumbling a soft, "Thank you," she avoided his eyes and the righteous look she was certain she would see there. Gingerly she stretched out her feet until the water, warmed at the shallow edges to a soothing lukewarm temperature, lightly caressed them. Raising her skirt slightly, she bent to splash some of its freshness on her legs and arms.

Realizing he was no longer needed, Adam dropped the torn fragment of her petticoat by her side so she might dry herself and turned away. The picture Amanda presented at the edge of the lake brought back too vividly the memory of that first night, and the silky feeling of her soft, white skin against his as he carried her into the lake.

"Call me when you're done. Don't try to walk back by yourself," he said over his shoulder as he made a hasty exit.

Amanda nodded absentmindedly as she continued to bathe, her mind already beginning to drift aimlessly.

Steadfastly refusing to look back, Adam determinedly returned to their camp, although the urge to turn and indulge himself, feasting his eyes on her beauty as she trailed the clear water across her soft, white skin was almost overpowering. Adam sat again, and for a moment, leaning his elbows on his knees, covered his face in bewildered disgust with himself.

What's wrong with me? She's beautiful and innocent, and only a child, at least to a man of my years and experience, he thought. This brought to mind a few of his most recent lady friends, who now appeared jaded and tarnished in his mind's eye. Desire was not a new sensation to him. He had felt it countless times for many women, but this feeling of deep and absolute tenderness that Amanda evoked in him, as well as the strong, soul-shaking desire he also

63

felt, and his overwhelming need to watch over and protect her, were passions that were tearing him apart. Since first setting eyes on her, his previously all-consuming fire to accomplish the vow he had made over his parents' graves had receded to the back of his mind as he had become obsessed by the little beauty now softly humming to herself at the water's edge.

Get hold of yourself, man! his mind railed. Put things in their proper perspective! Within the week she'll be feeling well enough to make a slow journey to Fort Edward and your duty will be over. Then she'll easily slip from your mind. Adam tried to think of the women he knew in the vicinity of Fort Edward, but the ruse didn't work. With a deep sigh, he stirred up the fire and turned his attention to their supper. While Amanda had been dozing, he had even managed to find some ripe juicy berries to provide a little variety in their menu, and had hidden them so the surprise might stimulate her appetite. He laughed silently to himself. Just like a love-struck schoolboy, he thought, and shook his head slightly, hardly believing his own actions.

Despite his resolve, his eyes returned to the water's edge. Amanda had managed to unbutton a few of the buttons on the back of her dress and pulling it down slightly in front, was sponging her neck and shoulders with a piece of material she had ripped from her petticoat. Watching her, he remembered how gently he had dried her slender body which had lain gleaming in the moonlight under his hands: her round, young breasts, the delicate pink tips an appealing invitation even then; her incredibly small waist; those only slightly rounded hips, down to. . . .

64

Damn! he thought, moving to sit facing the other direction so he could no longer infringe on her privacy. You are a fool!

Time seemed to drag by interminably until Amanda called, "Adam, I'm finished. You wanted me to call you."

Forcing himself to move slowly instead of following his inclination to rush to her side, Adam approached her, the battle within him causing a deep frown to appear on his face.

Amanda was startled by his dour expression. He told me to call him, but I suppose although he feels he knows his responsibility, he can't make himself enjoy it. And I suppose for that reason I should appreciate all he's doing for me even more, her mind countered. As a result of her reasoning, Adam's black scowl was met with a smile, and a look in Amanda's eyes that tore at his very heart.

Adam did not attempt to let her walk, but instead scooped her into his arms in one fluid motion, taking the only excuse he had to touch and hold her close.

"You'll make an invalid out of me, Adam, if you won't let me walk," she protested. In response he grumbled, "You'll have plenty of time to walk." Depositing her on the blanket, he turned abruptly back to the fire.

Within a few minutes his pensive gaze returned to Amanda again as she struggled to separate the tangled strands of her hair with her fingers. Noticing his attention, she said hopelessly, "My hair is so tangled. I'll have to cut it off if I leave it untended too much longer."

Cut off her hair! That gloriously silky mass! Never! He would never allow it! Wordlessly he began to search among the small number of things he had carried from Fort Carillon. There it was, the slightly yellowed bone comb, one of the few things he had found miraculously unbroken in the remains of his parents' cabin. He had remembered with great fondness his mother combing her long graying hair before bedtime, and had sentimentally carried it with him ever since the day he had found them. Walking over to Amanda, he put it into her hand. Amanda colored lightly as she looked at the delicate painted flowers bordering the gracefully carved comb, realizing it had belonged to a woman. Did he keep it as a reminder of an old love?

Answering her unspoken question, Adam said quietly, "It was my mother's. It's old, but it'll take out a few of those snarls."

Blushing even deeper because of the error of her assumption, Amanda said in honest appreciation, "I'm honored you would let me use it, Adam."

Adam appeared to want to say more, but changed his mind and abruptly turned once again to walk back to the fire.

He busied himself turning the rabbit he had skewered with a stick and rigged over the fire on a wooden spit. Adam glanced back now and again to silently watch as Amanda patiently took one section of hair at a time and combed the tangles free. She soon had just the back portion left where her head wound complicated the procedure. Her first attempt provoked a grimace of pain, and her second brought tears to her eyes Unable to stand it any longer, Adam moved to her side. Seating himself beside her, he took the comb from her hand and gently examined the wound.

"It's healing well," he mumbled under his breath. And then louder for her benefit he said, "But some of your hair has become stuck fast to it. When the healing is complete and the scab is free, you'll be able to comb that section of hair easily. In the meantime, I'll comb around it for you."

Then, surprising himself, Adam gently completed the work Amanda had started. When he was done, her hair lay in a shimmering gold and silver cloud around her shoulders. Gliding his hand over its shining surface, Adam said softly, "You have beautiful hair, Amanda. But I suppose you've heard that often before."

"Robert—did often compliment me on my hair."

Feeling a sudden stab of jealousy at the sound of that name again on her lips, Adam inquired lightly as he wound his hand again and again in the length of her tresses, "Who's Robert?" He saw her eyes fill with tears as she responded softly, "He's my be—betrothed." She faltered slightly, finding the word unfamiliar on her tongue.

"Your betrothed! That's impossible! How old are you, Amanda?"

"I'm sixteen years old. Quite old enough to be a wife," she said defensively.

"And how old is this boy Robert?"

"Robert isn't a boy; he's a man! He's twenty-six years old!" Amanda felt herself angering at his patronizing tone.

Adam's eyebrows raised with surprise. Twenty-six!

"And where is he now?" he questioned further.

The tears that had before been brimming in her eyes now spilled over and ran in two shining streams down her face as she sobbed out, admitting to herself at last, "He's dead. I know it. He's dead. I saw him fall!"

Finally released, the tears came pouring out in a torrent as Amanda leaned heavily against Adam's chest, sobbing convulsively. Adam drew her up tightly against him whispering soothingly, his face pressed against her hair, until he froze for a second in horrified realization. He was smiling!

Lord help me, he thought, still shocked and angered at his own inhuman reaction. I'm actually glad the man is dead! Experiencing a sharp sense of guilt, he questioned himself silently, What kind of an animal have I become that I'd rather see a man dead than lose her dependence on me? Shamed by his own instinctive reaction, he blatantly refused to face his confused emotions. It doesn't matter, his mind rationalized. She's alone and needs me, and while I'm needed, I'll be there.

With that solemn acknowledgement, his arms tightened around her possessively. He'd return her to Fort Edward and see her settled. Once they were in the fort and away from the intimacy of their situation, he'd be able to think more clearly and be more sensible. Then he would see.

Amanda, having finally sobbed out her grief until no more tears would come, remained placidly in his arms.

Pushing her gently from against his chest, he looked steadily into her sad blue eyes, where traces of tears still clung on her long, dark lashes, and smiling he said softly, "Come on, Amanda. I've been preparing this food for most of the day. It would be a shame to have it wasted."

He stood and drew her to her feet. Brushing back the bright cloud of hair that fell forward on her face, he slipped his arm around her shoulders and supported her lightly as she walked the few steps to the fire. After seating her gently, he gave his attention to the rabbit, which was a lovely golden color, and bursting with juice. Drawing his knife, he cut a piece and held it out to Amanda.

"Well, what do you think? Does it look ready?" His heart gave a little lurch as a small, tremulous smile appeared on her beautiful young face, and that tiny dimple winked at him speculatively.

Taking the meat from his hand, she took a generous bite and murmured indistinctly, "It's perfect, Adam."

Looking back to the roasting meat, Adam sliced another piece with a trembling hand. Whatever they were, his feelings for Amanda shook him to the very core, and it was a few minutes before he was again able to sit beside her and eat calmly.

In the forest evening arrived quickly on the heels of the descending sun. This night there was no arguing about the sharing of blankets as Adam, after tending the fire, walked to where Amanda lay and slipped easily beneath the blankets beside her. Sliding his arm around her, he whispered softly against her hair, "Go to sleep, Amanda, and don't be afraid if I'm not here when you wake up. I won't be far from you."

She closed her eyes in answer and was, within moments, fast asleep.

The next few days were spent in the same easy pattern, as Amanda grew in strength. The rest and the golden summer days brought a bright color to her smooth, white cheeks, and added the sparkle of health to her already glorious blue eyes. Adam had not believed it possible, but before his eyes she grew more lovely each day with returning health, until just to look at her caused him an agony of joy he had never thought to experience. The nights spent holding her chaste young innocence against him provided all the penance a sinner could expect on earth. But, as she grew stronger, Adam felt his confusion mounting. He seemed to alternate between the desire to keep her to himself and an eagerness to be away so he might test his feelings under more normal conditions. After four days had passed, he could see the decision had been made for him. He was certain Amanda was strong enough to be able to make the trip, provided they took adequate rest along the way. Hiding his reluctance, he spoke casually.

"We'll break camp tomorrow morning, Amanda, and start back." He saw her body stiffen and knew she was hesitant to return to a world where her family and betrothed had been murdered and she was completely alone. How he longed to ease her fears, but he knew instinctively she had no suspicion of his feelings, as well as he knew her feelings for him were nothing more than affection. Any declaration he would make now would only put an additional strain on an already uncertain situation. She was not yet ready to face her future.

Anxious to be away, Adam rose before light had completely penetrated the darkness of the night sky and almost completely erased the signs of their camp at the side of the lake. All that remained was to have a quick breakfast and start out. Once on the trail their meals would consist of dried venison strips he had taken with him from Fort Carillon and wisely conserved for the trek. The trails to Fort Edward were good and easy to follow, and if they were lucky, and Amanda's strength held out, he felt they could easily make it back in three days.

Touching her shoulder gently and restraining a strong desire to kiss open her sleepy eyes, Adam awakened Amanda and urged her to get up. His anxiety to be on his way did not go unnoticed by Amanda and she felt curiously let down to see he was so anxious to move on. *He probably can't wait to be free of me.* The thought stung, but she was determined to neither show it or hold it against him. *He certainly deserves a break from his nursemaid chores,* she reasoned. *Instead of being offended, I should remember I owe him my life.* But the thought subconsciously haunting her as she rose and rolled up the blankets was what she was now to do with that life Adam had so skillfully saved.

Once they were moving, Adam did very little talking, conserving his energy and directing his attention to the trail and the surrounding forest. He didn't expect to come across anyone on their three-day trek, but didn't dare let his attention become lax on the chance there were still some Indians in the area. Still, Amanda noticed he kept a watchful eye on her, constantly looking for signs of stress or fatigue and at every pause for rest, examining her face carefully and touching her forehead to check for recurrence of fever.

Her heart warmed at his obvious concern for her, and she flashed him a tired smile, which, in Adam's agitated state, was almost his undoing. His fear for the strain on her newly regained health only intensi-

71

fied his steadily growing feelings for her, and he felt in that moment an almost overwhelming desire to take her in his arms right then and there.

Misunderstanding the obvious tension her smile had evoked, Amanda turned her head. He thinks I'm not taking our situation seriously and is annoyed with me. The remainder of the day was passed in silence.

Their second day on the trail progressed in much the same manner, with very little conversation, as they conserved their strength for the trail ahead. It was more than midway through the day when an odor in the air caught Amanda's attention. Adam quickly turned to glance in her direction. He, too, had smelled the odor of burned wood and smoke that seemed to grow stronger every minute. They must be getting closer.

Amanda closed her mind to her surroundings and made herself follow resolutely in Adam's footsteps, thinking of nothing. She didn't want to think.

After a short while, she realized Adam had slowed his pace, and was glancing more and more often in her direction. Finally he came to an abrupt halt.

"We can't avoid the site, Amanda. In a while we'll be at Fort William Henry." His eyes were warm green again, as he looked sympathetically into her pale, stricken face. "Come on, you have to face it eventually."

He slipped his arm around her shoulder and walked beside her, for how long, how far, she wasn't certain. But suddenly it was there before her, the black, charred remains of the once proud and brave Fort William Henry. Even as she looked at the desecrated spot, she blinked in wonder. Nothing remained! Even the charred remains had been leveled completely!

Amanda felt the tremble that had started deep inside increase in intensity until her entire body was shaking convulsively. Then as a sharp, ragged sob tore through her, she began to run blindly, her only thought to elude the memories that were returning to haunt her as she stood at the site of a nightmare. On and on she ran, deep sobs stealing her breath as she stumbled in her wild desire to escape. Suddenly she tripped over a low limb; but the moment before she fell, she was scooped up into strong arms, and her wild flight was over. She buried her face against Adam's neck, her tears running down onto his chest in steady streams as she gave full vent to her emotions. Finally his step slowed. He stopped to sit on a boulder, still holding her in his arms, and whispered as her sobs subsided,

"Are you ready to go on now, Amanda? We've faced the worst now. It won't be much longer. We should reach Fort Edward tomorrow morning." His voice was deep with encouragement.

As she looked into his face, the steadiness of his gaze seemed to infuse her with the strength she needed to go on. Taking a deep breath, Amanda brushed away the remaining tears and nodded her head in silent assent. Adam's answering look was strange and, to Amanda, unreadable. He released her and then strode away wordlessly, his gait as steady as he dared, while she again took up behind.

Shortly before noon of the third day, Adam turned with an encouraging smile and took her hand as he said softly, "We're almost there."

Within minutes Fort Edward was visible, and

73

Amanda looked hesitantly at its walls, her uncertainty clearly visible. Slipping his arm around her, Adam pulled her forward to walk by his side in the cleared area nearer the fort. Unconsciously, Amanda noted they weren't challenged. Obviously Adam is well known here, she thought as they walked through the gates into the safety of the fort.

Amanda didn't look around, only up at Adam's suddenly beaming face. His happiness was apparent as a few soldiers called greetings and some slapped his back good-naturedly. "What did you bring with you this time, Adam? I see your taste is improving!" a bawdy male voice called out.

But before he could voice a reply, a high-pitched female voice cried out, "Amanda!" and a large, flaxen-haired woman rushed over to take Amanda in her anxious, motherly arms.

"Betty!" Amanda's cry of recognition was joyful as she recognized her mother's friend.

"Thank the Lord you're alive." Betty Mitchell sobbed out. "Your parents didn't make it, my dear," she added more softly.

"I know." Amanda's response was just as soft as she pulled slightly away to look into the woman's kindly, worn face.

"Betty, I'd like you to meet—" but her introduction was never completed as an unbelieving male voice called out, "Amanda? Is it you?"

She turned to face the voice, and there was absolute recognition and a joyous shout, "Amanda!"

Adam turned to see a tall, brown-haired young man rush to crush Amanda in his arms, his mouth cutting short her joyful exclamation, "Robert!"

74

Three

Robert here? Impossible, he's dead! Adam stood numbly for endless moments, stubbornly refusing to accept the evidence before his eyes as Robert swept Amanda wildly into his arms and kissed her again and again. Suddenly he was almost overcome with a deep, possessive rage and the desire to tear them apart. She's mine, she's mine! his mind screamed, but knowing he had no real claim to her, he merely watched with morbid fascination until the gnawing ache deep inside him grew so intense it was almost more than he could bear. The knot in his throat tightened, nearly taking his breath, and with a sense of utter futility, he finally turned away to escape the scene that was causing him such pain.

At that moment, gently extricating herself from Robert's embrace, Amanda turned her brilliant tearful smile on him. "Adam, isn't it wonderful? Robert's alive!" She turned back to stare for a moment at the young colonial, and repeated incredulously, "He's alive!" Then taking Adam's hand, she pulled him forward and said softly, "Robert, I want you to meet Adam Carstairs. He found me in the forest and treated my wounds. For the past week he's been my doctor and protector, but most of all, my friend." Her shining blue eyes looked up at Adam, unknowingly twisting the knife of pain he felt piercing his heart.

"He saved my life, Robert, and brought me back to you."

Adam wanted to shout, no, not for him. I brought you back for me. But with a supreme effort he calmly shook the hand extended to him in greeting, and with a stiff nod, acknowledged the profuse thanks that Robert offered, noting painfully that once his presence had been acknowledged, they seemed to forget his existence and were once again lost in each other. Adam could stand no more, and turning abruptly, he strode away to seek some privacy, only to be stopped by a young officer before he had walked a few feet.

"Mr. Carstairs, General Webb would like to see you, sir."

Nodding his head, Adam followed the soldier, appreciative of the excuse to leave the scene, for he suddenly realized he had been striding away with no destination in mind.

Adam was immediately ushered into the quarters of General Daniel Webb, and felt the same sense of distaste he had felt numerous times in the past when reporting the results of his surveillances to the commander of the fort. General Webb, he knew, must have been aware that Fort William Henry was under attack. Yet Amanda had told him they received no aid from Fort Edward. Why had he not sent help to the dying fort? In his heart, the heart of a fighting man, Adam knew the answer; and for that reason, his flesh crawled when speaking to the commander who had allowed so many of his countrymen to die.

However, in the absence of any higher authority, Adam was obliged to report, only too late, his recognizance of the French fort. He knew that in the past his undercover work had been very successful. As he spoke, Adam noted that the general appeared a bit more pale than usual, and he hoped the man's conscience was not lying dormant.

At the completion of Adam's report, General Webb's nasal tones resounded in the quiet of the room. "You have had a long, hard trek from Fort Carillon, Adam, but I would like to ask a favor of you. I have sent Major Putnam and his rangers to scout the area of Fort William Henry. They report the French have left by way of the lake. Major Putnam has filed a report that I'd like you to read."

Accepting the brief document handed to him Adam read:

The Fort was entirely destroyed; the barracks, outhouses and buildings were a heap of ruins—the cannon, stores, boats and vessels were all carried away. The fires were still burning—the smoke and stench offensive and suffocating. Innumerable fragments of human skulls and bones and carcasses half consumed, were still frying and broiling in the decaying fires. Dead bodies mangled with scalping knives and tomahawks, in all the wantonness of Indian barbarity, were everywhere to be seen. More than one hundred women butchered and shockingly mangled, lay upon the ground, still weltering in their gore. Devastation, barbarity and horror everywhere appeared; and the spectacle presented was too diabolical and awful either to be endured or described.

Adam concluded reading the report and looked up, his face devoid of color, as General Webb continued. "Why they did not proceed against Fort Edward after the destruction of Fort William Henry is unknown to us. We would like to know what they're up to, and with all the activity at Fort Carillon now, you would be the best man to get that information to us. Will you do it?"

Adam looked into the face of the portly, gray-haired officer, feeling the heavy weight of fatigue that the three days of travel and tension had wrought. But realizing he could no longer stay in the same fort that held Amanda and her betrothed, he snatched gratefully at the excuse provided him to leave.

"When did you want me to start, General?"

"I realize you are tired, Adam. Rest a few days."

"I'll leave tomorrow morning."

Surprised at Adam's quick acquiescence, but grateful nonetheless, General Webb extended his hand to seal the bargain.

"Done, then, Adam. Lieutenant Arthur will give you his room for tonight so you may rest undisturbed and leave as early as you wish. Good luck."

With a nod, Adam turned on his heel to follow the lieutenant to the privacy of his room.

Wild with elation, Robert struggled to regain his composure. Gone in one moment of explosive joy was the black depression of the past week when he had thought Amanda lost to him forever. Even now as he held her close, trembling with the myriad of emotions that engulfed his senses, he could not fully believe the miraculous turn of events that had restored her to him.

He had spent the past week in endless recriminations, reliving countless times the scene of the massacre when he had last seen Amanda alive, remembering with horror how the same Abnaki who had knocked him to the ground had turned and pursued her into the forest. He had struggled to his feet and started after them but hindered by his wound, had not reached Amanda in time to prevent the blow that struck her down. In his fury, he had managed to overcome the Indian just before he, too, had succumbed to his wound and fallen into unconsciousness.

When he had awakened, Amanda was not there. The Abnaki lay dead at his side, but Amanda was gone. He had then made his way back to the column, thinking she had been taken to Fort Edward with the wounded, but when he arrived, Amanda was nowhere to be found.

Although overcome with grief, he had been too weak from his wound to search for her, and to his despair, he realized that even if he had his full strength, he still wouldn't have known in which direction to begin. For all he knew, if she still lived, she was by that time on her way to slavery in the

North, or worse.

Today, a week later, he had emerged from the casement rooms at Fort Edward, having heard a commotion in the fort yard, and had seen Amanda's back, her unmistakable hair hanging to her waist, shimmering in the bright sun like a golden waterfall. Surely no one else had hair like that. He had called hesitantly, "Amanda, is it you?"

She had then turned to provide the face that fulfilled his dream!

"Amanda!"

Robert did not remember closing the remainder of the distance between them, but within seconds she was in his arms. His love! His angel! The memory of the sweet warm taste of her mouth did not quite meet the ecstasy of reality, of holding her so close again.

For a brief moment he had felt jealousy mar his happiness when he had been introduced to Amanda's friend, Adam Carstairs, and had looked up to see reflected in that blond giant's eyes all the agony of love lost, and had realized in that instant that Adam loved her, too. But then, glancing down at the shining innocent face of his beloved, he had thought simply, How could he not love her?

Now, reluctant to release her for even a moment, he continued to hold her in his arms, his face pressed against her shining hair. He spoke, his voice thick with emotion. "You're here now, darling, and we'll be married immediately. There's no need to wait. You know we had your parents' blessings."

Noticing as he drew back for her reaction that tears once again formed in her eyes, he hastened to add, "They put you in my care, Amanda, and they'd be happy to know you are being provided for."

Nodding lightly her throat too tight to speak, Amanda solemnly indicated her agreement.

Amanda sat in quiet contemplation her first few moments alone after the shock and excitement of Robert's reappearance, and her first thoughts were of Adam. Where had he gone? He certainly couldn't wait to be free of me, she thought grimly, amazed again at the way the thought stung. She had grown so very fond of Adam. He had almost become a part of her. She could still remember the sensation of his arms about her as she slept, his presence weaving a cocoon of warmth that was not all physical. It was a warmth that started deep inside when he took her into his arms, and continued to build as she lay each night with her head against his broad chest, until it enveloped her completely, covering her in delicious waves of an emotion she could only describe as total contentment. But obviously Adam had not felt the same. He had seen his duty and done it, and Amanda would be forever thankful. She only wished. . . .

Adam lay exhausted but unsleeping in his bed, thankful for the privacy of the lieutenant's small room. He stared up at the ceiling, seeing not its dull, warped surface, but a small beautiful face, blue eyes great and shining, a small perfect mouth in a wide, happy smile, that little dimple teasing him again. How many times had he wanted to feel that dimple beneath his lips? As he tossed restlessly on the narrow cot, his mind reconstructed with annoying clarity the scene that had taken place in the dining hall earlier.

Tom Higgins, his wide homely face flushed with rum, winked slyly at Adam as he said in a loud, suggestive manner, "You must have had a memorable week, my friend, all alone in the woods with that pretty young wench Robert Handly is so wild about. All the while he was here, bemoaning his lost angel, you were in the woods enjoying her charms, eh? Tell me, Adam," he said, poking him coyly in the ribs with his elbow. "Did you return her to Master Robert in the same condition she left him, or is she changed in a way poor Robert won't realize until it's too late?"

Tom had consumed far too much rum to notice Adam's face flushing with anger as he spoke; he also failed to notice the extreme care with which he slowly lowered his spoon to the table and turned to face him. However, once faced with the look of thunderous fury that distorted Adam's handsome features until he looked the picture of the wrath of God, his face paled; the leering smile disappeared to be replaced by an unmistakable expression of fear.

Adam spoke softly, his voice shaking with fury but carrying in the hush that had settled over the dining hall with the power of a shout, "I'll say this once and once only, Tom Higgins. Amanda Starkweather is a lovely, innocent girl. I found her wounded in the forest, as you heard her explain to her betrothed. She behaved and was treated as the sweet young lady that she is, and anyone I hear even intimate that anything other than that happened during the last week will answer to me!" After a moment's hesitation, Adam added in a dangerous warning voice, the cold glare of his icy green eyes causing the blood to recede even further from the drunken soldier's face, "Do you understand what I say, Tom?"

Tom's mouth had suddenly gone dry as cotton and the problem he had forcing words from his fear-parched throat was obvious as he quickly stammered, "Of—of course, Adam. I—I was only joking, you know."

"We won't have any more jokes at Amanda Starkweather's expense while I'm here." Adam's piercing stare finally left Tom's perspiring face and returned to his plate. After he had finished, he rose without a word and walked away.

One more word out of that drunken bastard and I would've killed him, Adam admitted to himself as he lay on his lonesome cot. Lord, how he missed Amanda in his arms! This was the first night in over a week that she was not sleeping beside him. I wonder, does she miss me, too? he mused. And then he berated himself for his foolishness. She has forgotten I ever existed now that she has her Robert back. Judging from the look on that young man's face, he won't be waiting long to take her to wife, and then she'll sleep in his arms, and he'll make love to her the way I—Adam's fists clenched in utter frustration, tightening until the tendons in his arms stood out like knotted cords against his smooth tanned skin.

"Damn, Damn!" he said aloud as thoughts of Amanda continued to plague him, deepening his sense of loss, dragging him lower and lower into depression. Memories of the past week continued to flood his mind, and it seemed suddenly incomprehensible that a week before he had not even been aware of her existence when he realized that now, since she had been removed from his care and was beyond his reach, the future seemed to stretch out empty and endless without her.

With a short, bitter laugh he ruthlessly mocked himself. How cautious you were in acknowledging your feelings. Your feelings couldn't possibly last; you were too experienced with women, immune to their charms. The attraction you felt for her would fade like all the others. What you felt for her was only a passing fancy. And if it wasn't, you had all the time in the world to make certain before you committed yourself. You fool! Stupid, arrogant fool! Did it take the pain of seeing her in someone else's arms to make you admit your love for her? And now it's too late for you, too late!

"Oh, Lord," he groaned. The agony of memory deepened his despair as he recalled Amanda in Robert's embrace, his arms straining her tightly against him, his mouth covering her warm, soft lips, tasting the sweetness of her mouth. The pain of losing her seared him, burning deeply into his chest, cutting and twisting until he felt he could bear no longer the cruel fate which had given Amanda to him for such a short time, only to snatch her away again. In a desperate attempt to shield himself from the torturous visions invading his mind, he flung his arm across his eyes. He was startled when he realized his face was wet with his own agonized tears!

Slowly, a small wry chuckle started inside him and grew until it was a loud, full-blown, raucous laugh, echoing like a voice from hell in the silent blackness of his room. He kept repeating between the laughter and the tears, "You fool, you fool."

* * *

The first rosy glow of dawn found Adam still tired and unsleeping in his bed. Damn, he thought. I'll do better to get up and start out than to lie here wasting time. With that determination in mind, he got up, dressed, and went in search of supplies for his solitary journey back to Fort Carillon. Within the half hour, Adam's gear was packed and he was ready to go; but still he hesitated, unwilling to admit even to himself the reason. Finally, after long minutes wasted in indecision, Adam approached the young, sleepy sentry at the gate.

"Jack, can you tell me where they've taken the young lady I brought back with me to rest for the night?"

"Captain Mitchell's wife took her to their quarters. She said Miss Starkweather is to stay with them until Ranger Handly and she are married."

Adam felt the stiff edge of pain stir anew in his chest, but he started moving in the direction indicated, and within minutes was knocking lightly at the Captain's door. There was no answer, but he had not expected any to his soft knock at such an early hour. Adam tried the door, and finding it unlocked, walked slowly inside into the small sitting room used by the captain and his wife as part of their living quarters. As his eyes slowly became accustomed to the darkness, he scanned the sparsely furnished room. A small rough table stood in one corner, obviously serving as a desk from the number of books, papers, and writing quills scattered on it. He looked further. A small fireplace stood on the outside wall; around it were grouped a number of hard, straight-backed chairs, one small upholstered chair, and a large, matching upholstered couch, all of which sat awkwardly on a colorless worn rug covering that section of hard oak floor.

What was that movement on the couch? Adam strained his eyes to see, as the blanket moved, a lock of bright gold hair that had slipped out from beneath the cover. Slowly he walked to kneel beside the couch and uncover and gaze at Amanda's beautiful sleeping face. He wanted to press forever into the recesses of his mind the picture she presented before his eyes. But as he did, he knew, even should he try, he could never forget it.

"Amanda," he called softly, caressing the silkiness of her cheek and bending to press a light kiss on the tip of her nose. "Amanda, wake up."

Slowly the long lashes lifted to uncover sleepy, brilliant blue eyes, that seemed to come alive as she recognized the voice calling her name.

"Adam! Where did you go? We looked for you, but you left so quickly. What are you doing here now? It isn't daylight yet!"

"I've come to say goodbye, Amanda."

"Goodbye?" Stunned, Amanda stared incredulously at him. He was leaving already? But she didn't want him to go.

"Why, Adam? Why must you leave so soon?"

"General Webb has asked me to ferret out whatever information I can at Fort Carillon because I have freedom of movement there. He thinks I can be of valuable assistance. I wanted to let you know I was leaving, Amanda, but I have to ask you to keep my secret or I can be of no further use to General Webb."

"Of course, Adam," Amanda said absentmindedly. The only thought on her mind at present was the fact that he was going away. "But how long will you be gone?"

"I really don't know. Why, will you miss me?" Adam's voice was light, but his heart accelerated beating in the desperate hope she would ask him to stay.

"If you go, you'll miss the wedding! Robert wants to be married as soon as possible. He said tomorrow, but Betty insisted I take at least a week to rest and recuperate completely."

The searing surge of pain her words induced made Adam oblivious to her uncertain expression as she spoke, and his last spark of hope died. Heartsick and defeated, he had an overpowering urge to escape the scene of his torment.

"Yes, I suppose I will." Adam rose slowly to his feet. "I'm sorry I won't be here for your wedding. I just came to say good-bye." Turning abruptly, he started for the door, only to be halted by Amanda's sharp cry from behind.

"Adam, wait!"

Adam turned as Amanda flung herself against him, her arms encircling his waist, her face pressed tightly against his chest. "Oh, Adam, I'll miss you so," she sobbed, her body trembling.

Adam raised her face, cupping her cheeks gently in his palms, "And I'll miss you, much more than you realize," he softly added.

Then, his lips only inches from hers, he whispered, "Will you kiss me goodbye, Amanda?"

At her small affirmative nod, Adam slowly closed

the short distance between them tasting, at last the sweetness of her mouth. Passion overwhelming restraint, he slipped one hand to the back of her head to hold her mouth firmly against his, then slipped his other arm around her to draw her up tight against him. Caressing her with his kiss, he separated her lips to taste her mouth more intimately. Claiming her was far sweeter than he had ever anticipated, and he pressed his kiss deeper, separating her lips further, savoring the taste of her. He devoured her sweetness, wanting all of her, knowing even as his hunger for her soared to desperate yearning that this was all he would ever have.

Relinquishing her mouth slowly, unwillingly, clinging until the last second to the ecstasy he realized he would never know again, Adam was trembling so violently that he did not feel the responsive shuddering of Amanda's small frame. Aware that he could not trust his voice as he drew back from her, Adam touched her lips gently with his fingertips before turning abruptly and leaving her standing silently behind him.

Amanda stood still for several moments, her reactions frozen by the swift passage of events in the last few hours. Suddenly coming to life, she ran to the window to watch as Adam bent to pick up his pack. He strapped it across his shoulders as the sentry opened the gates, and then walked through the gates and out of sight.

Amanda's sense of loss was acute. Feeling devastated and completely alone, she berated herself for her unreasonable reaction. She knew that she still had Robert, but somehow, that didn't seem to be enough. Filled with unhappiness and confusion,

Amanda returned to the couch to throw herself down and cry herself miserably back to sleep.

The next few days passed in an agony of confusion for Amanda. Robert, deeply in love, waited anxiously for the wedding set one week away by an adamant Betty Mitchell, who happily assumed the role of Amanda's parent.

"Would you take this poor child to your bed for the first time, realizing she is still weak from her wounds, and exhausted from her ordeals?" she had asked Robert in privacy as he continued to press for an earlier date.

"Do you think I'm brutal, Betty?" Robert had questioned her in return. "Don't you think I'll take into consideration her ordeals and physical condition, and be gentle? I don't only desire her, I love her. I'd never do her any harm."

"But I will not allow the opportunity for your passions to overwhelm your good sense. The wedding will take place in a week and no sooner!"

Finally resigned, Robert accepted the woman's stubborn decision and waited impatiently as the wedding day approached. Stirring his feelings of unrest still further was Amanda's strange behavior toward him. He was overwhelmed with love for her. Robert's eyes followed Amanda constantly, caressing her with an almost physical force. Strangely, Amanda avoided his glance with growing frequency, and as the second day turned into the third, she started even to avoid his touch, his kiss.

Afraid of her answer, Robert did not question her behavior, but tried to accommodate her feelings, unsuccessfully for the most part; for his passions too often overruled his head, and he often ended by stealing what she did not willingly offer, refusing to admit the possibility of Amanda's change of heart.

Amanda's confusion seemed to mount daily. She did not feel free to discuss with Betty her constant warm memories of Adam and the way in which his green eyes flashed before her each time Robert took her in his arms, the memory of his deep kiss of farewell spoiling every kiss Robert bestowed on her reluctant lips.

Amanda rose on the fourth day of her return with a mounting sense of panic. Would it be fair to marry Robert as unsure as she was about her feelings? But Robert wanted her, wanted to take care of her, and Adam didn't. What else could she do?

Rising early, Amanda slipped quietly through the doorway of the Mitchell's quarters, and walked across the still deserted yard toward the dining hall. She knew the cook would be preparing breakfast and she could occupy her thoughts for a short time in helping him. As she walked a sense of uneasiness started at the base of her spine, causing a prickling sensation to crawl slowly up the back of her neck. What was it, that sensation she had of being watched? Slowly she turned to scan the interior yard of the fort for the presence that caused her uneasiness. She stopped in shock as her huge blue eyes met and locked with glittering black eyes staring into hers in a look that seemed to penetrate her very soul. A scream rose in her throat with the memory of a similar pair of black eyes seen the second before a tomahawk had brought an end to consciousness; but she smothered her scream as she realized these eyes belonged to an

90

Indian who stood tightly bound to the punishment post on the far side of the fort. The young Abnaki who continued to stare at her so intently was a prisoner and unable to do other than direct the power of his menacing gaze in her direction. Even realizing this, Amanda was paralyzed with fear as his eyes held hers. How long the silent tableau would have lasted is uncertain. But at that moment an officer, emerging from a doorway near the bound Abnaki, saw the direction of the Indian's gaze. Seeing Amanda's stricken expression, he muttered inaudibly under his breath in suppressed fury and struck the Indian a powerful blow to the side of his head, causing the young hostage to slump into unconsciousness.

Too frightened to feel pity, Amanda now freed from his hypnotic stare, ran, her heart pounding, into the dining area. Hours later, calmed after having helped prepare and serve the morning meal, Amanda was once again in control of her emotions, and silently berated herself for her lack of courage. Robert had come in for breakfast more than an hour earlier, and had waited patiently for her to complete her self-appointed tasks for the morning. As he watched, the love, pride, and desire he felt for her was obvious in his adoring expression. Just three more days and she'll be mine! His heart quickened beating and his mouth felt suddenly dry. Then she'll have no more doubts or fears, he thought, acknowledging to himself for the first time the doubts he knew had beset Amanda's mind.

Robert rose from his seat as Amanda untied the huge apron she had worn to shield her borrowed dress, and started toward her, anxious to steal a

91

moment alone before she returned to her sewing with Betty Mitchell. Taking her elbow, Robert gently steered her out the door and into the bright sunshine of the interior courtyard.

"How is your sewing progressing, Amanda?" Robert inquired politely, hoping to break the stiff wall of silence that seemed to fall between them whenever they were alone. Gone was the easy banter, the familiar exchange of thoughts that once had existed between them, and Robert ached for their return. Amanda, my darling, his mind cried silently, please love me again.

Outwardly, Robert's expression did not change, the smile on his face was perhaps a little more stiff, but he was determined as they moved along the yard to bear with Amanda's nervousness, and pretend it was purely a result of her recent experiences. As they approached the far wall of the fort, Robert sensed Amanda stiffening, and following the direction of her gaze, he watched as Amanda, standing absolutely still, stared in horrified fascination at an obviously sorely beaten Indian who, his battered face swollen and bleeding, stared boldly back into her eyes.

With a roar of fury, Robert closed the distance between them, and delivered a smashing blow to the already badly beaten face of the Indian prisoner, causing a spurt of blood to flow from his mouth and down his chin.

"Robert!" Amanda's scream was too late to stop the blow before it struck, and she started to tremble as the bruised lip of the Indian immediately began to swell and blood dripped down his chin onto his chest. "Robert, how could you? He's bound and helpless, and someone has obviously beaten him already."

"Don't waste your pity on him, Amanda," Robert growled in a low voice, amazed that his blow to this ignorant impertinent savage would even phase her. "For all you know, he may be the very one who killed and scalped your parents!"

Amanda gulped at the savagery in his tone, and without a backward glance, ran up the stairs to the Mitchells' quarters. Letting herself in, she slammed the door behind her.

The rest of the day was devoted entirely to the creation of an adequate wardrobe, and a proper wedding dress for the bride to be, with Betty Mitchell fussing for the third day in a row in a manner quite befitting the mother of the bride. In truth, always having been extremely fond of Amanda, as well as having been her mother's best friend, Betty looked on it as her solemn duty to provide for Amanda as she would her own child.

Despite her conscious attempt to forget him, Amanda found herself being drawn again and again to the window to look at the forlorn figure of the beaten Indian still tied in the full sun through the heat of the long August day, standing as proud and disdainful as his battered face would allow. She could not explain the surge of sympathy she felt for the savage whose pride held him erect in the burning rays of the sun. Just days before she had been cursing all Indians, but—surely someone must have given him something to eat and drink, at least some water.

"Amanda, what are you doing standing by that window again? You've spent the greater part of the day just staring outside. You'll never be done in time for your wedding at this rate."

Seeming to be oblivious to her question, Amanda asked suddenly, "Do you think they have given him water, Betty?"

"Who, child? Who are you talking about?"

"The Indian, the Abnaki prisoner. He's been tied in the sun all day."

"Oh, I think not. Mr. Mitchell told me that he was captured near dawn today spying on the fort. He could've gotten away, but the other Indian that was with him was shot, and he obviously wouldn't leave without him, and couldn't get away fast enough carrying him. The other Indian died anyway, but General Webb ordered this one tied out there prior to his interrogation."

"Did he order him beaten, too?"

"No, Amanda. It's my guess that after what has happened these last two weeks, feelings are running quite high against Abnakis in this fort, and I think some have vent their hatred on him."

"But, Betty," Amanda's voice expressed the pain she felt, "he's a human being."

To which Betty Mitchell replied in a surprised voice, "Why, Amanda, whatever made you think that?"

Amanda lay on the couch in the Mitchell's quarters, desperately trying to sleep. She had spent almost all the daylight hours sewing, and the entire evening avoiding Robert's attempts to make love to her, until he had exclaimed, a note of desperate pleading in his voice, "Amanda, I know you're tense

94

after all that you've experienced, but I love you. Won't you at least let me try to comfort you?"

Finally she did allow him a few kisses, which only succeeded in evoking those same green eyes to her mind again, frustrating her even further. Finally, feigning exhaustion, she had persuaded Robert to leave. Just two more days and they would be man and wife. What would she do then?

She turned over to bury her face in her pillow. Amanda's mind returned again to the interior yard of the fort, where only minutes before she had looked out to see that Indian still tied, but now slumped against the pole in utter exhaustion. Had they given him any food or water yet? She knew they had not.

It's no use. I can't let a human being suffer like that, she thought. Mother and Father wouldn't rest if they were here unless he was given at least a sip of water. I can do no less.

Quietly rising from the couch, Amanda slipped Betty's robe over her nightgown, and filling the cup from the water bucket in the corner of the room, she opened the door and stealthily made her way down the stairs toward the punishment post.

She approached the sleeping Indian from the shadows. The bright silver moonlight on his face betrayed his youth; she guessed he was not more than twenty-one or twenty-two years old. His hair was dressed in the manner of the Indians of the area, cut closely to his head on both sides, leaving a cockscomb from the forehead to the back of the neck. The top of his hair was cut in a pompadour, while the remainder was of natural length, braided and trailing down the back of his head like a scalp lock.

His young face, guileless and defenseless in sleep, despite its still slightly swollen appearance, showed a clear wide forehead, high cheekbones, a prominent, straight nose and a full but well-shaped mouth. The coppery tone of his skin was darkened even further as a result of the day spent in the hot, broiling rays of the summer sun.

His most arresting feature, those coal-black, glittering, almond-shaped eyes, were now hidden from view, and Amanda took the opportunity to peruse his sleeping form still further. His frame, she noticed, was not of Adam's massive proportions, or even Robert's. He probably stood no taller than six feet, and his shoulders and chest were smoothly muscled, as were his slender powerful thighs, giving the impression of strength and an easy athletic grace, like that of an agile mountain cat. As she raised her eyes again to his face, she jumped in realization that his eyes were now open and staring silently at her. Slowly he raised his slumped body to stand erect and proud.

Softly, she came closer, not really sure if he could understand or even wanted to, and started to speak. "I was not sure if you had been given anything to drink today, and I couldn't rest thinking how thirsty you must be. I've brought you some water."

Raising the cup to his lips, she tipped the water against his mouth, and at first, he tasted it warily. Then, realizing it was water, he drank greedily. The water dripped out of the corners of his mouth in his haste to swallow the cool liquid, and ran down his chin and over his chest in shining wet streams.

He said nothing when the cup was drained, but

continued to look steadily into her eyes with a look Amanda could not fathom.

"Would you like more? But you must be hungry also. I'll be back soon."

Quickly she scurried back into the shadows of the buildings, and slipped into the dining room. She found her way cautiously in the dark to the kitchen and the pantry where she sliced a large piece of cold meat, put it between two slightly stale pieces of bread, and dipping her cup once again into the water bucket as she passed, closed the door behind her to slip back into the shadows. Within minutes, she was back at his side, and raised the bread, meat and water to his mouth alternately until all the food was consumed. Then dipping her handkerchief into the water remaining in the cup, she gently sponged off his swollen face. Except for the short moments that she ran the damp cloth over his eyes, the Indian's unrelenting gaze never left her face, but curiously, she was no longer afraid.

When she was done, she returned his stare for a moment, and muttering a soft, "Goodnight," ran quickly back into the shadows and to the safety of her room. She returned quickly to her couch, removed her robe, lay down, and pulled the blanket over her. She felt strangely content, and it was just seconds before she fell into a peaceful slumber that she realized in all the time spent in his presence, the Abnaki had never spoken a word.

Amanda awoke the next day with a greater feeling of contentment than she had felt since Adam left. She rose from the couch and ran immediately to the window to stare down into the yard. She was almost overwhelmed with pity when she saw he was still there, bound to the post. How exhausted and stiff he must feel! But at least he wasn't thirsty and starving as well.

Suddenly Amanda noticed movement at the other side of the fort yard and was surprised to see Robert leaning casually against one of the buildings, a look of abject unhappiness on his handsome face. With a tortured expression, he glanced up toward her window, and Amanda immediately stepped back from view. When she looked out again, he was still standing staring at the ground, deep in thoughts that obviously did not bring him happiness.

"He's waiting for me," Amanda realized, "and I'm the one who is making him so unhappy with my absorption in my own selfish feelings. What's wrong with me? This the same Robert who was so much a part of my life the past year, and in a few days he'll be my husband. Why do I make him suffer so?"

Overcome by pangs of guilt and remorse, Amanda dressed quickly and just as quickly ran a comb through her hair, which she left streaming down over her shoulders, not wanting to take the time to bind it up. She stuffed her hair ribbon into her pocket for later, and hastily opened the door and started down the stairs. Robert came immediately forward as she emerged from the doorway, and met her at the base of the steps.

Amanda's smile of greeting was brilliant, and her voice warm with feeling as she looked into Robert's eyes and said softly, "Good morning, Robert," and raising herself on tiptoe, kissed his lips lightly. The flush of pleasure that covered Robert's face, and the

98

obvious happiness she had given him with so small a gesture only added to Amanda's feelings of guilt.

"Did you sleep well, darling?" Robert's voice was slightly shaken with emotion. He despised his lack of control where she was concerned. Not waiting for her answer, he said in a softer voice, "Just two more days. The day after tomorrow you'll be my wife." Looking down into the clear beautiful innocence of her face, Robert felt his restraint crumble and he swept her tightly against him, holding her as if he would never let go. "Oh, Amanda, I love you so. I'll make you happy, you'll see. You'll never be sorry you married me, I promise."

Held tightly against his shoulder, Amanda listened as Robert continued speaking, only to have his voice fade from her hearing as she felt and turned to see the unrelenting glare of a pair of black eyes. Knowing Robert would be infuriated if he saw again the boldness with which the young Abnaki continued to stare, she quickly tore her gaze from his, and looking up at Robert, said softly, "I know, Robert." She kissed his lips lightly once more, and then slipped her arm through his, and began walking toward the dining hall.

Robert's heart felt pounds lighter! Just minutes before, as he had stood waiting for Amanda to awaken and come down for breakfast, he had been at his wit's end as to how to stir her love for him, which appeared to be waning more each day. He had known that if he was a less selfish person, he would give her more time and not press her into marriage when she was so obviously uncertain of her feelings. But Lord knows, he said to himself, I love her enough for both of us. He could not let her go for fear if he didn't marry her quickly, he would lose her forever. Adam Carstairs' expression when he had looked at Amanda the day of their return haunted him. He had heard of the scene in the dining hall that same night when Adam had become enraged at a drunken soldier's insinuation about Amanda, and he had a strong suspicion that Adam Carstairs would gladly change places with him. Adam's reputation for casual affairs with the ladies meant nothing where Amanda was concerned, he knew. Hadn't he been the same before meeting her? But now, with her slender, graceful hand resting on his arm, the future suddenly seemed immeasurably brighter.

Amanda stood looking into the mirror as Betty Mitchell slowly surveyed the result of her long days of sewing. Luckily she was a saver, and although her old ivory satin gown was yellowed with age and hopelessly out of style, even for this backwoods area, she had kept it, and the perfect opportunity had finally come for its use. With painstaking care, she had taken apart the old garment which was hopelessly large for Amanda's petite frame, and laundered the fragile satin material carefully. Then, after first pressing all the material flat, she had altered and reshaped the pieces, and sewn them into a gown of a completely different styling. The neckline was rounded in front and back, with inserts of delicate ivory lace over the bosom. The dress fitted softly to the curve of Amanda's shoulders, and the sleeves tightly to the elbow, where layers of the same ivory lace hung gracefully halfway to her wrist. Betty's masterful job of fitting gathered the dress tightly to Amanda's miniscule waist to flare wide in alternating panels of satin and lace. Amanda's face, as she looked in the mirror, reflected the ivory glow, giving her a soft luminescence. Her incredulous expression showed plainly her amazement. "I just can't believe it's me, Betty!"

Betty's eyes suddenly filled with tears as she exclaimed in a breaking voice, "You look like a beautiful golden angel, Amanda. I know your parents would be proud if they could see you now."

"Thanks to you, Betty," Amanda replied, her own voice breaking with tears. "Thanks to you."

Amanda had spent the remainder of the day sewing and then, due to Betty's insistence, resting. Her wounds had almost healed completely, but Betty's determination that she continue to rest could not be ignored.

As she lay on the couch, listening to the steady rocking of Betty's chair while she continued to sew, Amanda's thoughts returned once again to the prisoner in the fort yard. Unable to keep from the window a moment longer, Amanda rose and quickly moved to look out. The Indian still stood tied to the post, and several men stood nearby, making angry gestures. How much longer could he stand? It was now midafternoon, and he had had nothing to eat or drink since late last night. Surely they didn't mean to starve him to death! Just a few more hours. Be patient just a few more hours, she said silently, willing her thoughts across the yard, and I'll come again when it's dark, with food and water.

Slowly, as if in answer to her plea, the Abnaki raised his head and looked for a few moments toward her window. Amanda experienced a feeling of shock at the Indian's intuitive action, and silently repeated again, Just a few hours more. Be patient.

The day crawled on interminably, so anxious was Amanda to relieve the Indian's suffering. In her anxiety she had lost all conception of the young Abnaki as an enemy, and could only think of his silent endurance of the heat and burning rays of the sun, and the beating of some of the more vindictive men at the fort.

As night descended once again, Amanda stole out of her room, keeping to the shadows, and out of the bright light of the moon. Moving quietly in the dining room, she managed to cut a large piece of meat from the remains of supper, and picking up bread and water on the way out, closed the door and hastened to the Indian's side. Just as the night before, the Abnaki appeared to be sleeping, and she touched him lightly. "Wake up! I can't stay long. You must hurry and eat."

Once again the black eyes were instantly alert and he consumed the food anxiously. Before leaving, as the night before, she gently bathed his face with the remaining water. Taking one last look at his completely unreadable expression, she quickly returned to her room and to sleep.

The warm, heavy pressure of a hand covering her mouth, simultaneous with the sound of an unfamiliar voice whispering her name, awoke Amanda with a start. Black, glittering eyes looking directly down into hers froze her into immobility, and the pressure of a cold, sharp object against her neck stopped the scream that rose in her throat. Amanda caught the glint of steel in the shaft of moonlight streaming through the window, and realized there was a knife at her throat! The same menacing voice whispered again, "Do not cry out or I will kill you." Amanda lay obediently unmoving, fear dulling her mind as she came to the realization that she was completely at the mercy of the Indian from the fort yard!

Suddenly Amanda felt herself being yanked from the couch and pulled roughly to her feet. Then, slipping an arm around her waist from behind and pulling her tightly against him, the Indian pressed the knife to her side and urged her forward. With strength that seemed unbelievable after his long ordeal, he all but carried her from the room, her feet only touching the floor occasionally, and steered her down the stairs, and through the shadows to the side of the yard. There they joined another Abnaki who had been waiting in the shadows, and Amanda's puzzlement as to how this Indian had managed to escape was solved.

"What do you want from me?" Amanda managed to stammer past the tight knot of fear that seemed to close her throat. Her only answer was greater pressure on the knife against her ribs, and with a short gasp, she felt the sharp point cut her skin. Her heart hammered in fright and her blood thundered in her ears. Her knees went weak, which only caused the Indian, after a short glance, to take a firmer grip on her waist as they started for the gate.

We'll never get past the sentry, Amanda's mind

screamed. We'll be seen and they'll have to let me go and run. But all was quiet as the other Indian separated the gates wide enough for them to slip through and closed them again quietly behind them. Once on the outside, the reason they had not been stopped became all too obvious; for there, the blood still oozing from his body, his head horribly mutilated where his scalp had been stripped away, lay the young sentry. Amanda started to cry out, but felt the knife press harder into her side, and the warm sensation of her own blood as it trickled down from the cut that went deeper with her every sound.

Once outside the gates of the fort, they slipped into the woods. The arm around her waist was as firm and strong as a band of steel as they moved quickly and silently away. They moved swiftly without stopping to the river where the other Indian left them to go searching along the shore. The arm around her waist slackened its hold and Amanda slipped to the ground, her breath coming in deep gasps in reaction to their hurried flight and to the fear that seemed to paralyze her. For the first time since she had been awakened, Amanda had time to reflect on her situation, and pictures of the slaughter around her the night of the massacre came back to her mind. As her trembling increased, she managed to stammer to the Indian she had so pitied, who now held her so mercilessly captive, "Where are you taking me?"

There was no answer as the silent Indian looked at her through eyes now narrowed to slits, with an expression that seemed to her to be devoid of all human feelings. What had ever possessed her to feel so much compassion for this unfeeling animal?

Surely now she was reaping the harvest of her foolishness! If she had ignored him as so many of the other inhabitants of the fort had, she would probably be safely back in the Mitchell's quarters, instead of a prisoner of this thankless savage.

"Let me go," she pleaded softly. "You must realize you can travel faster without me, and stand more chance of not being followed if you're alone. My betrothed will start after me as soon as he realizes I am gone."

"*Tschitgussil!* Be quiet!" the savage hissed menacingly as he brutally gripped her wrist and pulled her to her feet. It was then Amanda saw the other Indian motioning to them and felt that unrelenting arm encircle her waist again to force her forward.

When they reached the water's edge, Amanda was immediately thrust onto the floor of an Indian canoe that had been hidden in the dense brush. The two Indians jumped in quietly, and the canoe moved noiselessly out onto the lake.

Hope faded swiftly as Amanda realized that by traveling in this manner at night, they would be miles away before anyone ever realized she was gone, and by then it would be too late to find her in this vast wilderness. The realization that she probably would never see Robert again, and desperate fear of her fate at the hands of these savages, swept over her. Overcome by her helplessness, Amanda lay her head on her arms and sobbed herself to sleep.

The bright light of morning found Amanda still on the floor of the canoe, although it was now pulled up on shore. Slowly she raised her head to see the whereabouts of the two Indians, hoping they would be out of sight, allowing her time to attempt an escape. But it was not to be that easy. Staring steadily in her direction, the young Indian, his face expressionless, chewed a stringy piece of dried venison. His eyes followed her every move as she got out of the canoe. She was painfully aware that she wore nothing but her nightshirt.

Gruffly he pushed a piece of the dried venison into her hands and, too hungry to be proud, Amanda accepted the meat and commenced eating. The other Indian sat a few feet away, seeming determined to have as little to do with her as possible, for which Amanda was immensely grateful. The young Indian finished eating and, his eyes still on her, approached Amanda silently. Kneeling before her, he picked up the small dirty foot that protruded from the hem of her shirt, and examined it, carefully noting the scratches and cuts that her barefoot flight through the forest had produced. Gently he lowered it to the ground. Moving to the canoe, he returned moments later with a piece of buckskin, and some rawhide strips. By cutting off two pieces, punching holes in the sides and lacing the rawhide strips through them and around her feet, he began to fashion a rough pair of moccasins as protection against the sharp stones and broken branches that had done so much damage to her unprotected feet.

His small gesture of consideration· boosting her courage, Amanda asked softly, "What's your name? I know you know mine, because I have heard you say it. I'd like to know what to call you."

His strong, slender hands stopped working for a moment at the sound of her voice, and he looked up

106

into her face, his previously softened expression now replaced by a look of wary suspicion.

But he answered softly, "I am called Chingue.[1]" Then motioning with his head in the direction of the other Indian he continued, "He is called Suckachgook.[2]"

Amanda's gaze was directed for a few moments to the other Indian, who kept his distance so haughtily. Like Chingue, he wore his hair in the traditional way, and was also bare to the waist, wearing only a breechcloth and the buckskin leggings they had donned for their flight through the forest; but there the similarity ended. Whereas Chingue's skin was smooth and clear where it was unmarked by the bruises suffered from beatings in the fort, Suckachgook's was tough and lined like old leather, his features large and coarse in comparison to Chingue's fine, sharply chisled facial structure.

"Chingue," Amanda continued bravely, "Please tell me what you intend to do with me. If you wanted a hostage, surely it would've been easier to take that sentry." Amanda's voice faded weakly as she recalled the young boy who lay outside the gates so pathetically dead. But there was not a suggestion of remorse on Chingue's face as the murder of the young sentry was recalled to his mind. In a deep, rough voice the young Indian answered, "I will give you to the mother of my friend who was killed when I was captured."

"Give me to her!" Amanda gasped, remembering only too vividly the tales of horror told by survivors

1. Meaning "Big Cat."
2. Meaning "Black Snake."

of the brutality of vengeful Indian women, recalling that they were considered by some to be even more vicious in their torture of captives than the men. "But why? Why do you single me out for your revenge? I tried to lessen your suffering, not intensify it. Why do you hate me so?"

Ignoring her questions, Chingue continued coldly, "Ninscheach[1] will decide what is to be done with you. If she desires revenge, you will be killed; but if she is merciful, you will be spared. It is not uncommon among us for a mother who has had one child taken from her in death to adopt another to fill the empty place in her heart."

"Do you really believe an Indian mother will accept a white girl in exchange for her dead son?" Amanda was incredulous that he could entertain such an unlikely thought for even a moment.

Once again, Amanda's question went unanswered.

Her moccasins completed, Chingue rose to his feet, pulling Amanda up roughly. Then he called over his shoulder to the Indian who sat silently at a distance, "Suckachgook, *Yuh, shimoltam!*"[2]

Without a word, the Indian rose, slinging his small pack on his back, and set off at a breathtaking pace. The strenuous gait was maintained for at least an hour before Amanda, breathless and weak, fell to the ground, unable to keep up any longer. With a cry of pain, Amanda felt herself being raised to her feet by a merciless grip on her tangled hair, and thrust roughly forward to continue the seemingly endless trek. So they continued through the day, with few

1. Meaning "She Bear."
2. Meaning, "Come, let us run off."

breaks for rest, until Amanda, her hair stuck to her perspiring face, breathless and exhausted, fell again. This time, even pain could not raise the trembling, disheveled young girl to her feet. Through the fog of her exhaustion, Amanda heard the deep, rough voice of her captor call out, "Suckachgook, *ne nipauwi!*"[1]

Through quickly closing lids, Amanda saw the other savage stop, turn, and start back toward them before she dropped into unconsciousness.

Amanda awoke, her face feeling cool and fresh in comparison to the rest of her aching, perspiration-soaked body. Her huge, blue eyes opened once again to find those same black eyes staring down into hers. She touched her forehead to feel a cloth soaked with water lying across it. Her face was damp to the touch, and Amanda realized with surprise that Chingue had bathed it while she had lain unconscious.

Grasping her ankle, Chingue gestured abruptly to the healing scars of her snakebite, and asked, "When did you get this wound?"

Surprised by his question, Amanda answered weakly, "About two weeks ago. What does it matter?"

Touching the marks of the fangs with his finger-tips, Chingue did not respond. Without further explanation, he moved from her side, to return within minutes with some water and another piece of dried venison. He raised her gently to a sitting position. Chingue supported her with his arm, and as he held the crude drinking vessel to her mouth, she gratefully gulped the water. Then, his arm still supporting her, Chingue watched silently as she

1. Meaning, "Stop there!"

hungrily tore the stringy meat with her teeth and chewed. When she finished her meager supper, Amanda looked up to see an almost tender expression on the face of the young Abnaki who supported her so carefully, and she felt a further sense of confusion.

This man is a maze of contradictions. First he looks at me with hatred, and then he performs an act of compassion in making me shoes. He then brutally abuses me when I cannot keep up his pace through the forest, and reverses himself again to treat me with the tenderness and patience of a lover when I collapse! Her eyes wide with bewilderment, she stared incredulously up into his, and was baffled even further by the smile that slowly spread across his face. The only thing of which she was then certain was that Chingue was a very handsome man, as the wide smile spreading across his features showed even white teeth that contrasted so well with the dark coppery tone of his skin. Yes, Amanda mused to herself, he is a very handsome murderer.

Chingue whispered softly against her cheek, "We will rest for the night now and continue again at daybreak. Before noon we should arrive at our village."

Terror gripped Amanda as her mind speculated on her fate at the hands of the Indian women, and her body began to tremble once again. Aware of the tremors of fear that shook her, Chingue continued softly, "If Ninscheach is generous and forgiving and adopts you, you will be given an Indian name with some meaning, not merely a word with a pretty sound as the white man uses."

The sneer that crossed the face of the young Abnaki as he spoke had not gone unnoticed by Amanda, and a flush of anger momentarily overcoming her fear, she responded hotly, "My name is from a very ancient language, and it does have a meaning!" His statement had brought to mind the many times her father's dear voice had whispered in her ear at bedtime when she was a child, "Yes, Amanda, your mother and I picked the right name for you."

"Then what is the meaning of this name Amanda?" Chingue asked, his smile slightly mocking and broadening at the flush that deepened while she hesitated and finally answered in a small voice, "Amanda means 'worthy to be loved.'" And she dropped her eyes to avoid the ridicule she was sure would be forthcoming from the young savage. In the silence that ensued, Amanda slowly raised her eyes to the gaze of the piercing black eyes now so intent on her, staring thoughtfully from an emotionless face, and was amazed to hear him whisper softly, his eyes never leaving hers, "Yes, Amanda, I believe your parents named you well."

Light faded quickly in the forest, and with it came the damp chill of night. Curling up in a tight little ball, Amanda pulled her nightshift tightly around her, struggling in vain for an extra measure of warmth that was not forthcoming. She stared jealously at the silent Indian who lay a distance from her, comfortably warm in the blanket he had carried in his pack, and shivered again as she closed her eyes.

Suddenly Amanda felt a soft layer of warmth descend as a blanket settled over her body. She looked up to see Chingue bending to lay down next to her, moving under the cover of the blanket, and curving his hard, warm body around hers. "Do not fear, Amanda. Chingue will keep you warm this night."

The haven of warmth provided by his virile young body did its work well, relaxing her aching muscles so that sleep almost immediately overcame her.

Daybreak arrived with incredible swiftness for the weary, footsore, and aching Amanda, and it seemed that no sooner had the first light broken through the night sky than she was shaken awake by hands that once again were rough and merciless. After consuming the last of the dried venison, Amanda took her place between the two Indians, and the trek commenced. They had been traveling for what seemed an eternity to Amanda when she realized Suckachgook had slowed his pace. The stoic Indian face then creased with a smile as he turned to Chingue and pointed across the stream. *"Penno wullih!"*[1]

Following the direction of his finger, Amanda saw a large Indian village in the distance and realized from the expressions of happiness on both her captors' faces that they had almost reached their destination. Amanda felt a gentle touch on her shoulder and turned as Chingue said softly, "We are almost at our village. Come, we must bathe and prepare ourselves."

They followed the small stream to an area where it widened to form a pool, and to her amazement, the two Indians boldly stripped off their clothes and walked into the water. The sight of the two naked male bodies caused a crimson flush to cover her face,

1. Meaning, "Look yonder."

and Amanda turned quickly in embarrassment. Here is your opportunity to escape! her mind urged, but common sense answered, Escape to where?

Amanda sank to the ground, her back to the pool of water, and became so engrossed in imaginings of her fate that she did not hear the quiet footsteps behind her, and jumped when Chingue's deep voice ordered, "Bathe, Amanda. I can not present such a dirty gift to the mother of my friend."

Anger once again overcame her fear and Amanda answered sharply, "What difference does it make if I die dirty or clean?" But she jumped to obey as Chingue's voice raised in command, "Bathe!"

Amanda crept behind a tree and, removing her nightshift, slipped into the water. The cool, clean water against her sun-reddened, perspiration-soaked skin was a balm to her lagging spirits. Amanda submerged herself completely, allowing the water to lift, along with the dust and dirt from the trail, the anxieties that threatened to overcome her. She lolled in the water, stretching the time for her bath, knowing that its conclusion meant entrance into the village and realization of her fate.

A deep command broke gruffly into her reverie and Amanda hastened from the water as Chingue said sharply, "Amanda, we leave now!"

Quickly slipping her nightshift over her shoulders, Amanda emerged from behind the tree, her hair plastered to her scalp, her shift clinging to her dripping body. A quick look of amusement slipped across Chingue's face as Amanda's eyes grew large at the sight of the two Indians, their faces painted colorfully, standing before her.

Chingue walked forward, slowly circling her, as if assessing her appearance, and taking a comb from his pack, began to comb the tangled mass of her hair. When he had completed his work, he surveyed her again, this time coming very close, to look down thoughtfully into her face and, as if speaking to himself, said softly, "*Wulisso.*[1] You do not require paint to color your face. I will present you as you are."

Slowly they approached the village, each Abnaki walking proudly, giving a series of happy hoots and cries to announce their arrival. Amanda walked between, her eyes on the joyful crowd that approached the two warriors in welcome. Standing slightly apart from the group of well-wishers stood an Indian squaw and two small girls, their faces reflecting the despair felt within. Within moments, Chingue left her side to approach and take the hand of the lone woman. As he spoke softly, the woman gripped the hand that touched hers, tightening at the pain his words inflicted. Tears formed in the dark, unhappy eyes of the squaw, and slipped down her lined, sun-darkened face. Amanda watched intently as Chingue continued talking, his face in an expression of utmost sadness. Then he turned and gestured in her direction. Chills ran up her spine as the pitiful expression on the squaw's face turned to one of burning hatred as her eyes fell on Amanda.

A look of concern came over Chingue as he watched the squaw's reaction to his words, and his voice continued in a soft, persuasive manner. Once he used the name Amanda, and the squaw looked up

1. Meaning "Beautiful."

at him questioningly.

At the conclusion of their conversation, her heart racing wildly, Amanda watched as the old woman turned without another glance in her direction, and walked away with the two girls. Chingue stared solemnly at the departing figures, then turned abruptly and walked back toward Amanda, his face no longer mirroring the confidence of his earlier mood. To her anxious, questioning look, Chingue answered gruffly, "Ninscheach is overcome with grief for her son. She will not decide your fate at this time."

"Then I must wait to find out what she'll do with me? Chingue, how long will it be? Tell me, please," Amanda begged, her strength and the last bits of composure fast fading away.

"You will wait until she decides!" Turning his back on her, he strode away, and Amanda, staring after him, suddenly felt an unceremonious push toward a wigwam that stood on the edge of the village. Into it she was thrust, and there she remained.

Amanda sat silent and alone inside the wigwam, awaiting her fate. With each sound of approaching footsteps, her heart accelerated beating, and she felt a dryness in her mouth, only to hear the footsteps continue past, or turn in another direction. Why was it taking so long? When would she finally be relieved from this horror of suspense that left her mind free to entertain morbid thoughts of all the barbaric tortures she had ever heard attributed to vengeful Indians.

Never had Amanda felt so abandoned. For a short

time, she had felt herself soften toward Chingue, despite his vacillating moods, but even he had now turned his back on her. Closing her eyes, Amanda saw before her the ghastly specter of her scalp drying on a scalp pole, and fear forced her to open her eyes to once again seek another horror—reality.

Despite Amanda's belief that she would not be able to bear another hour within her lonely prison, the hour stretched to two and to three, until Amanda could see through the hole in the top of the wigwam that it was almost night. Surely morning would seal her fate. But Amanda had guessed wrong again. Morning of the next day brought only a meager breakfast and a short trip outside to relieve herself, after which she was hurriedly rushed back into the wigwam. She was allowed to speak to no one and received no visitors, with the exception of the young squaw who escorted her outside a few times a day. All attempts at conversation were met with a cold, blank stare, and Amanda reasoned morbidly, Why should she speak? Who would want to talk to a dead person? For she was certain her fate was sealed, and all that remained was the order to carry it out.

The second day stretched interminably into the third, as Amanda, in an effort to maintain her rationality, relived her week in the forest with Adam Carstairs. Even as she went over each day in her mind, she could find nothing that inferred a commitment other than to return her to Fort Edward.

Robert, on the other hand, was another matter, He had declared his love for her so many times in so many ways, as to make her, in recollection, ashamed of the shabby treatment she had returned for his love.

116

If she were to return, Amanda told herself, she would beg his forgiveness, and marry him without delay. That is, if he still wanted her.

Then there was Chingue. Amanda had long since given up her attempts to understand his behavior.

Still another day dawned and passed uneventfully, until Amanda began to expect that this would be the pattern for the remainder of her life. "A rare torture indeed, Ninscheach has devised," she laughed hysterically. But still, no one appeared to confirm her fate.

The days dawned and faded into a week as Amanda kept her lonely vigil inside the wigwam, barely able, by this time, to keep her reason, so frayed had her nerves become as she sat anticipating the outcome of her imprisonment. She could no longer even feel the release of tears, and sat, dry-eyed, as the approaching footsteps this time stopped outside the wigwam, and Ninscheach entered. Amanda rose on trembling legs, and stood stiffly, awaiting direction.

"Undach aal!"[1] Seeing the pale, golden-haired girl who stood so rigidly in the center of the wigwam did not understand, she beckoned with her hand and turned as Amanda followed hesitantly. Once outside, they were joined by the two young girls Amanda had seen on the day of her arrival, and still uncertain as to her fate, Amanda followed them silently. They led her solemnly into a wooded area, where the small stream formed another pool. The two young girls pulled her now filthy nightshift from her body and led her naked into the water. Once submerged to the waist, the two girls took handfuls of sand from the

1. Meaning, "Come here!"

bottom of the stream and scoured her white skin vigorously until they raised a healthy pink glow. Then, pushing her under the water, they washed her hair with admiring exclamations Amanda could not understand. Their work accomplished, each taking a hand, they led her from the water to Ninscheach, who, with a face of stoic calm, rubbed her dry.

Amanda's mind was whirling. She felt she was being prepared for some ritual, but her frightened mind could think no further.

When she stood naked and dry before Ninscheach, the old squaw took in the glory of her perfect white form, her sparkling golden hair cascading to her waist, the huge blue eyes that so dominated her face, wide with apprehension. Mumbling to herself, she produced a buckskin garment similar to those worn by the Indian maidens, and slipped it over her head. She then gently combed her long hair until it hung in a shimmering flow of gold. Finally, she produced a headband delicately decorated with variously colored beads, and fastened it around her forehead.

Still without speaking, she drew Amanda along with her to her wigwam, and pulling her inside, motioned her to sit down in the center. Slowly, the wigwam began to fill with the women of the village, each sitting around her until she was completely encircled. Some touched her hair, ran their hands along the whiteness of her arms, other just stared, until Ninscheach finally began to speak.

While she spoke, the women listened attentively, and some began to cry, lamenting and carrying on as if in the throes of a great sadness. Gradually the tone of Ninscheach's voice began to change, as did the

118

expression on her face when she said Amanda's name. She began to speak happily and seemed transfused with a great joy that appeared to be contagious to the women sitting around her. When she concluded her speech, there was an air of celebration within the wigwam, and the women moved forward around Amanda in obvious attempts at welcome. Amanda turned to look at Ninscheach. The aged, round face was lit with true delight and she looked with pride on. Amanda, who now was suddenly certain she had been proclaimed Ninscheach's new daughter!

I'm free! They're going to let me live! Amanda's heart sang joyfully as she emerged from the wigwam. Never had she felt so alive, so appreciative of the warm sun beating down on her head, the fresh breeze in her hair. The world was suddenly more beautiful than it had ever been, and she had to restrain herself from celebrating wildly the sheer privilege of being allowed to live and enjoy it. Turning to take her first solitary walk within the village, she met once again the glance of familiar glittering black eyes. Wary and unsure of the manner in which to greet him, Amanda hesitated, awaiting Chingue's first move.

A warm, wide smile spread across his face, causing a slight tug in Amanda's chest. He said softly in his deep, rough voice, "Welcome, dear sister, Amanda. Welcome home!"

A week later, in the wigwam of her new family, Amanda reflected on her first week as an Abnaki. Ninscheach's family was without a man since the death of her son, because her husband had been killed many years before in battle. She was now forced to depend entirely on the generosity of the hunters in the village to bring her the meat they could spare to supplement the corn, beans, and squash she and her children raised in their fields. Even so, Amanda noticed no difference in the shares of food divided between them. She had covertly studied the faces of her new family many times in the last week, searching for some hidden resentment or animosity, but there was none, and finally realized that she had been totally accepted by them.

Her eyes followed her new mother as she moved around the wigwam. Ninscheach was a small woman, with a matronly figure thickened by age, whose round, lined face easily showed the years of hard work and her recent unhappiness. Her black, almond-shaped eyes were small, her nose and mouth quite large and coarse in comparison. Her long dark hair was generously streaked with gray and tied to the back of her neck, and her general appearance bespoke the years of care and worry she had seen. But then she looked up, catching Amanda's glance, and the spark that lit the depths of her small dark eyes seemed to expand to encompass her whole face, reflecting the true warmth and beauty of a mother's love. Amanda saw it and was amazed! She had never expected to feel the warmth of that special love again after that day outside Fort William Henry, and suddenly it seemed ironic that this love should come to her again from a member of the tribe that had murdered her own parents!

Amanda turned to glance at her "sisters." She had

120

been a lonely child who had always longed for a brother or a sister, and now, strangely, considering her circumstances, she felt doubly blessed!

Tscholentit, Chingue had explained, meant "Little Bird," and it was a very apt name indeed for her younger sister. She was about eleven years old, and her round smooth face bore a distinct resemblance to that of Ninscheach, but had a fineness of feature that her mother did not share. She was a pretty, happy child.

Mamalnunschetto, which meant "Spotted Doe," was a budding young maiden of about thirteen years. The first time Amanda had looked into her face, she had been transfixed by her new sister's immature beauty. Where her mother's eyes were small, Mamalnunschetto's were large, velvet black, almond shaped and fringed with long, silky lashes. Her other features were small and set in a facial structure that seemed so fine that Amanda was reminded of a porcelain figurine. Her body, not yet in the full bloom of womanhood, was slight and petite, lending her an air of delicate grace.

They were openly affectionate and proud of Amanda and often touched and stroked her hair as they walked through the village, as if to call the attention of those around them to its beauty.

Her family's patience with her ignorance of Indian ways seemed endless. Her education had begun the first day as she had helped her sisters carefully spread ears of corn to dry in the sun. She later found out that some of the corn would be pounded into meal, some would be stored in their wigwam in baskets hanging on the walls for cooking in the near future, and still others would be stored in large baskets and buried in the ground to be used during the winter with other vegetables, nuts and berries stored in the same way.

In the meager light of the small fire, Amanda's eyes scanned the wigwam that she now called home. It was constructed, as she had learned in one of her many lessons from Chingue, from an oval framework of poles bent in a dome shape and covered with slabs of birch bark. The inside walls were decorated with colorful mats, and baskets of all shapes and sizes hung from the walls, filled with seeds, corn, dried meat, and fish when the larder was full.

Amanda was sitting, as were her sisters and mother, on one of the benches covered with mats and fur skins that lined the walls of the wigwam; these doubled as beds at night and seats during the day. In the center of the wigwam, the fire that blazed in a small hollow surrounded by stones, provided her family with warmth, light, and heat for cooking. The smoke outlet in the center of the roof allowed the smoke to escape, and was a peephole to the sky.

Her family! How naturally those words already came to her mind. These were the same people for whom, just a few weeks before, she had professed undying hatred, called murderers, savages, animals who killed without reason. But they had suffered the same losses and tragedies as she, and mourned their loved ones as well. She found she could not bear a hatred in her heart for those who showed her love and willingly shared their lives with her. The past week had provided only one solution to handle the loyalties that were tearing her apart. In order to be able to bear the present, she must force the past from her mind. She found that even in her few moments of solitude she could not allow herself to reflect on her former life and those she had loved in a time that seemed so long ago. Even the smallest reminiscence brought her too much pain, and stirred feelings that were now senseless to harbor. The thought of the anguish Robert must have suffered when she had been taken from him one day before their wedding; the memory of those warm green eyes as they had looked down at her that last day; and Adam's farewell kiss that had so stirred her were deep scars that she would have to allow to heal without constant irritation of the wound.

What's the purpose of torturing myself over and over with things that are done and gone, and will never be again? she reasoned. I had better accept the life they have returned to me, for it is all that remains.

Although a part of her hated herself for her acceptance of her fate, her week of imprisonment had forced Amanda to the solemn realization that she valued her life, and she did indeed want to live.

Chingue had come each day to bring a share of the hunt to the family; sometimes it was a fish caught in the nearby river, a squirrel, or a turkey. He had returned again each night after they had eaten and spent his leisure time with Amanda, patiently continuing her education. With Chingue's help, Amanda was rapidly learning to understand Abnaki phrases and was proud she could communicate so well with her family.

One evening they had walked to a high spot at the edge of the village. The high poles standing upright in the ground, carved and painted brightly with masks of birds and animals piqued her curiosity, and she had asked candidly, "What are those poles, Chingue? Do they have a special meaning?"

With his customary patience, Chingue had explained in detail. "Every Abnaki has a guardian spirit, and his success in life depends on the good will of his spirit. The spirit is represented by animal or bird gods, or the being who created them. We believe there is a brotherhood of man, animals, and birds, and all are guarded by Welsit Mannitto, the Good Spirit. These are totems, pictures of our guardian spirits."

Amanda had shaken her head in wonder, her soft blond hair catching the last rays of the sun and reflecting the glow like a sea of gold. Chingue's gaze had remained on her face as she spoke unhappily. "I know I'm an Abnaki by adoption, Chingue, but I'm afraid my heart is still white. I'll never be able to accept such differences in our religions."

Chingue's eyes had traveled her softly tanned face, which provided such a striking contrast to the bright blue of her sad eyes, and he had spoken earnestly. "Wherein lies the great difference of which you speak, Amanda? Do not many of your people believe they have guardian angels, and do you not believe in one God who reigns over all men and beasts?"

"Yes, we do, Chingue."

"We also believe that the world was once destroyed by a great flood. Welsit Mannitto sent down four diving animals, one after another, until the last succeeded in getting mud from the bottom, which Welsit Mannitto made to grow into land and in that way recreated the world and man. Did not the missionaries tell me that a similar story appears in your holy book?"

Amanda's surprise was reflected on her face. "Yes. The great flood and Noah's ark."

Chingue had added softly, "Might not the greatest difference lie in the translation into different languages through many years, and not in the events themselves in which we believe, Amanda?"

Sitting in her wigwam, Amanda could still remember and feel the warmth that had filled her as Chingue had solemnly explained his beliefs in an effort to find a mutual bond between their religions and bring her closer to her adopted people. She could no longer regard him as her abductor, but thought of him as her friend and teacher, and in gratitude she had impulsively slipped her arms around him, hugging him lightly and pressing her face against his chest.

"Thank you, Chingue. You've done so much to make me feel one of your people."

His arms had then slipped gently around her, pulling her even more closely against him, and he had continued as if she had not spoken, "No, Amanda, there is no great difference between us."

Still feeling the warmth of Chingue's embrace, Amanda smiled softly as she lay down on her bench and finally drifted off to sleep.

The passage of time within the Indian village was rapid, marked most noticeably by the changing forest surrounding it. Each gust of wind seemed to lift a few more leaves from the brilliantly colored trees as September wore on, leaving them still in partial dress, but providing a dazzling carpet of color as well.

Amanda spent her time absorbing all the knowledge the Abnaki society had to offer. Chingue became a permanent part of the evening ritual of her family, and all seemed to take for granted that he would appear after their evening meal to spend some hours in their company. Other evenings they joined the old men around the campfires where they wove endless stories of Indian legends for the children, and Chingue appeared to derive great enjoyment from seeing that Amanda was as entertained as the children with the tales being spun.

Secretly, Amanda was amazed at her acceptance by the people of the village and remembered with shame the innate prejudice displayed by so many of her own people against the Indian. She could not believe in the wildest stretch of her imagination, had the situation been reversed, that an Indian being adopted into a white society could be accepted so thoroughly and be treated so completely as an equal.

Yes, Chingue, she mused silently, You are very wrong in one respect. There is a difference between our people far greater than you realize, and in this instance the white man falls short.

It was only occasionally that Amanda felt that she was an outsider in her new life. On one of those occasions, as she walked with her sister through the village, she found herself mumbling under her breath after her overture of friendship toward one of the maidens in the village had been again repulsed. She finally said aloud in exasperation, "Mamalnunschetto, why is it everyone seems to accept me here except the girls my own age? They seem to take a delight in snubbing me!"

Mamalnunschetto giggled softly, covering her mouth in an effort to hide the mirth that spilled over so spontaneously. To Amanda's questioning gaze, she replied softly, her eyes sparkling with mischief, "They are jealous, Amanda. All the maidens are jealous of you."

"Jealous!" Of all the reasons she had considered for her ostracism, jealousy had never entered her mind. "How could they possibly be jealous of me, Mamalnunschetto?" Amanda's tone held a note of disbelief.

"Oh, Amanda," Mamalnunschetto's sweet, young voice answered patiently, "do you realize that Chingue has long been admired by many of the young women in our village? Do you not think him handsome? Many of our young women have wished that he would take them to wife, but he has never shown an interest in any one of them. Then he returned with you, and brought you to us. He now spends much time in your company. All the young women can not open their mouths to speak to you for fear their jealousy will spill out!"

Mamalnunschetto laughed even more heartily, still attempting to stifle with her hand the giggles of utter enjoyment that came forth as she recalled the envious faces of the young women when they looked at Amanda. Her dark eyes still sparkling with merriment, she whispered softly, "They fear Chingue will take you to wife, Amanda."

"That's utterly ridiculous!" Amanda was completely incredulous. "Chingue has befriended me, but that's all." But the seeds of doubt had been planted in Amanda's mind, and even as she spoke, her voice lacked conviction.

That night when Chingue came as usual to visit with Ninscheach's family, Amanda found herself looking at him in a different light than before. As he approached, Amanda studied the fluid movement of his slender, smoothly muscled body. He walks with the silence and grace of a cat, she mused to herself, realizing for the first time the reason for his name, Big Cat. His dark, gleaming eyes quickly scanned the circle of people around the fire, seeking her face, and he then smiled, relaxing the sharpness of his chisled features. Those black, glittering eyes that had so mesmerized her that first day at the fort still had the power to trap and hold her azure gaze. Entrapped once again within their power, unable to turn away, Amanda smiled into their dark depths.

Chingue spent little time in conversation with her family and, after a few minutes, walked to her side, silently touching her arm to urge her gently to her feet. "Come walk with me, Amanda."

Without answering, Amanda fell into step beside him. They continued on without speaking until they came to an area beside the village that offered some shelter from prying eyes. Amanda felt obliged to keep her eyes downcast, feeling suddenly unnaturally shy in his presence. She felt Chingue's slender fingers on her cheek, and heard him ask as he cupped her chin in his hand, gently raising her eyes to meet his, "What is wrong tonight, Amanda? Why do you act so strangely toward me?"

A light flush covered her face, for she knew she could never repeat Mamalnunshcetto's words of that

128

afternoon. Looking directly up into his face at last, the familiar feeling of trust and warmth that she had come to feel in his presence returned, banishing her temporary shyness, and a spontaneous smile lit her face, the little dimple beside her mouth winking as she spoke.

"It was nothing, Chingue. Tell me of your plans for the hunt tomorrow."

But Amanda knew instinctively that thoughts of the hunt were far from his mind at that moment as his hand moved to caress her soft cheek and slide to the surface of her hair to touch it lightly. Amanda could sense his quickened breathing, and in an effort to divert his attention, she asked a question that she had long hesitated asking him.

"Chingue, there is one question I have wanted to ask you for some time." She saw she had captured his interest and continued. "I saw Ninscheach's face when you first told her you were giving me to her. She looked at me with a terrible hatred. At that time I was sure my death would not be long in coming. You continued speaking to her, and she turned away to reconsider my fate. What did you say that made a mother as loving as Ninscheach forgive and adopt a daughter of the people who had killed her son?"

Chingue hesitated for a moment before speaking. "As you said, Amanda, Ninscheach is a loving mother, and hated you without giving thought to reason when first she saw you. When she turned her look of hatred toward you my heart grew heavy, and I explained to her that her hatred was misdirected. I told Ninscheach of your parents' deaths in that same war that took her son's life, and that you were orphaned and alone as she was without a son. I explained to her that your spirit and Maschelameek's[1] were kindred, as you were as kind and beautiful as Maschelameek was generous and handsome. You both had strong feelings for life. Her son had died saving mine, and you had risked much to help me, a stranger to you in my great need. I told Ninscheach that I felt Welsit Mannitto had provided a daughter for her when he had taken her son, and that your name bore evidence of his providence, as it meant 'worthy to be loved'." He hesitated one more moment, and then continued, his voice dropping softly. "She now believes, Amanda, as I do, that you were named well."

Tears filled her eyes at the beautiful and almost poetic logic of Chingue's reasoning, and Amanda felt a knot of emotion tighten in her throat as Chingue drew her closer to him.

"Amanda." His deep voice was husky with the depth of feeling that held him in its grasp. "I believe Welsit Mannitto has provided you for me, also, for when first my eyes touched on you, it was the answer to a dream I had long carried within my heart. I will speak to Ninscheach tonight and ask to take you as my wife. Ninscheach looks on me as a son and will not refuse. I will take you to me as soon as I can complete the wigwam where we will live together."

Amanda was speechless. Never had she expected her question to result in a proposal of marriage! But suddenly she realized it was not a proposal she had received. Chingue had not asked for her acceptance, for in this society it was not needed. The decision

1. Meaning, "Spotted Fish."

rested with Ninscheach, and Amanda must do her bidding. But glancing covertly out of the corner of her eye at the proud, handsome man who walked beside her, the question raised in her mind was, Even if the choice was mine, would I refuse him?

When they returned to Ninscheach's wigwam, Chingue motioned her to go inside, and in true Indian fashion, Amanda obeyed without question, her heart beating rapidly within her breast. She pretended to be asleep when Ninscheach entered the wigwam, and Ninscheach made no attempt to disturb her. The next morning Amanda awoke with a feeling of nervous anticipation and went apprehensively about her morning chores. She had spent the wakeful hours of the night in intense contemplation of her life as Chingue's wife. To be an adopted Abnaki was one thing, but the thought of marrying and raising children as Indians, completely foreign to the society where she had been born, was another matter. Once she had become an Indian squaw, no matter how noble the Abnaki to whom she was bound, she would be forever outside the limits of white society, for she would have become tainted in their eyes. If I ever returned to the white civilization, she thought, would I be able to bear the look of contempt on Robert's face when he looked at me, or Adam's pitying glance? In her mind she had formally given up all hope of being rescued and returned, but in her heart hope was still alive. Marriage to Chingue would crush forever that hope and make her return to a white society an impossibility. Desperately, in the darkness of the night, she had begun to pray that Ninscheach would refuse Chingue's offer.

After their usual morning meal of small cakes of *Nokake*,[1] the girls continued their work of cutting squash and pumpkins into strips and hanging them on a line to dry in order to prepare them for winter storage. Ninscheach was unusually quiet and did not, in her usual manner, join in with the laughter and banter of her happy, exuberant children. It was obvious to Amanda that Chingue's appeal was being thoughtfully considered, and Ninscheach was having tremendous difficulty in making her decision.

The outcome of Ninscheach's refusal to permit her to marry Chingue, whether it would result in eventual marriage to another Abnaki in the future, perhaps with less appeal, was not even considered by Amanda in her frantic state of mind. One thought alone was her only consideration: If I marry, I can never go home!

The day passed in an agony of anticipation, and when Chingue brought a catch of trout for their supper, Amanda made certain she was hidden from view inside the wigwam. She could not face those eyes that seemed to see into her very soul and would know in a moment her desire to escape a union with him. She was also mortally afraid. She had never, with all the kindness and patience shown to her by Chingue, truly forgotten the wildly vicious look in his eyes when he had been aroused at the fort, and the bloodied body of that young sentry outside the stockade gates.

Chingue returned in his usual manner that night, but Amanda was not seated by the fire to welcome him. In a desperate attempt to avoid him completely,

1. Corn kernels pounded into a coarse meal and cooked in the fire.

she had taken to her sleeping bench directly after supper, and upon hearing a familiar step at the door of the wigwam, closed her eyes and feigned sleep. Within a few minutes, Amanda felt a warm breath on her cheek and the pressure of firm lips against her ear as a deep voice whispered, "Do not try to hide from me, Amanda, and do not be afraid. Ninscheach has given her permission and you will be my wife within the week." Turning her carefully to face him, he spoke gently, his eyes shining, and Amanda flushed at the love so openly displayed there.

"K'dahoatell, Amanda."[1]

Amanda's flush deepened, but she still could find no response.

Stroking her hair, his smooth beardless face pressed lightly against her cheek, Chingue spoke as if he had glimpsed into her soul. "You fear you will never be able to return to the whites once you have been an Indian squaw. That is true, Amanda, you would never again be accepted there; but you may put your trust in what I say." His deep voice shook with passion as he continued. "I will never give you cause to want to return to them. You will be my wife, and I will cherish you all of my life. We will live and grow old together. You will give me children and we will raise them as Abnakis, but with an eye to the time when we will all be brothers, red and white, we will teach them to respect what is good in the white man as well as our people." Raising her gently to her feet, he looked down into her face. Overwhelmed with emotion, he said in an impassioned voice, crushing her petite young body against his as he

1. Meaning, "I love you!"

spoke, *"K'dahoatell,* Amanda, *K'dahoatell!"*

It was decided. Chingue would take her to wife in four days, allowing him enough time to complete the wigwam where they would spend their marriage night and most of the winter, and allowing both of them to prepare themselves in a modest way for their new life.

Amanda saw very little of Chingue in the time following Ninscheach's acceptance of his terms. His day was spent in the building of their wigwam. His visits to Amanda were of short duration, and Amanda sensed that the tight rein kept on his emotions when Amanda was near sorely chafed, and he longed for the release he would feel within the next few days.

Ninscheach's demeanor was a mixture of happiness and sadness. In her characteristically quiet manner, she had come to Amanda to speak of the coming marriage. "Amanda, when first Chingue came and spoke to me of taking you to wife, I was sad. I did not wish to lose the daughter that had restored so much happiness to our family. But I have considered carefully and now realize that by the separation of one, I may gain much more in the time to come in the grandchildren Welsit Mannitto will provide me through you and Chingue. In that way I am happy to lose you, but still feel sadness to see your face depart my wigwam."

The core of tension that had been building within Amanda melted completely in the open declaration of love that came from the heart of her foster mother. Ashamed of the selfish and traitorous thoughts that had been uppermost in her mind for the past few days, Amanda slipped her arms around the shoulders of the old squaw and whispered softly as tears squeezed beneath her lids, "Thank you, *Mamintochimgussowagan.*[1]"

The third day came quickly. Amanda had been many times to the wigwam that Chingue had almost completed, carefully mounting on the walls baskets of dried corn, pumpkin, and squash that Ninscheach had so generously provided. Chingue's eyes followed her as she worked within the wigwam until the silence became so oppressive as to cause Amanda to glance self-consciously back into his face. Chingue's steady stare was completely inscrutable, and Amanda felt a tremor of fear shake her body. With complete disregard for the feelings that showed so plainly on her face, Chingue turned abruptly and walked out of the wigwam, only convincing Amanda further that she would never truly understand the complicated mind of the Abnaki.

The day before they were to be joined, Chingue brought Amanda before his solemn-faced parents. Their disapproval was obvious, but whatever their thoughts, they remained silent and nodded their heads in acceptance of Chingue's choice. But the meeting was quickly terminated.

Amanda's wedding day dawned bright and clear, and despite her obvious tension, it proceeded in the usual manner, the one exception being the nerve-racking giggling of her sisters when they noticed her nervous fumbling. Her nervousness was noted silently by Ninscheach, who took the first oppor-

1. Meaning, "Esteemed one."

tunity of privacy to speak to her.

"Amanda, do not fear. Chingue is a good, patient man, and has great regard for you. You need only go to him with love and trust in your heart, and all will be well."

Amanda nodded, wishing she shared Ninscheach's confidence. Chingue had been acting so strangely the past few days. As for her marriage bed, Amanda was almost completely ignorant of the part she was to play. How sorely she missed her true mother's presence, and her soft, gently guiding words. Would Chingue be angry or disappointed when he realized her ignorance of how to please a man? She recalled the stories she had heard of the savage Indian rapes of white women, and felt a slow flush cover her face as fear and apprehension assumed control of her mind. Whatever was to be her fate, it would soon be upon her.

The bright October day of her marriage was starting to wane when Amanda's two sisters appeared at the doorway of the wigwam, their pleasant young faces sparkling with excitement. Amanda looked up from the bench where she had been sitting in silent contemplation of the night to come, her beautiful young face reflecting her sober mood.

"Come, Amanda, it is time to prepare," Mamalnunschetto's sweet voice urged. Tscholentit stood slightly behind her, her hand covering her mouth as she giggled annoyingly. When Amanda made no attempt to rise, Mamalnunschetto's voice pleaded, "Come quickly, Amanda. Ninscheach waits at the pool."

Slowly Amanda pulled herself from the bench, her

legs as heavy as lead as she walked to the door. The two girls grabbed her hands and pulled her forward and on toward the bathing pool at the edge of the forest. They were bubbling with excitement. Amanda was acutely self-conscious at their knowing looks, and kept her eyes lowered as they dragged her past the rows of wigwams on the way toward the stream, certain all eyes were upon her.

Ninscheach stood by the pool, her dark, lined face stoic as Amanda approached. Amanda felt the grabbing, playful hands of her sisters pulling at her clothes as they pulled her shift over her head and, quickly undressing themselves, drew her laughingly into the water.

"Come, Amanda," their teasing, childish voices cried, "you must be shining and beautiful for Chingue tonight." Repeating their actions of the day of her adoption, Mamalnunschetto and Tscholentit again took handfuls of sand from the pool bed, and scrubbed her soft, white skin. With an air of solemn concentration, her sisters efficiently bathed her, and turned their attention to her hair. When satisfied they had done their task well, the two girls led her from the pool to stand before Ninscheach. As before, Ninscheach dried her thoroughly, as she would a child, sighing softly as she combed the long golden hair that had been bleached almost platinum by its exposure to the long summer days. The warm fall sun had started to set, and Amanda felt a chill as a small shiver passed over her body. She reached for her shift.

"No, Amanda," Ninscheach signaled sharply, and greatly puzzled, Amanda dropped her dress.

Ninscheach then turned and walked a few steps away to return with another buckskin shift, but one the likes of which Amanda had never before seen. Although cut in the same simple style, and sewn as the others with thin strips of leather, this garment was of a color so light as to appear almost white, and was deeply and delicately fringed at the hem and sleeves to create a gentle swaying motion as she walked. But most impressive of all was the delicate beading worked in an intricate pattern of blue and gold around the neckline and fringed hem of the garment. Ninscheach slipped the graceful shift over her head, and stood back to consider her for a moment. After carefully combing her hair a second time, she took a headband embroidered in the same pattern as her shift, and fastened it around her hair. Standing back a moment more, Ninscheach nodded her head approvingly, a small smile on her face, and Amanda turned to see a look of wide-eyed admiration on her sisters' faces. Suddenly Tscholentit ran hurriedly back to the village, and ducked into a wigwam on the edge, only to reappear within minutes and start back toward them, carrying something in her hand. As she approached, Amanda saw she carried an old hand mirror, obviously taken in a raid, and greatly treasured by the occupants of the wigwam who came out to watch Tscholentit's headlong flight back toward her.

Breathing heavily, her small round face flushed with exertion, Tscholentit held the precious mirror out to her.

"See, Amanda," she urged breathlessly. "See how beautiful you go to Chingue!"

Amanda took the mirror with apprehension. She had not looked on herself except in reflection in the pool since she had left Fort Edward, and she was unsure how her change in life-style had affected her appearance. Slowly raising the glass to her face, Amanda was stunned at the face reflected therein. Holding it still further back, she saw a small heart-shaped face, dominated by two huge, startled blue eyes, their brilliant blue color enhanced by the new golden hue of her skin, and by the silver-blond hair that cascaded in all its brilliant glory over her shoulders and down to her waist. Ninscheach had embroidered the headband she wore as her only decoration in the exact shade as her eyes, and looking at herself, Amanda knew instinctively she looked the role she was to assume tonight, that of a beautiful virgin Indian bride.

Her reflection having an almost hypnotic effect, Amanda felt herself accept at last what was to be the outcome of this night. No longer thinking of the world that would soon be lost to her, her thoughts were directed to the immediate future and to the night soon to be spent within Chingue's wigwam. Taking her hands, her sisters slowly led her back to the village and ceremoniously past the wigwams of her fellow Abnakis who stared with open-eyed wonder at her beauty, until she reached Chingue's wigwam. With a last solemn look, Ninscheach motioned her to enter, and added softly, "Chingue will come to you soon."

Amanda's mind was racing in hysterical confusion, but she did as she was bidden and entered to sit nervously on the bench and wait. Every nerve in her body seemed to be tingling in anticipation, and her blood seemed to be coursing wildly through her veins. She could not be certain how long she waited, but as she looked up through the smoke outlet to see darkness descending, she heard footsteps outside and jumped nervously to her feet as Chingue entered.

Amanda stared, her huge blue eyes wide with anxiety at the handsome young Indian who presented himself before her. He, too, had obviously just come from his bath. His slender, smoothly muscled body, clad only in breechcloth, gleamed with a copper hue in the light of the small fire flickering in the center of the floor. His hair had been dressed with care; the cockscomb down the center of his head shone darkly, and the long, natural length of hair that hung down the back of his neck was braided neatly and decorated with bits of colored shells. His glittering, coal-black eyes regarded her seriously from an intense, handsome face that was free of decorative paint; unknown to Amanda, this was in deference to the fear he had sometimes seen her exhibit at the painted faces of his fellow Abnakis. This night would not be a night to inspire fear.

"Amanda." Her name, whispered softly by Chingue, seemed to echo in the hush of the wigwam. "Do not fear me. Come."

Amanda stood rigid with fright as Chingue held out his arms, bidding her to enter within their confines. Her eyes appeared to grow wider as she stood, unable to force her body to move, and yet frightened not to obey his soft command.

Slowly, his face relaxing into a tender smile, Chingue approached her and grasped her shoulders

140

gently. "Amanda, have you never lain with a man before?"

At her puzzled look, Chingue clarified, "Have you never been to a man's bed to make love? Are you *wusdochqueu?*" Seeking the English word in his mind, he hesitated momentarily. "Are you virgin?"

Seeing the blush that transfused her face with red, and the slight gulping sound she made as she nodded her head meekly, Chingue's smile broadened. Gently drawing Amanda's quivering body against his smooth, hard chest, Chingue whispered, his lips pressed against her hair, "I felt desire for you, Amanda, and it mattered not to me if you were virgin, but I find it doubly pleasing now to know no one else has known you as I will know you this night."

Then, pushing her slightly away so that she might see his face, he continued, "I have lain with other women many times, Amanda, but in one way I am still virgin. I have never lain with one I love, for I have never felt love for a woman before you. Truly we will learn to love together, for it will be the first time for both of us."

Chingue felt an overwhelming tenderness for the slight figure trembling in his arms, and his touch was responsively gentle. He spoke softly as he unlaced the tie at her neckline, and raised the bottom of her shift to pull it over her head and from her body. "You were very beautiful in your marriage dress, Amanda," Chingue whispered huskily, and then looking at her exquisite naked form, he continued, his voice shaken with emotion, "but far more beautiful as you are now."

Chingue's eyes slowly traveled the slender body

that seemed to glow with its whiteness in the semi-darkness of the wigwam. Staring at her unbelievably lovely, though very apprehensive face, Chingue's eyes followed the slender column of her throat, touching on her petite shoulders, and across the rise of her chest to her full, round breasts, the small pink nipples standing out clearly and invitingly like two buds waiting to be caressed into bloom. His eyes continued down past the narrow rib cage to her waist, which appeared to Chingue incredibly small. Then he regarded her hips, slender but rounded well, the flatness of her white abdomen, and finally the tawny patch of curls that lay nestled between long, slender legs, the place where his body was soon to find happiness, satisfaction, and wonderous delight.

In one smooth movement, Chingue slipped the breechcloth from his body, revealing to Amanda for the first time the sight of a man's desire. Her eyes grew so wide in shocked disbelief as she stared at his swollen member, that Chingue, smothering a strong desire to laugh, gently scooped her up into his arms and carried her to the sleeping bench to lay her lightly on the mats, and then lay down beside her.

Pulling her naked form tightly against his, he began to stroke her tenderly, patiently talking to subdue the tremors of fear that shook her body.

"I have loved you since first I saw you in the yard at Fort Edward, Amanda. I knew then, should I escape, I could never leave you behind, for although my body would have been free, my soul would have remained your prisoner."

"But you threatened to kill me if I made a sound, and treated me so cruelly on the trail when I couldn't

142

keep up." Amanda's voice dropped off when she realized she had finally put into words her puzzlement with his eratic behavior.

"Yes, that is so, Amanda, but my threat had no substance in truth, for to have killed you would have been to end my own life." And then in answer to her second statement, he added softly, "Do you not know the fate of a hostage that can not keep up on the trail, Amanda?" To her look of sudden comprehension, he continued, "I did not wish to choose between you and my loyal friend, Suckachgook."

Amanda's trembling had abated slightly, partly from the resolution of her former misunderstanding of Chingue's confusing behavior, and also as a reaction to the deep, soft, hypnotic quality of Chingue's voice as he slowly and patiently broke down the barriers of her resistance. Encouraged by her response, Chingue continued earnestly, his hands stroking Amanda gently with a soft, relaxing pressure that drew the anxiety slowly from her body as surely as did his words.

"My people tell a story, Amanda, of a time long ago when Indians were first made, of one who lived alone, far, far from any others. He knew not of fire and subsisted on roots, barks and nuts. This Indian became very lonesome for company. He grew tired of digging roots, lost his appetite, and for several days lay dreaming in the sunshine; when he awoke he saw something standing near, which, at first, frightened him very much. But when it spoke, his heart was glad, for it was a beautiful woman with long, light hair, very unlike any Indian. He asked her to come to him, but she would not, and if he tried to approach her she seemed to go farther away. He sang to her of his loneliness and besought her not to leave him. At last she told him if he would do just as she should say, he would always have her with him. He promised that he would.

"She led him to where there was some very dry grass, told him to get two very dry sticks and rub them together quickly, holding them in the grass. Soon a spark flew out; the grass caught it and quick as an arrow the ground was burned over. Then she said, 'When the sun sets, take me by the hair and drag me over the burned ground.' He did not like to do this, but she told him that wherever he dragged her, something like grass would spring up, and he would see her hair coming from between the leaves; then the seeds would be ready for his use. He did as she said, and to this day, when we see the hair on the cornstalk, we Indians know she has not forgotten us.

"To the Indian, Amanda, corn is the seed of life. Like that Indian in the legend, I was lonesome and alone within my heart, and dreamed of a time I would find the one to fill my heart and remove the loneliness. Suddenly, when I saw you walk across the yard of Fort Edward, I knew I had found the one Welsit Mannitto had meant for me, for simply to touch my eyes upon you filled me with joy."

Chingue's hands had grown bolder with his passion, and now, gently caressing her buttocks, he began pressing her body lightly against his with a slow rhythmic motion, and she gasped, feeling the naked hardness of his maleness pressing so intimately against the tawny curls surrounding her virginity.

Still he continued, his shining black eyes reflecting the earnestness with which he spoke. "But unlike the Indian in the legend, I could never be content with just a remembrance of you, Amanda, for you are the seed of my life, the breath of my soul. Without you, there is no life within me, and for that reason I wish to bind you to me forever, to make my body part of yours, as you are part of me. Do not refuse me, Amanda." His voice pleaded with a sudden depth of passion that touched Amanda's young heart.

"Give yourself to me so that I may be a whole man again." Chingue's hands had moved sensuously up her back until they cradled her neck, and he bent his head to run his mouth slowly along the slender whiteness of her throat. Amanda felt unaccustomed shivers of delight as his mouth slowly descended, tracing the line of her collarbone with his tongue, then on to her shoulder with his mouth. In an ever descending motion, Chingue's mouth followed the curve of her firm young breasts until he found the soft, pink crest and covered it hungrily. Amanda gasped at the sudden surge of emotion she felt inside her, and the firm tugging in her groin as Chingue's mouth slowly caressed her breasts, touching, tasting, caressing, teasing, until Amanda felt a wildness within her rising like the ever increasing fury of a storm. Still he continued, his tongue teasing and fondling the swollen peaks until Amanda felt she could stand no more, so strongly had her emotions risen out of control.

"Chingue," she cried in a desperate voice, clutching his head tightly to her breast, "Please stop. My heart is pounding so hard, I'm sure it will burst!"

"No, Amanda." A tremor of passion was obvious in his breathless reply. "It will not burst, but expand to take me in."

Slowly Chingue's mouth continued its descent, his mouth and tongue exploring and tasting the sweetness of the smooth white skin of her abdomen, and continuing its downward path until it stopped at the silky golden curls that were to be his alone.

Looking up for a moment at Amanda's impassioned face, Chingue whispered softly in the stillness of the wigwam, "Amanda, my body longs to possess all of you, as does my mouth desire to savor all your sweetness." Slowly he lowered his face into the shining tawny curls, nudging and nestling gently, until of their own volition Amanda felt her legs separate to allow his tongue to enter the soft, private confines of her body. Amanda gasped suddenly at the thrills of pleasure piercing her as his tongue touched, probed, tasted and drew out her body nectar, until in deep shuddering groans of joy her body burst forth with exploding passion, convulsing in rapturous agony until she lay weak and exhausted within Chingue's arms. Then did Chingue lower his body onto hers, and begin a slow penetrating motion, driving his manhood deeper and deeper with each thrust into her exhausted body until, with a burst of searing pain, drawing from Amanda a sharp cry of protest, he came to rest completely inside her. Holding himself there, exalting in the occupation of her body, Chingue raised himself slightly to look directly into the soft blue eyes wet from the raging emotions she had experienced for the first time.

"I hold you now, Amanda, I possess you as no other ever has or ever will. You are part of my body as I am part of yours, and together we will meet the stars this night."

With a sensuously rhythmic action, Chingue began moving inside her, gently increasing the pressure of his motion until Amanda could feel her body's response intensifying with the rapidity of his movements. Faster and faster he moved, causing her heart to accelerate beating until she could hear nothing but its pounding in her ears, and feel nothing but her body's crying need for release. Slowly, carefully, Chingue took her with him to the pinnacle of his passion, pausing for a moment at its peak to savor as long as he dared the rapture that held them both, before bringing them mercifully and breathlessly to the ecstasy of climax. At the crashing, thundering finale of their act of love, Amanda did feel for a moment as if she touched the heavens, and as Chingue's spent body lay exhaustedly upon hers, she whispered shyly into his ear, "Yes, Chingue, you did truly take me to meet the stars tonight."

Through the long hours of the night, Chingue held Amanda tightly in his arms as he dozed intermittently, the short periods of sleep only serving to restore his strength and inflame the passion that had appeared spent such a short time before. He awoke again and again to caress Amanda's young, inexperienced body into fiery response to his unending desire for her.

The advent of morning found the two weary lovers locked in a sleeping embrace. Chingue, awakening, tilted up Amanda's chin so that he might view her beautiful face more clearly in the light filtering through the smoke outlet in the roof.

"Amanda," he whispered softly. "Amanda." The long golden-brown lashes lying against the smooth golden cheeks fluttered, and then lifted slowly in response to her name, and he stroked her smooth cheek as he crooned again and again, "Amanda, *N'dockqueum, K'dahoatell*. Amanda, *N'dockqueum, K'dahoatell*."[1]

The deep, soft sound of his voice, and his gentle caresses lulled the weary young girl back to sleep, and as she slept, Chingue took her body again with love.

The sun was near the midpoint in the sky when the two sleeping figures started to awaken. A deep, complete feeling of happiness washed over Chingue as he viewed the sleeping, naked figure of his wife lying next to him, her face clear and innocent as a child's, her hair forming long golden spirals as it lay in wild disarray around her. Gently he shook her, urging her into wakefulness.

"Amanda, come, the day has long since begun. Do you wish to sleep away your first day as my wife?"

Amanda's eyes opened slowly. It took her a long time to come to complete wakefulness, but when she did, she also came to the realization that she lay with Chingue stark naked in the broad light of day!

The look of horrified maidenly modesty which came over her face brought a wide smile from Chingue. Pulling her against him playfully, he chuckled and teased, "Come, Amanda, we can not lie abed all day, no matter the strength of your desire. We must bathe now, for at this time of the day the pool will be deserted, and we will have privacy." Pointedly ignoring the deep red flush that rose to

1. Meaning, "Amanda, my wife, I love thee."

148

Amanda's face, Chingue rose and dressed hurriedly, waiting patiently as Amanda pulled her buckskin wedding shift over her head. Then, snatching up his toilet articles, Chingue took her hand to pull her from the wigwam.

Amanda was too filled with embarrassment at their late rising and the obvious thoughts it implied, to be able to look around as Chingue led her proudly through the village to the bathing pool.

True to his prediction, the pool was deserted, and in the warm October sun, Chingue stripped off his breechcloth once again and started toward the water, only to stop and turn with a puzzled expression toward Amanda as she stood unmoving. Then realizing Amanda was once again seized by modesty, Chingue walked back slowly with a small smile, and stood before her. Gently, as the night before, he raised the shift over her head and dropped it to the ground. In one swift movement, he scooped his wife's small body into his arms and carried her into the water.

Memory stirred slightly, and for a moment the eyes looking down into hers were a soft, warm green, the chest lightly furred with golden hair, and she gave a start, shaking her head to clear away the vision. Chingue's arms tightened slightly in response to her movement, and he continued walking until they both were almost completely submerged.

A period of playful scrubbing was followed by a short, leisurely nap in the warm, drying rays of the sun. How lovely it is, Amanda's thoughts wandered vaguely as the sun warmed her naked body, and showed a fiery red against her closed eyelids. A sense of uneasiness slowly came over her, and she opened her eyes to see that Chingue had rolled over on his stomach and propped up on his elbows, he lay studying her sleeping face. The eyes that looked down into hers were pensive and serious, and Amanda felt an unreasonable fear pervade her senses.

"What is it, Chingue? What's wrong?" When he did not respond to her questions, but continued staring soberly into her face, Amanda ventured again, "Just moments ago you seemed happy and content, and now you've changed. Won't you tell me what's wrong?" she coaxed. When he finally started to speak, Chingue's eyes wandered to her hairline, where little tendrils of hair had formed small curls around her face, and he touched them gently.

"Amanda, your first night in my bed brought me great pleasure and happiness, and I desire to know if I gave you pleasure also."

Amanda's face flushed a bright red as Chingue stared directly at her awaiting a response. Slowly she stammered, "Y—Yes, yes, Chingue, I had not expected it to be so—pleasant."

Amanda's naive response restored the smile to Chingue's sober face, and seemingly appeased, he continued. "If that is so, Amanda, there is something I would ask of you."

Chingue saw Amanda's apprehension but continued slowly. "I watched in the fort yard as you greeted the man you called your betrothed." His eyes narrowing as he recalled the scene, he went on. "You raised your mouth and offered it to him, pressing your lips against his in a way that gave him much pleasure. You are my wife, Amanda, yet you have never offered your mouth to me."

Amanda's eyes widened, showing her surprise. Chingue was jealous of the kiss she had given Robert to appease her stricken conscience that morning at the fort! Now it was her turn to smile, and she did, broadly, unknowingly teasing Chingue even further as that small dimple darted in and out with her response.

"Chingue, I did not think it was the custom with your people to kiss as a sign of affection."

"That is true, Amanda." Chingue's face was solemn as he continued. "But I hope to erase the memory of his mouth against yours. I do not find it pleasant to recall that another man and you have shared a part of your body that I have not known."

Amanda found it hard to speak with the lump that had formed in her throat with Chingue's honest confession. Swallowing hard to fight the tears that began to fill her eyes as Chingue opened his heart to her, she wordlessly slipped her arms around his neck and drew him down against her. Lightly she pressed her slightly parted lips against his, slowly moving her mouth until she drew a response from his eager lips.

With a low groan, Chingue encircled her with his arms, pulling her to him until her naked breasts were crushed against his smooth, hairless chest. The taste of her had stirred in Chingue a driving desire for more, and his searching tongue probed deeper and deeper, reaching the inner depths of her mouth. He experienced not a feeling of satisfaction, but a growing sense of desire in his loins that he felt almost impossible to control.

As he drew himself away from her, he whispered softly, his voice shaken with emotion, "You will not do this again with any man but me, Amanda. Your body will be shared with me alone."

"And will you keep yourself for me alone, Chingue?" The question had slipped out unbidden past Amanda's lips, and once it was said, Amanda realized the doubts that had been on her mind regarding the solemnity of this Indian marriage.

With a look of utmost sincerity, Chingue answered, "There was no woman I loved before you, Amanda, and since I have had you, I will have no other. You are my life, my love, my soul, the breath that gives life to my body, and the spark that gives light to my day. I want no one but you, and will allow no one any part of what is mine."

Chingue spoke the last words with the heat of menace in his dark eyes, and in answer, Amanda drew his head down again to cover his lips with hers. Her small gesture of love had the inevitable result of a joining of their bodies that left them both rapturously breathless and exhausted. Slowly Chingue raised himself from her, a small smile on his face.

"Yes, Amanda," he then bent to whisper in her ear. "There are some customs of your people I find I am only too anxious to adopt!"

Four

The sound of male voices in conversation and low laughter outside her wigwam interrupted her thoughts as Amanda worked laboriously, grinding corn into meal. She suddenly remembered with amusement that before coming to the Indian village she had actually believed Indians never laughed! How wrong she had been! Her first month as Chingue's wife had taught her that humor, patience and understanding were integral facets of his character. Her ignorance of Indian ways only seemed to increase his efforts to guide her; her clumsiness in her work aroused his gentle humor; and her shyness in making love only appeared to kindle his desire and provoke a loving tenderness in him that touched her far more deeply than she had believed possible. Ninscheach had continued in her quiet manner to instruct her in her wifely duties, and Chingue's appreciation of her earnest efforts was obvious in everything he did. Unconsciously a frown knit her brow.

So, why am I not happy? she questioned herself for what was surely the hundredth time, still feeling that small core of unhappiness that would not be dispelled.

The small hand grinding the corn slowed to a stop, and she sat back on her heels to finally acknowledge to herself for the first time the thought that was dragging her down. She knew she would not know happiness until she accepted the truth: she was an Abnaki squaw, she could never go home now, never.

Golden October days passed into November, bringing a sharp crispness to the air which was the silent forerunner of the winter to come. Amanda knew the time for the yearly trek to the tribal hunting grounds had arrived, and her anticipation mounted. She knew that as Chingue's wife she would be included in the party of hunters and their families that traveled to the rich game area where they would camp until they had accumulated as much meat as they could carry back to the village before the winter snows. She was well aware that the outcome of the hunt meant either survival or famine for the entire tribe during the winter.

The day of the trek dawned bright and clear, with a flurry of movement within the village that created an air of excitement. At the first light of dawn Amanda was packed and eager to be off. Each family was responsible for carrying the essentials for cooking and living for a period up to two months, and every member carried his share of the load. Standing in the group that had formed as they prepared to leave, Amanda already felt the heavy weight of her pack, and glancing around surreptitiously, she was shamed by the effortless manner in which the other squaws

154

carried their portions of the burden. Of them all, it appeared only she was bothered by the weight she carried!

"Amanda." She turned to meet Chingue's worried gaze. Her discomfort had not gone unnoticed by him.

Without giving him the opportunity to comment on her weakness, she whispered softly, "Quickly, Chingue, we must take our places in the column!"

Noting the determination in her manner, Chingue reluctantly allowed her to proceed into the column, but for the remainder of the two-day trek, Amanda carried the double burden of her heavy backpack and the weight of Chingue's worried gaze, and was not really certain in the end which had been harder to bear.

Work began immediately upon their arrival at the camp two days later. The men erected shelters quickly and efficiently and set traps in deer paths and near freshwater springs. In the days that followed, Amanda joined the parties of women who checked the traps each day in an effort to reach any trapped animals before wolves or other animals could devour them. Each time a trapped animal was located, the women notified the men, who dragged the slain animals back to the bark hunting-houses, where they removed the skins to be treated later. The women then cut, dried, and prepared the meat for storage.

As another part of her instruction as an Abnaki wife, Amanda was taught the long, painstaking process of tanning the animal skins. Her sensitive stomach balked at the gruesome initial step of scraping the hides free of the remaining fat, hair, and flesh before softening them; but she hid her squeamishness behind an uncommittal facade. With hidden relief she proceeded to the second step of soaking the hides in oil for several days to provide weatherproofing and to wash them clean. In a room heated by a good fire they pulled and stretched the skins until they were soft and dry. Finally they sewed the skins up like a bag and placed the open side over a funnel under which a smudge fire of oak, cedar, or birch bark burned. The smoke provided the shading, from light to dark brown, whichever was preferred for the finished skins. The final step was the most enjoyable for Amanda, for it was then she envisioned the splendid clothing she would fashion in the long winter days to come.

In spite of her strict upbringing and early training, Amanda was not prepared for the grueling work that a hunting party entailed, and each night she needed only to feel the warmth of Chingue's arms around her before her tired, young body surrendered to sleep. In her exhaustion, she was not aware of the many hours Chingue lay awake. His strong desire for her impeded sleep, but he also realized the lack of privacy was an obstacle Amanda's delicate sensibilities could not overcome.

As the second week drew to a close, Amanda labored alone and listless in the warm hut where the skins were drying. The long hours had drained her energy and the concentrated heat in the hut sapped her strength. Wearily she raised her hand to tuck back a strand of hair that had escaped her careless topknot, when she heard a soft sound at the doorway. Turning swiftly she saw Chingue close behind her, and in a smooth, quick movement, he drew Amanda's small perspiring body against his to cover her pink, parted lips with his hungry mouth. Her short words of protest were smothered by the heat of his desire and the sensuous stroking of her body by his slender hands. His kiss deepened, and his hands slipped into the neckline of her shift to fondle the soft delicate roundness of her breasts. She groaned slightly as his fingers gently teased the sensitive nipples. His breathing ragged, he pulled his mouth from hers and whispered in her ear, "Amanda, my body aches for yours. Come with me now, so we may lie together and join our bodies until our desires are sated. I can stand no more of having you near without tasting the sweetness you promise. Come, now."

Without waiting for her reply, Chingue scooped up a blanket that lay by the door, and pulled her from the hut. Quickly, moving stealthily like two fugitives, they stole into the woods, and with Chingue leading, ran excitedly. After they had run some distance, Chingue stopped and looked around cautiously. Satisfied they had reached a spot of complete privacy, he lay the blanket on the ground and turned to Amanda, his black eyes shining. Quickly he stripped off his clothes to stand naked in the cold November air, too afire with passion to feel the chill as he began to undress her. Amanda reddened with embarrassment, not at Chingue's unabashed nudity, but at the excited feelings of eager anticipation surging through her. Finally she stood naked before him, incapable of words and trembling so wildly she could barely stand. As if reading her mind, Chingue snatched up her small body and laying it on the blanket, covered it with his. "Amanda," he groaned softly, reveling in the ecstasy of her flesh under his, "Amanda, *K'dahoatell*."[1]

Too far gone in his passion to delay any longer, Chingue entered her quickly and urgently, moving and filling her body as his rapid movements brought to a peak the answering passion within her. In a sudden moment of soaring glory, Amanda and Chingue met their time of climax together, attaining and expanding for short, estatic moments the beauty of love fulfilled and completed. Then they lay spent, side by side.

Fearing Amanda would chill as the cool air touched her perspiring skin, Chingue gently pulled her to her feet to slip her shift over her head and drape the blanket around her shoulders. He then dressed himself as Amanda stood, eyes downcast, filled with shame by her obvious abandon to his lovemaking.

Chingue finished dressing and turned back to her, seeing her discomfort in the way she avoided his eyes. He was completely attuned to her thoughts in his usual instinctive manner. Raising her chin gently so that her eyes met his, he said softly, "Amanda, you are my reason for life. Do not be ashamed to fill my life to the brim, but believe that I am honored by your love, and feel great happiness knowing that I can return by pleasing your body some small measure of the joy you give to me."

Once again Amanda was startled by his inborn perceptivity and his ability to dismiss with one sincere statement the cause of her discomfort. His glowing dark eyes stared with obvious love into hers,

1. Meaning, "I love you."

and Amanda, feeling a stirring of an emotion unknown to her, slowly slid her arms around his neck and, raising herself on tiptoe, pressed her parted lips against his. With a sudden intake of breath, Chingue crushed her against him, and Amanda gave herself up completely to the tide of emotion that once again swept them away.

A long time later, Amanda and Chingue returned to camp and silently, unaware of the knowing glances and suppressed smiles of the others in their party, resumed their work.

Two more weeks had passed before enough meat had been dressed and preserved to enable the weary hunting party to start home. Each heavily laden with packs of meat, some with drags attached to their back and shoulders, the men, women, and children began the journey back.

Amanda, unaccustomed to carrying burdens in this manner, struggled with her heavy backpack. Determined to do her share, she forged on as Chingue watched her covertly for signs of weakness or strain as the day progressed. Aching and exhausted, Amanda that night fell into immediate slumber as Chingue's arms closed around her. The second full day on the trail sorely tried Amanda's strained muscles, and more than once she was tempted to stop and call out her exhaustion; but pride and a sense of duty to her fellow Abnakis who trudged along beside her uncomplaining forced her to keep her silence and continue.

The weight of their burdens stretched their two-day trek into three, but they were not long past the noon hour of the third day when Amanda began to recognize the landscape. She turned with a smile to Chingue and said, "We're almost home, Chingue!"

Her spontaneous smile and the use of the word "home" did not go unnoticed by Chingue. Feeling a tightness in his throat, he returned her glowing smile. "Yes, Amanda, home."

The arrival of the hunting families and the new supply of meat was met with great rejoicing in the village, and while the exhausted travelers retired to their wigwams, a great feast was prepared. The celebration went on long into the cool, clear night as the happy, satisfied people of the village sang and danced their thanks and praise to Welsit Mannitto. Amanda, weary from her trek but content with her contribution to the party's success, sat by the fire, silently staring up into the black velvet sky, almost mesmerized by the ceaseless twinkling of the stars and the infinite beauty of the night. She felt again the sense of oneness that prevailed within their Abnaki town, and to her own amazement, she also felt an overwhelming sense of pride at being allowed to be one of them. Lost in her thoughts, Amanda jumped as a hand touched her shoulder, and a deep, rough voice whispered in her ear, "Amanda, it is time to retire to our wigwam. The days have been long, and we have earned our rest."

In answer, Amanda rose and walked beside him. Once inside, Chingue turned and reached for her, his face filled with the wonder of his love. "Amanda, my love and pride in you grows with each day you are at my side. Truly Welsit Mannitto looked down with favor when he gave you to me."

Slowly Chingue's mouth descended, his arms straining her tightly against him, and Amanda knew as she closed her eyes, her mouth awaiting his kiss, they would be a long time before sleeping that night.

With unbelievable swiftness the brisk, sparkling days of November shortened into the brief, bleak days of winter. The sharp, biting wind blew the last of the blazing color of fall from the trees, leaving only stark naked branches outlined against the gray sky. The deep, penetrating cold that covered the village seemed to settle within Amanda. Steadily, keeping pace with the onslaught of winter, she felt her sense of contentment and her fragile acceptance of her new life slipping away.

Outwardly she continued her wifely chores: weaving mats of cattail stalks to cover their wigwam as insulation against the cold, and carefully fashioning winter clothing from the tanned skins and furs in the traditional Indian manner, with a bone needle and thin strips of leather. But her former sense of accomplishment seemed to elude her, no matter the competency of her efforts, or the amount of praise heaped on her by a baffled Chingue. With a life-draining misery, she seemed unable to tear her thoughts away from memories of her former life, and reminiscences of the manner in which the last days of December had been spent in all her previous years of life: in happy, excited preparation for Christmas. The realization as that time slipped past that she would never again know the celebration of that great religious holiday within the confines of the Abnaki

161

town, reduced her to tears time and time again as she labored alone inside the wigwam in Chingue's absence.

Adding to her anxiety were her divided reactions to the fact that she had not had her monthly flow since first she had lain with Chingue. "I can't be pregnant," she repeated again and again to herself in the solitude of her wigwam, "It can't be, it's too soon."

Chingue paused at the entrance to the wigwam, a frown creasing his brow as he gazed at his wife's tear-stained face. Turning quickly in an effort to hide her tears, Amanda resumed her work on the moccasins she had fashioned, her face lowered furtively. Frustrated and unreasonably angered by her obvious unhappiness, which he felt so powerless to combat, he demanded roughly, *"Quatsch Luppackhan?"*[1]

Afraid to respond with the truth, Amanda stammered, *"N'matamalsi!"*[2]

The quick response in the Abnaki tongue from the small, delicate, golden-haired creature who looked at him with frightened blue eyes still wet with tears softened his anger and brought a tender smile to his stern countenance. Bending quickly to pull her up and into his arms, he whispered in her ear in a faintly disbelieving voice, *"Yuh allacqui!"*[3] and in a few quick strides carried her to his bed.

Chingue, always gentle in his lovemaking, strove to draw from Amanda with the sheer force of his love the spontaneous response that her unhappiness had

1. Meaning, "Why do you cry?"
2. Meaning, "I feel unwell!"
3. Meaning, "What a pity!"

stolen from him. Slowly, with the patience characteristic of all his dealings with her, Chingue, with soft, tender words and supreme gentleness, gradually overcame the sadness and fears that had loomed enormous in her mind. Slowly her inhibitions slipped away and, freed from their weight, the spark between them soared once again into an all-consuming blaze, leaving them both breathless, relaxed, and content for the first time in many weeks.

Happiness and pride stirred anew within him as Chingue slowly perused the beautiful features of the small woman who was his wife, and who lay at rest peacefully in his arms. Encouraged by their moments of loving intimacy, Chingue spoke softly, "Why is it you do not speak to me of the child that grows within you, Amanda?"

"Y—You know?" Amanda gasped, her eyes now open wide in shocked disbelief.

"I know that you have not bled since first we came together, and now," he said, resting his palm on her stomach where a faint roundness was visible, "I can see that my child grows within you."

Lowering his head, he gently kissed the white skin of her abdomen, resting his face there lightly as he continued to caress her.

"Do you not feel happiness to know my child grows within you?"

At the silence that ensued, Chingue lifted his head to look directly into her eyes and repeat his question. "Do you not feel happiness in thinking of our child, Amanda?"

She lowered her eyes as tears slowly slipped beneath her lids and whispered, "I don't know,

Chingue. I don't know. I'm so confused." Moving quickly, she clung tightly to him, her body trembling, and softly cried until the tears would no longer come.

Chingue's deep voice was filled with emotion as he whispered huskily in the silence of the semidarkness, "Would that I could share with you the joy that fills my heart when I think of the seed that grows within you, Amanda. I can perceive of no greater gift that Welsit Mannitto can give to a man than the child born of the love between him and his wife. Would that I could share with you the happiness that fills my heart, Amanda," he repeated as he tightened his embrace, "for surely my heart is filled to overflowing."

In the semidarkness of the wigwam Amanda, shamed by his obvious happiness, began to confess the fears that had beset and tortured her.

"Chingue, how can I be a good mother to your child? I know so little of Indian ways. Your people have been good and accepted me as an Abnaki, but in my heart I fear I'm still white. How can I raise a child to believe in something of which I myself am not sure? I've tried to pray, but I'm not sure that God will hear my pleas for guidance if I then raise my child to worship in a way that is completely foreign to me. Chingue," she cried in desperation, "I no longer even know how I should pray!"

Chingue's heart, so filled with love for the woman he held in his embrace, ached with her torment. He was silent for a few minutes, his expression that of deep contemplation, and then he ventured slowly, "Amanda, did you not say that like me, you pray to

164

an all-knowing, all-powerful God who reigns over all creatures on this earth?" At her slight nod of acquiescence, he continued, "And if he is an all-knowing God, do you not believe he knows and understands your life here within this village?"

Amanda nodded again, silently, her attention riveted on the handsome, serious face that looked into hers.

"Do you not think, then, that he has shown his approval of the love that flows between us by giving life to the seed I have placed within you?"

Slowly Amanda felt the burden of unhappiness being lifted from her with the magic of Chingue's words, and a small tremulous smile started to curl the corners of her soft pink lips. She softly whispered, "Yes, Chingue."

"Then come, Amanda. Let us now pray together to our mutual God as we will teach our child in the years to come." Drawing her to her knees, Chingue encouraged her to speak, and Amanda's small voice hesitantly broke the silence to pray, "Our Father, who art in heaven."

Chingue's voice echoed after her, *"Ki Wetocheme-lenk talli epan awossagame."*[1]

"Hallowed be thy name."

"Machelendasutsch Ktellewunsowagan."

"Thy kingdom come, thy will be done, on earth, as it is in heaven."

"Ksakimowagan peyeweketsch, ktelitehewagan leketsch yun Achquidhackamike elgique leek talli Asassagame."

"Give us this day our daily bread, and forgive us

1. Words of the Lord's prayer in the Abnaki tongue.

our trespasses, as we forgive those who trespass against us."

"*Milineen eligischquik gunagischuk Achpoan woak muvelendammauwineen n'eschannauchso-wagannena elgiqui niluna muveienilammawiwenk nik tschetschanilawequengik.*"

"Lead us not into temptation, and deliver us from evil."

"*Woak katschi n'pawuneen li achquetschiechto-waganink schukund ktennineen untschi medhick-ing.*"

"For thine is the kingdom and the power and the glory forever."

"*Alod, Knihillatamen ksakimowagan woak ktal-lewussoagan woak ktallowilissowagan ne wuntschi hallemiwi.*"

"Amen."

"*Nanne leketsch.*"

Their words of mutual prayer still ringing in her ears, Amanda looked up into Chingue's solemn face. Gone was the virile savage that her weeks of brooding and worry had conjured up in her mind, but in his stead was the darkly handsome, finely chisled face of her husband, whose black, glittering eyes mirrored so openly the depth of his love.

With a soft cry of remorse for the pain she had inflicted so thoughtlessly, Amanda rose to her feet and clasped him to her breast, silently giving thanks for the warmth, love, and understanding that was her husband, Chingue.

Amanda awoke the following morning with a deep feeling of contentment. Slowly she ran her hand

166

over her stomach, which before had been so very flat, delighting for the first time in thoughts of the child that grew within. The memory of Chingue's brilliant look of pride as he had pressed his lips against the slight roundness brought a flush of warmth to her face, and she turned to regard his sleeping countenance. Smiling softly at the appearance of vulnerable youth that softened his features when those intense, knowing black eyes were hidden from view, Amanda kissed the lips that were slightly parted in sleep. No sooner had her lips touched his, than his slender, muscular arms closed around her to lengthen and deepen the kiss to breathtaking proportion.

"Chingue!" Amanda shrieked playfully, pulling herself away, "You were awake all the time!"

Feigning an innocent look, Chingue shook his head and pulled her close again to hold her silently for a few moments, his face against the soft, fragrant cloud of her golden hair. His deep voice hoarse with the emotion of the precious moment, Chingue whispered softly, "Never draw yourself away from me again, Amanda. With you, you take the sun from my day, and the joy from my being, for you are the center of my life."

Then, as if to dispel the somber turn his thoughts had taken and restore the happy banter of before, Chingue suddenly pushed her away, smiling broadly and saying in a gruff, teasing voice, "Come, lazy one, I can not lie abed all day. I must be about a man's work."

Rising quickly, he pulled on his clothes and turned to look as Amanda rose, naked, in the cool wigwam, shivering slightly as she pulled on her clothes.

"You are cold, Amanda. Would you like to share my warmth this morning?" he asked suggestively. At that Amanda turned and repeated, a smile dimpling her face, "No, Chingue. You can not lie abed all day. You must be about a man's work!" With that, she turned abruptly and walked outside, the echo of Chingue's laughter still ringing in her ears.

After Chingue had left to go hunting, Amanda, still feeling the warmth of Chingue's happiness, went in search of Ninscheach and her sisters. Finding them at work inside their wigwam, Amanda took the opportunity to speak of the child she expected. Unabashed joy shone from Ninscheach's eyes as she turned them on Amanda, her round, wrinkled countenance beaming with happiness.

"You are a good daughter, Amanda," she said in her soft manner, "For since taking you to our bosom, you have returned a hundredfold the love we have given you. And now you bring me my first grandchild, for which I give you thanks."

Touched beyond words at Ninscheach's reaction, Amanda's arms encircled the ample body of the old squaw, only to hear a soft giggling from behind her. Turning she saw Tscholentit doing her best to hide the amusement that broke from her small body in fits of convulsive giggles.

"What is it that tickles you so, Tscholentit?" Amanda asked curiously.

"Oh, it is nothing, Amanda," Tscholentit responded, struggling to stifle her laughter. "It is just that now Chingue will treat you more like a princess then ever, since you carry his child. The other braves will find even more amusement than they have in the past with his treatment of you."

Shocked by Tscholentit's statement, Amanda inquired quickly, "Don't the other men believe I've been a good wife to Chingue?"

Darting a sharp, pointed look in Tscholentit's direction, Mamalnunschetto responded quickly in her stead, "Of course they believe you are a good wife to Chingue. It is just that the other men say they find great enjoyment in watching Chingue, the fearless warrior and brave hunter who could find no woman to please him in the village, so attached to his small, pale bride, so overcome by her smile and so weakened by her touch that he can not tear his eyes from her!"

"But it is not so!" Amanda protested vehemently.

"Oh, but it is." Mamalnunschetto's black, doelike eyes were lowered in shyness. "The men joke that Chingue's heart is no longer in his chest, but in his eyes when he looks at you."

"And the men say how jealous he is when Suckahokus[1] looks at you so warmly," Tscholentit slipped in, giggling wildly, before being chased from the wigwam by an angry Ninscheach.

"Do not listen to the wagging tongues of your foolish sisters, Amanda," Ninscheach urged softly. "If the men of the village joke, it is only their envy of the happiness you have given Chingue that speaks for them. For surely, the joy you have brought him is written on Chingue's face for all to see. And now that you bring him honor by giving him a son, Chingue's pride will know no bounds."

1. Meaning, "Black Fox."

Blushing furiously, Amanda lowered her head and murmured softly, "We do not know it will be a son, Ninscheach."

Her soft voice firm with conviction, Ninscheach responded lightly, "It will be a son."

The brief, dreary days of winter brought with them long, cold nights spent in Chingue's warm embrace. Ever loving, always patient, Chingue strove to bring to those nights a mutual, loving intimacy. In the hours spent making love, Chingue never failed to arouse Amanda gently, slowly raising her passions to a fever pitch, his slender knowing hands caressing her and drawing out her response, his warm probing mouth elevating her passion ever higher, ever increasing in violence, until his strong youthful body then drew her to crashing, tumultuous climax. And afterwards she would lie breathlessly satisfied against him. Amanda could not know that it was only at these times, as her small, young body lay vulnerable and breathless next to his, that Chingue felt secure in his hold over the woman who had come to be dearer than life to him. For this reason, he desired to lengthen and increase the pleasure of their lovemaking, hoping to bind her forever to him with her body, as he feared he never could in her heart.

Following their hours of passionate union, Chingue would hold her close against him, seeming never to tire of the sensation of her soft, naked body against his; and as his hands continued to caress her intimately, he would speak of his life as a child within his village. Understanding came slowly to Amanda, so different in many ways was the training a young Indian boy received in his childhood from that of a white child. But with that understanding grew a firm respect for the Indian ideas Chingue bespoke with such firm conviction.

"Our son, Amanda, will be a true Abnaki: firm and unafraid, braving all seasons and weather, risking all dangers, patient of hunger, thirst, and cold, displaying his bravery even in the midst of the greatest tortures. He will win against the wild beasts of the forests, the savage enemies in the wilderness, and, proud of his independence, he will strike his breast with exaltation and exclaim for all to hear, 'I am a man!'"

Listening to Chingue's words, Amanda recognized the Indian criteria for virile manhood, and knew, instantly, Chingue filled all those qualifications to the highest degree. She was unashamedly proud to have such a man for her husband.

On one such night, Amanda looked up into the dark, handsome face of her lover and husband and reached up to touch the high line of his cheekbone and run her fingers gently across his strong brow. She continued the line of her soft caress along the hollows of his cheeks, and finally drew the tips of her fingers across the firm line of his lips. The tenderness of her caress tore a soft moan from Chingue. He pulled her to him in a surge of loving passion.

"Amanda," he whispered urgently, his hoarse voice trembling, his arms crushing her against him with ever increasing force. "How dear you are to me! My love for you grows so great that I fear I soon will be consumed by it. What is your desire? I have no will to refuse it, for whatever brings a smile to your face, brings one to mine. Whatever strikes fear in your heart, strikes hatred in mine; and whatever brings you happiness, brings me joy unsurpassed! I have no life separate from you. My soul is so joined with yours that were you to go, I would be less than a whole man, and unable to go on."

Releasing her slowly, Chingue's hand went to caress the smooth bulge of her stomach, still only slightly visible, although the child had been growing for almost four months inside her. "This child you bring me, Amanda, will be the bond that ties us together. Through him you will feel yourself become part of me as I am already part of you."

"But, Chingue," Amanda protested, "I am.your wife, and already feel myself one with you."

"No, Amanda." Chingue's hand covering her mouth silenced further protest. His deep voice slightly shaken by the depth of his emotion, he continued, "Your feelings do not yet match the depth of mine for you, but while I hold you in my arms, I can be patient. I long for, and dream of that day when your love for me will equal mine for you, but until then I am content to hold you, to feel at least your body's response to my love."

Overwhelmed by Chingue's profound assessment, and the unashamed declaration of his ardor. Amanda lay silent and watched as his eyes slowly traveled from the small bulge of their child within, down her long slender legs to the small scar near her ankle. A small frown creased his face and he reached down to run his fingers across the marks of the small cross cut between the points of puncture.

"This wound was fresh when first I saw you, Amanda. Who was the one to draw the poison from

172

your body? Was it the man you called your betrothed?"

"No, it was not, Chingue. But what does it matter?" Somehow, Amanda was reluctant to recall to her mind that day in the forest and Adam's swift ministrations to her wound.

Chingue's eyes narrowed as he noted her downcast eyes and the manner in which she avoided answering him. Feeling the white heat of jealousy, he pressed for an answer. "Tell me who it is I owe my thanks for saving your life, Amanda, and how you came to be bitten."

Realizing her reluctance had only stirred his interest, Amanda responded. "After the battle at Fort William Henry, I became lost and was bitten as I wandered in the forest. The man who found me drew out the poison and, after nursing me back to health, returned me to Fort Edward."

"Who was this man, Amanda?"

"His name is Adam Carstairs."

As she spoke the name, Amanda noticed a tightening of Chingue's facial muscles while he struggled to contro the thoughts that swept over him. "I am not unfamiliar with that name. Adam Carstairs is a man of great reputation among the whites. The French soldiers joke of his prowess with women."

"Whatever is said of him, Chingue, he saved my life and treated me respectfully and gently all the while I was in his care. I will be forever grateful to him."

As he watched the resolute expression on his young wife's lovely face, Chingue, consumed by the

173

jealousy her statement had stirred, lowered his head to cover that small scar with his mouth, to rain kisses on her ankle and small foot, and return again and again with his mouth to the mark that had so inflamed his jealousy. Finally he raised his head, the fury of his passion having subsided. Amanda noted with shock that there was a brightness in his dark eyes that bespoke hidden tears. His hands trembled as they roughly clasped her shoulders. His deep voice shook as he pulled her fiercely to him. "I feel envy of this man because he drew the poison from your body, tasted your blood in his mouth, and bound you to him by saving your life. I wish to erase all memory of his mouth against your body, Amanda. It is to me you belong, and of me I wish all your thoughts to be. Chase his memory from your mind and heart, Amanda, so I may find some peace within me."

"Chingue!" Amanda's cry was soft and imploring as she slipped her arms around his neck and clasped him against her nakedness. "Put your mind at rest. There is nothing but friendship between Adam Carstairs and me. Don't torture yourself so foolishly."

Taking his face between the small, soft palms of her hands, she whispered lightly against his lips, "You have known me as no other man has, Chingue. I am bound to you. It is your seed that lives and grows within me, and of that I'm truly proud." And, as she spoke, Amanda knew in her heart the words she spoke were true.

Not all the time spent within the wigwam was spent in serious contemplation. Feeling Amanda's

174

eyes studying him on one winter night as they lay abed, Chingue asked perceptively, "What is it you wish to ask, Amanda?"

"What do you mean, Chingue?" Amanda's voice was surprised. She never failed to be startled by Chingue's uncanny ability to read her thoughts.

"I can see on your face that words lie on your tongue in fear of being spoken. Come, ask your questions. I wish to satisfy all your curiosities. You need not fear my anger."

"Well," Amanda's voice was hesitant as her stare became fixed on the tuft of hair that was allowed to grow on the top of his head. "The manner in which Indian men wear their hair has always seemed strange and a great amount of unnecessary trouble to me, Chingue. But as I've come to know the Abnaki, I've come to realize there must be a reason for dressing the hair in this fashion." And then in a perplexed manner she burst out vehemently, "But try as I might, I can't fathom what that reason might be!"

Hiding his amusement at her words, Chingue feigned a hurt expression. "Amanda, do you not find me handsome?"

Completely taken in, Amanda hastened to assure him, "Yes, Chingue, you are truly handsome and manly. It was just my curiosity that spoke so carelessly."

Now smiling openly, Chingue touched her face gently and explained, "When we go to meet the enemy, Amanda, we meet on equal ground and take each other's scalps if we are able. The victor is entitled to have something to show his bravery and his triumph. A warrior's conduct must be manly, or he is no man. A human being has but one head and one scalp from that head is sufficient to show he has been in my power. Were we to preserve a whole head of hair as the white people do, several scalps might be made out of it, and that would be unfair. Besides, the coward might thus, without danger, share in the trophies of the brave warrior, and dispute with him the honor of victory."

Amanda had seen numerous scalp poles since coming to the village, but did not share the Indian view of these trophies of war, and felt a slight wave of nausea sweep over her in recollection of the grisly sight. Speaking softly, Amanda averted her eyes. "I hope never again to view a scalp freshly taken on an Indian pole. To me, Chingue, you need not scalps to prove you are a man." Slipping her arms around him silently, Amanda lay her head against Chingue's chest until the sound of the steady, even breathing therein lulled her to sleep.

True to Indian tradition, as the middle of February approached, families from the village prepared for another yearly trek, to the grove of sugar maples. There the sap was drawn from the trees to be made into the sugar that would serve an Indian family the year around for sweetening. Such an outing was approached with joy, and whole families traveled the many miles to the grove, made camp, and remained until the task had been completed. On these occasions the wives performed the sap-gathering and sugar-making tasks, and the men erected shelters and did the hunting. But the sugar was the property of the

176

husbands to keep or share with other members of their tribe as each saw fit.

Amanda felt her excitement grow as the day to begin the trek approached, and it was with a strange sense of foreboding that she received the news that a French soldier had arrived at the village, and was in a meeting with the sachem. Slipping to a place where she could view the sachem's wigwam, her sense of foreboding increased when Chingue was called to the conference. Within moments Chingue emerged, to walk in her direction. On seeing her worried expression, Chingue led her back to their wigwam to seat her on the bench and speak urgently.

"We have received a call to a meeting at Fort Carillon with the men who speak for our Great White Father. The sachem has directed that several of our men should travel for him to speak with General Montcalm. And at the same time, we are to restock those provisions that have fallen low during this winter."

Aware of her disappointment, Chingue continued, "Do not fear, Amanda; we will still share in the proceeds of the sugar gathering, for the journey on which I travel concerns all the men of the tribe."

"Then I'm to stay at home when you leave, Chingue?" Amanda's eyes were heavy with tears at the thought of the lonesome days spent in his absence.

Touched by her plight, Chingue ventured, "If I so choose, I may take you with me. Would you like to accompany us, Amanda?"

The brilliance of her answering smile completely overcoming him, Chingue pulled his wife gently against him, saying softly, "We leave in two days time."

Amanda awoke on the day of the journey with happy anticipation, and hastened to prepare for the long trek to Fort Carillon. Looking at the beaver fur robes she had sewn so carefully for Chingue and herself during the long winter nights, she felt a fierce sense of pride in a job well done. She had made certain that all the fur ran in one direction so that rain could not penetrate the robe, but would run off its surface. Amanda realized that today they must, in the usual Indian manner, turn the fur to the inside so that it would provide greater warmth against the body. She had made the boots they would wear with their snowshoes in the same way, from dressed bear skins, the hair also turned inside for additional warmth.

Seeing the pride that radiated from her small, beautiful face as he donned the robe she had so carefully sewn, Chingue hid a smile, and then turned to aid her as she dressed. Despite the obvious happiness on the face of his tiny, young wife, Chingue was now beginning to doubt the wisdom of his impulsive decision to take her along, realizing the long trek on the frozen ground might be hazardous in her fragile condition. Still, despite a nagging voice in his mind, that warned of danger, Chingue could not bear to see the light fade from her face if he reversed his decision and told her she must remain behind.

The sun shining on the frozen surface of snow, gave a sparkling brilliance to the scene around them as the Indian column began its trek to Fort Carillon.

Amanda was fascinated by the fairy-tale quality of the forest in its veil of ice and snow and experienced a strong sense of adventure as she trudged in her place behind Chingue. First in line and functioning as unofficial leader of the group was Lintukseat,[1] the eldest of the group, and confidant of the sachem. Walking second in line was Suckameek,[2] the youngest man, an unmarried youth of about nineteen summers, but a proven warrior; and third walked Chingue, with Amanda keeping close to his heels. Hamruktit,[3] wife of Lintukseat, walked last in line, the many previous trips to Fort Carillon having dulled considerably her anticipation of the journey.

Unaccustomed to traveling in the deep snow on awkward snowshoes, Amanda felt heavily the long duration of the trek. But determined not to cause Chingue any embarrassment by falling behind, she kept up with the breathless pace, unmindful of the many anxious glances sent her way by a worried Chingue. As her step faltered again and again at the end of the first long day, Chingue cursed himself for his foolishness in allowing her to accompany him on such a difficult journey.

The second day proved an even greater challenge than the first to the weary Amanda, and its conclusion was greeted with even greater relief as she fell into Chingue's warm arms and the blessed sweetness of sleep. On the third day, knowing the journey to be near its conclusion, Amanda rose greatly refreshed and anxious to begin.

1. Meaning "Wild Wolf."
2. Meaning, "Black Fish."
3. Meaning, "Little Squirrel."

Before the sun had met the midpoint in the sky, the gates of Fort Carillon came within view. From her vantage point on a hill across from the fort, Amanda gazed in wonder at Fort Carillon. Due, in part, to Adam's explanation of the strategic importance of Fort William Henry, she was immediately aware of Fort Carillon's strategic location as the southern outpost of New France. Situated as it was, high on a rocky point of land, it commanded Lake Champlain as well as the outlet of Lake George, and she realized that whoever held Fort Carillon controlled travel between America and Canada.

Amanda noted that even in appearance, Fort Carillon differed greatly from Fort William Henry and Fort Edward. Instead of being a mud and log construction, it was almost entirely constructed of stone, and even at a distance, the artistry of the French masons was apparent. Although the fort was similar in shape to that of Fort William Henry, as it was four-sided, with bastions extending out from its four corners, it was further guarded on the land sides by two demilunes connected to the fort with draw-bridges, and on the south side an outer wall gave further protection to the area.

Amanda could feel the excitement building within her at the opportunity to see the interior so close at hand. Turning back to her companions, anxious to proceed, Amanda noticed the three proud men had paused to prepare themselves for their presentation to General Montcalm. They each took from the small grooming kits they carried at all times pouches of animal fat and different mineral and vegetable dyes which they mixed and began to paint on their faces.

Satisfied at last, they rose to their feet to take from their packs roaches of deer bristles dyed deep red, which they then fastened to the coxcomb of hair down the center of their heads, further heightening the striking effect of their face paint and the traditional cut of their hair.

Amanda, realizing that she would be expected to enter the fort looking her best as part of Chingue's party, hastened to groom herself and refresh her appearance, but she could not bring herself to make use of the vermillion face paint which Hamruktit had used and had so generously offered to share with her. Sadly shaking her head, she chastised herself for her inability to overcome her aversion to this Indian custom, and silently feared she would never become a good Abnaki.

Amanda, her gaze once again on the fort, did not notice Chingue's quick perusal of her appearance, or the small smile of pride he could not suppress as he viewed her pale beauty. Along with his love for her grew his pride in her achievements and her acceptance of the Indian way of life. Somewhere deep inside him, Chingue knew was a vanity that urged him to display to those at the French fort the angelic, blond young woman he had managed to win for his wife. Now, seeing her beside him, her long hair shining gloriously in the winter sun, her blue eyes bright with anticipation, her face clear and rosy from the bite in the frosty air, that small dimple darting in and out as she turned to smile at him, he had to stop and compose himself to present the cool, aloof appearance his position demanded.

Lintukseat, walking with the dignified air of an

Abnaki of consequence, led his party to the demilune where, once they were recognized, the drawbridge was immediately lowered. Once inside, they were immediately conducted to the office of the officer of the day, in the south barracks. The young officer, who had obviously been expecting them, snapped a salute as his eyes traveled over the small party, a fleeting look of surprise crossing his face as they touched momentarily on Amanda.

"Bon Jour. General Montcalm has been awaiting you and has asked me to escort you directly to him upon your arrival." He looked hesitantly at the two women, puzzled as to the arrangements to be made for them.

Chingue spoke, his deep, rough voice settling the problem for the perplexed young officer. "Hamruktit and my wife will choose the supplies we wish to take back with us." Then, addressing Amanda, he said, "Choose what you feel is necessary and that which will bring you more comfort in our wigwam."

Amanda flashed a shy smile at Chingue, as she realized he had given her license to choose whatever she liked, but lowered her face with embarrassment at the heat that smoldered in the answering look in his dark eyes.

The young officer's face was incredulous as he realized for the first time that Amanda was the wife to whom Chingue referred, but, swallowing hard, he managed to shake off his amazement and direct one of his men to escort the three ambassadors to General Montcalm.

Left alone in the room with Hamruktit and

Amanda, the slender, dark young man appeared at a loss for words, the shock of Chingue's disclosure seemingly having pushed all other thoughts from his mind. Staring at Amanda's small, heart-shaped face, so beautiful and innocent, looking at him from the depths of the huge robe she wore, he felt touched by anger that an ignorant savage had managed somehow to capture and sully the most beautiful girl he had ever seen.

Completely forgetful of Hamruktit's existence, he addressed Amanda cautiously. "It would be my pleasure to show you the fort, madame, before you select your supplies. Would that please you?"

The soft-spoken young man's heart quickened beating in the few moments he awaited an answer, as he found himself somewhat reluctant to part company with the small, compelling young creature before him.

"Very much, Lieutenant?"

"DuPres, madame, Michel DuPres at your service." The young officer's smile was bright and direct, and Amanda felt herself blushing slightly at his polite formal manner that so contradicted the warm look in his eye. Amanda continued "Hamruktit and I are anxious to see the fort more thoroughly, are we not, Hamruktit?"

At the other woman's affirmative nod, Amanda said quickly, "Please proceed, Lieutenant DuPres."

The enthusiastic lieutenant proved to be an excellent guide. Starting first at the southeast bastion, he showed the two women underground to the location of the powder magazine, above which, he explained, were the stables. From there he conducted them to the

183

boulangerie, or "bakery," its huge ovens also underground, with its vaulted ceiling and wood chute to the outside, where the wood for fuel was fed directly from the upper floor to a spot near the ovens. He then led them proudly across the parade grounds to the northwest bastion, which housed the fort's cistern. Michel DuPres was very mindful of the curious glances directed their way and felt a flush of embarrassment at the whispered remarks and knowing snickers that Amanda's appearance in her Indian dress caused among the men, realizing their reactions were similar to his, but were far more insulting in manner. He noted with a sense of relief that Amanda seemed too preoccupied with her observances of the fort to notice the rudeness of the soldiers and hastened to continue his tour.

Maintaining a steady flow of information, the young lieutenant, proud of the beautifully constructed fort, proceeded along the walkway by the outer wall, and while Amanda's eyes took in the magnificent view afforded from the fort's height, he allowed his gaze to linger, unobserved by Amanda, on her soft, pale beauty, realizing he envied strongly Chingue's possession of her. Regretfully pulling himself back to the task at hand as Hamruktit sent him a knowing glance, he continued by pointing out the west barracks, where the officers were quartered, explaining that the south barracks housed the regulars.

Lastly, Lieutenant DuPres led the two women to the southwest bastion, wherein were the rooms for stores and general supplies, and where he knew he no longer had an excuse to remain in the company of the lovely blond *poupee*[1] who had so charmed him. Accepting Amanda's thanks and regretfully bidding them *au revoir*, the slight young man saluted politely and left the two women to their perusals of the supplies.

Amanda felt a strong sense of relief that the tour conducted by the polite, able lieutenant was concluded. Her enjoyment had been considerably dampened by the curious looks and open sneers directed at her by many of the French soldiers. Blinking away the tears forming in her eyes in remembrance of some of their mumbled remarks, she turned to the task Chingue had set for her, driving all other thought from her mind as she considered the room and the abundance contained therein.

Feeling suddenly like a child in a candy store, Amanda's eyes flitted quickly around the room. Mostly concerned with the selection of stores entrusted to her, she did not remain long in consideration of the small group of French soldiers conversing in the corner, but continued assessing the contents of the room. After a few minutes, feeling too warm in her fur garment within the confines of the room, Amanda removed it in a quick fluid movement and, rolling it carefully, placed it in the corner, completely unaware of the effect she had on the group of men watching her every movement. The beautiful, if somewhat unusual picture she presented, her delicate figure encased in her fawn-colored Indian dress, her long blond hair hanging in a shining veil down her back, the small, perfect face so dominated by those huge, wondering dark-lashed blue eyes, now so

1. Meaning "doll."

serious in contemplation, left the men who watched open-mouthed in admiration.

Moments later, Amanda felt a moist, firm grip on her arm, and looked up into the leering, somewhat drunken face of a French soldier looking down into hers. Amanda felt a knot of fear tighten in her stomach as the drooping, bloodshot eyes looking at her from within a sweaty, heavily jowled face, wandered over her in open, lustful admiration. The hand that held her arm so securely slipped upward to her shoulder, drawing her closer as his thick voice slurred, "Ah, *mon petite*, you are a beauty. What is your name?"

Fear seemed to choke the words within her throat as she stared wide-eyed with fright at the corpulent, none-too-clean soldier assessing her so boldly.

"Come, *cherie*, tell Henri your name. I would like us to become very good friends this night," he coaxed.

Regaining her voice at last, Amanda replied softly, "Please, sir, let me go. You are keeping me from a task I must accomplish."

A spark of anger showed in his drooping eyes as she made an attempt to free herself from his grasp. "What is the matter, cherie? Have you lost your taste for white men after being shared by those red savages?" he hissed. "Or do you prefer to be treated in a different manner? Henri will oblige you, *mon petite*, and he will make you lose your desire for those red devils by showing you what you have been missing."

Pulling her roughly into his arms, he struggled to kiss her, his anger growing greater by the minute as

Amanda fought his amorous advances. Frantically Amanda glanced toward the other soldiers still standing in the corner, desperately seeking aid, and was stunned to see them smiling in obvious amusement at the scene being enacted before them. They were actually enjoying her debasement!

Her fury with the callousness of the French soldiers renewed her strength, and she struggled wildly to elude the drunken soldier's hands and mouth. She found herself almost gagging at the overwhelming odor of perspiration and the rancid staleness of his breath that seemed to increase with the ferocity of his struggles.

Suddenly Hamruktit's harsh voice sounded in the room, drawing Henri to attention. "This woman is Chingue's wife. If you harm her, he will kill you," she hissed venomously.

At the sound of Chingue's name, the soldier seemed to stiffen, relaxing his grasp, enabling Amanda to almost free herself. Still maintaining his hold on her arm, the soldier looked down, his rheumy eyes assessing her with added respect. "So, you are Chingue's wife," he said slowly, seeming to consider the situation as he spoke. "The particular Chingue has finally found a woman to suit him! I must say, cherie, I can find no fault with his taste." And then as if having reached a decision, he released his hold on her arm. "And, *mon petite*," he added with a note of regret, "if it is true, I have no desire to incur his anger and feel the sharp bite of his knife. Adieu, madame." With a short salute, he turned and walked unsteadily through the doorway, accompanied by loud laughter from the soldiers still observing idly from the corner.

Amanda glanced appreciatively at Hamruktit, and retired quietly to a corner to sit and await Chingue, too shaken to continue her task. Weighing heavily on her heart was the knowledge that she had been right in her assessment of the reaction her own people would have to her once it was known she lived with Chingue. It was obvious that the French soldiers felt she was no longer deserving of respect, and would not lift a finger to help her in distress. Only fear of Chingue's anger and retribution had saved her, and for that reason she remained in the corner, her eyes downcast, awaiting his return.

There she remained in silent contemplation of the cruelty of fate for a time, until suddenly, a familiar, booming laugh, accompanied by a high-pitched feminine giggle, cut into her reverie. Amanda snapped to attention, immediately seeking the source of that laughter, and moved forward in anticipation. "No, it can't be! It can't be!" her mind cried wildly.

Then, as if in answer to her denial, a tall, broad figure moved into view, and then through the doorway. His brawny arm was slung casually around a small, dark-haired woman who was obviously enjoying his attention.

Too overcome with emotion to speak, Amanda stepped forward and into the light as the tawny-haired figure turned in her direction. In the moment that the glance of those cool, green eyes met her tearful gaze, all movement seemed to stop, freezing for the space of a few seconds the dramatic tableau within the room, until, with a joyous cry, Adam rushed forward to sweep the small golden-haired figure into a wild embrace.

"Amanda! Amanda, darling..." Crushing her against him, Adam rasped her name over and again, reveling in the wonder of holding her in his arms once more. Revealing in that moment the love he had previously hidden so carefully, he whispered against the silkiness of her hair, "I've dreamed of this moment so often, but you're back in my arms now, and this time I won't let you go."

Before she could speak, the generous, smiling mouth she knew so well covered hers, cutting off and destroying all protest with its demanding kiss. All conscious thought seemed to leave her mind as Amanda was overcome by the intensity of the emotion stirred by Adam's appearance. His kiss deepened to claim the sweetness of her mouth for his own and Amanda's arms encircled his neck seemingly of their own accord as she responded instinctively to his embrace.

Amanda could feel the trembling of Adam's massive frame as he reluctantly drew his mouth from hers. Holding her tight against him, he looked down at her, incredulity lingering in his gaze as he searched her face. His vibrant voice was a hoarse whisper when he spoke again.

"I was frantic when I heard you had been taken by the Indians, Amanda. I couldn't believe it had happened! I blamed myself, cursing the day I left you. I searched for weeks to no avail. No one even knew the name of the Indian who had taken you! But you're here with me now..."

Amanda lay her head against Adam's chest as he spoke, the familiar masculine scent of his body filling her with a deep sense of peace. Enveloped in

the security of his tender embrace, she was unmindful of all around them as Adam held her possessively close, caressing her gently. A soft sigh escaped her
lips the moment before she opened her eyes instinctively, looking over Adam's shoulder to see Chingue
approaching stealthily, knife drawn, hatred burning
in his dark-eyed gaze.

"Chingue, no!" The cry tore from her lips, momentarily stopping Chingue and allowing Adam the time
to turn, release her, and face his attacker.

In the space of a second, Amanda was between
them, her hand on Chingue's as it held the knife.
"Chingue, no, please," she pleaded. "Put your knife
away. This is the man to whom I owe my life. I told
you of him, don't you remember? Please, put you
knife away!"

Jealous fury still obvious on his face, Chingue
slowly sheathed his knife as the two men measured
each other cautiously over her head.

"Chingue," Amanda ventured, her voice quaking
with fear, "this is Adam Carstairs."

Adam looked from Chingue to Amanda, noting the
possessiveness of Chingue's jealous stare.

"Adam, I would like you to meet Chingue," she
said hesitantly, unsure how to continue.

"Is this the man who took you from Fort Edward,
Amanda?" Adam's voice was rough as he measured
visibly the threat of the savage glaring at him with
such intensity.

Amanda nodded. Her mind in a turmoil as she
sought a peaceful solution to the explosive situation,
she unconsciously compared the two men. Chingue,
although tall himself, stood at least four inches

shorter than Adam. His slender, athletically muscular frame looked meager compared to Adam's massive height and broad proportions; but as he faced Adam, the fury of his jealous hatred burning from the depths of his narrowed black eyes, he made up in menace that which he lacked in size, and Amanda realized they were indeed well matched. And looking at the two men, she was not sure whom she feared for most.

"You have taken this woman from Fort Edward as a hostage, Chingue." Adam's voice addressed directly the Indian facing him. "Accordingly, I'll buy her back from you. Name your price and I'll meet it."

A look of contempt crossed Chingue's countenance as he spoke, his deep voice leaving an impact on the silent room. "This woman is not my hostage. She is my wife!"

Adam directed a quick, surprised glance at Amanda, who dropped her head to avoid his eyes, giving silent verification to Chingue's statement.

Adam's clear voice shook slightly as he replied, "Then I'll buy your wife from you, and with the great sum I'll pay you, you can buy many wives!"

The fury of Chingue's gaze intensified as he said contemptuously, placing his hand on Amanda's stomach, "And would you also buy my child which she carries within her?"

Adam looked to Amanda in shock, unwilling to believe Chingue's bold statement, only to see her gaze still averted from his as a tear slowly trickled from the corner of her eye, leaving a shining path on its course down her pale cheek.

Swallowing hard, Adam answered softly, "Yes, I

191

will. She'll keep the child, and you'll have many children from the wives you'll be able to buy."

"And none would be the equal of the son Amanda will give me," Chingue's voice replied haughtily. "But you speak needlessly, Adam Carstairs," Chingue continued. "Amanda is not mine to sell. She has been adopted into our tribe, and as my wife, and an Abnaki, she is free to leave me at any time to take another to husband. Why do you not address her as to her choice?"

Disbelief slowly faded from Adam's face as Amanda raised her eyes to meet Chingue's. The dark black eyes were unfathomable, and as she turned to Adam to see the loving confidence that now shone from his eyes, she felt violent fetal movement within her. Amanda's mind returned suddenly to the contemptuous way she had been treated and regarded by the French soldiers such a short time before, and she placed her hand on her stomach as if to still the movement she felt therein. No, she could not submit her child to the contempt she knew he would receive as a half-breed in a white world. She could not, even if Chingue would permit her to leave. Her feelings, whatever they were, were no longer of consequence. First came the child, who protested so bitterly within her. Don't be afraid, she thought, mentally consoling her unborn child, I won't do this to you.

Hardest of all was to turn to Adam and crush the dream that shone so brightly on his face. Her eyes brimming with tears, Amanda faced him, saying softly, "I'm sorry, Adam, it's too late now. I've been Chingue's wife for almost five months. I've lived with him, shared his life, and now his child grows

192

inside me." As she spoke, the tears hanging in her huge, blue eyes spilled over, flowing in steady, glittering streams down her face. "Please forgive me for hurting you, but I can no longer consider anyone but my child, who should be born to know and love his father. Forgive me, Adam, please." And turning, she looked to Chingue who returned her look, his face now completely impassive, and led her away.

Adam stared silently at the retreating figures of the Indian and the petite, pale girl-woman who had so suddenly stolen the joy from his life with her words, "It's too late now, Adam, too late."

The words kept running through his mind as he stared at the doorway through which they had disappeared. Unable to stand the room a moment longer, Adam strode forward, completely oblivious of the group of French regulars still standing in the corner as silent witnesses to the entire scene. Nor had he noticed the obese, slightly drunken soldier who had returned in time to hear Amanda's refusal of Adam in favor of Chingue, and who had watched her leave the room with jealous contempt glaring from his drooping eyes.

As Adam moved quickly past them, Henri caught his arm, saying in a loud voice, "Do not waste your time feeling sorrow for losing that one, monsieur. After that filthy devil has had his hands on her, she is no longer worth a white man's attention. She seems to enjoy being an Indian's whore."

The Frenchman's slurred words jerked Adam back to the present with brutal force, bringing the blood rushing to his head in blinding rage. Without speaking a word, Adam raised his arm, and in one quick movement smashed his fist directly into the mouth that had so defamed his beloved. The power of the blow slammed the drunken soldier against the wall, where he slowly slid to the floor unconscious, the offending mouth gushing blood as he fell.

Without a backward glance, Adam, too, left and headed directly to the small room where he was quartered during his brief visits to Fort Carillon. There he threw himself on the bed to stare unseeingly into space. I have to think, his mind kept repeating. I have to think. There must be some way to get her free of him. There must be, he thought desperately. He could not bring himself to believe or accept the fact that after all the months of aching longing, he should find Amanda again, only to lose her within minutes, even more completely than before.

Adam laughed wryly to himself as he thought of the last six months since he had seen Amanda. Six long, lost months spent in bitter self-recrimination and frantic, fruitless searching, while his heart ached with longing and his mind tortured him with pictures of Amanda being abused by some red savage, or worse, lying beneath him. How he had cursed his own stupidity and weakness at letting her go so easily, because of a betrothal that had taken place before he had met her. Why had he not realized then that the time they had shared in the wilderness had forged a bond so firm and true between them that it would have transcended all former commitments? He recalled the day a month or so ago when he had finally forced himself to face the fact he would probably never see Amanda again, and sick with

194

disgust and self-loathing, he had determined to go on with the only commitment of value in his life, the determination to be of help in concluding the war that was still raging.

How easy it had been to assume again the facade of the carefree bachelor while he resumed his under-cover work for the British. As many times as his body had been involved, his heart had never been touched, for without Amanda, that cold, dead spot within him had swelled again, and he was, for all his outward buoyant spirits, inside, cold and unfeeling—until today.

Remembering now the sudden, overwhelming joy he had experienced as his eyes had touched on her small, beautiful face, his throat tightened with emotion; and recalling the softness of her slight body in his arms just minutes previous, the warm delight of her mouth, the rapturous wonder of her response to his kiss, and the feeling of her arms wrapped tightly around his neck, he ached to hold her again, even more closely than before.

What a fool I was, he berated himself. I should have taken her for myself in the forest, when she slept in my arms. He thought back, remembering the many nights he had held her so close. The child, the child, the one inescapable fact. Then the child she is carrying would have been mine, mine. The deep anguish Adam felt was a burning pain inside his chest, squeezing, squeezing, until a ragged sob escaped him, releasing the tears that came cascading down his face in the solitude of the room. He cried out in a broken voice, his hand covering his face, "Oh, Lord, Lord, I think I've lost her."

Amanda followed a silent Chingue from the storeroom. Quiet and unobserved, Hamruktit had taken up Amanda's robe and followed them, and now catching up, hastened to put it around her quaking shoulders as they hurried across the cold parade grounds toward the officers' quarters. Hearing the shuffling feet behind him, Chingue turned and noticed for the first time Amanda's shivering. Taking the robe from Hamruktit's fumbling grasp, he quickly helped Amanda to slip into it, and drew it closely around her. Pausing to look down into the huge, blue eyes so full of anguish and tears, he said softly in his gruff voice, as he gently wiped the tears from her face with the palms of his hands, "Cry no more, Amanda. Tears do not suit an Abnaki."

The remainder of the day passed as if in a dream for Amanda. Even being introduced to the infamous Marquis de Montcalm could not seem to shake her from the tight, unfeeling world into which she had slipped after making her decision in the storeroom. Outwardly responsive to the general's flattering remarks to Chingue regarding his beautiful new wife, Amanda remained inwardly unaffected by all that progressed.

Amanda watched with relief the waning light of day, realizing it would soon be over, knowing they would be leaving for home at daybreak of the next day. She longed to be away from Fort Carillon, the scene of her humiliation. And she wanted to flee the despair of her memory of Adam's stricken face. Finally, Amanda found herself being led by Chingue to the room assigned to them in deference to

Chingue's beautiful young wife, and she breathed a sigh of relief as the door closed behind them, knowing she would soon have the escape of sleep.

Chingue turned to Amanda in the quiet of their room, and lifted her gently into his arms. Silently, he placed her on the bed, removed her moccasins, and took his place beside her. With his inborn, instinctive sensitivity to her innermost thoughts, Chingue did not attempt to make love to Amanda, but simply drew her into his arms, to turn her face up to his as he spoke. His eyes shone openly with the love he felt welling inside him, and his rough voice trembled slightly as he lay his palm against her cheek and spoke.

"This face is the light that brightens my day and gives breath to my soul. You are all things to me, Amanda. You are my life. When I entered the storeroom this afternoon and saw you in his arms, the light began to fade, and blackness was descending; my soul was dying." Pausing to regain his voice which was so hoarse with emotion, Chingue said softly, "I thank you for returning my life to me."

Without another word, he pulled her tightly against him, and held her thus until she finally slept.

Amanda awoke the next morning to see the first light of day breaking through the winter sky. Anxious to be away, she and Chingue rose quickly and prepared to leave. Once outside, they were joined by the other members of their party, and went to breakfast. Obviously, Lintukseat and Hamruktit had been busy during the evening, as all the supplies had been chosen and separated into packs so that each

197

might carry a share of the load. As they prepared to strap on their burdens, Amanda noticed movement against the wall, and turned to see Adam step forward to address Chingue.

"I would like to speak with your wife, Chingue. Do I have your permission?"

Chingue's eyes narrowed with suspicion, but he nodded his assent.

Moving forward, Adam took Amanda's hands in his. Amanda looked up into his intense, handsome face and steeled herself against the words he was about to speak.

"Amanda, I couldn't let you leave without speaking to you once more. After thinking things over last night, I realized I hadn't really given you much choice. It occurred to me that perhaps you didn't want to return with me, but"—Adam paused to force himself to say the words that were so difficult to speak—"you might want to return to Robert. If that is so, Amanda, if you'll agree to come with me, I'll do my best to see you're returned to him."

Amanda smiled, knowing that statement had cost him dearly, and replied quickly, "No, Adam, my past life is over now. All ties have been broken. But, if you'll do something for me, Adam, I beg you to tell Robert I'm well. Tell him, if he hasn't already done so, to put me from his mind and to take another wife, because I'll never return."

Amanda watched helplessly as the color drained from Adam's tortured face while she spoke. Not knowing what else to say, she whispered softly, "Goodbye, Adam."

Suddenly she was scooped against his broad chest

198

as Adam's massive arms crushed her to him, and he whispered agonizingly against her hair, "Amanda, please don't ask me to do this. Don't ask me to let you go."

After a few moments, Amanda's soft voice whispered firmly, "The choice isn't yours, Adam."

Slowly, Amanda felt the strong arms release her, and as they did, she raised herself on tiptoe to place a light kiss against his lips before she turned and walked back to Chingue.

Amanda did not look back as Chingue helped her to strap the pack on her back, nor did she look back as she assumed her place in the small column and walked from the fort. She did not want Adam to see the tears that streamed so ceaselessly down her face.

Her burden weighing heavily on her back, Amanda felt herself tire quickly, and before they were out of sight of the fort, she was panting and breathless, although uncomplaining. As soon as the fort slipped from view, Chingue fell back from his place in the column and stopped Amanda, at the same time motioning Hamruktit to continue ahead with the column.

Unstrapping the pack from her back, he proceeded to add her pack to his, leaving her free to walk unencumbered.

"No, Chingue, I won't walk freely while you struggle under the weight of both our packs."

Looking at her solemnly, Chingue responded, "You carry my child, that is burden enough. Come, let us catch up with the others."

When Amanda still hesitated, looking to the heavy load he was to assume, Chingue spoke softly, his voice deep and sincere as his pensive eyes held hers. "Do you not know, Amanda, when you tire and suffer, I also feel your pain? When you are gasping and breathless, I also can not breathe. To see your step lightened, your burden lessened, I am relieved, no matter the load I carry. Would you insist on your share of the burden and cause me to suffer needlessly? I beg your mercy, Amanda."

A slight smile touched the pale pink lips he loved so well, causing a sudden feeling of soaring happiness inside Chingue as Amanda replied softly, "As always, Chingue, you manage to lighten the burden on my mind as well as my body." She paused for a moment, then she continued, *"Yuh yehucke allemusketam."*[1]

Amanda passed the duration of the trek back to the Abnaki village in almost complete silence. Even unencumbered, Amanda found the journey particularly punishing to her small frame, as her aching muscles, unused to the clumsy snowshoes, cried out in protest at the seemingly ceaseless return journey. Many times her eyes strayed to Chingue's tall, spare frame, bent under the weight of the double packs he carried, and she fought the pangs of guilt that assailed her.

Chingue, well aware of both Amanda's exhaustion and her feelings for him, gathered her tenderly into his arms each night as they slept, whispering softly against her ear as he had their first night of love, "Amanda, *N'dockqueum, K'dahoatell.*"[2]

Forcing all other thought from her mind, Chingue's

1. Meaning, "Well, now, let us continue on."
2. Meaning, "Amanda, my wife, I love thee."

words of love lulled Amanda into two nights of exhausted slumber.

When finally, near the end of the third day, the Indian column approached the village, Amanda felt a sense of true relief. Now, at last, in the familiarity of her own wigwam she would succeed in driving from her weary mind the sad green eyes and handsome, stricken face that haunted her. Here, surely, she could forget him, she thought, admitting to herself at last her inability to shake Adam from her mind.

Suddenly feeling the weight of someone's gaze upon her, Amanda turned to see Chingue scrutinizing her pensively, and flushing guiltily, she quickly averted her eyes, only to feel the gentle touch of his hand on her cheek. She raised her eyes at last to see the pain and love so openly displayed in the face of the man who was her husband. Resolution flooded over Amanda. You will not give pain to the man who gives you only love in return, her mind demanded of her. Slipping her small hand into his, she gently pulled him forward toward their home.

Within the confines of her wigwam, as she prepared their night meal, Amanda realized for the first time she had given no thought at all to the results of the Indian delegation's talk with General Montcalm. Why was it they had been summoned so hastily to the fort? Chingue had been in conference with the sachem since his return from the fort and still he had not come back. What was it that warranted such prolonged discussion? Amanda could feel the apprehension building within her minute by minute, as her hand that stirred the cooking food trembled visibly.

A sound at the door of the wigwam caused her to look up to see, with a tremendous sense of relief, Chingue enter and seat himself near her.

"Tell me, Chingue, what was the result of your talk with the general and the sachem?" She knew without being told that a conference with General Montcalm boded no good for the Abnaki's peace of mind.

"The general has noticed an increase in the scouting of Fort Carillon by patrols of rangers. He fears an attack is being prepared, and would like us to send our men in alternating groups to aid him in fighting the enemy when it becomes necessary."

"Fight the enemy!" Amanda's voice was so soft it could hardly be heard. "You mean you'll go to fight the British, the rangers, my friends and neighbors, men who served with my father and Robert? Possibly you'll even fight Robert!" she exclaimed suddenly, her eyes widening in horror. "And whom shall I pray for, Chingue? Shall I pray that my husband be spared to kill my friends?"

All expression seemed to drop from Chingue's face, except for the glittering in his coal-black eyes, as he replied, "You, like me, are an Abnaki, Amanda. You will do as all other Abnaki women; await the return of your husband while he does what he must do to keep his manhood—fight those who threaten his village, his family and his friends. It does not matter whom we fight, for your place is to stay here and wait!"

"Chingue," Amanda implored, "You'll be trying to kill my friends."

There was a moment's silence before Chingue

replied softly, "If so, Amanda, remember, your friends will be trying to kill your husband."

The brutal truth of that fact hit Amanda with stunning force as she suddenly recalled only too vividly the pride many of her own acquaintances had displayed in the number of Indians they had slain, and she raised her eyes to Chingue, knowing there was no apparent answer to her dilemma. After a few moments she spoke. "When do you go, Chingue? With which group?"

His voice was dull and wooden; he responded almost immediately, "With the first group, in two days time."

Suddenly, before her eyes, the cold, hard look of Chingue's face faded, to be replaced by the warmth of the ardent lover, as Chingue pulled Amanda close against his chest, whispering softly, "I do not wish to leave you, Amanda, but I would rather take my turn now, while your time is still many months away. I would be here to see my son born, not many miles away as you give him life."

Looking at him, Amanda marveled once again at the part Chingue's concern for her played in all his decisions. Surely no other woman had such a considerate and selfless husband.

Warmed by the depth of his consideration, Amanda smiled responsively as Chingue's hands began to caress her gently. Slowly, persuasively leading her into passion, Chingue's caresses became more intimate. In a smooth, rapid movement, Chingue slipped Amanda's shift over her head, exposing the perfection of her petite form to his eyes. To Chingue, each time he gazed at her was as the first time, and he was suffused with love and desire. With shaking hands, Chingue scooped her easily into his arms to lay her gently on their sleeping bench. Pausing only long enough to divest himself of his garments, he then took his place beside her, pulling her full against him, her white skin pressed intimately and lovingly against his copper-hued body.

Feeling a tremendous sense of exaltation knowing that another battle for possession of her had been won, this time against Adam Carstairs, Chingue's passion grew with consuming intensity. But, ever watchful of Amanda's reactions, he kept himself under strict control as he continued his campaign of complete sexual arousal in the diminutive beauty that lay in his arms. Chingue's deep, rough voice murmured soft endearments as he pressed light kisses against the lids covering the brilliant blue eyes he loved so well. Feeling the soft tickle of her thick brush of dark lashes against his lips, Chingue smiled momentarily, and then continued to press his kisses against her ears, the hollows of her cheeks, the dimple that teased him so flirtatiously, and came to rest against the warmth of her soft, pink lips, now parted, awaiting him. Slowly, deeply penetrating the sweet wetness of her mouth, Chingue's kiss deepened, his tongue entering and searching, probing and teasing its warm confines until Amanda's heart leaped with excitement. Noting her response, Chingue's mouth then left hers to follow a burning, searching path down her body. All but devouring the slender white column of her throat with his adoring mouth, kissing the gently sloping shoulders, he came to the smooth swells of her breasts, so rounded and perfect, gleaming irresistibly in the light of the fire. A momentary stab of jealousy pierced him as his mouth caressed the soft, pink crescents now so erect with anticipation, knowing that soon they would not be his exclusively, but would provide the sustenance for his son who grew within her. Amused that he could feel jealousy for his own child, Chingue continued to caress with his hands and mouth the firm, white mounds that were for now his alone. The many days of abstinence from her body that the trek imposed on Chingue, as well as her near loss to Adam Carstairs, had aroused in him a hunger for Amanda so intense that he felt the constant need to check himself against unleashing its full impact, for fear of hurting or frightening this woman who was his life. Instead, gradually, with increasing passion, he smoothed, touched, and fondled her body tenderly, stirring in her the desire he had aroused so completely in the past. With a wildly beating heart, Chingue felt Amanda come to life beneath him, as her body, teased and tortured exquisitely by his lovemaking, responded heatedly to his touch.

Gradually overwhelmed with insatiable hunger for her and stirred beyond his greatest expectations by her spontaneous and growing response, Chingue felt his control slipping away, and for the first time lost himself completely in wild abandon. The kisses pressed against her fair skin, before so warm and controlled, were now hot and demanding, searching out the secret places meant for lovers alone. Unwilling to leave her breasts, but hungering for more, Chingue's mouth traveled down her body, his tongue and lips leaving a burning trail on her skin in their

205

steady course to the smooth, white thighs guarding the soft, golden nest that lay between them. The rain of light moist kisses on her stomach, navel, and legs raised Amanda's response to a fever pitch, where her only thoughts became of assuagement of the deep, throbbing need she felt within her. She seemed to relax all her muscles, as she felt the warmth of his kisses and the pressure of his mouth against those tight golden curls. With a will of their own, her thighs parted, allowing Chingue's tongue entrance into the warm, private place that only he had known. Slipping his hands under her buttocks, he raised her slightly as his mouth came to rest fully against the other lips also awaiting his kiss. Gently, drawing his tongue along the narrow slit and feeling the tremor that shook Amanda's small body, he plunged his tongue inside, intimately probing its secret innermost reaches, drawing forth her body juices deeply, greedily. So wild was his abandon, so complete his possession of her, that he took not the time to raise her passion to a level where it could be sustained. Within moments he felt her beautiful body tremble and shudder as a deep groan of exquisite rapture passed Amanda's lips and her body twisted convulsively in its shower of sweet body nectar.

As Amanda lay limp and spent, Chingue continued his persistent loving ministrations, his face pressed firmly, but gently, between her thighs. Unbelievably, Amanda felt her tired body rising again in response to his caressing tongue and loving bites, and her heart pounding crazily, she spoke in a gasping voice, "Chingue, no, please, I am spent. I can give no more."

Looking up at her blond beauty from where he nestled so rapturously, Chingue responded softly, "That is not true, Amanda. See already how your body responds to mine." He touched his tongue to her lightly, and a shiver of delight caused her body to quake spontaneously, bringing a triumphant smile to his face.

"See how your body answers my touch. See how it rewards me with its juice of life. Truly we are one, Amanda, and truly do you belong to me and with me. Tonight I will prove the power of my love. I will take you with me many times to the stars, until all doubt will be removed from your mind, and all thoughts of others purged from your memory. You are mine alone, Amanda. No other will ever know you as I have known you. Never will you forget this night, for my love will burn it into your heart forever."

At the conclusion of his impassioned speech, Chingue began a new loving attack on her body, and despite her disbelief, Amanda felt herself rising again and again on the brilliant wings of passion and brought to deep, shuddering, exhausting climax again and again as her body lay powerless against Chingue's tender onslaught.

Apparently insatiable in his desire for her, Chingue did not tire of his self-appointed, loving task through the long night. Amanda, weak from her endless spasms of love, lay helpless against his touch as Chingue took his fill of her time and time again. Many loving hours later, Amanda's body, now responding as by reflex to his arousal, fell from its pinnacle of passion once again in a night of seemingly endless ecstasy, to give Chingue further

207

proof of her vulnerability to his lovemaking. She heard a clear, joyful laugh and opened her eyes to see a shining look on Chingue's face as he devoured her with his eyes.

"Tell me now, Amanda," he demanded, "tell me now who it is that possesses you, body and soul, until you have no will of your own. Tell me whose body has made you his slave, only as you have enslaved his heart and mind. Tell me, Amanda, tell me who it is that has possessed you so completely as no other ever has or ever will. Come," he urged softly, sliding up to cover her body with his and look directly into the face he loved so well, "tell me his name."

In a voice quaking from the exertion of the past hours of raging passion, Amanda responded breathlessly, "His name is Chingue. He's the one who possesses me as no other ever has!"

His black eyes gleaming in loving triumph, Chingue plunged himself within her, driving deeply again and again only to fall, at last, in one long spiral of ecstasy from the passion that had sustained him for so many hours. Finally, he withdrew and rolled to his back beside his young wife and was silent, his labored breathing the only sound within the wigwam. Feeling his eyes upon her, Amanda turned her face to see Chingue staring, no longer triumphant, but serious and pensive.

Faced with her look of inquiry, Chingue whispered simply in a deep, throbbing voice the words that had been running through his mind over and over. "Amanda, you are my love and my life," and gathering her to him tenderly, he held her close until they both drifted off to sleep.

By mutual, unspoken consent their long night of love was not discussed between them, but many times Amanda raised her eyes to find Chingue's dark, penetrating gaze upon her, and found herself blushing at the intensity of his stare. In the two days that followed, very often that maidenly blush had brought them down to their sleeping bench, although it was not night; but each time, Chingue took care to exercise control and not proceed in the abandoned manner of that first night home. Fear of damage to the child within her made him cautious and angry with his loss of control. He had promised himself he would be more careful until the child was born. Afterwards would be time enough to allow his emotions full range, and his heart quickened beating at the thought. For now, he must be patient and gentle, and he was.

Their two-day respite from the anxieties of the present was over too soon, and Amanda awoke at daybreak of the third day to see in the pale light of the wigwam that Chingue had already arisen. He had started to dress for his journey to Fort Carillon, unaware that Amanda's eyes followed him.

Amanda felt a soft flush rise to her cheeks as she studied his naked, well proportioned body, marveling at his graceful, cat-like movements, and the play of smoothly rippling muscles under his shining copper-tinted skin as he pulled on his buckskin garments. Suddenly sensing her eyes upon him, he turned, his broad smile gleaming whitely against the russet skin of his face. Amanda's heart gave a small lurch as she acknowledged once again the splendid man that was her husband, Chingue.

Approaching her quietly, Chingue came to kneel by her side, his lips brushing hers before he spoke. "Day has come, Amanda, and I must leave." His warm, dark eyes caressed her, burning into his memory for the lonely weeks ahead the picture of her face, still rosy from sleep, shining appealingly from within the depth of the fur covering her. Lifting the covering for a moment, his eyes wandered warmly over the soft, white body he knew so well, coming to rest on the small mound of her stomach just beginning to protrude with growing life. Slipping into the language of his fathers, he whispered, *"Pennau, Amanda, n'nitschan wuliken. Wuliechen."*[1]

To his delight, Amanda responded shyly in like fashion, the small smile curving her lips bringing her dimple into play, *"Bischi,* Chingue, *Bischihk."*[2]

Slowly he lowered his head to press a tender kiss against the gentle swell, before covering her again against the morning chill of the wigwam. His eyes returned to hers, noting the brightness of tears that shone within their depths. Sliding his hands into the wild disarray of her long gold-and-silver curls, he held her face between his palms to cover her lips with his for a deep, lingering kiss. In a voice hoarse with unshed tears, Amanda said, *"Tschingetsch kmatschi,* Chingue?"[3]

"Before the new moon, and I will not leave you again until my son makes his entrance into this world."

Seeing his answer did little to chase the tears that

1. Meaning, "Look, Amanda, my child, it grows well. It is good."
2. Meaning, "Yes, Chingue, it is so."
3. Meaning, "When do you return home again, Chingue?"

threatened to overflow at any moment, he stated simply the words that came from his heart. "I must say goodbye, now, but the days will be long and dark until I hold you close again. How I love thee, Amanda."

Slipping his arms around her, he drew her tightly against him for a last, final kiss. Reacting deeply to their parting, Amanda's arms encircled his neck and clung fiercely to him.

Within moments Chingue was gone, and Amanda lay alone on her sleeping bench, unwilling to get up and start the day without him. Suddenly she jumped from her bed, drawing the blanket around her, as she ran to the doorway to seek a final look at the departing column. In the gray light of the overcast dawn, the silent column marched away, their snow-shoes breaking a new, wide trail in the fresh cover of snow that had fallen during the night. Amanda watched, unmindful of the cold, until the last of the fifty-odd marchers were out of sight, knowing a part of her went with them.

Time dragged by interminably for Amanda within her lonely wigwam. Before two days had passed, she had already found herself at a complete loss as to the manner in which to pass her day. Feeling miserable and alone, Amanda then left her wigwam to seek out Ninscheach and her two sisters. True to her expectations, within the hour the joyful chatter of the two young girls and Ninscheach's obvious happiness at her presence had restored her spirits, and her heart was lightened. Noting Amanda's pallor and depressed state when she had entered, Ninscheach extended the hospitality of her wigwam to Amanda for the remainder of Chingue's absence. More pleased than she could say, Amanda accepted eagerly, and returned for only a few minutes to her own wigwam to bring a share of provisions for her stay. And so, the next ten days of Chingue's absence passed more pleasantly than the first two.

Slowly eating away at her peace of mind during the duration of her stay with Ninscheach was her guilt at the complete estrangement between Chingue's parents and herself. From the first, Lingues[1] and Kahaketit[2] had displayed their disapproval of Chingue's choice of wife. Amanda had never held their disapproval against them, realizing the value they placed on their only offspring, the brave and noble Chingue, who had so disappointed them by choosing a white woman for his bride. To Amanda, their disappointment was justified, but now that Chingue's child grew within her, she was determined to overcome their objections in order that their grandchild would take his proper place in their affections.

Grim and determined, Amanda rose the next day, and taking an offering of some sweet cakes Ninscheach had newly taught her to prepare, she set off to bridge the gap that lay between them. However strongly she started out, with each step she took, Amanda felt her courage ebb, the memory of those two stoney faces greatly diminishing her resolve. Not as brave as before, but unable to retreat from the decision she had made, she called hesitantly outside

1. Meaning, "Wild Cat."
2. Meaning, "Little Goose."

the wigwam of Chingue's parents, awaiting an invitation to enter. After a few moments a harsh female voice, bearing no apparent welcome, bid her to enter. Once inside, Amanda was relieved to see Lingues was not present, for surely she was not up to facing the two of them together.

Swallowing nervously, Amanda gave Kahaketit the sweet cakes, with a timid smile, the words she had practiced saying freezing on her tongue in reaction to the icy stare that greeted her. Silently Amanda perused the face of the old woman seated before her, on which time had left its indelible mark in the many wrinkles that lined it so completely. At first appearance, the old woman looked fragile, being of small proportions and pathetically thin. Her features were sharp and hawklike, and her long gray-and-white streaked hair was tied carelessly back with a rawhide strip. Amanda thought, absentmindedly, how fortunate it was that Chingue favored his father so strongly. As if reading her thoughts, the old woman's glance held hers for a moment, her black eyes, so like Chingue's, glittering with hatred.

Amanda fell back a step, the force of Kahaketit's irrational antipathy stunning her with its impact. Gradually regaining her composure, and determined to proceed, Amanda spoke simply in an effort to establish a starting point on which to build a better relationship.

"Chingue has left with the first group on the scouting mission for the French as you know, Kahaketit, and it has come to me that now is the time for us to make peace between us for the sake of Chingue's child whom I carry within me. I can well appreciate your anxiety regarding Chingue's decision to take me to wife. I know I'm not worthy of him, and far better it would have been for a noble man like Chingue to have taken an Abnaki of true blood; but alas, the decision has been made, and the step taken. The seed that grows within me will soon be living proof of our union, and will bind us even more closely together. It is for this child that I ask your understanding, that he may grow happily and normally, unhindered by hatred within his own family. For him I ask your indulgence and beg your acceptance of me."

Amanda stared hopefully into the countenance of the old woman before her, her heart dropping as the fire of hatred continued to burn there. To her bewilderment the old woman said suddenly, "N'matunguam."[1]

Thinking she must have misunderstood the Abnaki tongue as Kahaketit spoke it, Amanda looked at her blankly. With a stoney stare, the old woman continued on in English. "On the first night Chingue brought you here, I had a bad dream. I dreamed Chingue walked on a long and lonely road for many days when he suddenly came upon you at the wayside. You were lost and alone, and he took pity on you and took you with him. As you walked side by side, you wove a spell over him, blinding him to all other women so he could see only you and want only you. Lovingly, he took you to a high mountain, at the top of which he built for you a great and glorious wigwam. There you both lived for many moons. Each day Chingue brought you more and

1. Meaning, "I had a bad dream."

more offerings of his love, until, finally, one day he brought you to the edge of the mountain. There he stood offering to you all, as far as your eyes could see, as proof of his love. You smiled and Chingue was content, but when he turned, his heart still full of love for you, you cast him off, to fall to his death on the valley floor below!"

An involuntary gasp passed her lips as the blood drained from Amanda's face. Kahaketit's dream horrified her! Her voice quaking in shock, she said desperately, "But Kahaketit, it was only a dream! You can't believe I wish to kill your son! He's the father of my child! How can you let one dream turn you against me?"

But even as she spoke, remembering the Abnaki's superstitious belief in dream omens, she knew it was to no avail. Her face still cold and unchanged, Kahaketit spoke, her feelings for Amanda apparent in the malevolence of her voice.

"I have had this dream not once, but many times. I have spoken to the shaman and my feelings are true. You will bring my son to his death! I have spoken to my son, but he will not listen to my warnings."

"You've told him of this dream?"

"He will not listen!" Kahaketit's face was distorted with rage, and faced with its fury, Amanda grabbed for the support of the wall as she felt her knees weaken.

"My son's love for you will be the cause of his death, and I will not make you welcome within my wigwam!"

As Amanda stood helplessly protesting her innocence, the enraged old woman shouted again and again, *"Palli aal, palli aal, palli aal!"*[1]

Tears streaming down her face, Amanda ran from the wigwam, the sound of the old woman's shrill cries echoing in her ears. Stopping breathlessly at last at the outskirts of the village, she retched violently in reaction to the horror that pervaded her.

Anxiety filled the remainder of the days spent awaiting Chingue's return. Even Ninscheach's quiet reassurances were ineffective in quieting the fear that had crept into Amanda's mind at the revelation of Kahaketit's supposed prophetic dream.

"Surely," her common sense argued, "I shouldn't let an old woman's superstitious anxieties become mine." But even as she debated with herself the validity of dream prophesy, she felt fear take a greater hold on her mind.

And so it was with a surge of overwhelming joy two weeks later that she raised her head to Tscholentit's excited, breathless cries as she raced into the wigwam where Amanda assisted Ninscheach in preparation of the evening meal. "The men are returning, the men are returning!"

Quickly dropping the bowl in which she was grinding parched corn, Amanda ran outside to gaze at the column of Indians as they approached the village, and hear again the blood-chilling sound of the scalp yell.

"They have engaged the enemy and were victorious! See how many scalps they carry on their scalp pole!" Tscholentit's high, childish voice squeaked even higher in excitement at the sight of the painted Indian braves walking in solemn procession, the six-

1. Meaning, "Go away, go away, go away . . ."

216

foot pole held in front of them, bearing countless grisly trophies of their victory.

Even as she watched, the blood-curdling scalp yells rent the cold March air again and again, the sharp sounds of "Aw-Oh," successively uttered, the last more accented and sounded higher than the first, drawn out at great length to be held as long as the breath would hold. Beaming with pride, the brave warriors were greeted by their families and neighbors, as Amanda stood, frozen with revulsion, silent and unmoving as a statue, her huge, blue eyes wide with horror. A tall figure, moving lithely, detached himself from the crowd and walked toward her. Sad understanding filled Chingue's eyes as they touched on Amanda's horror-ridden face.

"You've been in battle, Chingue?" Amanda's voice shook with emotion, torn as she was between happiness at Chingue's return, and horror at realization of the toll in human lives their bravery had taken.

"Yes, Amanda, we have seen battle with the enemy, but do not think now where I have been. Know only that I have at last returned to you and will not leave again." In mute invitation, Chingue held out his arms to her. The sorrow and silent appeal in his eyes proving at last too much for her to withstand, Amanda walked slowly into the haven of his arms, to feel them close around her, shutting out all other thoughts, as he drew her to the privacy of their wigwam.

That night the traditional dance of thanksgiving held on the occasion of each successful expedition was attended by all members of the village. Never

217

having been present in this type of gathering, Amanda was overwhelmed by the ceremony which was essentially of a religious character. The singing, always begun by one person only, soon became robust and harmonious as the others fell in, successively, until the general chorus began, the drum beating all the while to mark time. The voices of the women, clear and full, their intonations correct, were allowed in this ceremony only in chorus, and were excluded from the rest of the performance. At the end of every song the scalp yell was shouted as many times as there had been scalps taken from the enemy, marring the beauty of the celebration in Amanda's eyes, and causing her flesh to crawl with distaste.

Then began the recounting of the exploits of the battle, the oldest warrior starting first in a half-singing recitation and proceeding on down the line in order of seniority, the drum beating all the time, giving the narrations a greater sense of drama. It was at this point, as Amanda listened attentively, that her sense of uneasiness grew until it reached the proportion of physical distress, and she was forced to leave the gathering, a victim of her heaving stomach.

Much later that night as she lay in the solitude of her wigwam, warm in the circle of Chingue's arms, she confessed her feelings of inadequacy as his wife. Taking a deep breath, she whispered solemnly, "Surely, Chingue, I do you no honor in my obvious feelings of revulsion and resentment at feats that should be treated with pride and jubilance by a proper Abnaki wife." Her heart pounded with apprehension at his reaction to that which she was about to suggest. "I would be truly understanding of your actions if you were to petition to have me put aside as your wife and take another in my place, for surely I've embarrassed and disappointed you before your friends."

Chingue's sharp, surprised intake of breath was his only reaction to her proposal for many long moments, until at last his words sounded softly, deep emotion apparent in the tone of his voice as he scowled darkly, "Is it your desire to punish me for my actions taken against your former people in this recent battle, Amanda, even though it is my duty to destroy our enemies? If so, you may consider that you have achieved your purpose, for your barb has truly pierced my heart, and your retribution is won. If, on the other hand, you are sincere in your feelings of inadequacy, hear me now. Know that you bring me nothing but honor and joy as my wife. There is no other I would take in your place, for there is no light in a sky filled with stars that shines as brightly as my love for you."

Seeing the tears of relief that filled her eyes at his words, the scowl on Chingue's handsome face was replaced by a tender smile. "Then let us hear no more of this Amanda." Touching her with gentle intimacy, he whispered against her lips, "It is time to cease the discussion of my love, so that I may proceed to prove with my actions that which I claim in words."

True to his word, Chingue spoke no more that night, but spent many of the hours following in violent, loving demonstration of that which he had proclaimed.

* * *

The "Battle on Snowshoes," as the conflict later came to be called, was never a subject of discussion between Chingue and Amanda, but slowly, due mostly to the incessant chatter of Tscholentit and her slightly more restrained sister, the specifics of the bloody skirmish came to her knowledge.

On the afternoon of March 13, a deserter from the British forces having warned the garrison at Fort Carillon that a scouting force of Rogers' Rangers was setting out, a force of 600 Canadians and Indians set out from Fort Carillon to engage the enemy, protected by an advance guard of 96, mostly Indians. At midafternoon of that day, 180 rangers, a far cry from the 400 requested by Rogers and reported approaching by the deserter, hugged steep Mt. Pelee and kept an eye on the frozen rivulet which they knew the force from Fort Carillon would most likely use, as the snow was four feet deep, and the going very bad on snowshoes, Unknowingly, the advance guard, coming up the rivulet as expected, ran into the full force of Rogers' fire power, and at the first general discharge, at least half of the Indians were killed. The rangers then proceeded to rush the remainder, only to discover the remaining force of over 600 that followed.

Rogers' men dropped back, their rear protected by the mountain, and repulsed several French charges, the conflict continuing with only twenty yards separating the opposing forces. This fire continued for about an hour and a half, during which time over one hundred rangers and eight of their officers were killed.

It was then that Rogers, obviously realizing the

prudence of retreat, fell back, hotly pursued by the Abnaki warriors. Rogers' exact method of escape was still under dispute, Tscholentit claiming that some felt he had slid down the precipitous face of the mountain to Lake George, and others asserting that he hurled his pack down the incline, back-tracked with reverse snowshoes, and followed a gentler path to appear on the lake below. At any rate, the mountain was derisively renamed Rogers' Rock, and the bare stone of the incline facing the lake called Rogers' Slide by the scornful Indians and French.

It was during this hour and a half battle with twenty yards separating opposing forces, and the retreat that followed, that Chingue had distinguished himself with his bravery. Far from feeling the obvious pride that Tscholentit felt in Chingue's deeds, Amanda's mind continued to torture her as she pondered the identities of those one hundred rangers and eight officers that were killed. Could one of those scalps now hanging so obscenely on the scalp pole be Robert's, or possibly Adam's?

Amanda felt the rising of bile into her mouth as the thoughts continued to plague her, and once again those light green eyes that would give her no peace invaded her thoughts. Knowing she would get nowhere with this line of reasoning, forcibly ejecting the entire proceedings from her mind, and silencing Tscholentit more sharply than she had intended, she returned to her work.

Ever true to his word, during the months that followed, Chingue remained by Amanda's side, leaving her only for short, overnight hunting trips when the supply of meat became scarce within the village. His services as a hunter were in great demand now that the rotating groups reporting to help the French of Fort Carillon had cut so low the number of men remaining in the village.

Life took on a safe and easy pattern as spring came to the Abnaki town. Chingue believed as all Indian hunters, that hunger stimulated him to exertion by constantly reminding him of his wants, and a full stomach made him careless and lazy. Ever thinking of his home and using his time wisely, he preferred to be off into the woods before daylight on an empty stomach, the morning and evening hours being precious to him as the best for his purpose. He would then strive to be at home at ten o'clock in the morning when Amanda, having already pounded her corn, would have it boiling on the fire; and having baked her bread, she would give him a good breakfast. The day was then theirs to do with as they wished, until four, when depending on the needs of the village, he might return again to the forest to hunt in the evening hours.

It was during the months when winter turned to spring that Amanda grew in the knowledge of the Abnaki. Of the many things she learned, one striking fact impressed her mind: that "uncivilized" Indians should behave in such a civilized manner in their dealings with one another! Amanda had been witness to the many times groups of men who had hunted or fished in parties would divide their game among them when there were many shares to be made. On each occasion the participants received what was allotted to them without an argument, but then said *"Anischi,"*[1] as if having received a gift.

She also noted the great reverence the men showed for one another, which was foremost in all their dealings. She learned that their principle, the good and the bad can not mingle or dwell together in one heart, and therefore must not come into contact, seemed to guide them on all occasions. Unlike the white man, when traveling they were cheerful, never impatient, quarrelsome, or charging one another with fault; they were resigned to accidents that might befall them, even though they might lose by the neglect or carelessness of another. They were more inclined to overlook a fault and to commiserate than to punish if there was no malicious intent.

Their hospitality was ever a source of amazement to Amanda as she observed many times the delight and attention paid to a person on entering the wigwam of another, where the first word would be, "Sit down, my friend." There were seats for all, no matter the number, and the tobacco pouch was handed round as the first treat. Without a single word, the wife would prepare food for the company, considering the visit an honor, and never grumbling even if all her provisions were consumed, considering a friendly visit well worth any trouble or expense.

Amanda came to know the Indian belief in relation to the creation of man that the Whites were made by the same Great Spirit who created them, and that he assigned to each race of men a particular employment in the world, but not the same to all. To the Whites, the great Mannitto gave charge to till the ground and raise by cultivation the fruits of the earth,

1. Meaning, "I am thankful."

while the Indians he assigned the nobler task of hunting, and the supreme dominion over all the rest of the animal creation. She came to know they considered themselves the Lenni Lenape[1] that had existed unchanged from the beginning of time.

And even as she observed and absorbed all that progressed around her, Amanda was often aware of Chingue's covert glances, his pride in her and his delighted preoccupation with her bulging figure. On many occasions as she lay on the sleeping bench, and the child within took advantage of its opportunity to thrash around in his meager confines, Chingue would rest his palms against her stomach, his face transfused with happiness at the activity of his son.

One day as they lay in the hours before sleep, Chingue, excited by his son's vigorous activity, exclaimed, "See, Amanda, see how eager is my child for life. See how he moves and squirms to make his entrance into our world." And then in a moment of absolute solemnity, his dark eyes burning brightly, Chingue's hands moved to cup her face between them as he looked deeply into her eyes. "Truly, Amanda, you have made me the happiest of men, and the child you create within you from my seed will be my link to eternity. You have brought me joy unsurpassed, and should my life end tomorrow, I would consider it had been fulfilled."

"Chingue!" A cry of protest rose from Amanda's throat at his strange words, and she pulled him near to her in a sudden wave of panic. Unbidden, Kahaketit's dream had come to her mind, and she trembled with fear.

1. Meaning, "The Original People."

"Why do you shudder so, my little golden flower?" Chingue's voice was soft and teasing. "I did not say I intended to die tomorrow." And he laughed softly as she burrowed her face against his chest. "All right, Amanda, if it will please you, I promise to live at least one hundred summers, but only if you will consent to do the same!" Laughing again at the absurdity of their conversation, Chingue proceeded to kiss the tips of her breasts, and within minutes all rational thought was driven from her mind.

It was a warm, humid dawn in June, promising an unseasonably hot, uncomfortable day. Amanda, her time now only a month away, was bulky with child. Her small proportions, from the rear view gave no indication of that which the front presented, so unchanged was her figure; but when viewed from the front her stomach was hugely distended, her gait awkward and slow. Her long golden-and-silver hair had lost none of its sheen as some pregnant women found occurred, but instead seemed to glow with a white fire as the sun bleached it to an even lighter silver. Beneath the golden tendrils that surrounded her small, softly tanned face in the moist, humid heat of the presummer morning, her huge azure eyes bore light circles in silent testimony to the sleepless nights she had been experiencing due to the weight and discomfort of the child she carried. Far from detracting from her appearance, the slight shadows gave her an air of appealing fragility, as did the huge mound she carried so laboriously before her, her buckskin garment stretched to the utmost to accommodate its wide girth. It was this picture that stood before

Chingue as he prepared to leave for an overnight hunting trip. How he loathed to leave her for even that short a period, but he felt there was no danger, as her time was a full month away, and Ninscheach had promised to supervise the condition of her pregnancy during his short absence.

Now, as he considered the petite, swollen beauty of his wife, he found himself aroused and delighted. Her state of advanced pregnancy had done nothing to diminish the force of his desire for her, and in view of the way his heart quickened beating as he looked into her beautiful face, he felt perhaps it was best he gave her a short respite from his affections, which only seemed to increase with the passage of time. Amused at his own thoughts, he placed a chaste kiss on her lips.

"I will return tomorrow, Amanda. I will spend this night away from you, but in my heart I will be at your side."

Pulling her close for one last kiss, Chingue left to join the small group awaiting him outside. Amanda watched as the hunting party walked out of sight and then returned to her bed, not bothering to undress, in desperate hope of the ever elusive sleep.

Amanda dozed lightly, only to be awakened what seemed seconds later by a touch on her arm, and opening her eyes, she was startled to see familiar brown eyes only inches from hers as a large calloused hand covered her mouth. Stunned into disbelief, she lay staring upward for a few moments before she was able to make a sound. Then, as the hand left her mouth, she whispered unbelievingly, "Robert!"

Five

"Surely this is a dream!" she murmured, her heart pounding violently with shock, only to hear Robert's familiar voice in reply, "No, Amanda, this isn't a dream. I've come to take you home!"

Home! Amanda rose from the bench at Robert's urging, noticing for the first time the tall figure standing behind him.

"Adam!"

The sudden appearance within her wigwam of both men who had played such an intimate part in her life proved too much. Her vision wavering, Amanda felt herself swaying weakly, only to have strong arms grasp and support her—then in a quick movement pull her close. As if from a distance, she heard Robert's crooning voice. "Amanda, darling, you're all right now. We've come to take you home. Amanda, Amanda." Robert's voice continued calling her back to consciousness. "You must be strong now, darling. We must leave quickly before complete daylight."

"Robert," Amanda's voice was weak but purposeful, "I can't come back with you. Look at me. Surely I needn't explain the reason!"

Robert's eyes moved immediately to her distended abdomen, and quickly returned to her face, with an expression that was pained but resolute. "It doesn't matter to me that you carry an Indian child." Robert's face flushed slightly as he spoke, "I know it's no fault of yours. But I won't let it tie you to this life. You are my betrothed, and as soon as the child is born, we'll be wed as we had planned."

Amanda was aghast at the thought! Surely he did not believe they could just simply resume their lives as if nothing had happened! "But Robert, I'm already wife to Chingue and he—"

"Don't mention that savage's name to me, Amanda!" His voice snarled viciously, his hatred ringing with each word he uttered. "He is a dead man, for as surely as I stand before you, he will not live past our next meeting! You belong to me," he said, crushing her violently against him, "and no one will take you from me again!"

Amanda could do no more than gasp at the hatred that filled Robert's voice and glared so ominously from his eyes.

"Come, quickly now," he continued, completely ignoring the possibility of Amanda's refusal to return. "It grows lighter with each passing minute. We must hurry!"

Amanda shot a look of mute appeal to Adam, who stood a few feet away, silently observing, his face devoid of expression. In response to her silent plea he spoke quietly, "I've tried to reason with him, Amanda. I told him you were here of your own free will, but he wouldn't believe me. I only came with him so he would stand a greater chance of getting back alive."

With startling suddenness Kahaketit's dream returned to her mind, and Amanda felt the icy grip of panic as fear of its eventual realization possessed her. And in that moment she realized that the decision had once again been taken out of her hands, and her preferences would play no part in her destiny. Knowing her refusal would only result in the taking of lives, she hastened to follow Robert's directions. All she could hope to achieve at this point would be their bloodless departure.

Glancing briefly at Adam's impassive face, she turned resolutely to Robert. "We would not be gone long before it would be discovered that I'm missing and someone would start after me. You and Adam must leave now and wait for me in the forest behind my wigwam. I'll join you there after I have told Ninscheach that I am returning to my people."

"I will not allow—" Robert interrupted violently, only to feel the gentle pressure of Amanda's hand on his lips, silencing him.

"Don't worry, Robert," Amanda's voice was quietly reassuring. "Adam will confirm what I say. I am an adopted Abnaki and may leave any time I wish. I haven't been held here under duress. I've stayed because I felt I no longer had a place in a white man's world."

"Amanda, darling." Robert's voice was filled with the pain that had tortured him during their long months of separation.

"While you await me in the woods, I'll explain my decision to Ninscheach. I'll tell her to relate to

229

Chingue that my life as his wife is over. He'll respect my decision and we won't be followed."

"No, I will not let you out of my sight again." Robert's voice was strong and belligerent, but Amanda was just as determined. "These are the only circumstances under which I'll leave with you, Robert."

For a few minutes Robert stared into Amanda's resolute face, and then said suddenly, "I'll give you just a few minutes to return. If you're gone too long, I'll come after you."

With a silent sigh of relief, Amanda replied quietly, "Don't worry, Robert, I'll return. You have my word."

Amanda proceeded to snatch up her moccasins, her bulky figure making her movements less than graceful in her haste. Looking up, she saw a small smile on Adam's face as she bent awkwardly over the large mound of her stomach to secure them. Silently he took the laces from her hands, and proceeded to tie them as Robert looked out the doorway, scanning the area outside the wigwam. In an unguarded moment, the green eyes that looked into hers filled with pain, and Amanda felt her own fill with tears in response to his unintended appeal. Robert's anxious urging drew their attention.

"We'd better take our opportunity now to get into the woods. Soon it'll be full daylight." And turning to Amanda he said in a grim voice, "Remember, I'll come to get you if you don't come to me."

As both men slipped into the forest, Amanda made her way to Ninscheach's wigwam, her mind filled with apprehension. Her explanation to Ninscheach was of necessity short and her voice firm with resolution. "Tell Chingue the decision is mine, and I have returned to my people. I don't want him to come after me. I am no longer his wife!"

Putting aside the pain caused by her words, and pressing a hurried kiss on Ninscheach's wrinkled cheek, Amanda turned quickly to leave, but not before Ninscheach's observant eyes had seen the tears that had started down her face.

Fearing Robert's anxiety might cause him to act rashly, Amanda hurried to their meeting place, to arrive panting and breathless where the two men awaited. Without another word, they started out in single file, Amanda walking between, until they reached a place where three horses were secured to a tree. Then, after mounting up, they rode hastily away.

Feeling the luxury of clean white sheets against her skin, Amanda relaxed and closed her eyes. The softness of the feather mattress was a balm to her aching muscles, the result of their frantic escape to Fort Edward. Even now, days later, Amanda felt a sense of unreality as she went over in her mind the events that had transpired so rapidly and changed so radically the course of her future. There had been no time for consideration of preference on her part, for with Robert's and Adam's sudden arrival in the Abnaki town, no other course of action had been open to her except to leave with them. She had realized instinctively that hesitation or refusal on her part could have had dire results. But now, in the privacy of the bedroom provided by a joyously tearful

Betty Mitchell, Amanda realized the impact of the irreversible step she had taken, and she was overcome by doubts. Robert was adamant that they should be married after the birth of the child, and still she had not been able to explain to his satisfaction the reason the marriage could not take place. But how could she explain that which she truly did not understand herself? Surely, she should be glad Robert still wanted her, but. . . .

And there was Adam, ever watchful, silent, extending to her the comfort of his presence. More than once she had wanted to walk into the haven of his arms, to seek sanctuary from her anxieties, but Robert was ever present, a buffer between her and all who sought her company, or whose company she sought.

A bittersweet smile came to Amanda's face as she remembered the scene a few hours before. Finally able to convince Robert she was tired and wanted to retire early, she had indeed gone to bed, only to lie wakefully as now. Finally, she had gotten up and, slipping on a robe, had gone outside to walk in the mild June night, hoping the night air would clear her confused thoughts. As she walked, she suddenly became conscious of a figure in the shadows, and gasped with fright.

"Don't be frightened, Amanda, it's only me," Adam's voice whispered softly as he came to stand by her side. Understanding and sympathy shone from the green eyes looking down at her, and without a word, Amanda walked into his arms to release her tears. In her highly emotional state, Amanda was not aware of Adam's trembling as his arms closed around her and drew her to him.

Accepting Adam's presence as lucky chance, Amanda did not know of the hours Adam had spent watching the doorway through which she had disappeared after bidding a reluctant Robert goodnight. As he had done the previous night, Adam had watched, fighting the desire to go inside, to touch her, hold her, feel her lips under his. But realizing such a course of action would only alienate the bewildered Amanda even further, he had refrained. Instead he stood outside, knowing he was as close to her as he dared to be.

The sight of her small swollen figure emerging from the doorway, Betty's voluminous robe awkwardly covering her distended abdomen, and the perfect beauty and obvious innocence that radiated from her face as she turned into the light, caused a strange tightening in Adam's throat. "Oh, Lord, I love her," he thought helplessly, knowing his cause was all but hopeless. Had she not turned him down before, when he had begged her to stay. . . .

But the realization of their hopelessness could not change his feelings. Of all the women I have known, Adam mused silently, watching the small, awkward figure as she had unknowingly walked toward him, how is it this little golden creature has the power to give me more joy with one look than any number of women could in giving me their bodies?

Closing his eyes against the sweetness and the pain of holding her again, Adam thought silently, She doesn't love me, but she needs me now, and, Lord help me, I'm grateful for anything that will bind her to me. Softly he comforted her, reveling in her nearness, delighting in his power to console her.

"Amanda, darling," he whispered softly, inhaling the fragrance of her glimmering hair as he gently rubbed his cheek against its softness, "Don't be upset. Everything will work out. You just need some time."

"But Adam, I'm so confused. I no longer know what I want, or how I feel. I only know that when you hold me, I feel safe. Oh, Adam, you won't leave me yet, will you?" The eyes raised to Adam's were tearful and pleading, and Adam was startled that she would consider for a moment that he could leave her! Didn't she realize how much he loved her? And in that moment his question was answered. No, she didn't! Or she would never have walked so easily into his arms. She would have been stiff and uncomfortable as she was with Robert! Pulling her close once again to hide the emotion that was choking him, he answered simply, "No, I won't leave you, Amanda."

Amanda had returned to her bed greatly relaxed by Adam's gentle reassurances, his chaste kiss fresh on her lips, to find a sense of deep unhappiness slowly slipping back upon her, lowering her spirits until once again tears slipped heedlessly down her face as she desperately sought sleep's sweet oblivion.

A strange sense of uneasiness intruding into her disturbed dreams awakened Amanda to see Chingue kneeling beside her, and a quick feeling of exaltation swept over her. It was a dream after all, she thought in her semiconscious state, only to have Chingue's grim expression bring her rudely back to reality.

Lightly tracing with his finger the still damp path of tears down her cheek, Chingue asked softly, "Why do you cry, Amanda? Are you not happy in your new life?"

"Chingue, what are you doing here? How did you find me? You must leave! It's too dangerous here for you." Amanda's heart was racing with fear as Kahaketit's dream jumped vividly into her mind. "Quickly, you must leave!"

"You have not answered me, Amanda. Why do you cry? Do you not find pleasure in your new life?"

"I didn't leave you to find pleasure, Chingue." Amanda's response was barely audible as she turned her face from his intense scrutiny. "Fate took my future out of my hands once before, and it has taken it from me again by returning me to my home and my life here."

"And is this where you desire to remain, Amanda?" Winding his hand in the tangled golden curls that were stretched across her pillow, Chingue waited tensely for her reply.

"Truly, Chingue," Amanda's voice shook with the release of anguished tears, "I'm so confused, I'm no longer sure where I belong. Robert says my place is with him as my parents chose, and that we'll be married after I bear the child."

Chingue's hand tightened convulsively in her hair, this small movement going unnoticed by Amanda in her disturbed state. She continued, holding him fast with her sorrowful gaze. "But I'm no longer sure where my duty lies."

Chingue was silent for a few long moments, as he struggled inwardly with the desire to sweep her into his arms, but he knew with a frightening certainty that the time had come when he must face Amanda's decision as to her future. As an Abnaki, she was free to make her choice, and as an honorable man, he was bound to accept it. Drawing deeply on his inner strength, Chingue challenged her with his gaze. He spoke, fearing the finality of the answer he would receive.

"Of first consideration now, Amanda, is where your heart lies, for it is there your duty lies, also."

Amanda lowered her chin, breaking contact with Chingue's penetrating stare and Chingue's heart plummeted downward in despair. He felt a pain so deep as to be almost physical at the thought of giving up forever this pale, gentle girl-woman who had so filled his life and dreams. In those few short minutes, he began to doubt his ability to respect her choice if it went against him, for he saw with abrupt clarity that his life would be pointless and empty without her. He also knew that alone he would have neither the strength nor the will to continue, for in losing her he would lose part of himself, and as half a man, had no desire to go on.

After a few moments, her eyes still averted from his, Amanda spoke in a voice barely above a whisper, "I don't know where my duty lies, Chingue, but I know now that I've seen you again that my heart lies with you."

Incredulous joy held Chingue immobile for a few seconds as his mind digested the import of her words. Smothering the exulting cry he felt rising in his throat, he bent to crush her small body against him as he whispered incredulously, "Amanda, *kehella*?"[1]

[1] Meaning, "Amanda, is it possible?"

Her response was quick and sure. *"La kella,* Chingue."[1]

Enfolded in Chingue's arms once more, listening to his impassioned words of love and reveling in the feeling of his strong, lithe body pressed against her, Amanda felt joy return, and the contentment which had deserted her so completely in the past few days surged through her anew. Gone was her loneliness and desolation, and when finally Chingue lowered his head to cover her mouth with his, she knew she had truly returned home.

"Chingue," Amanda murmured breathlessly as his wild kisses stirred an even deeper emotion, "I know now your words are true, for it is now, back in your arms, that I feel truly complete."

At Amanda's breathless confession, the wild seeking kisses stopped abruptly and Chingue drew back to look into her face as if to find there the confirmation of her words. Touching her cheek gently, smoothing back the golden tendrils of hair that clung to the damp paths left by joyful tears, a glorious smile slowly dawned on Chingue's face, transforming the sharp planes of his features, while a brilliant glow of love shone from the depths of the ebony eyes that had burned so deeply into Amanda's heart. A deep, soft laugh sounded within Chingue's throat as he tossed back his head, all the time clutching her tightly to him in the unrestrainable joy her words had brought him. Finally, fighting the grip of emotion that threatened to overcome him, Chingue whispered softly, his rough voice reflecting his deep passion, "Amanda, *N'dockqueum,*

1. Meaning, *"It is so, Chingue."*

237

Cautiously, stealthily, Chingue led Amanda as they made their way across the deserted yard of Fort Edward. Hampering their escape was the brilliance of the full moon, which illuminated the yard almost to its fullest reaches, as well as the bulkiness of Amanda's advanced condition, which precluded rapid flight. Amanda's pleas that he leave her behind and escape to safety without her so that she might follow at a later time when there would be less danger to him, fell on deaf ears. His mind was set; he would not leave without her.

Her body stiff with fright, Amanda watched as Chingue silently stole up behind the sentry and struck him, wincing as she saw the young man slump to the ground. Consoling her conscience with the fact that Chingue had not struck a killing blow, she moved forward as he slid the lock on the gate and held it slightly ajar. But even as she breathed a short sigh of relief, the silence was broken by a sudden, sharp shout from the interior of the fort.

"Stop, who goes there?"

Running as fast as her condition allowed, Amanda followed Chingue into the forest. Behind her she heard the call to alarm as several other voices joined in. Feeling panic at the discovery of their escape, Amanda plunged wildly ahead, her breath coming in deep gulping gasps as she attempted to match Chingue's pace on the wooded path. She stumbled, quickly rising to her feet, only to stumble again, becoming more and more clumsy as she tired. Seeing

[1] Meaning, "Amanda, my wife, I love thee, I love thee."

the worry on Chingue's face as the pursuing voices drew closer, Amanda gasped, "Chingue, leave me here. I won't be harmed, but they'll kill you if you're caught!"

Even before his answer, Chingue's determined expression spoke for itself. "I will not leave you, Amanda." Urgently he pulled her to her feet. "Just a little way further and we will reach the canoe I have hidden. Once inside we will keep to the shadows on the water's edge until we are out of the range of their guns. Afterwards, they will be unable to catch us."

The voices behind were frighteningly close now, and Amanda recognized Robert's voice as she stumbled again. After running a few more feet, the pain in Amanda's side spread until it robbed her of breath completely, and she dropped to her knees.

"I can't—can't go any further, Chingue!" Amanda was gasping desperately now for breaths which she seemed unable to draw into her lungs rapidly enough. "Leave me—now. Go, I'll join you later!"

"No, I will not!"

Chingue's grip on her arm tightened as he attempted to raise her to her feet. She was struggling to get up when a sudden deafening blast stunned Amanda's senses, and before her eyes Chingue's body jerked upwards, a huge, gaping hole in his chest spraying her with blood as he pitched backwards heavily.

"No! No!" Amanda screamed, the words tearing her throat. "Chingue, Chingue," she sobbed as she crawled to his side, unwilling to believe the scene confronting her. Chingue lay on his back, a pool of blood quickly forming in great heavy gushes from the huge hole torn in his chest.

"Chingue, my darling, please don't leave me," Amanda sobbed hysterically.

With a great effort, Chingue's eyelids parted. Amanda heard the deep, gurgling sound in his chest as he struggled for each breath.

"You should not have come for me, Chingue," Amanda sobbed anew, touching his face gently with the palm of her trembling hand.

A small smile touched the lips that were now drained of color. "Did you not know—I had to come," he gasped. "A man can not live without—his soul." His hand moved weakly in an attempt to cover hers lying limply in her lap. With weak, short breaths, he whispered, "Truly, I was blessed. Many men seek, never to find in a lifetime of many summers—" A sudden shudder convulsed his body, briefly halting his words. With a supreme effort he continued, grasping her hand weakly as he rasped, "Soon you will give my seed life. Love my son, Amanda. Do not let him forget..."

The lips so pale with waning life were suddenly still. Staring helplessly, Amanda watched with horror as the last spark of life slipped from the body of her husband. Flinging herself forward, she clutched him wildly, her body heaving with deep, gasping sobs. "Chingue, my love, my love."

Robert's sudden deep voice penetrated her veil of grief as he demanded roughly, "Get away from him, Amanda! Get away, I said!"

Turning viciously, Amanda saw Robert, the gun in his hand still issuing the faintest spiral of smoke. Her eyes growing wide in horror, Amanda screamed,

"You killed him! You! Murderer! Murderer!" Springing to her feet, and screaming hysterically, she attacked him, wildly scratching and tearing at his face, shrieking again and again, "Murderer! Murderer!"

Robert dropped his gun, and grasping her arms roughly, twisted them behind her, leaving her helpless against his superior strength. Abetted by frustration, fury mounted to even greater heights within Amanda as she struggled in vain to get free of him. Finally, taking a deep breath, she screeched, "Murderer!" once more before she spat in his face!

In spontaneous reaction to her gross insult, Robert released her arms to draw back and deliver a resounding blow to her face. He then watched with a peculiarly stunned expression as Amanda took two reeling steps backward to crumple in a heap beside Chingue's body.

In her bemused state, Amanda was not aware of the action that followed as with an enraged bellow Adam sprang forward, his fist smashing into Robert's jaw, knocking him sprawling to the ground. Without a backward glance, Adam ran to Amanda's side to draw her gently to a sitting position in his arms.

Looking up in a dazed manner, a huge red welt rising on the smoothness of her cheek, Amanda said weakly, "He's dead, Adam. Chingue's dead. Robert killed him." Turning slowly back to Chingue, she looked solemnly at her husband's still form and, moving to his side, lowered her head to press a kiss on his still warm but lifeless lips. But even as she drew back, a sharp, paralyzing pain wracked her body. She drew in a deep breath as a jerking spasm convulsed her again, and agonizing fear replaced the receding contraction. She whispered in horror to Adam, "The child is coming, but it's too soon, too soon."

Her eyes shot back to Chingue's motionless body as she mumbled incoherently, "I can't lose the child, too. I promised Chingue." But even as she spoke, another ferocious pain doubled her over the second before she crumpled into a silent heap upon the ground.

Before Adam's eyes, Amanda dropped to the ground into unconsciousness, her swollen body, tiny and insignificant, lying next to the grisly scene of Chingue's bloody death. Fear and emotion choked his throat and clouded his vision as Adam bent and easily scooped the diminuitive but precious form into his arms, noting as he did the cut on her temple where her head had struck a rock as she fell.

"Oh, Lord," he silently prayed, "don't take her from me, please, please." He swiftly brushed past Robert who had risen to his feet and watched him in a bewildered manner with a look of incredulous dismay.

Amanda twisted and turned, caught in huge waves of pain which engulfed her in great undulating swells. Floating in and out of her tortured brain were visions of Chingue, his voice ringing in her ears, "Love my son. Do not let him forget, forget. . . ." Each time her mind's eye relived the scene of his death, Amanda screamed anew, calling his name, wildly hoping to call him back, change with the sheer power of her love the horrifying outcome of the scene being reenacted over and over before her. But each time, as before, she failed, and experienced again the agony of seeing Chingue's life slowly fade away.

In her delirium of pain, Amanda raised her heavy lids, her blurring vision focusing unclearly on the figures around her bed. There was Betty, a worried frown marring her expression. Amanda tried to smile to encourage the weary woman, but was strangely unable to accomplish that small task. Moving in front of Betty was a tall figure who grasped her hand as she struggled to make an identification. Robert! His face was creased with anxiety, his brown eyes moist.

"Amanda, forgive me, please," he begged earnestly. "I didn't mean to strike you. My darling, please say you forgive me." He bent to kiss the small hand he held so desperately in his grasp, and with his movement, reality came back to Amanda in a sudden flash.

Snatching her hand back in a swift, frantic gesture, she managed a hoarse croak in a voice raspy and broken from the hours of torturous dreams, "You killed him, murderer!"

Robert protested wildly, trying to draw her into his arms, "No, Amanda, no, he was trying to take you from me again. I couldn't allow him. Please, please let me explain."

"Palli aal! Ponihil! Kschingalel, kschingalel!"[1] Amanda's voice gained in volume as she lapsed into the Abnaki tongue, shocking the occupants of the room into silence for a short moment. Pretending an ignorance of her words, Robert continued to press his

1. Meaning, "Go away! Leave me alone! I hate you! I hate you!"

pleas. In desperation, Amanda's eyes wandered around the room, and came to rest on Adam who approached the bedroom door.

"Adam! *Witschemil!*"[1]

Her agonized cries tearing at his heart, Adam brushed all others aside, forcibly shoving the stricken Robert from her bedside.

Fighting her blurring vision, Amanda stared at the wavering figure peering down at her, until the image of thick sun-streaked hair, a broad, tanned, familiarly handsome face, green eyes serious with concern, cleared before her. An overwhelming sense of relief relaxed at last the tension that had been tearing at her small, aching body.

"Adam," she whispered softly, raising her hand to touch his cool cheek, "please don't leave me."

Consciousness slowly slipped away again as Amanda heard his deep, soft voice. "Amanda, my darling, I'll never leave you."

The hours following seemed to Amanda an eternity of endless pain and unspeakable horror as she was tortured intermittently by visions of a laughing, happy Chingue, when she in her confused state came to believe him alive again and was filled with a few moments of joyous exaltation, only to be plunged into deeper despair as her mind drew her back to the gory spectacle of his death. Suddenly, as the pain that wracked her body became unbearable, she screamed for Chingue, imploring his help, only to be visited again with the vision of his dulled black eyes as they closed forever. Pain and horror tore a

1. Meaning, "Adam, help me!"

244

piercing scream from her throat and she called, beseeching help from the only source of comfort she knew.

"Adam, Adam," she sobbed hysterically in her despair, "where are you? Why don't you come to me?"

The answer from her bedside was immediate as his familiar voice penetrated her agony. "I'm here, darling. Amanda?" Coaxing her back to fuller consciousness he answered again, "I'm here, darling."

A small, relieved smile curved the delicate pale lips he loved so well, tightening the knot in his throat until his voice almost failed him. Adam caressed her fevered cheek gently. "Just a few moments more and your child will be born, Amanda. Just a little while longer."

Amanda's face reflected the shock she experienced! So this was the reason. Of course. Chingue's son was about to be born. Elation overcame pain for a few glorious moments. Suddenly gripped by a deep, excruciating spasm, Amanda clenched the strong hand that held hers so securely, her nails biting into the calloused tanned skin and drawing little half moons of blood as she bore down in a supreme effort to give Chingue's child life. A sudden sense of release relaxed her body and Amanda heard excited exclamations from the foot of the bed. Looking up into Adam's strained face, Amanda gasped, "Is it a boy? Adam, is it a boy?"

Swallowing hard, Adam nodded his head as a small, weak wail grew in intensity to a loud, demanding cry. "Yes, Amanda, it's a boy."

A slight flush of color suffused her pale face for a

moment and Amanda called in a clear, proud voice, "Chingue, we have our son, we have our son!"

As Amanda's eyes closed once again in sleep, Adam stared down in fascination at the exhausted beauty lying before him, who so completely and unknowingly possessed his mind and heart. Slowly his eyes wandered over the small heart-shaped face, now so void of color, the dark bruise on her cheek and the small cut on her temple dark, blaring contrasts to the whiteness of her skin. The thick, golden-brown lashes resting against the paleness of her cheek were completely still, and small, glittering beads of perspiration stood out above her delicate lips, now slightly parted in an almost irresistible appeal.

Smoothing back the gold and silver tendrils of hair sticking to her face with perspiration, Adam was overcome with tenderness, love, and a deep, burning jealousy of the man whose life blood just hours before had drained into the rocky ground of the forest floor. Unable to stop himself, Adam slowly slid his arms under and around the unconscious body of the petite, pale woman lying before him, and gently cradled her against him, his emotion increasing the ferocity of his embrace until a soft groan escaped her lips. Suddenly frightened that he had hurt her, Adam released her tenderly against the pillow, only to feel a frightening sense of insecurity overwhelm him. He could not bear to relinquish his hold on her for even a moment. Lowering his head, he rested it lightly against her shoulder, submitting at last to the realization, to his despair. A son! Amanda had a son. And from the depths of his heart, he wished it was his!

Adam stared solemnly down at the squirming bundle of humanity in the wooden cradle. The child, wrapped in a simple white cotton blanket, was small, certainly not more than five pounds, but he possessed a tremendous strength and desire to live; of that Adam was certain. His face, stained an even darker red as he strained at the fist he sucked so greedily, was small, his eyes dark, and his hair abundant and a shiny black. How clearly he resembled his father! Once again jealousy and regret combined to squeeze unmercifully in Adam's chest. This child should have been fair and light eyed. He should have been mine!

Adam felt empty of feeling for the child who appeared an infant personification of all he had lost, as his dark features proclaimed so obviously his sire. For this, then, he thought contemptuously, for this Amanda still lies fevered with a sickness that threatens her life.

Adam watched as the small fist slowly dropped away, and the dark eyes closed in sleep, apparently induced by the vain struggle for nourishment. Suddenly the tiny delicate lips curved in a gloriously familiar smile, showing a surprising dimple that winked in and out miraculously as the smile grew to its full beauty. An unknown emotion stirred deep inside Adam as he recognized Amanda in the sleeping infant.

Of course! Realization came slowly to Adam as emotion grew and spread a warmth throughout him, He is flesh of Amanda's flesh and as part of her; how could I possibly not love him? Bending his huge frame over the cradle, Adam gently picked up the sleeping child, and smiled at the unfamiliar sensation of holding a baby in his arms. Gently he touched his cheek against the velvet softness of the copper-hued skin to whisper into the incredible delicacy of the tiny ear. "Yes, little man, you're Amanda's son, and as part of her you'll always have my love. But hear me now. I promise you, as surely as you will call Amanda mother, you will one day call me father."

As if in response to the solemn declaration, the tiny lips once again drew into a smile.

Amanda's small, premature Indian child seemed to grow and thrive from the moment of his first breath. The tragic circumstances surrounding his birth had not affected his tenacious hold on life, in marked contrast to his mother's continually weakening condition.

The small entourage attending the birth took heart at the infant's response to its care, only to feel an ever increasing sense of defeat when viewing the fever-racked body of his golden-haired mother.

Amanda's retinue of concerned was small. Of major importance was Dr. Cartwright, a portly man of some sixty-odd years, whose burgeoning size belied the gentle touch of his experienced hands. He had been in constant attendance since Amanda had been carried to the fort, and despite Amanda's ignorance of his existence, had turned the tide at the moment of birth when he had reached within her to manage in an expert manner the reversal of the child, who had been making his appearance feet first. His quick ministrations for a few testy minutes thereafter were credited by a thankful Adam with saving her life as he competently staunched the enormous flow of blood that had ensued after the difficult birth.

Then there was Betty Mitchell. Her large, sturdy frame stood her in good stead through the long, arduous hours of labor, the frantic activity at the time of birth, and the painstaking task of cleansing Amanda's blood-spattered, perspiration-soaked body when her labor was done.

And last, but far from least, was Adam. His presence was the rock on which Amanda's precarious hold on life clung, as each desperate, fevered glance from the small weakened woman in bed proved. His absence envoked a terror in the wide blue eyes that opened intermittently in delirium; and it was only when they again touched on that familiar, worried, green-eyed gaze that fear lost its hold, allowing her to slip back into a more restful sleep.

Kept on the outside of this concerned circle, much against his will, in deference to Dr. Cartwright's admonitions as to the harm the agitation of his presence would cause his patient, was Robert. It was his fate and punishment to wait outside the bedroom door, in the Mitchell's small sitting room, painfully ignorant of the minute-to-minute progress of Amanda's health, except for the fact that it was not going at all well for her.

Besieged on all sides by endless questions as Amanda's delirious condition continued, Dr. Cartwright's answer was maddeningly vague. "The blow Amanda sustained when she fell has complicated the already serious condition ensuing after her difficult delivery. She's had a great blood loss. These two facts of her physical condition are made more complex by the events preceding them, which she's obviously fighting not to accept. Right now her body is weak and her mind is in hiding. But she is young and strong, and very angry beneath her grief. I believe she possesses the strength to pull through, but it will take time."

"How much time? How much longer will her fever persist?" had been Adam's anxious query.

"We will just have to wait and see," had been the enigmatic reply.

On the second day after her child's birth Amanda's fever still raged. In the fear that her high temperature would force her into convulsions which, in her weakened state, she would not be able to survive, almost constant attempts were made to reduce the heat in her body with cold sponging. At first Betty's sense of propriety would not allow Adam's participation in their struggle against Amanda's fever, but as day turned into night and then day again, the weary doctor began to feel the full weight of his years, and retired to rest. Betty, her time divided between cradle and bed, without the benefit of sleep, realized she must succumb at last to necessity and allow Adam to participate actively in Amanda's nursing. Curiously, there was no offer of help from the other ladies within the fort. For their blind prejudice these women earned the small group's disgust and scorn.

Left to the freedom of his own discretion as day turned once again into night, and both the weary Betty as well as Dr. Cartwright were forced to seek a few hours sleep, Adam started to feel the pressure of panic. Amanda's temperature was rising, despite the cool compresses applied to her head and arms, and Adam knew it was time for more drastic measures. Ripping a larger piece from the cloth provided by Betty for compresses, Adam soaked it in the cold well water, and began to unbutton Amanda's nightdress. Raising her gently, careful not to disturb her body too greatly, he slipped her arms out of its confines and slipping it down, bared her to the waist. In his agitation to lower her fever quickly, he did not even stop to look at the soft white breasts bared to his view, but proceeded to squeeze the wet cloth almost dry, and then lay it across her burning chest, at the same time covering her arms and neck with its coolness.

A sharp gasp issued from Amanda's throat, and her eyes sprang open with shock as the cold cloth touched her burning skin. Speaking softly and consolingly, Adam's low voice almost purred, "Relax, Amanda, you'll soon feel better. Don't worry, darling. We've been through this before, don't you remember?"

A weak smile answered his query, causing a tight knot to form in his throat, against which he swallowed stiffly. He ripped another piece of cloth and soaked it in the bucket to use in alternating applications as the cloth covering Amanda's torso rapidly warmed from the intense heat generated by her fever.

Adam continued his patient applications and soft assurances through the night, stopping frequently to quickly draw fresh water from the well when the bucket of water warmed too much to be of benefit, and rushing immediately back to Amanda's bedside to continue his loving vigil. Finally, Adam began to see the results of his steady ministrations. Ignoring Amanda's chattering teeth, which he realized was merely the reaction to cold applied against her heated skin, he noted that the wet cloths were heating more slowly, and stopping, he placed his hand against her forehead. It was deliciously cool to his touch! Her temperature had dropped, and if it was not completely normal, it was, he was certain, far below the danger point.

Elation swept over him and Adam hastened to remove the cloth and desist his attentions, in sudden fear that a chill might overcome his beloved patient. Quickly he took the remaining portion of dry cloth and gently began to rub her dry before slipping back her gown. Starting at her throat, his attentions moved down to her shoulders and arms, and then lower, slowing to a stop as he seemed to consciously consider the picture before him for the first time. His gaze moved to the rounded white breasts, the crests still unbelievably pink, larger now since the birth of her child, and slid further to her waist for a moment in amazement that it had already almost returned to its former miniscule proportions. His eyes returned once again to the soft, white swells and he began gently to rub her dry. As he did, Adam felt a simultaneous tightening in his throat and groin. With hands that were now trembling, Adam completed drying the delicate white skin, and lifted her gently once again to slip her into her gown. As he tenderly raised her fragile young body, he softly pressed his lips to her breasts for a fleeting second, and was startled at the instantaneous jolt of warmth that spread through him. Hastily he buttoned her gown, covered her, and stayed kneeling for a moment in contemplation of the angelic vision before him. Without conscious volition, Adam lowered his head to cover the cool, pale lips with his own generous mouth, drawing deeply for a short, beautiful moment from its unbelievable sweetness. As he reluctantly pulled away, Amanda's weary eyes fluttered open for the breath of a second, and a flicker of a smile passed over her face. Adam placed his work-toughened palm against her cheek and felt the heat of tears beneath his lids.

She'll recover. She'll regain her strength, and then she'll need me more than ever.

Getting quietly to his feet, Adam pulled a chair to her bedside and sank down to close his eyes for some well-earned rest.

Gradually Amanda opened her eyes. It was so difficult! Why were her eyelids so heavy? She stirred restlessly in bed, and found her limbs like lead weight as she attempted to move them. With unbelievable difficulty, Amanda turned her head to scan the room where she lay, and only through a deep, sustained effort was able to keep her eyes focused as she did. Immediately her gaze came to rest on a huge, broad-shouldered figure lying sprawled in a small, upholstered bedroom chair, his massive frame over-lapping uncomfortably the small structure, giving the impression of great discomfort. A weak smile lightly lifted the corners of Amanda's mouth as her eyes swept over the dozing figure whose tawny hair fell boyishly forward as his head lay uncomfortably against his shoulder in sleep. His handsome face seemed drawn and tired, and even in repose the dark circles beneath his eyes disclosed his sleepless nights. Light brown stubble covered his usually clean-shaven cheeks and chin, and the simple, tan broad-cloth shirt he wore was wrinkled and untidy, in silent testimony to his hours of complete devotion to his nursing chores.

As if sensing her silent perusal, Adam stirred and opened his eyes. His weary features brightened immediately as his eyes met hers, and his wide smile flashed, evoking in Amanda a spontaneous warmth which showed itself in her own weak but growing smile. Adam immediately left his chair to kneel by her bed and lay his hand against her forehead warily. Its coolness relaxed the tension that had built in the many anxious hours before, and in response to his tremendous relief, Adam slipped his arms around her gently, to hold her closely for several silent minutes.

Although Amanda's mind was still a jumble of confusion in her weakened state, she felt strangely content to lie quietly in Adam's arms, cradled against his broad, familiar chest. She could feel the warmth of Adam's breath against her hair as he spoke softly. "You've been very ill, Amanda, but you're getting better now. Soon you will be completely well."

Amanda struggled to talk as Adam released her to lay her tenderly against her pillow. How strange she felt, as if she were climbing from a deep, dark well. She was so tired. It was so difficult to speak.

Suddenly memory returned to flood her weary mind with the multitude of events that had tran-spired within the last few days. She slid her hand over the flatness of her stomach, and managed in a weak, hoarse voice, "My son. How does he fare? Is he well?"

"He's fine, Amanda. His progress has been far better than his mother's the past few days."

"Please, Adam, I want to see him. I've never seen my son." Amanda's weary blue eyes filled with tears as memory continued to inundate her mind with the gruesome details surrounding his birth.

"I'll get him for you, darling. Betty!" Adam's voice was boisterous in reaction to his lightening spirits as he rose and walked quickly to the door. Betty Mitchell stood poised over the small cradle in the sitting room where she had spent her restless night. Anxiety fell quickly from her expression when she viewed Adam's happy face.

"Amanda would like to see her son!"

Both unthinkingly ignored the morose silent figure who sat across the room, as far from the cradle as possible, his eyes watching jealously as the happy pair brought Amanda her child.

Amanda felt her pulse quicken, and small beads of perspiration broke out on her upper lip as excitement strained her meager strength even further. A tired but beaming Betty lay the small blanketed bundle beside her, and lifting herself slightly, Amanda looked down for the first time into the face of her son. Her eyes touched on the smooth, copper-hued skin, noting the delicate slant of his dark eyes and brows, the blackness of his abundant hair, the shape of his face, which even at such an early age evidenced his father's fine, chisled features; and she felt for the first time a great burst of motherly love and pride. Suddenly her waning strength was exhausted, and Amanda collapsed weakly backwards, only to strain desperately to lift herself again in order to view her son. Adam moved quickly to sit beside her and lifted her gently, supporting her against his chest as she gazed in wonder at the innocent beauty her pain had wrought. Directing a proud look at Adam, she said weakly, "He's beautiful, isn't he, Adam?" And at his silent nod of assent, she continued quietly, "He's truly Chingue's son."

She looked back to the infant in time to see a smile flick across his face, displaying the disarming dimple, and to hear Adam's deep voice whisper in her ear, "And your son, also, Amanda. As his features cry his father's name, so does his smile cry yours. He is truly a son to be proud of."

Amanda raised her face to Adam's in silent gratitude, moments before her eyes closed again in contented sleep.

It was decided the following day that the child would be named Jonathan, after his grandfather, and each consecutive June day thereafter added its share to Amanda's growing strength. To her delight, within the week her vitality, although she was still cautiously confined to her bed, was such that she was finally allowed to nurse her child. Eagerly taking the hungry baby from Betty with trembling hands, Amanda placed him against her breast. The infant began to nurse hungrily, making small, smacking noises in his wildly anxious efforts to sate his ever increasing appetite. Amanda laughed softly at the almost comical look of rapture on the tiny face as his empty stomach began to fill. Transfused with a deep, consuming love for the babe at her breast, Amanda felt a thickness in her throat, and Chingue's face flashed before her. Softly she whispered to the baby she held so close against her, "Your father is dead, my little son, but his memory will live forever in my heart. Although you will never see his face, you'll come to know him and remember him always, and you'll become as proud as I that Chingue was your father."

Adam observed silently from the doorway, unnoticed and temporarily forgotten by the small, golden-haired beauty who, now undeniably the center of his existence, spoke quietly to her child. As he watched, he felt sadly excluded from their circle of love and felt a sudden flash of jealousy. An unexpected, quietly mocking voice in his ear voiced his silent thoughts. "You thought you'd usurp her love, Adam, but now you know where her heart lies."

Robert's voice was venomous as he took his opportunity to inflict pain on the man who had taken his place at Amanda's side. "She loves that savage. He's the only man in her heart. You're as much an outsider as I am, and as much a fool."

Abruptly Robert turned and stormed angrily out the door, leaving Adam to the silent contemplation of his bitter words.

Golden day followed golden day, and Amanda's contentment with motherhood was reflected in her rapidly returning health. Finally satisfied with her improved physical condition, Dr. Cartwright recommended at last that she venture outside for some sun, in the same breath warning her against the dangers of excessive activity, excessive sun, excessive excitement, etcetera. His deep fatherly concern was obvious in the frown that creased his serious, heavily jowled face. Impulsively, Amanda leaned forward to place a short kiss against his ruddy cheek, and said with mock severity, "I promise, sir, I will not overdo!"

Her smile concealing her great trepidation, Amanda slipped her arm under the hugely muscled one Adam gallantly offered and walked outside. Her heart accelerated beating as they strolled slowly around the yard of the fort, so great was her dread of her first encounter outside the circle of loving friends who had surrounded her so faithfully during her time of crisis. Although the subject had been deliberately ignored during her recuperation, Amanda was greatly aware of the absence of visitors and well-wishers that usually accompanied a birth, and awaited nervously her confrontation with the world outside her room. Unaware that the warm June sun beating down on her uncovered head reflected brightly on the shining gold and silver threads, turning them into a shimmering, molten gold, Amanda felt only its deep, penetrating warmth warming her body, slowly relaxing her taut muscles.

Her deepening feeling of tranquility conveyed itself to Adam. He had begun to relax and enjoy his sojourn within the walls of the fort when Amanda's sudden spontaneous stiffening jerked him to attention. Mrs. Prentice, wife of Lieutenant Prentice and the source of Amanda's concern was striding in their direction. With the briefest of nods, the previously friendly woman of some thirty-odd years continued past, never slackening her pace, and Adam felt the small hand that clutched his arm tighten involuntarily. Looking swiftly down at Amanda, he noted the slight tremble of her lip as she lifted her head a notch higher in defiance of the slight, and continued forward without sparing the woman a backward glance. They continued their walk without speaking, each new encounter proving the same as the last, indicating her complete ostracism from the white world of Fort Edward, and her intense determination to hold herself above their scorn.

So, this is the way it's to be! Adam's fury mounted with each step. Look down on her, do they? his mind raged. There's not a person within these damned fort walls fit to clean her shoes. Abruptly deciding he had had enough, he spoke softly to Amanda in an attempt to disguise his raging anger.

"I think it's best we return now, Amanda. I'll put a bench outside Betty's door so that we can rest a while in the sun."

Still avoiding his gaze, Amanda nodded her assent. As they later sat wordlessly side by side in the sun, Adam slipped his large hand over the small, soft hands clutched so tightly on her lap, and tilted up her chin with his finger to give her a short encouraging wink.

"Don't worry, Adam." Amanda's face was sober, her voice resolute but tinged with anger. "Jonathan and I won't allow their prejudice to upset us."

A fierce swelling of pride almost overwhelmed him at her spirited defiance of her rejection. Suddenly unable to speak past the lump in his throat, he damned the fate that held him in full view of the fort and kept him from sweeping her into his arms then and there.

The sound of rapidly approaching footsteps drew Adam's attention to the slender young soldier who headed toward them. Noting his purposeful manner, Adam felt a vague sense of apprehension prickle along his spine. Flashing a smile at the silent Amanda, the young soldier said sincerely, "Glad to see you're feeling better, ma'am." Directing the rest of his remarks to Adam, he continued, "General Webb would like to see you, Adam. He asked me to add that it was a matter of utmost importance."

Absurdly grateful for the young soldier's small pleasantry to Amanda when he saw her smile, Adam turned to refuse graciously, only to be stopped by Amanda, who had anticipated his response.

"Please go with him, Adam. I've had enough sun for the day, and our walk has made me more weary than I expected. I think I'll rest for a while."

Adam watched until the door closed behind her before turning to the young man. "Well, Harry," he said abruptly, "let's see what the general has on his mind." Adam's natural curiosity added haste to his steps as he strode in the direction of the general's office.

The general's manner was serious and worried as he extended his hand in greeting. He spoke, going directly to the point as was his usual custom, his agitation obvious in his short, nevous movements. "You could not have timed your return better for the sake of your country, Adam. Since you've been engaged in a personal search for the past few months, and have found those same personal affairs demanding your constant attention since your return to Fort Edward, I don't believe you are cognizant of the activity presently underway at the site of Fort William Henry, or the expedition intended to be launched within the next few weeks."

"You're right, general." Adam's voice was wary, "I have no knowledge of an expedition or what it may have to do with me."

In the face of his obvious reluctance, General Webb proceeded hesitantly. "At present General James Abercrombie has gathered at the head of Lake George the greatest army ever assembled on the American continent, almost fifteen thousand men. He has erected over three hundred buildings, storehouses, barracks, and hospitals near the old entrenched camp and has thrown up earthwork and mounted several pieces of small-caliber cannon on the former site of Fort William Henry. It is his intention to launch an attack and overwhelm Fort Carillon."

Adam could feel the steady acceleration of his heartbeat as the general continued speaking. He was intrigued by the scope of the attack and the impact a victory of that magnitude could have on the eventual outcome of the war.

"General Abercrombie and Lord Howe are presently calling for all possible intelligence on the area. Your intimate knowledge of Fort Carillon and its surroundings, as well as the nature of the personnel within the fort, would be invaluable in drawing up and executing the plan of attack. I've sent those two worthy gentlemen word of your return, and they're presently awaiting your advice."

"I'll be glad to furnish all the information I have to

you, General, so that you may in turn forward it on, but I'm needed here and I don't intend to leave."

The general considered Adam speculatively for a few silent minutes. His face reflected his careful deliberation before speaking. Finally, as if having come to his decision, the general started, embarrassment and shame growing on his face as he proceeded in a determined if faltering manner, his voice soft and devoid of his occasionally haughty manner.

"Adam, although we've never spoken of the events that occurred at the battle of Fort William Henry, I know you're aware of all the facts. You're also aware of my decision in refusing to send help to the besieged fort in fear of weakening Fort Edward's defenses. I realize now that my intervention would probably have been the key to turning the battle in our favor. Except for me, that gallant fort may have been standing today, inhabited by the very people who now lie buried beneath that same ground. This is a guilt I bear, and not lightly, I assure you."

With an earnest expression, General Webb continued, his discomfort in speaking so openly on this painful subject obvious in the pallor of his skin and the nervous clenching of his smooth, slender hands.

"I speak frankly to you now, Adam, so that you might understand that I'm not without experience when I speak of the weight of guilt. I can't impress upon you too strongly the value of your contributions to a successful attack. The very knowledge you contribute could save the lives of many of our men who would ultimately meet their deaths without the aid of well-rounded, accurate intelligence in an area where you are well versed."

General Webb sat abruptly to cover his face with a weary gesture before continuing. His voice a shade softer still, the general resumed his plea, looking up to lock gazes with Adam as he spoke. "The burden of guilt in knowing that your help may have spared the unnecessary loss of lives even in victory would be hard enough to live with, Adam, but should this attack fail without your fullest cooperation, your burden would be nigh impossible! I tell you this now, not in an attempt to lighten the burden I carry through confession, but to spare another responsible fellow human being the agony of regret I have endured and will endure until my heart beats its last."

Wearied to the point of exhaustion by his intimate confession, General Webb did not wait for Adam's response, but concluded, "Consider what I've said, Adam, and come to me with your decision tomorrow morning. General Abercrombie expects to launch this operation within two weeks, and any further delay would be inauspicious."

Adam had yet to say a word when General Webb rose to his feet, extending his hand as he did, "Until tomorrow, Adam."

The general's words weighing heavily on his mind, Adam retraced his steps back toward the Mitchells' residence. He had been deeply stirred by his confession and felt the weight of responsibility that gentleman had placed on his shoulders. So many men! It could either be a great victory or a resounding defeat. Pricking his conscience most sorely was the realization that all that the general had said was true. Although many knew the area surrounding the fort, with a force as great as 15,000 men, they would all be needed to guide those soldiers through the unfamiliar wilderness. He also had a knowledge of the defensive structure of the fort known to very few.

Still, his mind cautioned, how can I leave Amanda now, when she needs most the reassurance of my presence in the face of the open hostility displayed against her?

In the end it was Amanda who took the decision out of his hands. Her observant eyes had fastened on him the moment of his return. Patiently she coaxed the entire story from Adam's reluctant lips and at its conclusion hesitated only a moment before saying softly, but with deep conviction, "You have no choice, Adam. You must do all you can to help. We both remember only too vividly the horrors of defeat."

Smiling wryly, she continued, "Fortunately, the greatest cost here will be my discomfort, for I'll miss you sorely while you go to confer with General Abercrombie; but in this case, I really don't think my feelings should take precedence." Covering his huge hand with her small one, she waited until his eyes rose to meet her gaze.

"Don't let worry for me cloud your decision, Adam. I have Betty, Captain Mitchell and Dr. Cartwright—my guardian angels—to look after Jonathan and me, and I'll be well taken care of until you return."

With those words, his decision was made.

Morning came too quickly and Adam felt the warring factions within tearing him apart as he joined the small group making the sixteen-mile trek to conference with General Abercrombie. Part of him longed to remain at Amanda's side, while the other part knew full well where his duty lay and was anxious to contribute. Adam was engrossed in his own thoughts, and the sixteen miles seemed to fade away. In a surprisingly short time, he was confronted with the impressive and stimulating sight of 15,000 soldiers preparing for war.

Just as had been described by General Webb, the camp was a beehive of activity. The force gathered for the attack was varied and composed of about 6,000 British regulars, with the remainder being made up from the ranks of the provincials of New England, New York and New Jersey. The picture confronting his eyes was bright with the color of banners and bugles of different regiments. Among these were the Highlanders in their picturesque traditional dress, with red jackets, and their bagpipes proudly displayed. It seemed as if an entire town had sprung up where the rangers' camp had once stood, except that this town was composed almost entirely of men, jubilantly and confidently preparing for battle.

Once in the presence of General James Abercrombie and George Agustus, Viscount Howe, it was not long before the true leader of the expedition became apparent. General Abercrombie, a heavy man of some fifty-two years, although the official leader, had not succeeded in obtaining or earning the confidence of his men and, it was sorely evident, had not the great strategic military mind of young Lord Howe. In the days that followed, the well-ordered, concise questions of Lord Howe gleaned from Adam's mind every detail he had to contribute to the success of their operation, and at the conclusion of their conference, Adam's esteem for Lord Howe's ability as a strategist and concerned leader of men was great indeed. It was because of this hard-won respect that Lord Howe's appeal carried so much weight in Adam's mind when Adam declared his intention to return to Fort Edward. Lord Howe's patrician countenance creased with alarm. "Surely you don't mean to depart before we leave for battle, Adam. Your presence and contributions will be greatly missed."

"As much as I'd prefer to see this battle through to the finish, sir, I have obligations elsewhere which press me sorely."

"I ask you, Adam," Lord Howe persisted, "would these obligations suffer from your absence of another week or two? I beg you to reconsider. Outside are British troops that are almost completely untried in warring under circumstances such as they'll soon encounter. True babes in the woods in that respect. They are desperately in need of men of your ability to offset their inexperience. I plead most earnestly your cooperation."

Lord Howe, a wise judge of man, had hit the exact note on which to press his point, and seeing Adam's resistance waver, he pressed further. "I'll be only too happy to dispatch a courier with any message you feel it necessary to send to Fort Edward, and will be endlessly grateful for your compliance with my request. You see, Adam, each one of my men's lives are dear to me, and I'd not lose even one that could have been spared as a result of your expertise."

The last of Adam's resistance fell away at the

266

eloquence of Lord Howe's plea. He gave a short nod of acquiescence and responded simply, "I'll stay."

The next morning a courier left the temporary camp bound for Fort Edward with a message delivered later to an anxious and startled Amanda.

My dearest Amanda,

Contrary to my original plan, but as a result of Lord Howe's urgent request, I have decided to see this matter through to the finish. We will soon be embarking to make our assault on Fort Carillon, and at the conclusion of our duties, I will return to Fort Edward with all possible haste.

I trust you and Jonathan are faring well, and are not experiencing any discomfort, for it is this anxiety that is uppermost in my mind. My only consolation is that I know you understand this is something I must do.

Your loving servant,
Adam.

Staring down at Adam's wide scrawl, Amanda felt an acute sense of loss. ". . . . see this matter through to the finish." That would mean he intended to go into battle with the main force. Unreasonable fear took a momentary hold on her senses as she considered the dreadful possibilities of battle.

"Oh, Adam."

With a start, Amanda suddenly recalled that the young courier still stood nearby, patiently awaiting her response. Forcing all other thought from her mind, she walked rapidly to the desk in the corner of the small room and penned her reply.

Dear Adam,

I thank you for the consideration of your
note, although its contents do not bring me joy.
But you are correct; I do understand your obli-
gation, and my thoughts and prayers go with
you.

Jonathan and I are well, and I am sure you
will be surprised with his growth the weeks you
will be away. Do not concern yourself with our
welfare, but expend all your efforts in keeping
yourself safe. We will be here when you return.

Until then I remain,

Sincerely,
Amanda.

Quickly folding the scribbled note, Amanda sealed
and handed it to the weary young man. "Thank you,
soldier. I wish you Godspeed." Within moments the
letter was on its way.

What a travesty that letter had been, Amanda
thought wryly as she stared at the closed door. In
truth, Jonathan's and her situation had seen rapid
deterioration from the moment of Adam's departure.
The inhabitants of the fort had grown openly hostile
toward her when she refused to exhibit an element of
shame she did not feel. Her obvious pride in her
child, as well as her adament refusal to accept the
stigma they tried to force upon her, seemed to
inflame their prejudice. Even the doctor's and
Captain Mitchell's strong words in her behalf had no
effect on them, and feelings had progressed to such

an emotional level that she feared for Jonathan's safety and had begun to keep him indoors the entire day.

And there was still Robert. In the few times she had gone outside to walk or sit in the sun, he was always within view, watching, his eyes now unreadable. Where formerly his presence had radiated a warm familiarity, she now felt only revulsion and the coldness of death when she looked on his countenance, feelings which unknowingly reflected on her face and inspired a responsive infuriating anger in Robert. Amanda sensed inwardly he was merely marking time for some indefinable reason, for his look was often sly and calculating, and her apprehension began to build more with each new day. She realized that the time for a determination of her future was at hand; but despite the support of her loyal friends, she felt strangely lost without the rock of Adam's presence and steadfastly put off any decision until his return so she could seek his advice. A chill suddenly swept over Amanda as a new consideration came to her mind. She would have to revise her thinking slightly. She would put off her decision. She would wait not until he returned, but if he returned.

Amanda lay in her bed, wakeful and edgy, partly due, she was certain, to the realization that Adam was soon to go into battle against the French, if indeed the force had not already embarked for that purpose. Her days since receiving Adam's letter had been spent with an underlying tension existing just below the surface of her conscious thought, as if she were in a state of emotional suspended animation until the battle was over and she would, she hoped, be able to take a deep, relieved breath. She felt doubly alone tonight, as she found herself in the unusual circumstance of having the Mitchells' quarters entirely to herself. Betty had been called out earlier to help a young mother battle her child's croup through the night and the captain was on an overnight scouting mission. Amanda's eyes roved over the small sitting room that she had insisted upon occupying since her return to health, thereby returning the use of their bedroom to the captain and Betty. The well-used couch was once again her bed, and the small wooden cradle stood close by. Glancing down at Jonathan's tiny face, serene and innocent in slumber, Amanda felt a rush of love, and was relieved that at least he rested well. The room was silent and eerie and, in the absence of sleep, countless pictures crowded her mind, the most frequent of which was Chingue's face. It was only in times like this, when sleep eluded her, that Amanda was unsuccessful in driving all thoughts of Chingue from her mind, although she tried most desperately. But alone in her bed she was completely vulnerable to the memory of Chingue's strong, athletic body lying next to her, the strength of his arms as he pulled her to him, the pressure of his mouth on hers. It was then that the pain would start afresh, when she realized that his loving tenderness was lost to her forever, and that the strong, handsome, beautiful man who was her husband had been removed from the face of the earth by the force of unrestrained jealousy. And, as her love for Chingue was stirred anew by the stimulus of bittersweet recollection, so was her hatred for Robert inflamed to greater heights.

Tortured so for countless nights, Amanda tried again vainly to keep Chingue from her thoughts and concentrate on her child. And although during the day she had been largely successful, tonight Chingue was ever lurking in her mind, his coal-black eyes still able to stir her love in memory. She reasoned to herself, Why can't I forget, or at least be able to drive him from my thoughts? He's dead, coldly, irreversibly dead. She knew the tears streaming down her face could achieve no useful purpose, and sobbing softly, Amanda murmured hopelessly into her pillow, "Chingue, *Witschemil. N'schawussi, N'wiquihhalla, N'wischasi woak K'dahoatell.*"[1]

Amanda awoke abruptly in reaction to the warm pressure of a hand over her mouth. Her short cry of fright was stifled as the hand bore down more heavily and fear prickled along her spine. It was Robert! She struggled in vain, attempting to remove his hand, only to hear Robert's voice in her ear as he demanded harshly, "Stop struggling! Give me your word you'll listen to what I have to say and I'll remove my hand. Is it a bargain?"

At Amanda's short nod, Robert slowly withdrew his hand, ready to clamp it back if she started to scream. But Amanda had no such intention. Her voice was sharp, and hatred flashed in her eyes as she demanded, "What are you doing here, Robert?"

"I've come to take you away with me. There's no

1. Meaning, "Chingue, help me. I am weak, I am tired, I am afraid, and I love thee."

life for us here. We'll go where we're not known and start anew."

Amazement left Amanda speechless for the space of a few seconds, until she uttered incredulously, "Do you really believe I'll go with you? If you do, you must be insane!"

"Of course you'll come with me, Amanda." Robert's voice held a note of impatience, as if speaking to a wayward child. "It was your parents' wish. They knew that I loved you and would take care of you. They knew what was best for your welfare."

Unable to believe that he could be speaking so confidently in the face of her open antipathy, she said coldly, "You know as well as I that whatever feeling once existed between us is gone. It died the minute you fired the gun that killed Chingue, and is more dead in my heart than Chingue is right now."

"That's not true!" Robert's voice took on a wild note as he disclaimed her remarks. "You still feel some sort of crazy loyalty to the savage, but it will pass, you'll see."

"No, no it will not. I'll never forget what you did." Amanda's voice rose as he started to draw her into his arms and she pushed him away violently.

"You're coming with me now, Amanda, tonight."

"I won't go with you," she ground out from between clenched teeth as she fought vainly to be free of his powerful grip. Still struggling, she shot him a look of pure loathing, only to feel the first prick of fear as she observed his wily expression. His voice was coldly confident.

"You're very fond of that half-breed baby in the

272

cradle, aren't you, Amanda?"

The insinuation was clear. Her first reaction was shock, then outrage! Fury shook her voice. "What do you mean by that, Robert?"

"It should be obvious. That child means no more to me than any other Indian, and you've seen how little I value their lives."

Amanda could feel the blood draining from her face as the coldness of fear began to spread through her veins. He continued coldly.

"You know there would be no questions asked if he suddenly disappeared. As a matter of fact, I think I can safely say most people here would be grateful to see him gone."

"You won't. I won't let you touch him!" She gasped.

His face bearing a diabolical sneer, Robert pressed closer. "Do you really believe you can stop me, Amanda?"

Amanda looked up, beginning to feel true horror as his words echoed through her brain and his hands held her helpless. She stared, seeing a man whose countenance, dark and ugly with cruelty, bore no resemblance to her patient, gentle betrothed of a year before, and saw victory in his eyes as fear for her child swelled within her. Still unwilling to submit to his threats, Amanda strained to sound confident, but did not quite succeed.

"You couldn't harm a child. That's merely an empty threat. You couldn't."

"Do you want me to show you how I really feel about the offspring of that savage?"

Robert's face was suddenly contorted with rage,

and Amanda was once again struck by the thought that the man had slipped beyond the limits of reason. Without waiting for her reply, Robert moved quickly to the cradle to roughly grab the child within, jarring him cruelly from sleep. As she watched with incredulous shock, Robert raised the crying infant over his head as if to smash him to the floor, a demonic smile on his face. A small cry issued from her lips and he spat out venomously, "If you call for help he is dead, now!" He laughed wildly at her frozen expression.

"This is your last chance, Amanda."

Amanda sprang from the couch to reach for her child held high above her head, beyond her reach. She no longer doubted Robert's ability to kill her son and sobbed hysterically, "Please, give him to me. Please give him to me."

"Will you come willingly with me?"

"Yes, yes, I'll come. Give me my child."

Slowly Robert lowered the screaming baby, prolonging Amanda's agony as long as possible, delighting in his power over her as she begged softly, "Please, Robert, please."

Finally Jonathan was in her arms, and Amanda held him close to comfort and quiet the trembling infant who was breathless from terrified screaming. The sobs slowly quieted to a low whimper and then to silence as the exhausted child drifted off to sleep.

"Get dressed and put some of your clothes together. We must hurry."

Amanda hastened to obey and started to move into the other room to dress.

"No, you'll dress here. You won't leave my sight again until we are away!"

Without a word, Amanda turned her back and began to slip her nightdress to her waist and, pulling her dress over her head, proceeded to clothe herself as modestly as she could manage. She turned to see that Robert's eyes had never left her. He stared as if transfixed, fascinated by her actions. Suddenly seeming to snap from his daze, he said roughly, "Pick up the child and we'll leave."

"No, leave him here. I'll go with you alone!" Amanda knew Jonathan would be far safer with Betty than he would be in Robert's company, but Robert smiled evilly.

"I'm not that much a fool, Amanda, that I would leave my leverage behind. Pick him up quickly or there'll be no further need to discuss his future!"

Snatching Jonathan hastily against her, Amanda bent to scoop up some of his clean linen before preceeding Robert out the door. Within minutes, they were at a spot where two horses stood saddled and loaded with provisions. Lifting her with unbelievable ease, Robert put her in the saddle, a triumphant smile on his lips, and swung up onto the first horse. Taking her horse's reins in his hand, he urged him toward the gates, which were opened as they arrived by a smiling sentry who winked at Robert conspiratorily as they passed through. Within a very few minutes, Fort Edward was left behind.

July 5, 1758—Excitement tingled along Adam's spine as the force of 15,000 made ready to embark. It was obvious from the high spirits of the brawny group of rangers around him that their confidence in the success of their venture was high. He joined in their laughter and ribald jokes in an effort to dispel the presentiment that nagged viciously at his mind and was relieved when he finally succeeded for a short time in shouting it down. But, as he watched the first of the great number slowly filling the bateaux and whaleboats that eventually covered Lake George in a six-mile flotilla, he could no longer supress his feeling of anxiety, and a new shiver of premonition at the ominous thought, How many will return?

Traveling with the rangers and the light infantry of Lord Howe in the advance whaleboats, as Lord Howe had requested, Adam's progress up the lake was maddeningly slow, giving him time to review in his mind the plans to gain control of Fort Carillon. The plan of attack was very simple. They were to disembark at a landing place approximately seven miles from Fort Carillon and to march from there in four columns upon the enemy, dispatching one column to capture the old sawmill a short distance from the fort. The rangers, Howe's light infantry, and the marksmen were to head up each of the four columns. Simple and sure. There would be no problem. And as the day wore on, Adam's mind drifted off to more personal matters.

The time that Adam had spent with Lord Howe in preparation for the attack had seemed much longer than two weeks. But July 5 had finally come, and Adam found his thoughts racing ahead to the time, a few days hence, he hoped, when he would be free to return to Fort Edward and to Amanda. The past weeks spent with groups of British regulars in an attempt to acquaint them with the area they were

276

about to enter had been full and tiring, but the silent nights had seen an invasion of a different sort. In the quiet darkness of his tent, Adam needed not even close his eyes to picture the incredibly beautiful, angelic face of Amanda before him: Amanda smiling, her huge blue eyes brilliant and sparkling; Amanda weeping, her petite frame shaking with sobs; Amanda holding her child to her breast, her beauty that of the Madonna as it became transfused with love; Amanda with head held high, in silent disregard of the disapproving glances sent her way; and most poignant of all, Amanda's face raised to him in the silent, trusting appeal reserved for him alone. Lord, how he yearned to return to her!

It would be difficult at first, he knew, to turn that trust into love, and it would require patience in allowing Amanda time to grieve and to heal. But soon, soon he would be back by her side to take her under his wing once again, until she would allow him to take her forever into his life as his wife.

July 6, 1758—The sun rose over Lake George, spreading its golden glow on the impressive spectacle of one thousand small boats moving relentlessly on their course toward Fort Carillon with oars glistening, uniforms and banners proudly displayed, and men alert and eager to encounter the enemy on the wild, virgin shores. Unexpectedly, they landed unopposed and fell into columns as planned and headed into the forest.

Adam was part of the second column to enter the wooded area and was not marching long before he was passed the word that a small group of 400 of the enemy, including some Indians, had set fire to their camp and fallen back as the British force pressed onward. Encouraged by the French retreat, they marched steadily on through the dense swamps and dark woods with Adam's column following behind the lead. But it was not too much longer before it became obvious that the denseness of the summer foliage had proved too much for even the most experienced woodsmen and their whereabouts were temporarily in question. Exasperated by the confusion, the guides and Lord Howe stopped to reconsider their position, when the noisy thrashing of another party echoed through the wooded area. The order for complete silence was unnecessary, as each man strained his ears to make out the voices as they came ever closer. The other party was also apparently lost and seemed to be the same French force that had retreated and burned its camp that morning. The party drew nearer, and a sudden deep voice broke the uneasy silence as it called out, *"Qui vive?"* A quick thinking ranger with an unfortunate English accent called back, *"Francais!"* Within seconds gunshots echoed on the heavy forest air.

Adam fell to a position behind a large tree and began firing as Lord Howe attempted to gather his light infantry to engage the enemy and allow the remainder of the columns freedom to continue their advance. Cautiously he moved with his men to the crest of the hill, arriving just as a burst of fire sounded. Adam watched unbelievingly, stiffening in shock, as the brilliant soldier's body arched with the impact of the bullet that entered his chest, and shuddered slightly before falling heavily to

278

the ground!

Adam's jaw sagged with shock. Lord Howe dead? How could it be? So quickly, before the battle had really begun? Glancing quickly around him, Adam saw his sense of unreality was shared by the men surrounding him, and it was obvious it was only the heavy gunfire that rang repeatedly over their heads that kept them under cover and away from their leader's side.

As the day progressed, the impact of Lord Howe's sudden death became more and more apparent as his men's confidence was replaced with indecision, their enthusiasm with confusion, until, by nightfall, it was indeed a surprise to Adam that they had managed to come out of the skirmish the victors.

July 7, 1758—Adam awoke to find the mood of the men had only deepened as the dispirited column prepared to bear Lord Howe's body back to the landing place. After the long dismal trek their mood was so apparently despondent that they were ordered to remain and refresh themselves and another column, under Colonel Bradstreet, was ordered forward to dispossess the enemy of their position at the sawmill. At the end of the long, weary day, Adam learned that the French, having been warned of the column's approach by an advance scout, had set fire to the mill and bridge adjoining and fled. But before too long, the British had secured the position, restored the bridge, and were ready to move on.

July 8, 1758—The day dawned clear and humid in the heavily wooded area. Having benefited from their hours of rest and awakened with an eagerness to avenge their leader's death, the men of Adam's column quickly formed again to march against the enemy. By then it was common knowledge that General Abercrombie had established his base at the abandoned sawmill and intended to direct the attack, on the advice of his chief engineer, from that distance. Adam was struck again with the thought that the true leader of the expedition had already been killed, and with a twinge of premonition which he firmly refused to acknowledge, he took his place in the column, his light-brown brows drawn together in a worried frown.

The anxious columns advanced through the hot, sultry forest much of the morning, only to stop abruptly, causing the men at the rear of the column to mumble their incomprehension at the unexpected halt. Fighting his way to the head of the column, Adam joined the other members there as they stared in open-mouthed disbelief at the sight that met their eyes. There the forest had painstakingly been cleared and an incredible wall of logs, obviously erected at the order of the Marquis de Montcalm, went on endlessly, appearing to span the entire peninsula of Carillon! The wall was uncommonly high, and the ground in front was covered with a thick abatis of trees, their branches sharpened into points and laid so thickly as to be almost impregnable! From behind the wall came the fire of French troops, heavy enough to suggest a considerable number and, from the conviction of their invincibility, steady and accurate enough to inflict unbelievable damage. Faced with the awesome obstacle, the British troops fell back to await word from the couriers who were immediately dispensed to General Abercrombie's headquarters.

Adam squatted on the forest floor with the men of his column, absentmindedly slapping mosquitos and awaiting the general's orders. To have come so far to be stopped so abruptly was disheartening, but Adam knew, as did the rest of the men, that an assault on such an obstacle by infantry and muskets was hopeless. And so it was when the courier returned that General Abercrombie's orders fell on incredulous ears. They were to storm and take the defensive position of the enemy!

Standing with the astonished men, Adam awaited the first disgruntled refusal to obey the suicidal command, but instead watched the gallant soldiers begin to form and ready their attack.

This is madness! his mind shouted. Surely they realize they haven't a chance.

Quickly scanning the faces around him, Adam saw in them the knowledge of the futility of attack, but he also saw on the stubborn countenances unqualified acceptance of the order.

Taking the position ordered his group, that of providing cover fire for the advancing forces, Adam grimly watched for the command to commence attack.

Through the long, hot July day he continued to watch as, again and again, wave after wave of brave, doomed men stormed the wall, only to be caught in the abatis and hung there as perfect targets for the French marksmen. The rare few that actually made their way through the tangle of branches, only succeeded to find it their fate to be cut down at the wall by French bullets or sabers.

The horrendous death toll mounted as the day progressed, and it was obvious to Adam that the Forty-Second Highlanders, the famous Black Watch, had been all but annihilated, their blood joining with that of the Royal Americans and the countless colonial soldiers who had fallen in the doomed storming. And still the near hysterical couriers who carried the message of the bloody death and destruction of his regiments to General Abercrombie in his position of safety at the sawmill repeatedly returned white-faced with the unqualified order to press on!

Adam sat in the position he had held most of the day. His senses were outraged at the stupidity of the old man's order to continue an attack that was utterly futile from the beginning. No longer firing, he became almost hypnotized by the sight of men continuing to advance, to fall, their blood draining into the damp forest floor, only to be trampled by the next ill-fated wave of men who met the same end. The air was filled with the sound of gunshots and the moans of the dying. The choking odor of gunsmoke mingled with the more nauseating odor of blood and death that hung over the scene, filling Adam's nostrils until the taste of bile burned in his throat.

Senseless, bloody slaughter, his mind raged, ordered by a doddering old fool willing to sacrifice the lives of his men for his stubborn pride! Sickened and unable to comprehend the mentality that would order the bloodbath to continue, Adam rose with one thought in mind, to make his way back to General Abercrombie and demand the cessation of the senseless attack.

Adam moved hastily forward, only to feel a sudden, thudding burst of pain slam into his chest, the force rocking his huge frame almost off his feet. Dazed from the impact, Adam sank to his knees, clutching his chest, his pain deepening as he gasped wildly for breath. Feeling a hot, sticky wetness seeping through his fingers, Adam looked down and saw with a sense of unreality that his hands were covered with his own blood! Blackness was rapidly descending, and the sounds of battle were being shut out by the great roaring in his ears, and Adam felt himself sinking helplessly to the ground. His mind raced as the last bit of light began to fade before his eyes.

"Oh, Lord," he implored silently, "don't let it end this way. After all that's happened, never to return, never to see her again, never to. . . ."

Wearily, endlessly, the two horses were urged forward. Amanda's body was stiff and aching from the two long days spent in the saddle, and even Jonathan's meager weight had seemed to grow until her cramped arms could barely support him. But she dared not complain. As the long days had stretched on, Amanda had watched Robert grow increasingly more irritable and tense until even the slightest hungry whimper from her uncomfortable child was met with a murderous glance. Watching the back of Robert's head as he cautiously scanned the area through which they passed, Amanda was astounded with the change that had come over him. Gone was all trace of pity and solicitude from his personality. This was a new and frightening Robert who seemed devoid of all human feelings except hatred and revenge. In his present state of mind, she dared not question their destination or their fate, but hoped desperately once they arrived and Robert had had a chance to relax, some semblance of his former self would return so she could at least feel free to reason with him.

Glancing sharply over his shoulder as if sensing her silent perusal, Robert's eyes were cold and hard, sending a chill of fear down her spine. What was it he had in mind for the two of them? There was not even the pretense of love between them now. But there was no answer for Amanda during that long day, or even the next as their journey continued.

Just before noon of the fourth day, Amanda noticed a change in Robert. The planes of his face seemed to sharpen and bear an even more tense expression as he halted the horses and turned to signal quiet. Dismounting silently, he moved forward, and it was then that she noticed for the first time a small cabin almost hidden in the woods a short distance away. Robert advanced quietly, slipping out of her line of vision for long minutes at a time as he moved within the heavy foliage. Stealthily he approached the cabin, which to all outward appearances was deserted and, moving with a sudden, snapping action, pushed open the door and entered.

Amanda's heart hammered violently in her chest. What was it Robert expected to find? His sudden reappearance at the doorway of the cabin startled Amanda from her frightened conjectures, and she noted with relief the relaxed manner in which he strode back in their direction. Whatever was within the cabin, it did not constitute a threat; of that she was certain.

Without a word of explanation, Robert scooped up the reins of the two horses and led them forward. The closer they drew, the shabbier the cabin appeared, and it became obvious that it had been uninhabited for a long time, and was in an advanced state of disrepair. Looping the reins around the hitching post in front, Robert turned and swung her lightly from the saddle to the ground, announcing with a sober expression as he did, "We're home, Amanda."

"Home!" The single word escaped Amanda's lips in a startled gasp. "Do you mean you expect us to live here? You're insane!"

"This cabin fills an important requirement."

"You talk in riddles, Robert." Amanda was fast losing patience, even as she realized the danger that lay there. "What is it you mean to say?"

"Just this." Robert's voice was coldly impersonal as he spoke. "We're completely isolated here. There's no way you could possibly escape, should that thought cross your mind. You know as well as I the dangers of being lost in this wilderness. And you must think of the child's welfare." His voice, at the mention of her child, became a nasty sneer. "You will live here with me as my wife. The sooner you accept that fact, the better. Now we must make this place habitable."

Turning abruptly from her, he strode into the cabin, leaving Amanda to digest the portent of his words. It was at this point that Jonathan's uncomfortable squirming interrupted her confused thoughts, and realizing the source of his discomfort, Amanda walked inside and scanned the filthy room for an area to lay him down. Spotting a large bed in the corner, Amanda lay the whimpering infant on it and went back to the horses for clean linen. Before reentering, Amanda hesitated a moment, watching as Robert stood over the child, distaste obvious in his demeanor. Noting Amanda's return, he strode away without a word, and within minutes could be heard outside busily sawing and hammering as she settled to nurse her freshly changed infant.

Amanda held her small, warm gift of life to her breast, and gloried in the sensation of giving sustenance to this living reminder of her lost love. Chingue's son! The coal-black eyes shining so clearly up at her as Jonathan nursed so blissfully tore at her heartstrings; they brought so clearly back to mind the vision of his father. Filled with love as she looked at the dear little face, Amanda cooed softly to her child, *"Schiki a na lenno."*[1]

From the doorway Robert's harsh, angry voice startled her out of her reverie. "Stop using that heathen language!" Striding forward, he roughly placed a crude cradle on the floor in front of her. "This is for your son," his voice sneered. "I will not have him sharing our bed!"

Our bed! The words echoed in Amanda's mind as she stared incedulously at Robert's angry face. Before she could voice a comment, Robert continued. "You've wasted enough time with that child. Put him down and let's start putting this cabin to right before nightfall."

1. Meaning, "That is a fine, pretty man."

It was obvious from his expression that further discussion was pointless while he was in such a foul mood, and knowing she could not afford to anger him any further if she was to reason with him later, Amanda hastened to do Robert's bidding. Stopping only for a quick meal of dried venison and coffee brewed over the fire in their freshly cleaned fireplace, they worked until night.

Feeling the full weight of exhaustion, Amanda looked around, wearily assessing the condition of the room. The rough floors and walls had been dusted and swept. The crude table and chairs standing not far from the huge fireplace had been reinforced and scrubbed until the incredible filth had been removed completely from their surfaces. The limp rags used to cover the windows had been hastily washed, dried before the fireplace, and rehung again, giving the room a somewhat fresh, if still shabby appearance. The small supply of dishes and cooking utensils still usable in the cabin had been washed thoroughly and replaced in the small cupboard that had also been given the same attention. The huge old bed in the corner had been aired, its tattered linen washed, dried, and replaced on the bed, and even its lumpy discomfort looked a blissful haven to Amanda's tired eyes.

Well, at least the cabin is livable now, Amanda thought dejectedly, wondering just how long she would be forced to endure its confines as she glanced to the cradle where Jonathan once again fussed anxiously. Amanda turned as she heard a sharp, scraping noise at the door, in time to see Robert enter, dragging a large metal tub behind him.

A bathtub! Her eyes widened in wordless inquiry.

"It was outside in the rear of the cabin. I thought you might enjoy a warm bath. You've had a long, tiring day, Amanda."

His sudden sympathetic concern was unexpected and she nodded dumbly. Confounding her even more in her exhausted state, Robert continued softly, "Feed your child now, Amanda. I'll ready the water so you'll be able to take your bath as soon as he sleeps."

Unable to understand his vacillating moods, but hopeful he was experiencing the return of reason, Amanda retired immediately to the bed to nurse her child who was beginning to moan loudly. She watched as Robert heated two large kettles over the fire and made trip after trip to fill the large copper tub.

After what seemed an eternity, Jonathan, finally sated, fell off to sleep, his small face angelically content as she laid him in his cradle. Pouring the last of the kettles of hot water into the tub, Robert placed a small cake of scented soap nearby, explaining as he turned, "I'll wash up in the stream. The cabin is all yours until you're done."

No sooner had the door closed behind him than Amanda jumped from the bed. The sparkling water drew her like a magnet and almost beside herself with eagerness, she removed her clothes. Hastily pinning up her hair, she stepped into the tub. Releasing a deep sigh of contentment as the heavenly warmth caressed and soothed her aching muscles, Amanda lay for long minutes as the soft, pulsating heat eased the tenseness out of her exhausted body, and the stiffness of their four-day journey slowly slipped away.

After a while, Amanda took the soap and, rubbing it briskly, smoothed the lavender-scented bubbles over her body. The subtle fragrance wafted up into her nostrils, adding to her deepening feeling of unreality, and cupping her hands, Amanda lightly trailed the warm, scented water up her arms, and watched in an almost childlike fascination as the bubbles ran down her arms and into the tub.

A small sound from the doorway suddenly drew her attention, and turning, she saw the door, already partially open, swinging open even further.

"Robert, I haven't finished bathing yet," Amanda called in alarm, only to see the door continue opening until, to her embarrassment, she was in full view of Robert, who stood on the threshhold, a strangely intent expression on his face. He wore no shirt, having obviously just come from his bath in the stream, judging from the dampness of his heavy brown hair and freshly shaven face. His broad chest, lightly furred with dark brown hair, heaved heavily. He moved forward slowly, as if the small exertion taxed him sorely. Trying vainly to hide her nakedness, Amanda watched helplessly as Robert advanced to kneel beside the tub, staring as if fascinated by the vision before him.

Finally able to find her voice, Amanda protested, "Robert, you promised me privacy while I bathed."

Heedless of her words, Robert's eyes glowed with wonder as they traveled the full length of her body. Starting at her golden tumble of curls shimmering in the light of the fire, they moved slowly downward, resting a few moments on the angelic perfection of her face, descending to the slender column of her neck, the small shoulders that belied her sturdy

289

strength, the white globes of her breasts, now swollen with milk, but still firm and pointed in their enlarged state, the still-minute circle of her waist, the smooth flat stomach leading to the golden brown nest almost hidden from his view, and on to long, slender legs.

He whispered, his voice heavy with emotion, "I knew you would look like this: fragile, delicate, as perfect and lovely as a porcelain statue, your skin so white and flawless."

Glancing up to her face, he smiled softly and touched the light golden tendrils of hair that curled on her cheeks and forehead from the heat of the water. "You were wearing your hair this same way the first time I saw you, do you remember, Amanda?" He chuckled lightly at the memory. "You were washing one of my shirts in the laundry at the ranger camp, and scrubbing so hard at a spot you couldn't remove, your face all concentration and effort. How old were you? Fourteen? But I loved you then, from the first moment I saw you, and I knew from the first that I would never want any woman other than the one you would be in a few years. Your father knew how I felt, and asked me to wait until you were a little older, and I promised him I would try. I kept my promise, Amanda. I waited almost two years. You were almost sixteen that night in Fort William Henry. But I couldn't wait any longer. I was afraid I would lose you."

And then, as if his words brought to mind an unpleasant thought, Robert frowned. He continued, caressing her cheek gently as he spoke, "You loved me then, Amanda. Do you remember that night?" Robert's eyes implored her to relive the memory with him. "I held you in my arms and you gave yourself up to me. I could've taken you then; you know that, but I didn't. You loved me then, Amanda," he repeated softly.

"That was a long time ago, Robert." Amanda's voice was kind but firm as she continued. "So many things have happened since. I'm not the same inexperienced girl I once was. I'm a woman now. I've been married and borne a child."

"No!" Sudden, heated rage showed in his face as Robert exclaimed wildly, "You weren't married. You were taken by a low, filthy savage who has paid for his abuse of you."

Amanda was startled by his sudden violent outburst, but protested vehemently, "You're wrong, Robert."

Interrupting her as if she hadn't spoken, his voice was once again calm.

"But let's put that from our mind, Amanda, and look to our future."

"We don't have a future, Robert, not together. I don't love you. Too many things have passed between us. I can't forget what you did."

"Please, Amanda." Robert's voice was pleading as he spoke. "Tell me what I must do to make you love me again. Just tell me and I'll do it. Please."

As Robert spoke, his ardent face slipped from view to be replaced in her mind by a familiar, copper-hued image, black eyes gleaming, penetrating her thoughts and mind. The memory of him was still able to stir her emotions; she remembered his full lips parting in a smile to reveal teeth that flashed a sparkling white in contrast to the russet tone of his skin. She heard his deep rough voice whispering passionately, "You are the breath of my soul, Amanda, my very life. One cannot live without his soul."

The agony of Chingue's loss seared through her body once again as strongly as the first time, causing her to squeeze her eyes shut against the pain that tore at her chest, twisting until a deep, single sob escaped her throat, and tears cascaded down her cheeks. Robert's voice slowly penetrated her benumbed state, and, in response to his pleading she opened her eyes to see his handsome face humbled and broken, his brown eyes moist as he continued, "Please, Amanda, just tell me what it is I must do to regain your love, and I'll do it. I swear, you have only to tell me."

"You can't do anything, Robert." Her voice was cold and lifeless, and she moved to avoid his hands as he reached in despair for her slender shoulders.

"I'll do anything, anything." Robert implored, until Amanda answered at last, looking directly into his eyes.

"Can you bring Chingue back to life? It's only then that I'll be able to forgive you what you've done!"

Robert's eyes blinked as if he had suddenly been struck a blow in the face. His expression changed rapidly, hardening until all softness was again replaced with the glare of his irrational hatred.

"No, I can't bring him back to life, and wouldn't even if it was within my power. He took you, stole you from me just the day before you were to become my wife. He took your innocence." Robert's voice broke momentarily and he paused to draw a deep breath before continuing. "He defiled you, impregnated you with his child. I killed him and I would kill him again if he were standing before me. And I tell you this now, Amanda," Robert's voice became low and menacing. "If the need arises, I'll kill again to keep you. I've spent two years of my life loving, desiring, and waiting for you, and the greater part of another year living with the torture of knowing another man possessed you as I never had. It won't happen again! I'll never give you up!"

Amanda could bear no longer the burning hatred in his gaze or the thought of living her life as wife to the man who had killed her love. In desperation she rose from the water, her intention being to run from the passion of his fury, but she was suddenly stopped by the gasp that issued from Robert's throat as she was revealed in her full, glorious nakedness. Glancing hastily in his direction, Amanda was stunned with the look of undisguised wonder and yearning that transfused his formerly hate-ridden countenance as he looked up at her. Slowly rising to his feet, his body visibly trembling with passion, Robert whispered in a low, husky voice, "You're so beautiful, my darling, my Amanda. Now our time together has finally come."

Scooping her wet body up and pressing her against his bare chest, he strode to the bed and laid her down. Quickly divesting himself of his breeches and boots, he slipped into bed beside her, and pulled her naked body against his with a deep rapturous sigh.

The sudden touch of his flesh against hers broke the spell that had held her immobile for those long moments, and Amanda began to struggle wildly, crying out as she pushed, scratched, and beat at the man who sought to take her to him.

"No! Let me go! You're a murderer, a murderer, and I despise you!"

Her words seemed suddenly to enrage Robert as

her actions had not, and flipping himself over to lie atop her, he pinned her arms over her head with one hand, forcing her legs apart with the other as he growled venemously, "You'll be mine tonight, now, and then you'll know who is master here!" With a quick movement, he lowered his body and thrust savagely within her.

The sudden gasp of pain his enforced entry into her body caused was drowned out by Robert's deep groan of pleasure as he savored for a few short minutes the sweetness of her body enclosing around him. He continued his rapid, penetrating movements, increasing the fury of his movements even as she cried out in pain and struggled ineffectively beneath his imprisoning weight.

Chingue's face appeared once again before her and she cried out in remembrance and futile yearning for his endless patience and the gentleness of his passionate lovemaking, even as Robert's extended cry of climax sounded in her ear, and he collapsed atop her in exhaustion.

Nauseated and repelled by Robert's vile attack on her body, Amanda felt the acid taste of bile in her throat and, with a frantic, supreme effort, pushed his limp form from her and ran urgently to the corner where she bent over the basin and retched violently until her stomach was emptied.

Staggering slightly with weakness, she walked to the tub to rinse her perspiring face, only to hear Robert demand softly as she straightened up, "Come, Amanda. It's time you returned to bed now. I'm waiting."

Six

Oblivious to the warm August sun that beat down on his head through the leafy cover of trees, Robert sat, despondent in his voluntary exile, and ran his hand nervously through the shock of wavy brown hair that fell forward as he rested his elbows on his knees. He had to get away, to sit and puzzle out this whole miserable situation that only seemed to worsen by the day. Just a short time before, he had angrily grabbed his gun and stormed out of the cabin on the pretext of going hunting, making sure to take the horses with him to hide them in the usual place. He knew from experience Amanda would take the opportunity afforded her to attempt to escape. He snorted disgustedly. After a little over a month, he still did not feel safe in leaving them behind; but he knew she would never start out to escape on foot with the child.

The child! The living, breathing thorn in his side, festering and spreading the poison of jealousy throughout his system. A reminder to both Amanda and him of an experience he wanted to erase from her mind, and which she was unwilling to give up. Quite the contrary, she clung to that Indian's memory, silently using it, he was certain, to remove herself mentally from their more intimate moments together. Damn him to hell! How do you fight a dead man?

Robert could feel a familiar sense of desperation coming over him. Why couldn't she understand how much he loved her? It had been his right to destroy that animal when he had threatened to steal Amanda from him again. It was a mystery to him how that Abnaki had managed to get such a firm hold on her emotions. They were all filthy savages: barbaric, bloodthirsty, little more than animals. How could she suffer him to touch her, much less revere his memory? He could understand that no more than he could understand her pride in their red-skinned offspring. Her beautiful face, always expressionless and cold in his presence, glowed with love when her eyes touched on that obscene little bastard! Just the other day Robert had returned unnoticed by Amanda, who sat outside the cabin, her child at her breast. He had seethed with angry jealousy as he had watched Amanda's fragile features, alight with love as she gazed adoringly at the infant. She had been singing softly, and it soon became obvious the infant had had his fill, as his sleepy eyes closed and his little mouth released the nipple he had formerly held so tightly. Smiling softly to herself, Amanda had laid the child in her lap for a moment in order to button her dress, and then had picked him up to return him to his cradle inside the cabin.

Robert's eyes had followed her inside, feeling his hunger growing. He hungered insatiably for the love she would not give him, and in his desperation he had entered the cabin in a violent seizure of jealousy and had demanded what she would not give freely. The hatred reflected on her face as she turned to him had driven him to wild, obscene threats against the helpless infant, and had finally provided him a willing partner to his lovemaking. Afterwards, as she lay beside him, he had felt shame at his treatment of the guiltless, beautiful woman whose only crime was that of being loved too much. He had turned toward her and spoken in a defensive manner, as if to relieve himself of the blame for his behavior.

"Did you also drive your Indian lover to such fits of passion that he was forced to vent his anger on you?"

Amanda's voice had been soft as she had lain rigidly beside him.

"For Chingue's gentleness, endless patience, understanding, and love, I gave myself freely."

Robert had stiffened as her barb hit its mark. Slowly he had raised himself, his eyes looking down at Amanda growing wild with rage as he, with great deliberation, raised his hand and struck her a devastating blow to the face. Her surprised blue eyes had fluttered almost shut as she came close to losing consciousness from the blow, and a small trickle of blood made its way from the corner of her mouth across her cheek. Within a few moments the fogginess had cleared from her eyes, and she had whispered in that same soft voice, a faint, taunting smile on her face, "In all the time I lived with that 'savage,' he never struck me."

Amanda's flaunting of her Indian lover's conduct at that minute had seemed to push him over the edge of rational behavior, and blind with fury, he had struck her repeatedly until she lay unconscious, bruised and bleeding beside him. His arm had been raised to strike her still another blow when he had come to the realization of his actions. Suddenly frightened beyond belief, he had called her name frantically as he touched her bruised cheek.

"Amanda, please, darling, I'm sorry. Wake up, darling."

At her silence, panic quickly ensued, and he had jumped from the bed to get water and a basin and had begun to bathe her bruised face. Her one eye, puffy from his numerous blows, was already turning black; her cheeks were red and marked from his hand; and her lips, her soft, deliciously warm lips, were swollen and bleeding. He had bathed her face gently, waiting anxiously for the first spark of consciousness to return and had been so relieved when her eyelids began to flutter and then opened that he had found it difficult to control the sobs rising in his throat.

He had continued to bathe her face, whispering softly as he did, "Amanda, forgive me. Please, forgive me."

That night he had waited patiently, as he had done many times before, until Amanda had fallen asleep, making sure her breathing was deep and even, and then had gently pulled her into his arms. He had come to realize that it was only then, when she was unaware that she lay in his embrace, that she would relax against him, cuddle to his side as he held her. He was then free to kiss her lightly, whisper his love against her fragrant golden curls, and pretend for a short time she enjoyed his embrace. But that night he had whispered forlornly as he held her, "Amanda, my darling, I didn't want it to be this way between us."

Robert ran his hand nervously through his already rumpled hair. He had to concede at last that he was frightened, truly frightened. Amanda's silent, adamant refusal of his love seemed to awaken in him a latent brutality, a facet of his personality of which he had until now been totally unaware, and which caused him deep shame. But greater still than his shame was the fear he felt as he acknowledged to himself at last that each day, as frustration drove him past the bounds of restraint, he was less and less in control of his actions. He was frightened, cold with fear, at what he might do if things continued this way.

He remembered with painful clarity the night not long before when he had held Amanda tenderly in his arms. She had almost seemed to respond to his passions, and he had let his hopes soar, firmly refusing to believe that fear for her child's safety might cause her to feign a response. Deluding himself that she was beginning to return his love, he had unthinkingly begun to speak of his plans.

"When we leave here, Amanda, you'll choose the area where we'll settle. We'll go anywhere you desire. You'll have as many neighbors as you wish to visit with."

"When do you intend to leave here, Robert?" Amanda's question was hesitant; a faintly hopeful note was in her voice. Robert had answered honestly with the plan he had cherished in his mind from the first.

"It won't be long before you carry my child,

Amanda." Ignoring her sudden intake of breath, he continued, "When you're near your time, we'll go to the nearest settlement, where we'll be married; for surely then you'll no longer entertain any wild notions of escape in your advanced state of pregnancy. We'll remain until you bear my son, and will proceed when you are able to travel again to seek our new home."

The beautiful picture Robert had painted in his mind of their domestic bliss was shattered by Amanda's outraged voice as she exclaimed, "God could not be that cruel. He could not allow a child born of your lust to grow inside me!" Slowly her voice had gained in volume as her hysteria mounted, "No, I will not bear your child. I will not! I don't want the child of my husband's murderer to grow inside me!"

Frantically, she attempted to jump from the bed, only to have his iron grip close on her arm and drag her back toward him. Robert had been white with fury as he faced her, looking into her eyes as he forced her back upon the bed.

"But you will bear my child, Amanda, and once you hold him in your arms you'll love him, and through him, me. We'll have a bond that ties us together forever, and you'll never leave me."

But just this morning, the first victory had gone to Amanda. She had won temporarily. She had announced with a mirthless smile that her monthly flow had just begun.

Amanda sat wearily at the table, her head resting on the hand that covered her eyes, shutting out for a brief moment grim, stark reality. Thank the Lord he had gone out, for her brave facade was fast wearing thin, and was indeed cracked in so many places that it threatened to give way at any moment and expose to Robert the full depth of her fear. And once he realized the weakness that lay behind her affected pose, Robert would exploit it to his best advantage, she was sure. Hatred, prejudice, and jealousy had combined to create a monster of the man who for years had been an accepted member of her family. The Robert who lived and slept with her was a virtual stranger who inspired only ambivalance and terror in her heart. But the panic she felt most deeply was not for herself. Slowly Amanda tilted her head to view the child who lay contented, though unsleeping, in his cradle, his dark eyes curiously scanning the area around him.

He is so pure and innocent. How can Robert despise him so?

Amanda's eyes filled with tears as sorrow took greater hold on her senses. She knew instinctively that Robert was fast crossing the boundary of rational behavior, as well as she knew that his lapses of control, during which he beat her so unmercifully, shocked him as well as they did her. Her secret, innermost dread now was that he would turn his rage on Jonathan, and to this fear she had become subservient, to the extent that she had prostituted herself, feigning a response she did not feel to Robert's lovemaking. Amanda felt her stomach revolt as her mind jumped back for a moment to the occasions she had sold herself to Robert, giving him pleasure in her simulated passion to gain a few moments more security for her child. She felt old, dirty, used, and for the first time in her life, knew what it meant to be defiled.

For a few unguarded moments, Adam slipped into her mind, twisting further the knife of pain in her chest. Why was it the fates conspired so effectually against her, first taking Chingue from her forever, and then removing from her life the only consolation and protection left to her? Over a month had passed since Adam had left for the site of Fort William Henry. The result of the assault on Fort Carillon as well as Adam's fate were unknown to her. Determinedly she again forced them from her mind. She now had a more immediate problem to face: that of the safety of her child.

To this purpose Amanda devoted every waking moment of her day from that point on. Robert's failure in their first month together to impregnate her with his child only served to make him more determined to succeed. Had Amanda not been so concerned with her son's safety, Robert's pitiful, desperate attempts to win her love might have had a greater effect on her emotions; but she needed only see the look of distaste on his face each time the child was put to her breast, and his intolerance and impatience with the pleasant infant's smallest whimper, to nourish her hatred and be reminded of the danger that lay behind the loving looks directed at her from those soulful brown eyes.

In the desperate days that followed, despite her attempts to placate Robert and endure his constant, passionate attentions with a semblance of loving response, occasionally her mask slipped and her true repugnance showed through. Robert responded with ever increasing violence, and after his rage had been vented on her small, defenseless body, he was always truly horrified at his actions, stricken with extreme remorse, which then resulted in a few days of the most tender treatment, until his endless lust for her grew beyond his control.

At the end of the second month, Amanda's monthly flow once again began. This time she did not react with the elation which the first had inspired. True, she no more wanted Robert's child now than she had before, but deep apprehension of Robert's reaction to his second defeat overshadowed her joy.

That night, putting off her declaration as long as was feasible, Amanda prepared supper, working to create a special meal with the meager stores remaining to them. She had tried a little harder than usual a pleasant atmosphere as a prelude to the declaration which was of necessity soon to come as the night drew on. After Jonathan had been retired for the night, and Amanda could see by the increasing heat of Robert's glances that they were soon to do the same, she managed to say in a voice she hoped carried a casual note as she averted her face from his.

"My monthly flow has begun this evening, Robert."

Amanda's statement was met with a quiet so intense that even the fire in the hearth seemed to stop crackling for a few moments. Finally, Amanda raised her eyes to Robert, who still stood frozen in the action of raising his pipe to his mouth. Slowly, before her eyes, his face began to crumple into a picture of despair, and throwing down the pipe, he quickly closed the few steps between them to crush her in his arms.

"That makes you happy, doesn't it, Amanda?" His voice was muffled against her hair as he held her tightly. "I've pretended to myself your response to me within this past month was genuine, not inspired by fear, but I know it isn't true." He pulled her closer still, forcing her to take short, shallow breaths as he whispered, his body trembling, his voice broken from emotion, "You've won again, but I'll win next month, or the next. We won't leave this place until my child is growing inside you, and I'm assured of my possession of you."

Releasing her in a quick movement, Robert bent to scoop up her petite form and carry her to the bed. Putting her down gently, he began to undress her with trembling hands, pausing, as her breasts were bared to view, to press warm, tender kisses on their rounded, white surface. As he continued to undress her, Amanda gasped, "Robert, you know you can't enter. My monthly flow."

Still Robert did not desist in his attentions until she lay naked except for her small underdrawers. Quickly divesting himself of his clothing, he slid into bed beside her, pulling her full length against him as he did. Amanda could feel the swell of his passion, which was not affected by her body cycle, and felt a deep relief when he whispered in a shaky voice, "No, I won't enter, Amanda. I only want to hold you next to me, to know I really possess you." There was a moment's hesitation before Robert spoke again, softly, "I love you so, Amanda. You'll learn to love me. You will."

Fall was fast approaching, quietly heralded by the brightening foliage around the cabin where Amanda and her son remained confined more effectively by the dense, colorful woods than by iron bars. True to his word, Robert began to prepare for winter in silent determination: smoking meats, drying berries, gathering nuts, not depending on Amanda's cooperation to effect preparation for a stay to which she was opposed. The passage of time, contrary to Amanda's expectations, had not lessened Robert's adoration for her. His desire was insatiable and his possessiveness had become stifling in its intensity. He never seemed to tire of watching her, caressing her, and touching her intimately. A direct challenge flashed in his eyes each time she pulled away from his hands, and he would increase his intimate caresses, daring her to dispute his mastery over her. Finally, weary of the battle, she allowed even his most intimate touch, unflinching as she continued her work, pointedly ignoring the look of victory that shone from his eyes.

From the outside appearance, Amanda had changed little since her enforced confinement with Robert, except for a dullness in her eyes that bespoke the change within. But spiritually she felt drained, the only spark remaining that of the love for her child. She no longer felt free to think of Chingue, as she no longer felt worthy of the beautiful, almost sacred emotion that had existed between them. She no longer entertained even the slightest hope of gaining her freedom. How much longer could she be lucky enough to escape pregnancy from Robert's constant attentions? He had not yet won, but would, eventually. It was inevitable. She was defeated, lost, defiled, without hope, and past despair—the beautiful, empty shell of the warm, loving person she had been.

Fall's glory was on the wane as the bright, glorious days of October began to shorten and turn cooler. With the end of October also came proof that Amanda had still not conceived Robert's child. Robert had accepted his defeat with a grim determination that bespoke what was to come in the long winter nights ahead, and realizing this, Amanda steeled her mind against all thoughts but those of her son. Jonathan, her bright, robust, dark-eyed son—the only true light in a life that had turned dark with shame.

Quickly picking up Jonathan's newly washed linens, Amanda walked outside, eager to take advantage of the bright, midday sun that would dry her laundry quickly. Robert had gone hunting early in the morning. The slow dread that slipped over her at the thought of those long winter nights threatened to put a damper on her precious moments of freedom from his presence, and determinedly, Amanda chased all dour thoughts from her mind as she proceeded to hang her laundry, reveling in the warmth of the autumn sun against her skin.

How bitterly this autumn contrasted with the last. For a few brief moments Amanda allowed herself to lapse into memory of last October, with its beauty of love discovered and explored, appreciated and indulged. Chingue! Even now, when Amanda had been sure all feeling inside her had been destroyed, she could still feel the pain of his loss. She closed her eyes briefly against the overwhelming picture of black eyes sparkling from a masculine, russet-toned face, the broad, tender smile reserved for her alone. Unable to bear the torture of memory a moment longer, Amanda forcibly emptied her mind of all thought except the chore before her.

So absorbed was she in her task, that she failed to hear the movement in the bushes behind her, until a deep, soft voice called hesitantly, "Amanda?"

Amanda stood rigid with shock, as her startled mind identified the voice that came from behind. Gradually, she turned, until her azure gaze locked with a familiar, level, green-eyed stare. A bright flush of warmth suffused her face, only to drain away as quickly as it had come, leaving her weak and shaken, visibly swaying, giving Adam the excuse he awaited to rush forward and take her into his arms. As his strong, muscular arms held her close, Adam closed his eyes to savor the moment he had dreamed of for three torturous months. Amanda, my darling, my love! his mind silently cried, as his mouth spoke consolingly to the small shaken girl in his embrace. It seemed to Adam that every effort he had expended in the past three months had been toward this very moment.

He remembered unclearly his awakening in the makeshift colonial hospital, with a pain in his chest so severe that he had been unable to speak. He had not found it necessary to inquire as to the outcome of the battle, for it had been all too apparent on the faces around him that they had paid a bloody price for defeat. His eyes searched the room hopefully, seeking that one important face, but then he chided himself for thinking Amanda would be free to attend the wounded sixteen miles from Fort Edward when her son needed her. But his desire to see her was not lessened by the practicality of her absence. Finally spotting a familiar face, he called to Dr. Cartwright, who was moving between the rows of wounded and dying that crammed the crudely constructed building.

"Dr. Cartwright!" Adam's hoarse voice snapped the heavily jowled face of the doctor from his patient to look in his direction. With a small smile, he walked toward Adam, hand extended in greeting.

"Adam, my friend. I'm glad to see you so greatly improved."

Too anxious for formalities, Adam took his hand, asking as he did, "What of Amanda, Doctor? Is she well? Does she know of my wound? I wouldn't want her to be caused any senseless worry."

The jovial doctor's countenance fell for a moment, and Adam's heart began to race in apprehension as he noticed the doctor's obvious reluctance to speak.

"What is it, Doctor? Is something wrong?"

Adam's chest was heaving, his breath becoming painful and uneven as his tension mounted. Realizing the toll his silence was taking on Adam's meager reserve of strength, Dr. Cartwright spoke evenly, "No, Amanda isn't aware of your condition. Before the battle was over, she had already disappeared from Fort Edward with Robert Handley!"

Adam was unbelieving, and certain his wound had made him fevered as he whispered, "You're saying she left with Robert Handley freely, of her own choosing? That I can't believe! You know as well as I do that she despised him!"

"Nevertheless, Adam, the guard at the gate stated he saw them leave. She held her child as she rode, free and unbound. She was obviously not coerced, and accompanied him freely."

"I can't believe—" Adam gasped, but was unable to complete his sentence as the deeply shattering pain returned to pierce his chest, stealing his breath as he struggled to speak.

"You must relax now, Adam, and not excite yourself." Dr. Cartwright's voice was stern and disapproving. Noting Adam's labored attempts to catch his breath so that he might respond, he continued solemnly, "I won't discuss this matter with you any further, Adam. You now know everything I know regarding Amanda's departure from Fort Edward. No one spoke with her before she left or has seen either of them since. If you disagree with the general consensus of opinion that she left because the pressure of resentment against her and her child became too great to bear, then you must seek your own answer." Lowering his head to look directly into Adam's agonized gaze, he continued a bit more kindly, "If you would seek them out, you must first regain your health and strength, and I'd recommend strongly that you expend all your energy in that direction for the present, if you want to be well enough before the trail is too cold."

Realizing the wisdom of Dr. Cartwright's advice at that time, Adam had not been able to do more than nod his agreement and bide his time.

After his convalescence, months of endless searching had led him here. But the moment his eyes had touched on Amanda, her silver-blond hair lifting gently in the autumn breeze as she worked, unaware of his presence outside the cabin, he had known the long arduous search, fraught with dead ends and disappointments, had been worthwhile. But as he held her, he sensed instinctively something was amiss. Her expression was that of shock, an emotion he could well understand, but she appeared to be clearly devoid of joy!

A sudden angry voice behind Adam interrupted his thoughts.

"Being an old friend doesn't entitle you to hold my wife in that manner, Adam!"

"Your wife!" Adam's voice was incredulous as he stepped back awkwardly to look down into Amanda's white face.

A look of venemous hatred shone from Amanda's wide blue eyes as she spat out her refute. "I am not his wife!"

Robert's tone spoke volumes as he declared insidiously, "You're my wife in all ways except in the eyes of the law, and that, too, will be arranged before too many months have passed."

Adam felt a strong sinking sensation at the manner in which Amanda dropped her gaze, appearing to confirm Robert's statement.

"Is that your horse tied up beside mine in the woods, Adam?" Robert inquired, and at Adam's nod he walked forward and slid his arm around Amanda's waist in a possessive gesture. "He'll be safe there for the time being. Come inside. Amanda and I'll show you our little home."

Adam followed behind, stunned into silence at this unexpected turn of events, when a small sound from within the cabin took his notice. Amanda broke away from Robert to run forward and scoop a small bundle from a crude cradle in the corner. Her face as she turned toward Adam held the first trace of the Amanda of old as she walked proudly toward him.

"Look, Adam, how Jonathan has grown since you last saw him!"

Adam reluctantly tore his gaze from Amanda's shining face to look at the child she cradled in her arms.

"Is it possible," he exclaimed as he looked unbelievingly at the child Amanda held so proudly for his inspection, "that he could have grown so in such a short time?" Adam was truly astonished, for the thin, red, squirming infant of three months before had turned into a bright-eyed, appealing child, who looked at him speculatively with his shining black eyes. He reached forward to take the child as he spoke, marveling inwardly at the intelligence shining from his small face. "How truly his appearance bespeaks his father, doesn't it, Amanda?" Adam was unaware of the veil of contempt that covered Robert's face as he, too, looked at the child and nodded in silent agreement.

As Adam spoke, Jonathan's face broke into a wide, appealing grin, eliciting a responsive smile in return. "And his mother," he said softly, the familiar smile warming him deeply. Instinctively, Adam lowered his face and kissed the soft copper-hued skin, amazed at the pleasure he derived from holding

Amanda's child again in his arms. "He's a beautiful boy, Amanda," he said solemnly, returning the gurgling child to his mother, whose smile was genuinely warm, and whose eyes were bright with tears.

For a few moments Adam had almost forgotten Robert's presence, until his voice broke harshly into the tender moment. "You're welcome to stay for supper, Adam, and the night if you wish. You can make up a pallet by the fire. The only bed here is the one Amanda and I share."

Robert's reference to their common bed was an obvious attempt to flaunt his intimacy with Amanda. Blushing profusely, she returned Jonathan to his cradle.

Waiting to see the progress of events before committing himself, Adam nodded silently. The remainder of the day was spent in an agony of frustration as Robert painted a painstaking picture of domestic bliss for Adam, and Adam, in return, awaited vainly an opportunity to speak to Amanda privately. With every statement and possessive caress from Robert, who seemed to gain more confidence hourly from the awkward situation, Amanda seemed to retreat further inside herself. She would no longer even glance in Adam's direction, and by the arrival of suppertime, he could barely elicit a response from her white lips. At the conclusion of supper, Amanda arose to gather the dishes, aware that Robert eyed her openly with desire. Flushing under the heat of his gaze, Amanda continued her work without comment and, at its conclusion, took Jonathan from his bed to retire to the corner where she put him to her breast.

Adam's gaze drifted longingly toward Amanda as she sat, her face bright with love as she caressed her hungry child's shining black hair. Robert's annoyed tone caught his attention in time to hear him say firmly, "I'm sorry we can't offer you our hospitality any longer than one night, Adam, but you can well see our cabin is small and won't accommodate a much longer stay." Adam made no response to the obvious statement, and Robert rose, stretching widely. Turning to Amanda, his tone was sharp as he spoke. "The child should be sated by now. Come, it's time for us to retire."

Amanda shot Adam a pained look, but hastened to do Robert's bidding, and when Robert and Adam returned from their short excursion outside, Adam's pallet was made up in front of the fireplace. Amanda stood in her nightdress, unaware of the enticing picture she presented, her hair sparkling in the light of the fire, which outlined her slender figure through the light fabric of her gown. Robert's scrutiny of Amanda was intense and heated, and realizing instinctively it was not feigned, she stepped backward involuntarily as he approached. His manner was increasingly embarrassing in its intimacy as he slid his arm around her back and under her arm, his hand resting against the side of her breast, where he caressed her slowly. "Goodnight, Adam," he said knowingly, "Sleep well."

Wordlessly, Adam turned to his pallet. Robert waited until Amanda had slipped into the bed and then, quickly undressing, slid in beside her. He pulled her from the far edge of the bed where she had moved to escape him, and held her roughly in

313

his grasp.

"Robert!" Amanda's whisper held a horrified note. "You would not!"

"No, I'll restrain myself tonight, Amanda." Robert's voice was deep with suppressed passion. "We'll have many more nights together, you and I, during which we'll make up for this one a hundredfold." Then, pulling her even tighter within the circle of his arms, he closed his eyes to sleep.

Morning was long in coming to the unsleeping Amanda. Adam's arrival, had it come a few months sooner, would have been the answer to her fervent prayers. But she had long since stopped praying. It was too late. Robert had done his work well and had managed with his relentlessness to stifle her will to defy him. He had used her too often and too well. Lovingly, brutally, sadistically, in whatever manner his mood demanded, until he had turned the act of love, which she had only known to be a beautiful intimacy, into a demeaning, vile, animalistic experience that left her feeling defiled past redemption. She felt no longer worthy of Adam's concern and could not ask him to risk his life to remove her from Robert's oppression. In essence she knew it would come to that, for Robert would never voluntarily release her.

So, Adam had been wounded. How her heart ached for the long, painful days of recuperation that he had spent without her attentions, for surely she owed him that much and more. How many times had he saved her life? Amanda had a sudden reckless urge to laugh hysterically. Saved her life for what? For this travesty of love and the existence in which she was now trapped? For all she knew, Robert's seed had already taken hold inside her, for he had not missed a day in his attentions since the conclusion of her last flow. His hunger for her was insatiable, his possession of her a fact he impressed upon her with his persistent demands on her body. No, it was too late for her, too late. Where could she go now? Who would take her in? An Indian's squaw? A white man's whore?

At the first light of dawn, Amanda stirred, eager to be up and away from Robert's clinging embrace, which he had not relinquished even in sleep. Raising her head slightly, she glanced toward the fire, and the pallet on which Adam slept. Surprisingly, her glance was met and held by warm green eyes trained on her, silently begging an explanation. They seemed to bore through her and she felt almost compelled by their intensity to jump up, run to him, and beg his consolation. How she longed for the sanctuary of his embrace; she ached.

Suddenly, as if warned by a sixth sense of impending danger, Robert opened his eyes in time to see the look of longing displayed so openly on Amanda's face, and reaching up, he roughly pulled her down beside him and covered her mouth with his in a deep, devouring kiss. Her eyes widened frantically, and she shook her head to deny that which she feared would follow, as tears coursed down her cheeks and she moaned softly. Amanda knew she need utter just one word of protest and Adam would jump to her defense. Then the inevitable confrontation would result. No, she could not risk Adam's life. She wasn't worth the risk. As Robert lifted his mouth from hers a thunderous look in his eyes, his breathing deep and rigid, she whispered softly, "Please, Robert, don't. I won't say anything." And then she closed her eyes against the dawning of his bright, victorious smile.

The morning, with its necessary, endless tasks, seemed to fly by, and before Amanda was prepared, Adam stood ready to depart. Amanda packed some provisions and a freshly baked loaf of bread for his journey, and he stood listening as Robert said his good-byes, making certain as civilly as possible that Adam would consider them final.

Amanda's eyes were free to wander over Adam's person as his attention was held so completely by Robert, and a small smile teased the corners of her mouth. He had changed little since the first time she had seen him that day in the forest. His hair was a little longer, but still wavy and streaked by the sun; his skin was tanned, but with a slight darkness beneath his bright green eyes that attested to his recent wound. But the handsome face, formerly so often covered by the wide, contagious grin that had the power to warm her heart so easily, was now creased in a frown. Taking her mind from that disturbing thought, she slowly slid her eyes across the incredible width of his shoulders, the breadth of his muscled chest, the small waist and powerful muscular thighs. His impressive figure in his buckskin garments bespoke strength and power, and completely belied the extreme gentleness of which the appealing woodsman was capable.

Suddenly the arm around her shoulders tightened and the hand squeezed her arm unmercifully as

Robert attempted to elicit a response. "I told Adam we would probably not be seeing him again, because we intend to move from here soon, be married, and start afresh where we're unknown."

Amanda could feel her face drain of color as she repeated, realizing for the first time, "Not see him again. . . ."

Within moments it was happening. Adam was leaving as Robert maintained a firm grip on her shoulder. The last sad look of desperate appeal from those direct green eyes seemed to burn into her soul. He turned and moved quietly away and Amanda's breathing began to quicken until the pounding of her heart turned to thunder in her ears. His tall, brawny figure had all but disappeared in the remaining foliage as he walked to the area where his horse was secreted, when suddenly an involuntary cry tore from her lips as she wrenched herself from Robert's grasp.

"Adam, please, don't leave me here with him. Adam, take me with you, please."

Amanda started to run forward, only to be jerked violently backward as Robert's fist crashed against her cheek and blinding pain knocked her to the ground. Sobbing wildly, her vision slightly blurred from the force of Robert's brutal blow, Amanda struggled to get to her feet, still calling wildly, "Adam, Adam, wait, please."

Robert gripped her arm, his face contorted with rage and knocked her down once again. As she attempted to rise the second time, Robert loomed over her and drew his knife from the sheath at his waist. His eyes were wild as he raised it and whispered viciously, "I told you I'd never let you go, Amanda."

The bright midday sun glinted blindingly on the blade as the knife descended with a powerful thrust toward her chest, and Amanda closed her eyes as the thought flashed through her mind, it's over, at last.

But the sharp crack of fist against bone snapped Amanda's eyes open in time to see Robert flung backwards, sprawling in the dirt, as the knife seemed to fly from his hand to a spot some distance away. Incensed to the point of madness, Robert sprang forward to grasp Adam by the throat, squeezing and maintaining his maniacal hold as Adam struggled to free himself, growing whiter and weaker by the second. With one supreme effort, Adam broke Robert's tenacious grip, and in the next second followed up with a bone-splitting blow to the jaw that again sent Robert sprawling, but this time into unconsciousness.

Within moments Amanda was on her feet and within Adam's arms, trembling, her face pressed to his familiar chest, her arms around his waist, holding him as tightly as Adam's arms held her. Suddenly Amanda felt Adam push her roughly away and jerk her hastily behind him, and she turned to see Robert rising to his feet. But as Robert began to speak, his voice pained and broken with emotion, she could feel the tension draining from Adam's body. "Take her with you, Adam. She never wanted to come with me. I forced her, held her child's safety over her head. I told her I'd kill him if she didn't come with me, and I would've, too. She knew it. I forced her to let me make love to her." Adam's hands balled

318

into fists again, but Robert continued, "But she never loved me back, never. She only loved that filthy, red-skinned savage, never me."

Unexpectedly, Robert's face crumpled and tears rolled helplessly down his cheeks as he sobbed uncontrollably, "But I never meant to kill her, never. Amanda," he appealed, begging her understanding, "you know that, darling. I never meant to kill you." Then, shaking his head in a bemused fashion, he said softly, "But I would have. Take her with you, Adam. I'm not responsible anymore. I can't be trusted. If she stays, I'll eventually kill her, and then myself."

Turning away, Robert walked slowly into the woods, as Adam gestured for Amanda to gather her belongings. Frantically, Amanda ran back into the cabin and began throwing clothes and Jonathan's clean linens into a bundle. Hastily she wrapped more food for the journey and, as Adam entered, thrust them into his waiting hands and ran to take Jonathan from his cradle. As they quickly made their way across the yard, Robert's voice halted them once more as he emerged from the woods to the side of them. Amanda turned to see his eyes red from weeping as he spoke softly to her.

"Amanda, forgive me, please. I beg you, please. It was all a mistake, a nightmare. Just remember I love you."

Robert had stopped speaking, but his brown eyes wet with tears looked imploringly into hers. Unable to respond past the lump in her throat, Amanda, gripping Jonathan a little more tightly, turned to follow Adam into the woods.

The pace was slow through the densely wooded

landscape, and torturous to Amanda, who was beginning to feel the full impact of Robert's brutal attack. Lulled by the steady monotonous sway of the horse, Jonathan had fallen asleep almost immediately, and her arms were numb from his weight. Her jaw, bruised and swollen from Robert's vicious blows, throbbed unceasingly; the pain was compounded by her pounding head and the stiffness on her right side where she had fallen during Robert's attack. Still she said nothing as she followed silently behind Adam. She dared not complain, for she was getting her most fervent wish: escape from Robert.

Again and again Amanda's vision blurred as fatigue took greater hold, and so groggy had she become that she was unaware of Adam's constant worried glances in her direction. Suddenly, Amanda realized that the swaying motion had stopped, and looking down she saw Adam beside her as his strong arms reached up to lift her from her saddle. He attempted to put her on her feet, but Amanda surprisingly found her legs unable to support her. Swinging her lightly back up into his arms, Adam carried them to the side of a small stream, where he lay them down gently. Adam took the sleeping child from Amanda's stiff embrace, and lay him beside her, and then turned to briskly rub her aching arms for a few minutes, eliciting a soft moan as the circulation slowly returned to her tortured limbs. Adam then moved away, to return a few moments later with a cloth which he dipped into the icy cold water of the brook, and began to bathe her face.

Amanda smiled faintly as the water touched her perspiring skin, but winced as Adam attempted to cleanse the bruise on her jaw.

"My battered angel," Adam declared with a soft smile as he dipped the cloth once again into the water and held it against the swelling. "Hold this, Amanda." Taking her hand he positioned it to hold the cloth as he would a child's.

He returned a few minutes later with two blankets. He folded one as a pillow, and with the other he covered Amanda as he gently pressed her against the pillow's softness. "Your son is still sleeping. Take advantage of this time to rest. You've had an exhausting day, and you'll need all your strength to take care of this little man when he awakens," he said, indicating the ruddy little cherub lying next to her.

Amanda protested, attempting to rise. "I must help you ready the food."

Pressing her firmly backwards, Adam would accept no argument. "Sleep now. Sleep heals."

Adam watched intently as Amanda's delicate features relaxed, and she drifted off to sleep. Her bruised lips, parted slightly, beckoned with an almost irresistible appeal, and his throat tightened as the tenderness she aroused in him became almost overwhelming. Oh, Amanda, his mind cried, how many times have I failed you?

Adam was almost overcome with regret at the heartbreak and degradation she had been made to suffer in the last months, and he shook his head, bemused by his own stupidity. He reviewed in his mind what he felt was his complete bungling of their lives. A kind fate had seen fit to thrust Amanda into his arms at the most crucial moments in her life, and although from the first he had desired her, he had managed at each opportunity to allow Amanda to slip through his fingers. But Chingue had been no such fool! He had seen Amanda, recognized her worth, and against impossible odds, stolen her away. Adam knew instinctively that Chingue had not been the ignorant savage Robert had claimed him to be, for he had taken Amanda's innocence and used it well, easing her into maturity in a way that had earned her respect and love. Adam closed his eyes momentarily against the pain as he imagined the Indian's loving ministrations to Amanda's virgin body. He burned with jealousy that he had not been the man to indoctrinate her soft, fragile loveliness into the rites of love, and he blamed only himself. Chingue had been more the man than he in knowing and admitting his desire and taking positive steps to fulfill it. Adam knew full well that now, no matter how great his efforts, no matter how deep his love, to Amanda he would always be second best to Chingue's memory, and the knowledge was a bitter pill indeed.

But he had been a fool not once, but twice! No matter the pressure of the situation, he should have recognized Robert as a potential danger after the birth of Amanda's child. He should never have left her alone, and for his stupidity Amanda had paid most dearly.

"But I won't fail you again, Amanda," he whispered softly as he touched the tips of his fingers to the golden curls that lay across her makeshift pillow. "Not again."

*   *   *

Amanda awoke to see the sun slipping from the horizon, and to a strange sense of peace. She realized immediately where she was and knew from her aching breasts that it was Jonathan's suppertime. She glanced back to where her child had lain when she had fallen asleep, but he was gone! Wild panic set Amanda's pulse to racing, and she started to rise. Her throat was choked with fright, until her hysterical glance touched on the broad figure near the fire, who held her child so carefully on his lap as he amused and tickled him with a brightly colored leaf. Fat, sturdy little arms waved wildly at the twirling leaf, and an excited gurgling could be heard above the crackling of the fire. Adam's face as he looked down on her son was a mixture of pain and delight, and Amanda felt the full weight of sorrow once more, knowing Chingue would never know the pleasure of holding his son. But now was not a time to look back, and taking a deep breath, Amanda rose to walk toward the fire, a sincere smile on her face as she met Adam's embarrassed countenance.

"Your son is easily amused, Amanda," Adam stated self-consciously. "Did you hear how he laughs at a brightly colored leaf?"

"Perhaps it isn't the leaf he finds so amusing, but the face of the person who holds it!"

Laughing lightly as Adam shot her a wry glance, she took her son from his lap and smiled into the little face that was growing more perplexed as hunger pressed its urgent demands. He began to whimper. Turning her back to Adam, Amanda sat and began to unbutton the front of her dress as Jonathan squirmed on her lap, his hungry cries growing louder. Amanda admonished him teasingly, *"Sehe! Quatsch luppackhan, Pilawetit?"*[1] And then as his hungry mouth found her breast and he began to suck noisily, she whispered softly, *"Schiki a na Lenno. E gohan."*[2]

After staring solemnly for some moments at her nursing child, she addressed Adam quietly, "He responds well to his father's tongue, doesn't he, Adam?"

Feeling a vague premonition, Adam was unwilling to give an affirmative response. "I think, rather than the words, it's his mother's voice he responds to so quickly."

Adam's answer was met with silence, and he rose to use the time the child fed to prepare their food.

With the setting of the sun, the October air took on a sharp chill, piercing the cotton garments Amanda wore as if they were paper. Her slender shoulders began to quiver noticeably and Adam rose to drape a blanket around her shoulders. Giving him a quick, thankful smile, Amanda's eyes did not linger long enough on his face to see the loving tenderness in his gaze.

Within a short time, Jonathan's lids grew heavy and began to droop, as his mouth reluctantly relinquished the nipple in favor of sleep. Quickly changing his linen, Amanda wrapped her contented child in the blanket and lay him to sleep a short distance from the fire which crackled invitingly. When she again sat, Adam gave her the meat he had warmed by the fire and freshly brewed tea, spiced

1. Meaning, "Hush, why do you cry, baby boy?"
2. Meaning, "That is a fine, pretty boy. Yes, indeed."

medicinally with rum, "To soften the aches of a tiring journey," he advised solemnly, and sliced the bread Amanda had baked that morning.

Before too long, Amanda, like her son, found her lids growing heavy and a warm languor stole over her. "Oh, Adam, she said softly, "I'm afraid you're going to spoil me. Then what will I do when you leave and I must fend for myself again?"

Amanda's voice was soft and teasing, but Adam was startled by the inference that they would be parting at some point soon. Realizing that this was neither the time nor the place to get into a serious discussion, he imitated her teasing manner, "Well then, I suppose I'll have to stay around indefinitely."

Amanda shot him a quick, unreadable look and then rose. "I think I'll go down the stream a little further and refresh myself before I turn in, Adam. Will you watch Jonathan for a few minutes?" At Adam's affirmative nod, Amanda moved away, to return a short time later looking freshly washed, her hair combed and glimmering like moonlight in the dark forest. Adam had cleared the remains of their meal and banked the fire for the night, now he sat awaiting her return.

Glancing around, Amanda inquired, "Where will you sleep, Adam?"

"Here, where I sit," was his answer.

"But where is your blanket?" Amanda's eyes searched the area for a sign of his bedding.

Smiling wryly, he answered, "Once again we're without the required number of blankets, Amanda."

It was then Amanda realized that Adam's blankets were in use, one wrapped around Jonathan, and the other around herself, and she laughed as her question was answered. "Well, I suppose we must then share our blankets once again."

Unwrapping herself, she hastily lay down beside her son, and covered herself again and holding up the corner invitingly, she urged, "Hurry, Adam, I'm cold."

With his heart pounding so loudly that he was certain Amanda could hear it, Adam moved quickly beneath the cover, taking her in his arms so that they might wrap the blanket around them more securely. The touch of her body against his seemed to sear his skin, and his arms tightened involuntarily. How long had he waited to hold her again? On the pretext of tucking the blanket more closely around them, Adam pulled her even closer, until her head rested on his chest and she was full length against him. But this time, unlike their first days together in the forest, Amanda was not ignorant of the demands of a man's body, and she felt herself stiffen in his arms.

She began to tremble as Adam's proximity brought back to mind too vividly the many nights she had endured Robert's caresses, the feeling of his mouth against her breasts, his often savage plundering of her body, while all the time her flesh crawled with horror. Suddenly she was sobbing wildly, with all the pent-up sorrow and anguish of the past months, for the demise of her innocence and trust.

Reading immediately the reason for her panic, Adam continued to hold her gently as he reassured her quietly, "You know you never need fear me, Amanda. Do you think me such an animal that I would force myself on you?" Lifting her chin with

326

his finger, he forced her to look into his face. For a moment he was struck breathless by the strength of her sweet appeal. The wide blue eyes lifted to his were brilliant with apprehension, and fresh tears clung to the long dark lashes that framed them so evenly. The smooth skin of her cheek was damp as he tenderly caressed it.

"Don't fear me, Amanda. I've always had your trust and will do nothing to prove myself unworthy of it. Close your eyes. You must sleep, for we rise with the sun to begin our journey back to Fort Edward."

Adam saw a slight flicker in her countenance at the mention of Fort Edward and was not too surprised. She had suffered dearly at the self-righteous snubs of the "good people" of the fort, but he knew he could depend completely on Betty Mitchell for her support until Amanda was free of her memories and ready to love again. And this time, no other man would come between them!

Dutifully, Amanda followed Adam's suggestions and closed her eyes, but Adam was well aware that she did not sleep for many hours.

Adam woke sharply with the chirping of the first birds of the morning. Night had not completely left the sky, but Adam had no eyes for the heavens. To Adam, heaven was in his arms, sleeping against his chest, hair askew, soft, pink lips inviting him to taste the sweetness within. Adam felt his body swell with desire, and was inordinately glad that Amanda still slept, for although he could control his actions, his body responded to his innermost desires, and those were, at this time, too painfully obvious. Patience, he cautioned himself. He didn't want to suffer Robert's fate, for he knew the poor, love-crazed man had managed to kill every last shred of feeling Amanda had ever felt for him, and to her, Robert was more dead than Chingue would ever be. Only distaste and fear lingered on. And they were a great obstacle in his path toward her love.

Patience man, he repeated to himself, and almost laughed aloud at the situation he found himself in. Who would believe it? Adam Carstairs, always successful with the ladies, any ladies, all ladies. Womanizer, seducer of anxious young wives and willing young women, any and all women who fell victim to his manly blond appeal and quick, warm smile—until now. Now he lay bewitched, himself the victim, caught in a situation where his easy charm would not suffice. He must learn a new tactic in this game of love: patience.

Raising his eyes to the heavens for the first time that morning, he whispered with a grimace, "Lord, give me strength." And returning his hungry gaze to the fragile little beauty in his arms, he said to himself with a wry smile as he shook his head, "I'll need it."

Adam would not allow himself to sleep again. He wanted to savor the feeling of holding Amanda close to him, for he knew it would be a long day and too long a time before he would hold her again. When she began to stir, he bowed slightly to temptation by touching his mouth to hers for a short, warm kiss. Desire was so strong in him as he drew his mouth from hers that his body trembled. Luckily, Jonathan took that moment to voice his first appeal of the morning, drawing Amanda's attention, and Adam rose quickly. After disappearing for a short while, during which he made liberal use of the icy water of the brook, he returned to the camp.

Smiling warmly as his eyes touched on Amanda, who held her famished child to her, he commented, "Well, since you can't handle two meals at one time, I suppose I'll have to prepare our breakfast."

Adam was rewarded with a fleeting dimpled smile, and feeling more than amply paid, he began his chores.

Adam was feeling better than he had for months. His spirits high, his heart lighter, and hopes for the future shining brightly on his horizon, he was amused by his own feeling of euphoria. *I suppose I must be in love!* For too long love had meant only heartache for him, but now things would be different. Directing toward Amanda a brilliant smile, he felt a sharp pang of apprehension as she turned to avoid his eyes.

Breakfast was finished, the camp broken, and they were ready to mount up before Amanda turned toward Adam and began to speak. Her child lay on the ground beside her, and her appearance was that of grim resolution as she squared her small frame and faced him levelly.

"I would ask one more favor of you, Adam. I came to a decision last night." Looking steadily up into his eyes, she said firmly, "I'm going to return Jonathan to his true people. He isn't welcome at Fort Edward. I'd like you to go by the Abnaki village before returning to the fort."

Adam was stunned! He asked unbelievingly, "You'd give up your son?"

Amanda's irate answer confused him even further,

but only momentarily. "Of course not! I'll stay there with him!"

Speechless, Adam stared for a few moments before asking hoarsely, "How long do you intend to stay there?"

Amanda's voice was soft, her eyes downcast. "I'll never return, Adam."

With that short statement Adam felt his world rocking crazily beneath his feet. He stood dumbly, too shocked to speak, finally managing to stammer out one outraged word.

"No!"

The tone of his voice snapped Amanda's eyes to his face and she hastened to explain, her words pouring out in a long, unhappy torrent. "I couldn't bind you to me with my need, Adam. You should be free to choose your own woman, or just enjoy your life as you have in the past. My problems are my own. There's only one place that will welcome my son, and, I hope, me, through him. I beg you to take me there."

Her eyes were pleading even as he shook his head violently and thundered, "I won't. You aren't binding me with your need, Amanda, don't you realize that? Did you think I had just stumbled on the cabin where Robert had you hidden? I searched for you for three long months! I knew I would have no peace until I saw you again. I love you! Can't you accept that fact? I love you with all my heart, all my strength. You are part of me, Amanda. To be separated from you is to lose part of myself."

Adam's words rang frighteningly familiar in her ears, and covering them with her hands, she exclaimed wildly, "I won't listen, I won't listen."

"You must," Adam demanded, roughly pulling her hands from her ears. "Didn't you suspect I loved you from the first? That day in Fort Carillon I begged you, but Chingue was alive then." Anxiously swallowing, Adam continued softly, "I can accept that you loved him more than you'll ever love me, but he's dead, he can never return. I'm alive, and I'll accept any measure of love you're willing to give me."

Amanda's reply was soft, almost inaudible, "I have none to give, Adam."

Amanda looked into Adam's stricken face. She hadn't wanted to hurt him. She owed him so much. But she would not pay with herself. He deserved more, a full measure of devotion. "Adam, there is nothing left inside me. Only love for Jonathan. I must have him grow up to know love. His grand-parents will welcome him as they never did me. I'll stay with my adopted family, and Jonathan will see them often. He'll grow up happy and secure to revere his father's memory. You're deserving of more than I have to offer, Adam. You deserve a woman that you can be proud of. Not one who has been used."

Adam broke in heatedly, "I want no one else, only you." Warm green eyes caressed her in silent appeal. "To me your name will always describe you far better than any other woman I know. You'll always be 'worthy to be loved' and I'll love only you. I won't let you go."

"What will you do, Adam? Confine me as Robert did? Try to impregnate me with your child to bind me to you as he did? How do you expect to elicit a

love that I don't have to give? Please, take me home,
Adam. I belong with my son."

"Amanda!" Adam's voice was an agonized cry as
he implored her to relent. "You ask too much. You
ask me to give up hope. There is no life without
hope."

Amanda's voice was relentless. "Please, take me
home."

For long moments Adam stood looking down on
Amanda's determined countenance. Suddenly without warning, he swung her angrily onto her horse,
handed her the child, and mounting himself, led
them away.

The beautiful autumn day progressed as an icy
silence developed between them. Anxiety began to
take hold of Amanda's senses as she came to fully
realize how dependent she was and had always been
from the moment of their first encounter on Adam's
integrity and good will. She had never seen him
angry, not at her, but knew instinctively the ruthlessness of which he was capable. Ruthlessness in
this virgin land was necessary to survival, but
Amanda had only known Adam's gentleness and
protection. Apprehension at this unknown facet of
his personality seemed to rule her senses, and
glancing up toward the back of his head as he
continued to lead on, she hastened to quiet Jonathan
in fear of bringing Adam's wrath down upon them
both. But, after several hours of riding, Jonathan,
wet and uncomfortable, could be silenced no longer.

Still without speaking, Adam turned, glancing
sharply in their direction, and continued on. It was
not long before he led them to a spot beside a small

stream, where he dismounted, and then lifted Amanda from the saddle. He spoke gruffly, for the first time since the morning, "Your son needs attention. I'll prepare our food while you tend to him."

Within a few minutes, the partial source of Jonathan's fretfulness had been removed, and once again clean and dry, a portion of his sunny disposition returned. Not waiting to hear a resumption of his hungry wail, Amanda sat, her back supported by a tree, and once again put him to her breast. Even in times of tension, Amanda found she could enjoy these private moments with her son, for it was then she could put all other thoughts from her mind and be free to study the ruddy-complexioned little angel and delight in the miracle that had given him to her. Although her child was already almost three months old, she still regarded him in wonder, feeling true joy as the passage of each new day stamped more clearly on the small face Chingue's mark as his sire. Truly, he was his father's image! Amanda felt her eyes grow warm with gathering tears, but looked up in response to a sudden uneasy feeling to see Adam, crouched by the small fire, staring intently in her direction. His eyes were no longer cold, but warm with passion, and her heart started thudding in her chest as he slowly stood to his full massive height and walked toward her, his eyes never leaving her person.

He stood towering over her for a few moments before he crouched down beside her, his adoration shining in his face, his green eyes so brilliant with love that she flushed under his scrutiny. His handsome face relaxed into a small smile as he laughed lightly, all the while gently playing with the soft hair at her temples. "Does my love embarrass you, Amanda? I've kept it hidden for so long that it is a relief to finally let myself look at you unrestrained." Adam's voice dropped a notch as the smile left his face and he whispered, "You're so beautiful, my darling Amanda."

His hand had left her hair and was caressing her cheek, as he slowly lowered his mouth to cover hers for a lingering kiss. "You're like a beautiful, golden madonna," he whispered softly as his eyes dropped to her breast and the child that suckled there so contentedly.

Amanda felt her flush deepen as Adam's eyes dwelled so openly on her bared bosom, and he slowly lowered his head to lightly kiss the smooth copper-hued cheek of her son. He then moved to press a warm, lingering kiss on the swell of the breast at which her child suckled. At her startled intake of breath, Adam looked up, his eyes hot with emotion, and moving quickly, he slipped a hand behind her head and held her firmly as his mouth covered hers once again in a kiss that, unlike the first, was deeply passionate. He was trembling visibly as he withdrew his mouth from hers.

"I love you, Amanda." Adam's voice was shaken as he spoke earnestly. "Don't ask me to give you up, please. You asked me once before at Fort Carillon, and I complied because you loved another, but now there's no one standing between us."

"But there is, Adam."

"The only things that stand between us are memories, good and bad, but they'll fade in time, you'll see." Obviously trying to regain some semblance of his control, Adam said softly, "I'll wait, darling, no matter how long it takes for you to be free of your memories. But don't ask me to give you up to a life that will take you away from me forever. You couldn't be so cruel."

"It would be less cruel to make the break cleanly now, Adam." Amanda's response was soft.

Adam stiffened visibly at her words. "Are you trying to tell me that there's no hope at all that you'll ever return my feelings? Amanda." Adam's voice was desperate. "Is there nothing in me that you feel you can one day come to love? Do you find me so obnoxious, so loathsome?"

"Adam!" Pain was obvious in Amanda's sharp response. "The fault doesn't lie with you, it lies with me! I'm dead inside, I tell you! All love is gone, except for Jonathan. Just him, just him." Amanda began to sob violently as she clutched the child who still nursed at her breast. "Please forget me, Adam. I am dead inside, dead, dead."

Adam looked desolately at the woman he loved, as, her face averted from his, she continued to cry softly. Finally, in silent resignation, he rose to his feet and walked back to the fire.

The following three days of their journey proceeded uneventfully. Amanda had several times caught Adam's eyes on her when he had thought her otherwise engaged, and his unguarded looks betrayed enough of his innermost thoughts to prohibit her from asking the questions she most desired to have answered. What was their destination? Where had Adam decided to take her?

As they lay awaiting sleep that night, Adam spoke hesitantly, apparently uncertain of the manner in which to begin. In the semidarkness Amanda was unable to see well the expression on his face as he spoke.

"We'll soon reach the point where we must choose the turning toward Fort Edward or the Abnaki village. Do you still feel strongly about returning to your Indian life, or do you want to return to Fort Edward for a while before making your final decision?"

Tensing inwardly at the pain she knew she was going to inflict on the man to whom she was already so heavily in debt, she said softly, "I want to return to my Abnaki family, Adam."

Amanda saw the slight shudder that passed over Adam's strong frame at her quiet statement, and suppressed the tears gathering in her eyes at his silent pain. He gave no response, except a short nod before closing his eyes to sleep.

The next morning a tenseness existed between them that Amanda could not dispel. Adam continually avoided her eyes as if unable to face her, and completely ill at ease with his behavior, Amanda found herself responding in like fashion. During their preceeding days of travel, Adam had taken to assuming the burden of Jonathan for most of their hours on horseback, relinquishing the child to Amanda only when he became fretful. This morning he again pulled his horse to her side after he had mounted, and took the happily gurgling infant from her arms. His eyes, as he looked to the child who smiled so happily at his appearance, were filled with

336

a pain that pierced Amanda's heart also. As Adam resumed his place in front to lead them forward, gently cradling her son in his strong, muscled arm, Amanda felt doubt shake her resolve for the first time, but shaking off her momentary weakening, she strengthened herself for the step she knew she must take.

The tension between them seemed to build steadily as they traveled, until Adam turned and stated in a flat tone, "We'll arrive at the Indian village by mid-afternoon."

Amanda gasped inadvertently at the sudden statement, but ignoring her reaction, Adam silently resumed his position in the lead and moved forward. It was a few hours past noon when Adam halted his horse abruptly and, dismounting, turned to swing Amanda down from her saddle. Holding the sleeping child casually in the crook of his arm, he curved his other arm around Amanda's waist and led her silently forward. From their position on a slight rise of ground, Adam and Amanda looked down in silence on the Abnaki village she had once called home.

Gently laying the child down on a small mound of leaves, Adam turned and faced Amanda, his eyes ablaze with the torment he had suffered so silently and so long.

"Amanda." Adam's voice was deeply emotional as he spoke. "I've done as you asked. I brought you to the place you've chosen to hide for the remainder of your life, but as surely as I stand now before you, I know this is wrong. That village is no longer your home. Your life there is done, finished with Chingue's death, and no effort on your part can restore him to you or bring you any closer to him than he is within your own memory. I beg you to reconsider your decision before it is too late."

Adam hopefully awaited her response, only to be filled with despair as Amanda stated simply, "My decision remains the same, Adam."

Rendered speechless by the intensity of the emotion engulfing him, Adam stared, seeming to pierce her very soul with his unhappiness. His hand moved awkwardly to her shining hair, and stroked it gently as he spoke. "I'd like to say my good-byes to you here, privately, Amanda. Once we enter the village all opportunity for privacy will be lost."

Herself too filled with emotion to speak, Amanda nodded her assent, and Adam drew her slowly into his arms as his mouth descended toward hers. With the first touch of her lips, all the love Adam held inside him for the small golden woman in his arms seemed to explode within him. Crushing her small body against his in a wild embrace, he separated her lips to taste the sweetness within. A low groan issued from deep inside him and he drew her even tighter, his tongue driving deeper and deeper into her mouth. When finally he withdrew, he continued a tender barrage of kisses, on the lids, covering the glorious eyes he loved so well, the creamy smoothness of her cheek, the tip of her delicate nose, the spot where that fleeting dimple was hidden, the graceful column of her throat, to return in a surging rush of emotion to the mouth he so longed to taste again. When his deep, searching kiss came to an end, Adam was trembling violently, and he whispered hoarsely against her hair, "This is your home now, Amanda, here in my arms. This is where you belong, and where you should stay, not down there. Stay with me, please, for the love of God, I beg you. I can't do without you anymore."

Amanda's tear-filled eyes were trained on his tortured face as she drew herself away. "My decision has already been made. I must return my son to his home."

Adam stiffened as all hope died, his face growing bleak with pain. Turning abruptly, he strode away and returned within a few minutes leading the horses. Without a word, he lifted Amanda to her saddle, and bent to scoop Jonathan into his arms, hesitating momentarily as he handed the child over to his mother.

"Strange," he said to himself almost as much as to her, "how I'd come to look forward to hearing him call me father." Then with a short self-derisive laugh, he relinquished the child and turned to mount quickly.

The rapid procession of events as Amanda solemnly urged her horse on behind Adam seemed to blur in her extremely agitated mind. As they drew nearer the village, Amanda became aware that a small group was forming, their faces impassive as they watched the approaching riders, and although most were familiar to her, no greetings passed their lips. Indeed, there was no sound at all, nothing but silence to greet them. Despite her confident assertions to Adam, Amanda was far from certain of her reception, and although she had no fear for Jonathan's safety, she suddenly realized that if she risked her life, she also risked Adam's and a new anxiety was born in her mind.

"Adam, please help me down." Amanda's voice sounded unnaturally loud in the prevailing silence as they reached the village border.

Dismounting, Adam walked quickly to Amanda and, lifting her from the saddle, stood behind her, tense with apprehension and ready for immediate action if the explosive situation should turn against them. Frantically Amanda searched the crowd, seeking a certain familiar face, to no avail, until a movement at the rear of the small gathering caught her eye, and a short, matronly figure came within her view. The first glimpse of that round, lined face that had grown so familiar and loved, released the tears that she had suppressed for so long. But still Amanda hesitated as she searched Ninscheach's countenance for a sign of welcome. Slowly, a small smile grew on the old woman's face, and she held out her arms, saying softly, *"N'nitsch undach aal!"*[1]

Clutching Jonathan tightly against her, Amanda ran forward, managing to throw her free arm around the woman she had learned to love, sobbing softly, *"N'ahawees, N'ahawees!"*[2]

Within moments, two more pairs of arms were thrown joyously around Amanda, and Mamalnunschetto and Tscholentit, laughing and squealing happily, joined in her welcome. Jonathan's sudden, angry wail separated the happy crush, demanding attention and drawing admiring exclamations from her happy family. It was at that moment that

1. Meaning, "Come hither, my child."
2. Meaning, "My mother, my mother!"

Amanda suddenly remembered Adam, and turned to see him watching her solemnly from where she had left him. Motioning him forward, Amanda waited until he had drawn close enough to take his hand, and turning to Ninscheach, introduced him simply and sincerely, *"N'tschutti, Adam."*[1]

Adam's horse moved steadily forward, although the hand on the reins was lax, guiding carelessly. He followed the trail to Fort Edward with unseeing eyes, as he relived in his mind the last twenty-four hours in an attempt to find a way to accept the fact he found so difficult to face.

He remembered distinctly the inscrutable faces of the Indians gathering as they approached the village, and the unmistakable expression of welcome and love shown by the old woman, Ninscheach, and her daughters, which had turned the tide of feelings so distinctly in Amanda's favor. Slowly, one by one, others had come forward to express welcome at her return, and he had kept silent watch over those remaining, searching their faces for any signs of hostility toward Amanda and her child. The knot in Adam's stomach tightened as he recalled the face of the one young brave in the rear of the crowd that had assembled. He had caught the young Indian in an unguarded moment as he looked at Amanda, desire for her so obvious in his expression that Adam had barely been able to restrain his impulse to wipe that look from his face with the power of his naked fist! Suckahokus,[2] Chingue's friend, as Amanda had later

1. Meaning, "My dear, beloved friend, Adam."
2. Meaning, "Black Fox."

introduced him. And Adam had mentally added, who hopes soon to replace Chingue in your bed.

Adam shook his head sadly at that thought, for it was obvious she had no idea of the young man's feelings. He knew he was being unfair to Amanda, who had room for only one man in her heart, and that man was Chingue. But Chingue was dead, and Amanda had chosen to stay with his people. How long would it be before she became lonesome enough to accept another man? Whenever it was, Adam knew he would not be that man, because Amanda had sent him firmly away with an admonition to forget her and continue his life as if she no longer existed.

Adam's thoughts returned once again to the Indian who had watched Amanda so covetously, and he felt the heat of jealousy stir his emotions. "All right, Amanda," Adam whispered softly through clenched teeth, "you'll get your wish. I'll forget you as you instructed. You may dream of your Indian lover in peace, and when his memory grows dim, replace him with the anxious young Abnaki who is waiting to follow in his footsteps. My empty arms ache now," Adam consoled himself, "but they won't be empty long, and I'll eventually lose your face among the many that will follow you!"

Feeling fortified by his new sense of resolve, Adam urged his horse forward. He was anxious to begin to forget.

The onslaught of winter came suddenly with the arrival of the first bitter-cold weather in mid-December, followed the same week with the season's first snowstorm. The startlingly beautiful blanket of white stirred in Amanda a new wealth of memories. She remembered Chingue's pride in the fur robe she had so carefully sewn for him; the glow in his eyes as he praised her work; her first, hilarious attempt at snowshoes, and Chingue's amused patience at her incompetence; the cold night they had first discussed the child she carried in her womb, and Chingue's dreams for the child he had known instinctively would be a son. But most of all, Amanda recalled with a deep, inner longing the many long winter nights spent in Chingue's arms, the endless hours of love that, due to Chingue's ceaseless patience and gentleness, were all-consuming, exciting, and breathlessly rewarding. How empty and alone she felt on her lonely sleeping bench. Her body ached for the touch of his slender, skillful hands, and the warmth and intimacy of his strong young body against hers. In the silence of the winter nights, Amanda recalled to mind again and again the sound of his deep, rough voice as he spoke his almost poetic words of love. Amanda missed his guidance, his love, and his strength of body and mind—everything that was Chingue.

But, as time slowly ushered in the new year, Amanda came to accept the fact that dwelling on her memories would not only keep alive the pain, but retard the progress of the future, and painfully, with great remorse, she began to delegate thoughts of Chingue to the special part of her mind reserved for happy memories, and to busy herself with the future.

Despite the cold and isolation of winter, time moved quickly within the Abnaki town, and Amanda threw herself completely into her womanly

343

routine. Determined as she was to be a true Abnaki mother, Amanda spent her days delighting in Jonathan's growth and health, and her evenings, after her child had been put to bed, in the gatherings of the old men and children where the recitation of countless Indian legends and tales of youthful bravery were spun. Amanda opened her mind and heart to all around her, hoping to absorb the spirit of the Indian into her soul, so she might better encourage her son to grow in his father's image. Looking down into Jonathan's sparkling black eyes and rosy copper cheeks, the dimpled smile on his face declaring to the world his state of contentment, Amanda thought solemnly, I don't want to fail you, my little son, or your father through you. I pray I'll have the strength to persevere.

Winter stretched relentlessly on and Amanda began to notice subtle changes in the life-style in Ninscheach's wigwam. The meals, although shared equally as always, were becoming smaller and they were eating meat less often. It was then that Amanda began to realize the extent of her imposition on Ninscheach's hospitality; for their provisions, accumulated with only three in mind, had suffered a great depletion with the addition of her and her child. But it seemed Amanda was not the only one to become cognizant of their dwindling supplies, and to her family's delight, Suckahokus began to deliver a portion of the proceeds of his hunt to their wigwam each day that he ventured forth.

Amanda watched, smiling to herself at Mamalnunschetto's shy, hidden glances in the young man's direction. With a feeling of surprise, she realized that her lovely, doe-eyed sister would soon be at an age considered favorable for an Indian maiden to be taken to wife, for surely, she was Amanda's junior by no more than two years. Amanda turned to consider Suckahokus for the first time in a new light. Her wide blue eyes studied him intently as he spoke with Ninscheach, motioning to the rabbit he had delivered for their supper. Suckahokus had not Chingue's height or athletically slim proportions, but was of medium height, of broad stature, his wide shoulders, powerful chest and thick, muscular neck ample evidence of his strength and prowess as a wrestler. He had not the fine, chisled features that had made Chingue's countenance so strikingly unforgettable, but was rather coarse of feature, his saving grace being the softness and warmth that shone from his direct black eyes. He appeared to be quite young, but surely mature enough for Mamalnunschetto, as he had, at least from outward appearances, seen twenty summers.

Suckahokus flushed suddenly under the intensity of her silent perusal, and smiling quietly to herself, Amanda turned to attend to her fussing child. Realizing suddenly the cause of his impatient whining, Amanda hastened to open the ties of her shirt and put him to her breast. Carrying Jonathan quietly in her arms, Amanda turned to make herself comfortable on the softness of her sleeping bench as her child took sustenance. Looking up, Amanda saw Suckahokus stopped in midsentence of his discussion with Ninscheach, gazing intently and warmly in her direction. This time it was she who flushed under his scrutiny, her embarrassment finally turned into a smile at his amused reaction. She then chuckled as she mused silently, All right, Suckahokus, you're right. Now we're even!

Not too long after the turn of the year, Amanda began to have another visitor to her wigwam. At the first appearance of Kahaketit's thin, wrinkled countenance, Amanda's inclination was to hide her child from the old woman's penetrating gaze, but Amanda knew she should not succumb so easily to fear. The old woman looked her direction with the animosity of the past, but the cold, tired eyes of Chingue's mother seemed to come alive as they touched upon his child. Amanda saw clearly written on the old woman's face the love and pride she too felt when looking on her sturdy, appealing son, and as the two women's glances met over the head of the contented Indian baby, a solemn bond was forged between them.

Kahaketit spoke softly, muffling the sharp edge of her normally shrill tone of voice, "He is a strong, handsome boy. He is truly Chingue's son."

Amanda's response was as soft, but her voice was steady and clear as she spoke, "And of that I am well proud."

With Kahaketit's acceptance of her child, Amanda felt the final impediment to her peace had been overcome, and she would be able at last to live at rest with her conscience in her new life. But still, peace of mind eluded her. Never far from her thoughts, nagging pitilessly at her conscience, was the picture of Adam's face as he had bid her good-bye. To owe a man so much, and repay him with such unhappiness! The persistent voice inside her mind would give

346

her no respite. Finally, in sheer self-defense, she recalled Adam's wide reputation with women, and she scoffed at her misgivings. Laughingly she thought, he has probably drowned my memory by now in a sea of willing ladies, and is unable to even recall my face. Unhappily, that thought sobered her. I should not like that at all, her mind countered, for Adam will be forever enshrined in my memory. He's too dear to me to forget.

Amanda, now resigned to her life as a husbandless matron, amused herself with the agonizingly slow progress of Mamalnunschetto's hidden love for Suckahokus. It was obvious to Amanda that the serious young man was observing the Indian custom of sharing the fruits of the hunt with the family of his chosen one, for each night, after dropping off his kill, he would return to spend time in their wigwam. The quiet young man's regard for Jonathan was obvious, and his few, well-chosen words of praise for his intelligence and rapid growth endeared him to Amanda. Amanda's sole annoyance stemmed from Mamalnunschetto, who appeared unnaturally shy in Suckahokus's presence, and withdrew into an abnormally silent state, forcing the burden of conversation on her. Before long, it was Amanda who held the task of entertaining their provider on his visits, and she began to lose her patience with her sister's backward behavior.

On one such evening as Suckahokus closed the flap of their wigwam behind him after leaving, Amanda burst out angrily, "Mamalnunschetto, you begin to anger me greatly with your foolish shyness. Why do you not speak with Suckahokus when he visits? He is a fine young man, and I know you are not immune to his attraction."

A surprised expression crossed the young girl's face before she silently lowered her eyes.

Amanda felt her annoyance increase to the point where she demanded bluntly, "Surely you realize Suckahokus is pressing his suit for marriage."

Mamalnunschetto nodded, her eyes still downcast, and Amanda burst out in exasperation, "Then, why do you not respond?"

Her eyes still avoiding Amanda's, Mamalnunschetto answered softly, "Because I am not the one he seeks. It is you he wishes to take to wife!"

Amanda's eyes flew wide in surprise and disbelief as she vigorously denied the statement, "No, no, Mamalnunschetto, you're wrong! It's you he seeks. He knows I'm still in mourning for Chingue."

Looking at her sister's downcast eyes, Amanda turned to Ninscheach for support. "Tell her, *N'aha-wees*.[1] Explain that it is she Suckahokus seeks out."

"I cannot do that." Ninscheach's quiet voice cut the silence of the wigwam as she delivered the final surprise. "It is you, Amanda, whom Suckahokus has asked to take to wife!"

Amanda stood still and unbelieving. It couldn't be true! Surely Suckahokus realized that she loved Chingue, still loved him. No, no, she couldn't. She was finished with that kind of love. She couldn't face it again! Filled with a true sense of horror, she was unable to meet the glances of her family and ran from the wigwam to the silence and privacy of the woods. There she remained, her mind stunned into numb-

1. Meaning, "My Mother."

ness until the sharp winter cold forced her to return and crawl silently into her sleeping bench to sleep.

On the following day Amanda arose, impatient for her first opportunity to speak to Ninscheach alone. Grasping it, she spoke softly, her eyes worried, "Ninscheach, I would speak with you in private. Would you walk with me for a few minutes after the morning meal?"

A silent nod indicated Ninscheach's acquiescence as she continued her work. The preparation of the meal then stretched on interminably for the anxious Amanda until Ninscheach stood to leave the wigwam, motioning her to follow.

They walked a short distance in silence before Amanda began lamely, "Ninscheach, I am troubled by what you said last night. I didn't know Suckahokus desired to take me to wife. Indeed, I believed it was Mamalnunschetto that he sought. Surely he realizes that she is a better choice for wife to him than I?"

"It matters not whom you believe to be the better choice, Amanda, for Suckahokus has made his choice. It is you he seeks. Did you not realize," Ninscheach's shy dark eyes lowered as she spoke, "that he desired you even while Chingue lived? He bore the brunt of many jokes for his covetous glances in your direction, and now that you are without a man, he has lost no time in declaring his intentions."

Amanda was stunned by Ninscheach's words and what appeared to be her acceptance of Suckahokus' suit, and exclaimed with heated fervor, "But I don't want him! Now that Chingue is gone, I don't want another husband! I won't take another husband!"

349

Ninscheach raised her wise dark eyes to Amanda, and regarded her solemnly for a few moments before beginning to speak. "Amanda, my daughter, you are a grown woman and know the hard ways of life. You are young, with a strong son to care for and raise. How would you provide for this son?"

Amanda's words of protest were stopped by a silent gesture as Ninscheach continued. "You must realize that we owe much to Suckahokus' generosity, and that without it our fare would have been very meager these many weeks."

Ninscheach's searching stare forced Amanda to nod her begrudging acquiescence.

"The winter of your grief will soon be past, Amanda, and as the sun comes to melt the snows, bringing forth new life from the earth, you must allow your grief to slip away, and begin your life anew. You are young, and have many summers before you. Your son will need a father as well as a mother to guide him into manhood."

"But you didn't take another man, Ninscheach." Amanda's voice implored her understanding.

"I was old before my husband was taken from me, Amanda, and had a grown son to care for me, but you are young and have a son who needs a man's guidance. You must put your grief behind you. Suckahokus is patient, but his patience is not without end. However, if his suit is hopeless, you must be kind and tell him, for each day you grow dearer to him and the pain of loss will be greater."

As if seeing Amanda's desire to put a quick end to Suckahokus' unsolicited offer, Ninscheach added quietly, "But if you do so, you must be ready to accept

350

another, for as great as my love is for you, daughter, I, a woman alone, will be unable to provide for you all of your life until your son is grown. Indeed, it was only through Suckahokus that we passed this winter in comfort."

The bluntness of Ninscheach's statement staggered Amanda for a moment, and seeing her confusion, Ninscheach pityingly offered consolation. "Suckahokus is a good, kindly young man. He feels deeply for you, and would be honored to call your son his own. You would do well to accept his suit."

"But Mamalnunschetto cares deeply for him." Amanda's voice trailed off as Ninscheach easily dispensed with her objection.

"Mamalnunschetto is but a small flame that is overshadowed by the brilliance of your fire in Suckahokus' eyes. It matters not what she feels, for it is you Suckahokus desires. You may turn him away, but you must be prepared to accept another if you would raise your child within our village.

Ninscheach's words filled Amanda with a sudden panic.

"But I can not, I will not take another husband. I will not." Amanda flushed with the heat of intensity as her words dwindled away.

"You need not decide now, Amanda. Suckahokus does not demand an immediate response. But do not take too long," she cautioned finally, "for in the end, it must be either Suckahokus or someone else."

The last, short phrase was to repeat itself in Amanda's mind many, many times in the hours following, until, in the darkness and silence of that night as she lay abed, the words seemed to pound in her brain. "It must be Suckahokus or someone else."

Her mind responded with a final, No! There will be no one else! And the decision to leave the village was made.

Adam felt a sharp pang of guilt as soft brown eyes looked guilelessly up into his. It was not the first time in the four months since he had bid Amanda good-bye that he had felt the prick of conscience, but this was by far the strongest twinge yet. He looked down into the innocent young face of the girl in his arms.

What the hell is happening to me, he thought in disgust with his blatent disregard of her tender feelings. It was obvious his short campaign to win her affections had been as successful as his other numerous affairs in his attempt to drive Amanda from his mind. Whatever had appealed to him in the first place in this small, shy young woman? There was no need to answer that question, because the reason for his attraction was obvious. Her youth and innocence, coupled with her diminuative size were enough to strike a reminiscent chord, and it was that similarity to Amanda alone that had drawn him like a magnet from the arms of his last lady love. But she was not Amanda, and the trust in her face was too bitter a pill to swallow.

Sickened with himself, Adam pulled her slight young body against his, and held her gently while he tried to assemble the wild confusion of feelings that assailed him. After a few moments, one fact above all became clear, and releasing the young girl's willing form, he said softly, "It's time I take you home."

That night in his bed, alone for the first night in

many, Adam began to take stock of the last four months. He tried to remember the faces of the steady procession of women that had lain by his side. Some were old friends, eager to renew his acquaintance, other new faces to fill the aching void inside him. He had smiled at, charmed, and cajoled each, but had, after four long months, not succeeded in lessening his sense of loss. He had, in fact, only confirmed the absolute necessity of that pale, small young woman to his happiness.

Adam closed his eyes momentarily at the swell of emotion inside him as her face flashed before his mind. "Amanda, my love," he whispered softly, "It's just no good without you."

Adam urged his horse steadily forward, with far more urgency than he had traveled this same trail in the opposite direction just a few months previously. Once his decision to return to the Abnaki village had been made, he could not seem to move quickly enough on his way. Stubbornly refusing to face the changes that the passage of four months time might have wrought in Amanda's situation in the village, he had loaded a spare horse with provisions, his excuse for returning, and had started out with great haste. He chastised himself mentally for abandoning Amanda to her grief.

I shouldn't have let her drive me away. She wasn't responsible in her state of mind for her actions. Robert had shamed her until her only thought was to hide. But someone as beautiful and desirable as Amanda could never hide long.

Adam's mind flew back to the face of the young

Indian he had first seen at the rear of the crowd as they arrived. "Oh, Lord," he prayed softly, "let me not be too late."

Amanda sat quietly mending the torn blanket as her child slept angelically beside her. There was a great, welcome silence within the wigwam, allowing her mind freedom to wander, but her thoughts were troubled, a state of mind she had found too constant of late. The long winter nights had been put to the purpose of planning her future. Within the month she would accompany the first column to the fort. Her departure was now a fact her family accepted, but without joy. Suckahokus had taken her refusal of his suit without comment, but still continued to bring a portion of the hunt to her family, and the glow in his eyes when they rested on her revealed only too plainly that hope still lived within his heart. Now alone in her wigwam, looking on the face of her sleeping child, Amanda felt doubt soar inside her. She had not been allowed to retreat from the world and live for her son as she had hoped when she had come to the village, and now she was forced to return to a life that stretched out in a long void of uncertainty before her. The Abnaki column would soon take her and her son to Fort Ticonderoga, but how she would get from there to Fort Edward was still a question.

Her mind, unguarded for a moment, allowed the image of a familiar blond giant to come before her eyes, and angry with herself for allowing Adam to enter her thoughts again, she shook her head vigorously. She had sent him away. She had done the right thing. He was deserving of a woman he could call completely his own, not one haunted by the memories of a dead love. He deserved a woman who was pure and clean, not one defiled and used by a man possessed with lust. Yes, she had done the right thing.

Rising slowly, she folded the repaired blanket and turned toward the entrance of the wigwam when she heard movement at the doorway. Amanda gasped as her eyes touched on the manifestation of the image she had driven from her mind just moments before, and she swayed with shock.

"Hello, Amanda." The image spoke her name softly, in a familiar voice, proving itself to be real, and Amanda felt a sudden surge of joy. Her happiness drove her spontaneously into his arms, to encircle his powerful chest with her petite, limited reach as she hugged him tightly, exclaiming softly against him, "Adam, I've missed you so!" And in that moment Amanda realized the truth of the words she spoke.

Even while feeling the warmth of her embrace, Adam was almost unbelieving of his welcome, so prepared had he been for a reprimand at not acceding to her wishes. His arms encircled her, warily at first, fearful that a release of his burning hunger for her would cause her to withdraw her impetuous embrace. But despite himself, his arms tightened as he whispered, straining to suppress his rioting feelings, "All the way here I invented excuses for my return so you wouldn't be angry, but the truth is, I couldn't stay away any longer. I had to come, to bring you back. Amanda, please come back with me. I—"

"Things have changed considerably since you left, Adam." Amanda interrupted in an attempt to explain her situation and he stiffened noticeably as he drew back slightly, seeking her gaze.

"What are you trying to tell me?" Adam's voice was sharp, filled with tension.

"It's just that I've found I can't hide from life here as I desired. It just hasn't worked out that way. I've decided to return to the fort and make a life for Jonathan and myself there."

Suspicion clouded Adam's eyes. He knew she was holding something back, but did not want to take the time for questions. Far better to get her away while her resolution to leave was still firm, and later. . . .

"Then put your things together, Amanda." He took her hands gently in his. "We'll start back today."

Amanda opened her mouth to speak, but a deep, growling voice interrupted from the doorway. "She will not leave with you. Amanda is to be my wife. She is now, as she has been since she came to our village, under my protection." His voice then dropping lower until it was almost a snarl, Suckahokus continued, "And you will take your hands from her now."

His threatening command had not the reaction for which it was intended, even though Adam dropped her hands, for he stepped in front of her, facing Suckahokus squarely, his intention clear as his huge hands balled into fists, and his countenance changed to a steely look of determination.

Amanda turned to face an angry Suckahokus, quite unlike the young man to whom she had become accustomed. Faced with his wrath, Amanda felt herself suddenly at a loss, but stepped between the two men and began to speak haltingly.

"Suckahokus, my good friend. You have always been so generous and understanding. I give you my thanks for your friendship and beg your forgiveness, for you are a worthy man. But I must return to my own people. I ask you to accept my decision."

"You will not leave with this man."

"Adam is my friend. It is he who brought me here to mourn my husband and bury my grief. It is fitting that he be the one to return me to my people. But know now, Suckahokus, that a part of my heart will remain forever with my Abnaki family and good friends here, and the bond of blood that runs in my son's veins will never be broken. I ask you to allow us to leave in peace."

For a few long minutes Suckahokus' coarse, blunt features mirrored the pain felt deep inside. Slowly his gaze hardened as the stoic mask of the Indian slipped across his features, and he finally responded in a gruff voice, "The decision is yours." Without another word, he strode past her and through the doorway.

Adam ordered quickly, "Put your things together. We'll leave immediately."

Amanda's hasty good-bye's to her family were as blurred in her mind as her entry into the village. She remembered only the tears shed bidding her mother and sisters good-bye, her brief farewell to Kahaketit, and her solemn vow to bring Jonathan often to visit so he might know his father's people. Lastly, she remembered the solitary figure of a broad young

Indian brave who stood alone, watching her departure from a distance, and her heart was saddened. But even as she watched, a slender Indian girl detached herself from the group waving farewell and went to stand beside him, her lovely face turned compassionately up to his.

"Thank you, Mamalnunschetto, for the peace of mind you have just granted me."

Amanda's appreciation was silent and sincere.

With a relentless pace, as if endeavoring to put as much distance between them and the Abnaki town as possible before nightfall, Adam guided them through the forest. The unseasonably warm March afternoon soon cooled as the sun began to set, and Jonathan's fretful squirming in Adam's arms made further travel impossible until he had been made comfortable and fed. Within the hour, Adam had found a suitable spot to camp for the night and, lifting Amanda down from her horse, relinquished her son to begin the business of setting up camp. Even as they tended their individual chores in the manner of those accustomed to traveling together, Amanda was aware of Adam's eyes upon her. He seemed to follow her every move, and so self-conscious did she become under his gaze that her hand trembled as she untied the fastenings of her shirt, her face flaming a deep red as she put Jonathan to her breast. When Jonathan's warm little body had settled against hers, suckling noisily, Amanda lifted her face, only to see Adam still staring intently, his eyes serious. He rose and walked forward to stand towering over her as she sat on the worn blanket nursing her child. Slowly he lowered himself to sit beside her and, drawing her back against his chest, supported her as she fed her child, his arms encircling them both possessively.

Within the half hour a full stomach and a clean change had accomplished its purpose, Amanda's completely sated young son was asleep. A loving warmth suffused her as his small mouth, milk still dribbling from its corner, fell open, and she looked back into Adam's face. The tenderness displayed so openly in his expression stunned her, and suddenly embarrassed, she averted her eyes and readied her son for the night.

Their short meal, accomplished after Jonathan had been settled, was eaten quickly and in silence, and Amanda, still by the fire, watched as Adam rose abruptly to prepare their blankets for sleep. Feeling strangely tense, Amanda rose for a few moments' privacy. Adam, crouched by the fire, stood as she returned to their camp and, walking slowly forward, gently took her into his arms. Holding her a small distance from him, he pensively searched her face. Amanda could feel the trembling in his massive frame as he began to speak.

"We have many things we must settle between us, Amanda." At her inquiring glance, Adam continued, "Now that I've found you again, I don't intend to lose you. We'll be married as soon as we reach Fort Edward."

At her sudden gasp, Adam whitened slightly and said in a choked voice, "Do you think I'm such a fool that I'd let you go again? I won't allow us to be separated another time. You'll be my wife. It was meant to be, can't you see?"

"I will not marry again!"

"You will marry me!"

"No, no!"

A sudden fury overwhelmed him at her adamance, and he gripped her shoulders angrily. "And how do you propose to care for yourself? Feed your child?"

"Betty and the Captain, they'll help me until I can find some work, laundry perhaps." Her mind was frantically reviewing again the alternatives she had considered all winter long.

"You'd take their help, impose on their kindness, but won't accept what I offer. Amanda, I offer you a home, security for your son, protection."

"But you want too much in return!"

"I ask for nothing."

"You want my love, Adam. I can't love you as a wife loves a husband. Robert—he—that part of me is dead. I don't have that love to give. It lies with Chingue. It will be with him forever."

Adam was silent for a few moments while Amanda's searching gaze pleaded his understanding.

"If your heart is closed to love, I won't ask that you love me, Amanda. Just that you allow me to love you."

"No, no." Amanda shook her head, vehemently denying his request.

"Think before you refuse me again, Amanda. You say you can't love again, but you must go on living. You must survive, you and your child. I need you. My life is pointless without you. You are my joy, my reason for—"

"Stop! I won't listen to you. Stop, stop!" Panic

inundated her senses at his passionate tirade. The words were too familiar to her ears, spoken by another voice at another time and place.

"Would you destroy my life? Do you hate me so that you wouldn't even allow me to love you if I don't ask your love in return? Just let me love you, Amanda." Adam's voice trembled with the intensity of his plea. "I must be able to hold you, touch you." He drew her gently into his arms, murmuring against her golden hair. "After you sent me away this last time, I tried to find you in every woman I held, but none would do. Only you, only you." His voice trailed off as emotion choked his words once again, and he crushed her breathtakingly close.

Amanda felt the pain of his embrace. It was not a physical pain she shared, but the soul-draining pain of unrequited love that was tearing him apart, and she could stand his suffering no longer. Pushing herself slightly away from him to look into his eyes, she touched his cheek with the soft palm of her hand.

"Adam, would you bind yourself willingly to a woman who can never return the depth of your feelings? Is this what you truly want?"

"If that woman is you, yes."

She looked at him for endless moments, a deep sadness in her eyes, and finally whispered, "Then, if you're certain, I will marry you, Adam, and I pray that you'll never regret this day."

Amanda closed her eyes against the exhilaration that suffused his face, and in the light of his happiness her last shred of resistance was abandoned. He held her close in his love-filled victory and whispered against her ear, his voice deep and hoarse as passion throbbed wildly in his veins.

"Tonight, will you let me love you tonight, Amanda? Now?"

He pulled away to look into her eyes for confirmation. "So I will know our pact is sealed and I won't lose you again?"

A sudden coldness spread through her body and she stiffened instinctively, but a small voice inside her mind was his ally. You can't allow him to marry you blindly, to have him firmly bound to you beyond recall before he realizes what his future will hold."

Adam watched the play of emotions across her beautiful face as the fear crawling up his spine threatened to devour his reason. Suddenly, her face was calm. Her voice shook, but her glance was level and sure.

"Yes, Adam, tonight."

Joy exploded within him, and he swept her up into his arms and carried her to the blankets. He lay her down and began to undress her with shaking hands. Swiftly he unlaced her blouse and slipped it off, stopping to allow his eyes just a few short moments to linger before continuing. Swallowing visibly, he then slipped off her skirt to sit back on his heels and gaze in wonder at the exquisite symmetry of her naked form. Finally he stood in a swift movement. He divested himself of his garments and stood looking down at her.

Her eyes moved to his great, naked splendor, and as he returned her gaze he swelled with obvious passion, and she dropped her eyes. Slowly he lowered himself to lie beside her, and taking her into his arms, he said in an unbelieving voice, "Oh, God, at last."

At the first touch of her pale, velvet skin, Adam was swept into a delirium of exaltation, and his hands, as they stroked her soft, white breasts trembled severely, forcing him to close his eyes momentarily in an intense effort to regain some segment of control. A deep groan escaped his lips as they covered hers and he once again tasted the sweetness of her mouth. Free at last to indulge his passion, Adam's tongue drove deeper into that innate sweetness until his frenzy of love drove him relentlessly on, to cover her face, neck, and shoulders with a shower of kisses, coming at last to dwell luxuriously on the rounded swells of her breasts. Gently he caressed the enlarged pink nipples with his tongue, noting regretfully the tenseness in Amanda's body as she held herself aloof from his caresses. Slowly, endlessly, he continued his caresses until, with a small groan, Amanda was unable to restrain her body's instinctive response any longer. Stimulated by her reaction to his lovemaking, Adam increased his ministrations to her passion as his hands fondled and smoothed the most intimate reaches of her slender white body. His pursuit of her desire was inescapable, as his loving hands and mouth aroused and stimulated each nerve in her body until she shuddered with passion. Finally shaken by her body's betrayal, Amanda cried softly, tears streaming down her face, "Please, Adam, please take me now."

When still he persisted in his loving attentions, she begged for release. "Please, Adam, now."

Adam stopped for an incredulous second to stare into Amanda's impassioned face. With a joyful sound he covered her mouth with his as he arched his body, his manhood seeking the warm, moist place his hands had explored and aroused so wildly only moments before. With one penetrating thrust, Adam entered her, drawing a small, low moan from Amanda's lips as her mouth opened further to allow his tongue the freedom he desired. Again and again he thrust rhythmically inside her, and within moments her body's response was complete as she matched his ever increasing impetus, striving, aiding his passion to peak in a blinding burst of joy that held him suspended for long, glorious moments before dropping him panting and consumed by the moments they had shared.

For long, quiet minutes Adam held Amanda's small, perspiring body against his, overwhelmed by the beauty of their first mutual experience in love. He was, for all his knowledge, the novice this time. A satisfying physical act had become for him an exhilarating, sensually uplifting, joy-filled experience, the aura of which filled him still after its completion. But even as he gloried in his happiness, an uneasy feeling stole over him as he realized that, for all his reluctance to release her from his still hungry embrace, Amanda's arms no longer clung to him as they had in the tumult of her passion. They lay limply at her sides. His arms tightened instinctively, in an effort to elicit a similar response, but there was none.

Finally releasing her to look into her face, Adam found Amanda's eyes lowered, avoiding his. Greatly he raised her chin until she looked directly into his eyes. Hardly able to hear his own voice over the pounding of his heart, he whispered softly, "What's wrong, Amanda? Did I hurt you?"

"No, you didn't hurt me, Adam." Her whispered voice was barely audible.

"Then tell me."

"There's nothing wrong, Adam, nothing."

"But there is. You shared my passion, I know you did, for a little while."

Noting the quick flush that covered her face at his words, Adam continued, "Tell me what's wrong."

As he waited the response that did not come, the answer became only too clear in his own mind, and he said quietly, "The problem is simply one thing, isn't it. I'm not Chingue."

Amanda's eyes filled, confirming the truth of his words, and for a few short moments the pain constricting in his chest, as hatred and jealousy overran his emotions, almost stole his breath. But slowly reason gained control, and he admitted simply to himself, I'll share her with a dead man now, if I must, but someday. . . .

Reaching over, Adam took the blanket and pulled it across them, whispering in her ear as he drew her gently into the circle of his arms, "Sleep well, my only love."

The following two days passed in much the same pattern as the first. The unseasonably warm, sunny days continued, facilitating their travel, and the sharp, clear nights seemed to Adam to be made for love. Despite his urgency to reach Fort Edward to legalize their union, it was only through steadfast self-control on his part that they kept to their forward pace, for desire seemed a flame that was kindled within him each time his eyes touched on Amanda's small, golden figure.

At their midday stop on the third day of travel, Adam's eyes leisurely dwelled on Amanda as she sat nursing her child. Her long, silky hair, bleached an almost silver white by three days travel in the sun, was unbound, falling from a center part in a long, shimmering cascade against her cheeks. Her eyes were on her dark, copper-skinned child, and her long, dark lashes seemed to fan out gracefully against her smooth cheeks, now more golden still from the days on the trail. Her face in profile showed a short, delicate nose, and the lips slightly parted in a small smile of pleasure were finely drawn, but full and appealing. She still wore the light tan buckskin clothing and moccasins she had worn the day of their departure from the village, and appeared to Adam in her rough garments the living image of the corn maiden that filled Indian legends.

So small and beautiful, he thought as his eyes continued to consume her, like a fragile golden doll. And she belongs to me at last. Adam's throat grew tight, and at that moment Amanda looked up, catching his eyes on her, and flushed modestly, unknowingly unleashing a flood of tenderness inside him. Rising slowly, he walked to sit beside her and pull her back against him, allowing her to rest her back against his chest as they had sat many times before. Lightly he covered the shimmering hair with kisses, and raising her chin gently, he showered kisses on her smooth, lightly tanned face, before coming to rest on her slightly parted lips.

Reluctantly drawing away, he whispered with a brief, unbelieving laugh, "I'm almost afraid this is a dream, and I'm going to wake up at any minute and find myself without you again."

Then, as if that bitter thought was more than he could bear, he covered her mouth with his in a long, deep kiss, calculated to reassure himself that she truly belonged to him, and continued softly, "In those long nights filled with dreams of you, I was beginning to think I had blown all out of proportion the joy I could expect from our joining. But I know now, Amanda"—Adam was tenderly caressing her cheek and punctuating his remarks with light kisses— "that my dreams of the happiness you would bring me were modest, for you've stirred in me feelings that I hadn't believed possible in my wildest dreams. Our joinings bring me beauty and love unsurpassed in my experience, and I thank you, Amanda."

Adam paused a moment to consider carefully his next words. "I know you don't share my feelings. Maybe you feel a fragment of shame when we come together because our vows haven't been solemnized, but soon you'll be able to dismiss that from your mind." Looking down at Jonathan's peaceful face, Adam whispered, "Your son sleeps. It's time to go on."

Bending his head to give Amanda one last kiss, he rose quickly and took the sleeping child from her arms so she might fasten her shirt. He looked hungrily at the gleaming white breasts before they were hidden from view and thought wonderingly, she's finally and completely mine.

It was midway through the fourth day of travel when Fort Edward came into view and anxiety and apprehension combined to leave Amanda shaking nervously. She adjusted her buckskin dress, smoothed her breeze-ruffled hair, and then looked to her child who was wide awake in Adam's arms, surveying his surrounding with keen interest. As they drew close to the gate, Adam shouted good-naturedly, a familiar, wide, engaging smile covering his face. "Open the gates, Dan. Don't you recognize a friend when you see one?"

Immediately the gates swung open as the sentry called a rowdy greeting. They entered the fort yard and Amanda waited anxiously as Adam dismounted and came to swing her down easily from her horse with his one free arm. He turned Jonathan over to her and began to shake hands affectionately with a few soldiers that had gathered. As he traded jokes of welcome with his friends, Adam noticed the gaze of a young colonial drawn steadily past him where he stared as if bewitched. Turning quickly, he saw the enchanting vision that had so mesmerized the young man. Amanda was standing hesitantly where he had left her, the sun sparkling gloriously on her pale hair, her blue eyes wide with uncertainty, glowing like azure jewels against her golden skin. She was holding her robust, copper-skinned child against her, as his curious, black, almond-shaped eyes openly assessed the crowd that appeared to be forming in the yard. Feeling a tremendous burst of pride in the knowledge that that vision belonged to him alone, he walked to her and encircled her waist with his brawny arm, stooping to plant a casual kiss on her head as he asked in a voice calculated to be heard by all the curious onlookers, "Tell me, Dan, is Reverend Briscomb within the fort? There's a wedding I'd have him perform today!"

A few startled gasps could be heard from the disapproving crowd, and Adam gave a short laugh.

"The reverend won't return for two days at least,

368

Adam. He had some baptizing to accomplish."

The frown that creased Adam's brow at the soldier's words was short-lived. Suddenly a female voice called happily, "Amanda!" And Betty Mitchell pushed her way through those gathered about and snatched her into her motherly arms. Jonathan's squeal of protest quieted the two joyously tearful women and turned their attention on him, to his obvious pleasure, as he dimpled appealingly. Then, smiling warmly, Betty turned to Adam.

"Welcome home, Adam, and thank you for returning Amanda to me."

Adam laughed, moving toward them as he spoke. "I've done nothing of the sort, Betty. I've merely brought my future wife back to be married!" Then, nodding his head at her incredulous look, he answered solemnly, "Yes, Amanda and I will be married as soon as Reverend Briscomb walks through those gates!"

"Hallelujah!" Betty's instinctive response left no doubt as to her reaction, and happily they turned toward Betty's rooms and away from the scrutiny of the curious.

Adam's eyes wandered unseeingly along the roughly hewn boards of the ceiling as he lay in bed in his temporary quarters, his arms crossed behind his head. Temporary! Humph! It had been five long days since he had brought Amanda to Fort Edward, and still Reverend Briscomb hadn't returned. The enforced separation from Amanda was getting harder each day. Their four nights on the trail had only whet his voracious appetite for her, and his frustrated desire was a deep, throbbing ache inside him. He knew, of course, they had no recourse but to wait; and now that Amanda was once again temporarily her charge, Betty had again become the fussy mother hen, watching over her, using every spare waking moment to prepare as best she could for her charge's coming nuptials, and making suitable clothing for Amanda and Jonathan. With the frenzy of womanly activity, Adam had begun to feel sorely neglected, and suddenly amused by his own thoughts, Adam laughed aloud.

"I'm even jealous of Betty!"

But his mirth was not longstanding. The unanticipated delay was making him edgy. Too many unforeseen occurrences had happened in the past to interfere with the orderly progress of their lives for him to accept the delay without concern. Surely the reverend would return today. With that positive thought in mind, he rose and dressed. He knew Jonathan awoke early and Amanda would be feeding him soon. It had become his custom to sit with her in these early morning hours in Betty's sitting room, where she was temporarily quartered, and while she tended her son, to discuss their plans.

Adam had also put his enforced wait to use. Certain that privacy would be a prerequisite to the success of their wedded life during the initial period, Adam had decided they should journey to the site of his parents' cabin and inhabit the cabin he had hastily reconstructed before leaving. He had begun to accumulate supplies accordingly. Living would not be difficult there. Hunting and trapping would provide adequately for the three of them.

Nagging annoyingly in the back of his mind was his abandonment of the vow he had sworn over his parents' graves. Had General Abercrombie's attack on Fort Carillon been successful, and the French been driven into Canada, he would have considered it fulfilled, but that fiasco had only put a heavier burden of guilt on his shoulders. Still, until Amanda was safely his wife, he would know no peace of mind, and thoughts of her swept all others away. Guiltily, he realized that Amanda was more important to him than the sanctity of his vow, the outcome of the war, his very life itself!

Hurriedly he finished dressing and headed for the Mitchells' quarters. A soft response answered his light knock and Adam entered the sitting room, his anxious eyes touching immediately on the object of their search. She had just finished changing Jonathan's linens and was attempting to dress him in his newly made clothing. But the squirming, energetic child had not the patience to await his breakfast, and protested vigorously, his loud angry squawl shattering the silence of the room. Worried lest he should awaken Betty and the captain at such an early hour, Amanda said with an air of exasperation, "All right, you little imp." Scooping him up and wrapping a blanket around his unclothed body, she sat him on her lap as she unbuttoned the front of her dress. Jonathan's hungry mouth quickly seized on the object of his quest, and he settled down peacefully.

Amanda then raised her eyes to Adam, who had moved to sit beside her on the couch. She smiled at the familiar, handsome face looking so warmly down on her and again mused for a moment on the striking differences in appearance between this man and Chingue. Whereas Chingue had been tall, his slender, athletic build did not give him the massive, powerful appearance of Adam's wide-shouldered, muscular frame. Chingue's sharp, black eyes, his classically handsome features, and his proud bearing had bespoken cunning, swiftness, agility, and above all, pride in his people and his heritage. Adam's demeanor, on the contrary, was understated, his huge size speaking for itself with quiet authority. He drew people easily to him with his mischievous green eyes and engaging grin, and was generally friendly and outgoing. But Amanda had also seen the other sides of Adam: Adam the hunter and the hunted, his green eyes cold and wary; the angry, menacing Adam, whose huge size screamed devasting, overwhelming power to those who had raised his ire; and the tender, loving Adam, his green eyes soft and glowing, amazingly gentle when making love, for all his size, and endlessly patient and forgiving with all her inadequacies and indecision. Their outward appearances contrasted so vividly, but their gentleness, patience, and love for her were common traits. Adam surely deserved her love, but if so, what prompted the feelings of guilt that suppressed so heavily her response to his affections?

"I think your mind is very far from me right now, Amanda." Adam's voice was soft as he whispered against her cheek. "Come back to me, quickly. I don't want to kiss a girl whose mind is on other matters."

Adam's manner was teasing, but his eyes were strangely serious. With a small smile, Amanda lifted her mouth to his. What was meant to be a light kiss, owing to the child who nursed so busily at her breast, slowly deepened as the taste of Amanda began to heat his blood, and groaning audibly, Adam finally pushed himself from her.

Looking directly into her face, he whispered hoarsely, "Amanda, I ache to lie with you again in my arms. To have you so near and yet not be able to love you! If Reverend Briscomb doesn't return soon, I'm afraid you'll marry a madman!" Then suddenly he added, smiling, "But you'll marry me, mad or not, my little lady." Looking down at Jonathan's full, bright cheeks, he whispered softly, "Hurry, my little son, and get your fill. I'd like some time with your mother without you between us."

Contrary to this request, Jonathan was particularly slow in his feeding, stretching Adam's patience almost to the breaking point. When finally his little dark head began to droop, Adam felt hope rise. Perhaps Betty would sleep five minutes more.

Amanda lay the child in her lap as she quickly buttoned her dress, then lifted him to continue his dressing.

"Oh, no," Adam whispered firmly. "Put him to rest as he is. The blanket will keep him warm until he awakens. We only have a few minutes left to be alone."

Amanda did as she was asked and turned from Jonathan's makeshift crib to be pulled tightly against Adam as his mouth covered hers hungrily. She could feel the large, heavy bulge of his manhood, and was aghast at her own body's reaction to its stimulus. Finally pulling his mouth away from hers with extreme regret when he heard movement in the next room, he whispered against her hair in an agonized voice, "Soon, Amanda. Reverend Briscomb must return soon."

Seven

Adam stared ahead of him and fought to suppress the whoop of joy he felt rising in his throat. The stimulus for his sudden state of exaltation was a tall, thin, rather bedraggled-looking gentleman, whose narrow, lined face was strained with fatigue, his skimpy gray hair tied artlessly back with a narrow leather thong. His travel-stained clothing consisted of a shirt that had once been white, but now showed a distinct gray cast, a narrow black tie, a black cloth coat which had seen much wear—all contrasting rather sharply with the buckskin breeches and moccasins he also wore. He was a rather pathetic sight, who nonetheless brought Adam striding forward, his hand extended in greeting, as the weary gentleman walked through the gates of the fort. The broad grin and warm welcome extended by Adam was met rather suspiciously as Reverend Briscomb regarded him steadily through the glasses perched so precariously on the bridge of his sharp, hawklike nose.

"Welcome back, Reverend Briscomb. I've been awaiting your return most anxiously!" Adam's hearty handshake was accompanied with an even

374

heartier slap on the back, which almost succeeded in dislodging the delicately balanced spectacles.

Reverend Briscomb's response was a trifle less hearty, and a bit cautious as he spoke softly. "Thank you, Adam, and what may I do for you?"

Amanda surveyed her image in the mirror, a look of astonishment crossing her pale young face. Surely that lovely image could not be she! It seemed to Amanda in that moment of discovery that Betty Mitchell had indeed performed a miracle and changed her into a princess, so unaccustomed was she to her own appearance in such finery. She turned to view more closely the dress Betty had sewn so carefully for her wedding. Although of simple design, it was by far the finest garment she had ever worn. Made of a fine, softly spun, ice-blue cotton, it was cut in a square neckline in front and back, with the sleeves hugging the arm tightly up to the elbow, where a wide ruffle trimmed with sheer white lace flared out gracefully. The ruffles of the same white lace carefully sewn into the neckline of the dress to afford some modesty still failed to hide completely the rise of her full, white breasts. The bodice tapered down to a gentle point at the waistline, emphasizing its narrowness. From there the skirt flared out dramatically into a graceful bell. More striking still was the splendid manner in which the dexterous Betty had dressed Amanda's hair, pulling the sparkling, champagne-colored mass to the top of her head, where she had woven it intricately to fall gracefully in the back in a tumble of shimmering curls. At the crown of her head she had placed a small, delicate fan of lace and minute blue bows.

The upswept hairstyle exposed the slender curve of Amanda's shoulders and neck and drew attention to her high cheekbones and the delicate planes of her face, further enhancing her fragile, china-doll quality. As she stood gazing in awe at Betty's handiwork, she failed to realize that the gown she wore, which was lovely in its own right, was transformed into a frock of overwhelming elegance only by reflecting her own inordinate beauty.

Unable to find the words to express her appreciation, Amanda turned and embraced Betty spontaneously, with great warmth, drawing happy tears to the older woman's eyes.

In another section of the fort Adam stood waiting with great impatience. Glancing absentmindedly around the dining hall, which was to be the site of their vow taking, he noted that it no longer bore even the slightest resemblance to the room in which they had eaten earlier. A small smile lightened his grim expression momentarily as he mused, Betty must have put to good use the many favors owed her to have accomplished such an elaborate change in the short time since Reverend Briscomb walked through the gates this morning. He ran his gaze lightly over the room again in amusement. The long tables had been moved to one end of the room, and the benches arranged in rows, to create an aisle down the center. At the head of the aisle, using one long dining table, a white tablecloth, and numerous tall, tapered candles, she had fashioned an alter of sorts, in front of which stood Reverend Briscomb, now appearing quite a bit more presentable than he had earlier in the day. In the time spent within the fort awaiting Reverend Briscomb's return, Adam had been aware of a gradual softening of the manner in which the inhabitants of the fort had treated Amanda, and he was surprised and pleased to see the benches almost filled. Although he personally cared little who attended his wedding, he knew Amanda would be relieved to be accepted once again, and for that reason alone was grateful for their presence.

The nervous groom stared anxiously at the doorway from his location at the head of the center aisle near the alter. His thick, sun-streaked hair had been carefully brushed back, and he wore proudly beneath his buckskin jacket the white broadcloth shirt Amanda had sewn for their wedding. But his expression was tense; his light brown brows were drawn into a frown; his huge fists clenched and unclenched as he awaited Amanda's arrival.

The rotund figure of Dr. Cartwright stood beside him, in readiness to perform his role as best man, amused by the groom's obvious agitation.

What can possibly be detaining Amanda so long? Momentarily close to panic, Adam's mind raced wildly. Perhaps she's changed her mind and decided against our marriage! Starting forward urgently, he stopped by a firm grip on his arm and a low voice as Dr. Cartwright asked calmly, "Where are you going, Adam?"

"I'm going to find Amanda."

Smiling reassuringly as he maintained his steady grip on Adam's arm, he whispered, "Have a little more patience. She'll be here soon."

The sudden sound of surprised gasps interrupted

their conversation and snapped their attention to the doorway where Amanda stood, a stunning vision of ethereal loveliness, her arm resting lightly on Captain Mitchell's as she prepared to enter. Slowly she proceeded down the aisle, escorted by the slim, gray-haired captain, with Betty and Jonathan following closely behind, and Adam's heart swelled with love and pride in the woman who was to become his wife. His gaze caressed her warmly, noting the apprehension in her wide blue eyes as she approached. Tenderly extending his hand, he drew her near, his eyes never leaving her face, as Reverend Briscomb began the ceremony. Amanda's gaze was drawn to Adam's where it clung almost mesmerized by the warmth in its depths.

Hardly conscious of his words, Amanda listened as Reverend Briscomb's voice droned on, and Adam recited his vows in a firm, clear voice. Within moments Reverend Briscomb was addressing her, and as if from a distance Amanda heard her own voice stumbling softly in response. To her mind a small eternity elapsed before the reverend's sonorous tones proclaimed their wedded state.

The whole scene seemed stiff and unreal to Amanda, so different from the event of her first marriage. But Adam wore a look of unmistakable joy as he pulled her tenderly into his arms, whispering softly against her lips before they met his, "Amanda, my wife."

The next few minutes were spent in a flurry of congratulations, as those who had withheld their friendship from Amanda for so long shook the couple's hands and wished them well. In the midst of

378

the confused scene, a sudden angry wail drew Amanda's attention from the guests, and she turned to see Jonathan squirming angrily in Betty's arms as he strained and leaned toward her, his fat little arms outstretched, his dark eyes filled with pleading tears. Without hesitation, Adam turned to take the unhappy baby, smiling coaxingly into the sad little face until the appealing child returned his smile and relaxed against him, his arms encircling Adam's neck. It was then that Adam turned back to Amanda to see her tense, hesitant expression replaced with a warm smile as she regarded them both; and appearing to relax for the first time since entering the room, she moved to casually slip her arm through his.

Rubbing his cheek lightly against the child's shining black hair, Adam thought, Thank you, little son, for the gift of your mother's as well as your own acceptance.

Walking beside Amanda, his arm around her slender waist, holding her far more casually than was his inclination, Adam was thankful that the small reception arranged by Betty was over at last. Jonathan had obligingly fallen asleep in his new father's arms and had been taken to the room of a friend where Betty and the captain were spending the night. At Betty's insistence, the privacy of her rooms had been turned over to them, knowing they were to set out for his cabin in the morning. "You must have a proper wedding night," she had insisted as they protested her generosity. She would not hear their refusal. Inwardly, Adam was pleased to accept, as he desperately wanted everything to be perfect on this most important night.

A short time later, Adam turned from lighting the lamp in the Mitchells' small bedroom, to find Amanda nervously avoiding his eyes. It seemed to him, as his eyes touched on her, that he had waited most of his life for this particular moment, and he did not wish to spoil it with impatience caused by the waves of desire he felt sweeping over him. Gently he drew her to him, raising her chin so that her eyes met his, and inquired softly, "What is this, Amanda, maidenly anxiety? Did our nights together give you cause to be afraid of me?"

"Oh, no, Adam," Amanda hastened to assure him. "It's just," she stammered uncertainly, "that I'm afraid you'll regret our marriage someday." Her doubts expressed, Amanda emitted a soft sigh and turned her face again from his.

Regret! The thought was inconceivable to Adam. Gathering her close, he closed his eyes momentarily at the overwhelming sweetness of her nearness. "Don't you believe me, Amanda, when I say I love you?" he whispered shakily against her hair.

"But why do you love me, Adam? I've caused you nothing but trouble and pain since first we met." In a trembling voice, she added softly, "I can't even bring you my virginity."

Instinctively his arms tightened as jealousy flooded his senses, but firmly shaking its hold, Adam stated softly, "I can tell you the many things I love about you, my darling, but I can't tell you why I love you. Loving you came naturally to me, as naturally as breathing, and loving you is as necessary to my life as my breath itself. Without you, my life has no purpose. This has been proven to me over and over, to my sorrow, and I won't suffer separation from you again. You're my wife now, Amanda, and one day you'll come to love me."

"Adam, you promised. You said you wouldn't expect—"

Hesitating only a second. Adam said slowly, "I remember my promise, and I'll keep it. But now you must keep yours."

Adam scooped her up into his arms and walked wordlessly toward the bed. Depositing her solemnly there, he began to undress her with trembling hands. Amanda's heart ached at the pain she had inflicted, hating herself for her inability to lie and say the things he so wanted to hear. Quickly and efficiently Adam had, within minutes, stripped away her clothing until she lay naked before him. Slowly he removed the pins from her hair until it was unbound and loose against her pillow. He then stepped back to remove his clothing, and when he was done, he stood looking hesitantly down at her. Aware of his sudden uncertainty and pained at his distress, Amanda raised her arms and held them out to him in graceful invitation, whispering huskily as she did, "Come, Adam, my husband, come and love me."

With a small groan, Adam lowered his body to cover hers, a sharp electric tingle coursing through his veins as his flesh touched hers. "Amanda, my darling, my darling," he whispered again and again between deep, passionate kisses. He was overcome by the all-consuming desire that this petite doll-like woman inspired in him. Her innocent sexual allure drove his senses wild, and each taste of her only seemed to whet his appetite for more. He covered her face and hair with frenzied caresses, and soon the sweet, warm inner reaches of her mouth against his probing tongue were not enough. His warm lips and gentle, taunting hands seemed to be everywhere at once, titillating her senses so wildly as to raise her heartbeat to a raging thunder in her ears. But for Adam the fire could not be quenched. His wild need and desire for her drove him on, tasting, probing, caressing, reveling in the joy her beautiful body gave to him.

With a dull ache inside him, Adam realized he would not easily be sated this time, not until Amanda cried in need for him, the same need that was burning and tearing now inside him. Wild abandon seemed to overcome him as his lips left the swollen peaks of her breasts to follow a steady, torrid, downward path. Softly his face nuzzled the shining golden ringlets nestling between her thighs, and Amanda gave a sharp, sudden cry of protest. No one other than Chingue had ever known her so intimately, and she struggled briefly as Chingue's memory returned like a physical presence between them. But Adam, restricting her legs with his body, pinned her flailing hands to her sides as he whispered in a shaking, passionate voice. The lamp still glowed brightly, illuminating his face clearly as he raised it to look into hers. "Aren't you my wife, Amanda? Weren't our bodies joined as one? Don't deny me tonight. I have a deep, aching need of you that will not be assauged. I must possess all of you, my darling. All of you." Adam's voice broke then, and his face was clearly lined with the pain he felt deep inside.

Her eyes still on his tortured expression, Amanda slowly relaxed her tense body, and separated her thighs. With a broken cry, Adam's mouth swooped down to cover the soft lips nestled within the tight golden curls. At his first taste of her, he was lost to his passion. Driving deeper and deeper, he probed the tender inner confines of her body, seeking his own appeasement and drawing forth the deep, sensuous response he so desperately needed from her.

His probing tongue and wild assault on her senses could not be denied, and gradually Amanda was transported beyond conscious thought, her body reacting instinctively to the throbbing need building inside her. Writhing with desire, hating her traitorous body for its weakness, she sobbed as Adam's all-devouring mouth drove her past the limits of her control, and with groaning, shuddering convulsions she tumbled breathlessly from the pinnacle of passion.

Tears of happiness welled in Adam's eyes as he accepted her body's tribute to his lovemaking. I have made her forget him for a little while, he thought exultantly, but I won't rest until I'm firmly ensconced within her heart.

Slowly Adam slid his body up over hers, to hold her close against him as her ragged breathing returned to normal. "Amanda," he said simply against her hair, "I didn't know it was possible to love someone so deeply."

Gently he entered her, purposely restraining his actions to stretch as long as possible their enjoyment of each other. Adam's slow, rhythmic penetrations continued, gradually increasing until Amanda once again scaled the heights of passion. Suddenly Adam's restraint was gone, his crashing, explosive release eliciting the same from her as they climaxed together in simultaneous abandon.

Feeling the perspiration of their mutual passion against his skin, Adam held her fast, unwilling to withdraw and end their glorious moment. Slowly he rolled to his back to release her, but a sudden loneliness caused him to draw her close once more as he whispered, "I will never stop loving you, never have enough of you." Within moments he proceeded to prove the truth of his solemn statement.

When, many hours later, Adam lay asleep, his arm still curved possessively around her, Amanda allowed her tears full reign. Glittering black eyes seemed to haunt her mind, and she sobbed softly, "Chingue, my love, forgive my weakness. You who were so true, so loving, who gave your life for me, forgive me. This man needs me too. He will care for your son and me, but he needs my consolation. My darling, Chingue, I love only you."

Amanda awoke slowly to the security and warmth of a gentle embrace. Her contented feeling of well-being was not new to her, and in her drowsiness a familiar name came to her lips, only to be silenced by the insistent pressure of warm lips against her own. Opening her eyes, she was momentarily stunned to see light skin and tawny hair so close to hers, and, as he drew away, not dark, but soft, green eyes lit so brilliantly with the light of love. Brought back to reality in a blinding jolt, she suddenly recalled her marriage and the night spent in her marriage bed.

384

Her cheeks flaming, Amanda tried to look away, but found her face held firmly with a broad, calloused hand as Adam chuckled, "What's bothering you, Mrs. Carstairs? Do last night's passions heat your blood again?"

In answer, Amanda blushed even more vividly, and Adam laughed, charmed and amused by her reaction.

Lowering his head to gently trail his lips across her temple, he whispered huskily, "Need I coax you, or will you follow me willingly down the path of passion, my love?"

Before Amanda could stammer her response, a sudden soft knock sounded on the door, and with a small frown of impatience, Adam called out, "What is it?"

Betty's soft, apologetic voice was heard in response. "Jonathan needs his mother and will not be put off any longer."

Reminded of her motherly duty, Amanda responded quickly as she scrambled out of bed. "Please bring him to me, Betty. I'll be ready in a moment."

As she hurriedly began dressing, Amanda turned to see Adam's eyes boldly roaming over her still unclothed figure, and once again felt hot color in her cheeks as she stammered shyly, "I believe it's time Jonathan be weaned. I've been selfish and avoided the task because I've enjoyed his closeness, but now. . . ."

Unable to find the words she desired to finish her statement, Amanda hesitated. Adam rose from the bed, unmindful of his nudity, his broad, well-proportioned body seeming even greater and larger in the light of day. Amanda's eyes widened as he came to press a light kiss against her lips and then aid her in dressing, speaking softly as he did, "Yes, I believe now would be a good time to start."

The small entourage urged their horses steadily onward, and Amanda felt her anticipation growing. Adam had warned her to expect little in the way of comfort at first, for the most that could be said for the structure he had hastily erected after clearing the debris of his parents' burned-out cabin was that it would be a roof over their heads and a hearth on which to cook. Adam was inwardly thankful that his desire to mark the land on which his parents had lived and given their lives had driven him to reconstruct the cabin, however crudely, as he now felt the inner peace of bringing Amanda home.

His mother's warm, lined face returned to mind for a moment, and Adam smiled. How she would have loved Amanda, he thought sadly, knowing his sweet, lovely bride was the answer to Helen Carstairs' many prayers. His grin broadened as he imagined the reaction his tall, quiet father would have had to his beautiful young wife. His lecture on the treatment this small, delicate woman should receive would have been delivered with a comradely wink and a hearty slap on the back.

The sudden appearance of the overgrown clearing where the cabin was situated caused Adam to urge his horse to a faster pace, and he turned to look momentarily into Amanda's face.

Amanda's heart began to race wildly as her new home first came into view, and she assessed it hesitantly. The simple log cabin was small and hastily constructed. This was obvious in the absence of the finer details of construction that marked a completed dwelling. But it appeared strongly built, and surely would prove adequate for their needs with a little work. This she perceived in one look at the neglected, partially dilapidated, one-room dwelling that Adam viewed so despairingly. His handsome face, as he turned toward her once again, was apologetic and embarrassed until it met her pleased expression.

"Please help me down, Adam." Amanda's face was eager as she waited impatiently for him to lift her and Jonathan to the ground. "Do hurry," she urged, "I'm anxious to see the inside."

Astounded by her obvious eagerness to see the interior of a cabin that would have instantly repelled the average woman, Adam lifted her down and followed behind as she moved urgently forward, stopping her only as she came to the doorway so he might inspect the premises for unwanted occupants of any species.

Satisfied at last that the cabin's cold, dank interior held no danger, Adam turned to allow Amanda entrance, smiling quietly at her obvious optimism and dreading the disappointment he knew would soon follow. Adam's eyes remained fixed on her face, awaiting the first sign of disenchantment as her wide, blue eyes scanned the dark room. But Amanda did not see the crudely constructed floors and walls that were unsealed and allowed the brisk March wind to whistle through, nor the roughly hewn ceiling, hanging from which webs in all shapes and sizes were evident. Nor did she notice the obvious lack of furniture with which to begin their housekeeping. Instead, she saw the rough beginning of a dwelling that would soon be clean, warm, and comfortable. It was her first real, permanent home since Jonathan's birth. She looked to the side wall, a gasp of delight escaping her lips as her eyes touched on the huge fireplace that dominated that area. Although it had suffered greatly from neglect, Amanda had never before seen such a beautiful hearth. Spacious enough to accommodate the most hearty fire, its entire face was covered with delicately painted blue-and-white tiles, each obviously set with painstaking care, achieving, even stained as they were by soot, a look of elegance quite out of place in the humble surroundings.

In answer to her look of silent inquiry, Adam responded, "That fireplace is all that remains of the original dwelling. It was my mother's pride and joy."

"And it will be mine also, Adam," Amanda whispered softly as she turned to face him. Then, with a sudden burst of enthusiasm, she said purposefully, "Well, we might as well begin right now." And turning, she set herself to work.

Time moved quickly for the newlyweds as they worked diligently to put their home to right. In an area where even the simplest piece of furniture had to be constructed from scratch, Adam found himself working steadily, with his fair-haired, determined wife matching the steady pace he maintained. If Adam found himself working harder than ever before, he also found his happiness and contentment far greater than he had ever dreamed, for his work brought him the satisfaction of knowing the fruits of his labor would be shared with Amanda and Jonathan.

Adam was both amused and touched at the diligence with which Amanda attacked her wifely chores, and he knew joy beyond measure when each night, no matter the labor of the day, she accepted his love with a willing response. But still, gnawing steadily at his happiness was the suspicion that Amanda's response to his lovemaking was motivated simply by gratitude, and that the great, overwhelming passion he felt for her was not returned.

Despite the nagging doubts in Adam's mind regarding Amanda's love for him, there was no doubt whatever of the great, growing attachment forming between Jonathan and himself. Adam's entrance into the cabin brought great squeals of delight from the bright youngster, his leaving having the reverse effect of earsplitting howls of despair. Jonathan's noisy, fussy behavior on these occasions frustrated his tiny mother immensely, but was the source of great amusement and pride to Adam, who reacted with obvious pleasure. He would laughingly swing his dark-haired son into the air amid the child's loud cries of utter joy. Determined as Amanda was to reprimand her son for his open display of temper, her heart swelled with happiness in their obvious enjoyment of each other.

On his few short absences from the cabin, Adam had grown to anticipate with pleasure the happy domestic picture of his family when he returned. On such an occasion, returning from the hunt after a long morning in the woods as April began its second week, he was stunned to find the cabin empty and no sign of Amanda or Jonathan. Fear slipped its icy fingers along his spine, and he loudly called Amanda's name to have silence his only response. His heart pounding, he walked back outside, searching the area for a clue to their whereabouts, when a faint, scraping noise caught his attention. Anxiously following the sound, he came to a cleared area a small distance behind the cabin, the site of his parents' graves. He stood silently watching, unobserved, as Jonathan played happily on the ground and Amanda worked putting the last touches to the rock enclosure she had constructed around the graves. Her hair, which had been hastily pinned to the top of her head, fell in light, feathery wisps on her neck, and small, shining beads of perspiration were apparent on her upper lip. A long smudge of dirt ran across her perspiring cheek, and as he watched, she got up abruptly and stood back, arms akimbo, admiring her work.

She gave a startled gasp as Adam's voice broke the silence.

"My thanks for your tending of my parents' graves, Amanda." A sober expression accompanied his words.

Amanda offered quietly in response, "We've both suffered great losses in this war, Adam, but I have no graves to mark mine. These will be the markers of our common loss."

Adam's answer was wordless as he slowly walked to stand beside her and, slipping his arm around her, drew her to his side. But that night, long after

Amanda had fallen asleep, Adam lay awake, the uncompleted vow made over those graves nagging him into wakefulness.

Adam glanced casually up into the cloudless blue sky as he wearily wiped the perspiration from his forehead with the back of his arm. The warm April sun had forced him to shed his heavy homespun shirt an hour earlier, exposing his broad chest to the warm rays that glinted so brightly on the mat of fine, golden hair as he continued chopping wood. Noticing for the first time the profusion of budding trees and plants and greening grass, he slapped absentmindedly at the swarms of gnats taking their first opportunity of the year to make their presence felt. Spring has come in a rush, he thought. Then he laughed to himself, realizing his preoccupation with his new bride had almost made him unconscious of the passage of time and the change of season. Even now, after a month of marriage in complete seclusion, his thoughts never roamed very far from her or his bright, energetic young son.

Amanda, his heart sang, his eyes following her as she crossed the yard to hang her laundry on the line stretched in the sun. His gaze lingered lovingly on her slim form, and he felt a great warmth suffuse him as he watched her at work. He smiled again in contentment. They had accomplished a great deal in their first month of marriage. Adam had hastily sealed the cabin's log walls securely, eliminating the drafts that had caused such a great discomfort at first, and Amanda had cleaned and scoured the inside of the cabin until the log walls appeared to glow, and the tile fireplace was restored once again to its original beauty. Their household furniture presently included a table, four chairs, a crib for Jonathan, a large bearskin rug salvaged from the remains of a shed behind the house, and a big, comfortable bed that had already seen many long, loving nights. The small clearing around the cabin, which had been overgrown with weeds, was clear again; and Amanda had located and restored almost to its original state his mother's herb garden, which was putting forth the first shoots of the season. He had worked for the past hour and a half chopping and stacking wood, and a generous supply lay near the cabin for fuel and cooking purposes.

Adam felt a deep sense of fulfillment and knew the sole reason for his happiness was busily hanging her laundry in the sun. His eyes returned to the petite blond figure as the April breeze pressed the folds of her dress against her slender young body, outlining the soft curves he had come to know so well. Amanda, my Amanda, he thought again. She is all things, everything to me. A momentary seige of jealousy stirred his blood as he thought of the distant look he occasionally saw in her eyes, when he was reminded her heart was not completely his. Chingue still haunted their marriage bed at times. Adam knew this instinctively. But he also knew that, although Amanda had not declared her love for him, he was dearer to her than any living man, and he had decided to content himself with that. He was alive and Amanda belonged to him now. His eyes still on her, Adam dropped his axe and started forward, approaching quietly, without her notice, until he stood directly behind her. Slowly, he slid his arms around her slender waist, pulling her back tightly against him. After her initial start, Amanda relaxed in his embrace.

Burying his face in her fragrant cloud of golden hair, he luxuriated in the waves of pleasure her nearness stirred within him. "This is not the time to hang your laundry," he mumbled softly.

"But Adam," she protested, "it is a perfect day for drying."

Turning her quickly in his arms, he murmured, before his lips covered hers, "It's a perfect day for making love." And scooping her quickly into his arms, he started toward the cabin.

At that moment a sudden call shattered the quiet, freezing Adam in his steps. Slowly lowering Amanda to her feet, he turned in the direction of the shout, and within seconds a figure was visible in the brush. A dark frown covered Adam's face in response to the friendly smile of the short, red-haired fellow who walked forward.

"Hello, Adam! Good day, Amanda!" The young man was obviously happier to see them than Adam was with his presence.

"Hello, Jeremy. What brings you here?" Adam's smile flashed reluctantly as he grasped the stubby, freckled hand extended in greeting. He sincerely liked the friendly young colonial standing before him, but the youth's sudden appearance so far from the fort stirred his suspicions. He was certain the eager soldier had not come all this way without a definite purpose in mind.

With a quick glance, Jeremy's eyes took in the

happy domestic scene, coming to rest more appreciatively than suited Adam on Amanda's sweet, inquiring countenance. Finally tearing his eyes from her face, he addressed Adam directly. "You seem to have accomplished a lot since you came here, Adam."

"Yes, we have, but what brings you such a distance from Fort Edward?"

The youth was obviously reluctant to declare the intention behind his visit, but Adam pressed his inquiry doggedly as he ushered the tired fellow into the cabin for refreshment. "I'm sure you didn't come all this way to inspect our progress. Colonel Webb must have more important duties for his men than that."

Finally, his serious brown eyes looking intently into Adam's, Jeremy began. "You must have realized, Adam, that another attempt would be made to take Fort Carillon this year." At Adam's nod, he continued. "We have a new commander for this assault, Adam. General Amhurst isn't a befuddled old man like General Abercrombie." The young soldier sneered as he spoke the name of the general whose stubbornness the year before had resulted in the needless loss of so many lives, as well as the battle itself.

"General Amhurst is a brilliant leader. He's careful and painstaking in planning and detail. We'll be certain to take Fort Carillon this time."

Adam eyed the freckled young face peering so earnestly into his as they sat companionably around the table, and could feel Amanda tense for his reply, as he ventured, "That's all very good, but you haven't yet stated the purpose of your visit here. What does all this have to do with me?"

Jeremy looked quickly to Amanda's expectant face and flushed a bright scarlet. He was aware of the tender scene he had interrupted with his arrival, and was obviously loath to declare his purpose, sensing the resistance with which it would be met. Looking for a moment at Amanda's delicate beauty, he admitted to himself, from the experience of his nineteen years, that if he were Adam and this lovely, young woman were his, he would be greatly disinclined to heed a plea that would take him from her side.

"Jeremy!" Adam's sharp tone jerked back his wandering attention, demanding a reply.

A new flush of color covering his face, the young colonial hastened to answer, "It's because General Amhurst has earned his nickname, the Cautious Commander, that I've been sent to enlist your aid in setting the strategy of attack, Adam."

Rising to his feet, all the while shaking his head negatively, Adam said emphatically, "No, I won't have anything to do with this. I've seen enough bloodshed. I'm through with it all."

"The General was informed of your familiarity with Fort Carillon, Adam." Jeremy's zealous plea was insistent. "You needn't join in the actual battle. General Amhurst merely seeks the advice only you can offer him."

Turning his back rudely, still shaking his head, Adam walked toward the fireplace. "I'll have nothing to do with this assault, I tell you. I've been through all this before. My help didn't make much difference the last time, and I don't intend to go through it all again. I'm needed here and here I'll stay."

"But Adam—"

"Any further discussion will merely be a waste of time."

"But Adam—"

The young man's persistence was met with an angry glare, cutting short any further argument as Adam turned and warned quietly, "You're welcome to stay the night only if you'll accept my answer, Jeremy. Otherwise, you may leave right now to return to your general with my answer."

Jeremy's pleading glance toward Amanda met lowered eyes, and finally conceding defeat in the face of Adam's glaring hostility, he murmured in a low voice, "As you wish, Adam. I'll be pleased to accept your hospitality for the night."

Within a day, Jeremy Stone had departed their cabin, but his arrival had precipitated a vague, practically indiscernible change in their lives, one which affected Amanda deeply. His visit had introduced an element of anxiety into their days. Adam was increasingly moody and uncommunicative at times, and although his love for her was obvious in all his actions, his lovemaking had developed a frantic, desperate quality that caused an apprehensive fear to be born within her. Amanda grew more frightened by the day, with a vague, undetermined cause the basis of her anxiety. A silent, torturous air of expectation completely devastated her peace of mind.

*　　*　　*

A bright, sunny day a month later had drawn Amanda outside the cabin to bask in the warm sun during her precious moments of leisure while Jonathan slept. A sudden impulse took her up the path toward the walled graves behind the cabin, only to stop abruptly as her husband's solemn figure came into view. Standing silently beside the graves, Adam wore an expression of tortured remorse. So stunned was Amanda at the pain reflected there that she felt suddenly breathless, and in a flash of realization Adam's words in their discussion during their first days together in the forest were returned to her: "I buried my parents' mutilated bodies and made a solemn vow over their graves to avenge their deaths, to be part of at least one major progressive step toward peace and the end of the senseless murders."

In that instant the cause of Adam's anxiety was clear. He had selflessly abandoned his vow that she might keep the peace and tranquility he had been able to give her. But in doing that, Adam's own peace had been damaged. His mind was at war with his heart; one demanding adherence to his word and commitment; the other unwilling to leave her.

Slowly she walked to stand beside Adam at the graveside. Slipping her arm around his waist and leaning lightly against him, she whispered softly, "You must honor your vow, Adam."

Snapped from his reverie by her quiet statement, Adam stared down at her, amazed at her silent reading of his thoughts.

"If you would honor our marriage vows, Adam, you must also honor your previous commitment. I won't have you abandon your integrity on my behalf.

I won't stand by as the years pass and watch as your conscience destroys you. Come on." Gently she urged him back toward the cabin. "We'll prepare to leave for Fort Edward. When you go, Jonathan and I will go with you."

Adam's eyes were filled with wordless gratitude for her understanding as they slowly walked toward their home.

The decision having been made, it seemed no time at all before they were once again on the trail to Fort Edward. Amanda's farewell glance at the cabin brought the brightness of tears to her eyes, but conscious of Adam's intense scrutiny, she quickly diverted her face and urged her horse on behind him. It was obvious from Adam's solemn demeanor that he had no more desire than she to leave their haven, but both had agreed that personal choice had no place in their decision.

Countless worries continued to plague Adam's mind as he persevered on their determined course. He directed another backward glance at his bride's face as she determinedly urged her horse forward, and then he looked at the child resting quietly in his arms. He had been fool enough to let other matters take precedence over Amanda before, and the result each time had been disastrous. These two human beings had become most precious to him, and were, indeed, as important a part of him as his very eyes or limbs. With the realization that alone he was no longer complete came a startling sense of panic. He could not lose them!

Sensing his anxiety, Amanda managed an encouraging smile, and Adam, feeling the warmth it generated down to his very bones, was hard put to continue moving forward without stopping his horse to take her into his arms then and there.

To Adam's surprise, his arrival at the fort was not completely unanticipated, for Colonel Webb, judging his character shrewdly, had counted on his eventual capitulation to General Amhurst's summons. Before much time had elapsed, Adam found himself across the table from the man who was soon to lead the attack against Fort Carillon.

Adam scrutinized General Amhurst. To his appraising glance, the general appeared an intense, serious man, filled with the responsibility and importance of the success of his mission. At his side his aide, Major John Hawks, listened attentively, as did Colonel Webb and himself, while the general outlined the basic plan of attack.

In his quiet, characteristically military manner, General Amhurst explained that a force that would eventually number 12,000, half British regulars and the other half colonials, had begun to assemble at the site of Fort William Henry. Demonstrating the caution that had earned him his nickname, the general had ordered that the entire area be burned, particularly the site of the old military cemetery, which had been violated by Montcalm's Indians. And then he had the entire area covered six inches deep with sand from the beach. This was a sanitary precaution always taken when his army camped, so they might pitch their tents on clean ground. His plans were simple. He intended to follow General Abercrombie's route to Fort Carillon, occupy the trenches of Montcalm and, protected in this way from the guns of the fort, begin formal seige. As the meticulous Britisher continued to speak, a begrudging admiration for his intelligence and perception grew inside Adam, and when urged, he launched into an in-depth description of the area, illustrating his remarks with roughly sketched maps of the terrain. He next analyzed and dissected the interior defenses of Fort Carillon. The meeting was still in full progress when Adam realized they had been in session for almost four hours. Suddenly conscious of the fact that he had casually turned his wife and son over to Betty Mitchell's eager hands without any knowledge of their accommodations within the fort, he was assailed by guilt and hastened to depart, after a promise to resume their discussions the following day.

Adam walked across the now darkened interior yard of the fort, finally acknowledging to himself that his assistance would be in demand until the attack was launched at the end of July. It would take him that long to draw up and copy detailed maps and to familiarize the troops with the terrain. Without conscious volition, Adam had become infected by General Amhurst's contagious sense of purpose and dedication. He also remembered only too well the scores upon scores of bodies lying where they had been mercilessly cut down in their valiant attempts to penetrate the *abatis de bois* the previous year, and the uppermost thought in his mind was that their failure must not be repeated.

Suddenly possessed by a deep, overpowering longing to see his family, Adam quickened his step toward the Mitchells' quarters.

Dependable and generous as always, Betty had already arranged her sitting room to accommodate his family and him for the duration of their stay at the fort. The circumstances of the past two years had succeeded in allowing her to think of Amanda with the possessiveness of a parent, and with this abundance of warm feelings in her heart, Betty had come to look upon Jonathan as her own grandchild. So it was to Jonathan's deep, gurgling laughter that Adam entered the room to see Betty proudly assuming the role of doting grandmother. At the first sight of Adam, the child's laughter turned into loud, demanding shrieks as he almost tossed himself from Betty's arms in an effort to reach him. Feeling a familiar sense of pride, Adam took his sturdy young son, who strained so heavily in his direction, eliciting a wide, toothless, dimpled smile as the child mauled his face lovingly. The others in the room observed with wordless satisfaction the strong bond that had grown between them.

Many hours later, far too many for Adam, who had grown accustomed to the isolation and privacy of their cabin and had long since tired of people around them, Amanda and he were finally alone. During the long hours since his meeting with General Amhurst, he had been impatient to share with her his impressions of the Cautious Commander, and the plan of attack against Fort Carillon. But now that they were alone, he felt himself fast losing his inclination to talk. He sprawled casually at the end of the couch where Jonathan lay blissfully sleeping, his broad frame slouched down against the softness of the

401

pillows, his long, muscular legs extended in front of him. Despite his casual posture, his partially closed green eyes watched appreciatively as Amanda began undressing. His heart had accelerated beating the moment her fingers had touched the first button on her dress, and he felt a familiar tightening in his loins when her perfect young body was revealed to him ever so briefly. Would he never cease to be awed by the wonder of her flawless beauty, and the even greater wonder of her purity of spirit, which was reflected so brilliantly in her huge, silver-blue eyes? Surely I have captured an angel for my wife, he thought as he stared at the woman he loved so completely. But, despite his momentary desires, he knew there were matters that need be settled between them. And so it was with an air of apprehension that he watched as Amanda began to prepare a bed for them on the floor beside the couch, the only place available in the crowded fort. Betty had generously offered her bed for the duration of their stay, which they had declined immediately. When they refused, she had offered to share her bed with Amanda, suggesting that the captain and Adam sleep in the barracks. That suggestion was met with a look from Adam so black as to send the color flying into Betty's pale cheeks as she remarked quietly, "I must be getting older than I realized to have proposed that arrangement!"

Adam and the captain had laughed uproariously, and Adam had encircled the matronly figure in a brief, affectionate hug to ease her embarrassment.

Adam felt a momentary stab of guilt realizing that, except for his selfishness, Amanda would be sleeping in comfort on a soft, downy mattress. But he did not

402

experience true regret at his refusal to be separated from her. There would soon be too many nights when they would be forced to be apart. He could not bear to begin the separation any sooner than was necessary.

His eyes following her every move as she settled their blankets, Adam delighted in Amanda's natural grace of movement as she moved around the room, and he admitted to himself with a sigh that each moment, each hour, he became more enamoured of his lovely wife.

Having arranged their pallet to her satisfaction, Amanda quickly slipped beneath the light covering that was necessary even on this June night. Adam rose, careful not to disturb Jonathan, and, divesting himself of his clothing, joined her. Taking her into his arms, marveling at the sheer magic of her touch, he proceeded slowly to relate the events of his meeting with General Amhurst. At the conclusion of his narrative there was a brief silence before Amanda's soft voice sounded warily.

"How long will you be needed here? How long will it be before we can start home?" The softly whispered questions had taken on an anxious note.

Adam had not extinguished the lamp before joining her, and tilting up her chin so that her bright, hopeful eyes looked directly into his, he answered quietly, "We both know what I have to do, Amanda. Neither of us will know any peace until Fort Carillon is under the British flag and Fort William Henry is avenged." Amanda remained silent, her eyes still on his face, and he continued. "General Amhurst will stay here until the end of the week and then leave to join his men encamped at the site of Fort William Henry. Before the month is out, I'll leave to join them."

Amanda listened wordlessly, her face stiff and unmoving while her heart seemed to turn into a lead weight within her chest. The tightness in her throat precluded any comment, and her mind tortured her with visions of the death and destruction of the previous year's battle.

Misconstruing the emotionless manner in which she appeared to accept his leaving, Adam gripped her arms in frustrated anger.

"I've agonized over this decision and face separation from you with a dread that is almost unmanly, and you accept it without the barest trace of sorrow."

Suddenly his anger drained away and Adam embraced her to hide his tortured expression in her hair. "Won't you miss me at all, Amanda? My heart is torn with the agony of this decision. I'm suffering even now in anticipation of our separation. Haven't I managed to win even a corner of your affections?"

The emotion frozen inside her melted in the heat of his open despair, and Amanda whispered, her voice catching as she spoke, "Oh, yes, Adam. We'll miss you. Jonathan and I will miss you every moment you're away."

The sincerity of her words showed plainly on her face, and Adam's spirits rose slightly, awaiting her next words. But the declaration of love he had hoped to hear did not come. Finally, accepting once again that her love and loyalty still belonged to the man who lay dead for many long months, he spoke no more, and commenced to show his feeling for her lovingly, gently, so completely as to leave no doubt.

A true ranger's daughter at heart, Amanda easily adjusted to the military regimen at the fort, and began to settle in for an extended stay as Betty's guest. General Amhurst's scheduled departure at the end of their first week signaled the end of daily conferences, and Adam's days were then devoted to the drawing of specific, detailed maps of the area between Fort William Henry—their planned point of departure— and Fort Carillon. His knowledge of the forest and terrain around Fort Carillon as well as the fort's interior defense was unmatched, and his skillful recounting of his detailed knowledge filled many long hours and days. His preoccupation with his map-making chores seemed to fill his mind completely. But slowly Amanda became aware that, to the contrary of appearances, Adam studied her covertly as she worked around him in the small sitting room that had become their home, glancing quickly away as soon as she became aware of his perusal. Carefully evading her questions each time, he would once again immerse himself in his work. Amanda realized something other than the impending attack weighed on his mind, but all attempts to ascertain the cause of his distress met with complete frustration.

After a full morning of work, Adam's attention slowly drifted from the maps before him, as Amanda moved silently around the room. Jonathan had been put down for his nap, and was sleeping angelically. The sunlight filtering through the open doorway caught and sparkled gloriously on Amanda's silver-blond tresses as she hesitated momentarily in its rays. Thinking herself unobserved, she wore a perplexed expression, her delicate light-brown brows drawn together in a frown.

Even a frown can't mar her beauty, Adam mused absentmindedly, his eyes lingering lovingly as the deep, dull ache inside him sprang to life again. Prior to this time, without separation from her awaiting him so relentlessly a few days hence, Adam had tried to feel content with his lot. The woman he loved was his wife; her beauty of mind, body and spirit was available to him at his slightest inclination; their days were content, their nights filled with love-making that was mutually enjoyed—of that he was certain. He knew it was in his power to stir Amanda physically, and he also knew her love was a different matter, it did not belong to him. Oh, Amanda was fond of him, of that he was also certain. She had come to depend on him and trust him and his judgement completely; that was also true. She also enjoyed his company and esteemed him greatly, and until now he had convinced himself that all that was enough. Time had been his ally, for he had been sure that its passage would eventually earn him her love. But now his ally had become his enemy, for within a few days he would leave, still never having heard her say the words he so longed to hear. It was growing late. Time was running out. Panic seemed to wash over Adam, setting the hand with which he held the quill to shaking. Perspiration broke out on his forehead and upper lip as he foresaw in his mind the possibility of his death, and Amanda once again alone, forced to look to another man for protection. Adam felt the pain twist in his chest at the thought of another man holding his Amanda as he had held her, loving her as he had loved her.

Tortured beyond control by the vividness of his fancy, Adam sprang to his feet and took Amanda's arm possessively. Had he been assured of an hour's privacy, he would have taken her to bed and assuaged his torment with the balm of her soft, sweet body, but there was no privacy here. Her eyes were wide and startled as they looked up into his, and he felt he could drown in the depths of those fathomless blue pools. His desire mounting to even greater proportions, Adam whispered urgently, "Come on, Amanda, let's go for a walk outside the stockade. I feel restless. I need some exercise."

"But Jonathan is asleep, Adam. I can't leave him."

"We'll send Betty back to stay with him. Come with me," Adam's voice urged. And his eyes, still filled with the pain of his torturous thoughts, pleaded with her.

Hesitating only a moment longer, puzzled by the urgency of Adam's request, but realizing his need, she smiled with a flash of a mischievous dimple and put her hand in his. "It's a fine day for a walk, Adam."

Within minutes Betty was on her way to Jonathan, and Adam and Amanda were walking through the gates. Once within the cover of trees, shielded from prying eyes at the fort, Adam swept her into his embrace, covering her face with frantic, hungry kisses, as he murmured over and over, "Amanda, my little love." His passion having exceeded the point of control, Amanda soon found herself lying beside him on a bed of new moss as he followed his tumultuous feelings through their course to the ultimate conclusion. Eventually, lying spent beside her, the labored breathing of passion returned to normal, Adam began to feel guilt at his hungry demand on her body. Turning on his side, he cupped her chin in his hand to raise her face to his.

"Darling, I needed you desperately."

Looking levelly into his tortured face, Amanda replied softly, "And I'll always be here when you need me, Adam."

Unknowingly striking just the right note with which to soothe his anguished mind, Amanda felt herself swept tightly against his broad, muscled body once more, as he buried his face in her hair and, with a low groan, held her for a very long time.

Taking the first opportunity the next day, Adam caught Betty alone and earnestly faced the motherly, flaxen-haired woman.

"I'd like to ask a favor of you, Betty. If I don't return, I'd like you to give Amanda a home so she won't be forced to accept the first man who offers for her. I don't want circumstances to force her into marriage again for the security of her child."

Realizing the implications of his statement and the cause of his despair, Betty hastened to challenge their veracity. "You're wrong, Adam. Amanda obviously cares for you."

"I don't want to belabor the point, Betty." His voice was weary. "I only want to be assured she won't be pressured by necessity again."

"Adam, this is all so senseless. You'll return."

"Will you give me your reassurance, Betty?" Adam's face held a silent plea.

Noting the tension reflected there, Betty answered simply, "You have my word."

With a solemn nod, Adam smiled, a great weight having been lifted from his heart and mind.

June had come to a close, and the warm, sultry month of July was ushered in at Fort Edward with a buzz of activity that was completely unsuited to the weather. The buildup of the attacking force at the head of Lake George was almost completed. Approximately 5,000 British regulars were already encamped at the former site of Fort William Henry, and a like number of provincials had also arrived, with their number still increasing. Adam had completed drawing his maps and could no longer with honesty find a reason to linger at Fort Edward. He had already decided to leave with the next group of men traveling to the encamped force the following morning, but had delayed informing Amanda of his intended departure.

Lifting his eyes from the last of his work, he watched silently as she bathed her cheerful, laughing son in a small tub on the table. Jonathan's bright black eyes glowed with excitement as his fat little hands slapped wildly at the water, splashing himself and everything around him with glee. His joyful frenzy elicited from his spattered mother a severe reprimand, which, in truth, did little to dent his enthusiasm. Greatly amused, but realizing his willful son was in need of some discipline before he completely emptied the contents of the tub, Adam raised his voice so it might be heard over the shrieks of mother and son.

"Jonathan, you are getting your mother wet!"

The dark eyes, before alight with delight, filled with tears at his idol's harsh tone, and the small mouth drew into a sorrowful quivering pucker, which appeared to be the forerunner of a loud, forlorn wail. Completely won over and unable to suppress a smile, Adam declared in an encouraging tone, "Now you are a good little man. Let your mother finish your bathing and we'll go for a little walk."

True to his word, within the hour the striking family made their leisurely way through the stockade gates for the promised outing. The handsome, tawny-haired giant of a man walked casually, easily supporting the weight of his dark-haired son, whose large, black, almond-shaped eyes looked around curiously while he clutched his father's shirt collar possessively with his small, copper-tinted hands. At their side walked the small, doll-like mother of the child, still more girl than woman, her glorious golden hair knotted casually at the top of her head, her pensive face turned up toward them, wide blue eyes thoughtful. But her pride was obvious as she casually slipped her hand through the crook in her husband's arm, to be rewarded with a slow, warm smile.

Once outside the gates, Jonathan, who was now almost at the point of walking unaided, was lowered to the ground, where he walked awkwardly, supported on each side by his parents' hands. Slowly they made their way to the moss-covered bower that had served their purpose so well once before, and there collapsed lazily. Adam's eyes followed Jonathan as the child, dropping to his hands and knees, began exploring inquisitively, and he avoided Amanda's eyes as he began to speak.

"I've completed my map-making, Amanda. I'll be leaving with the next group of provincials to join General Amhurst."

At her sudden intake of breath, Adam's eyes moved quickly in her direction to see the color drain from her face, taking with it the happiness that had glowed there so vividly only moments before. Her eyes wide and apprehensive, she whispered, "When will you be leaving?"

"Tomorrow at daybreak."

The slight color remaining after his initial declaration completely drained away, leaving her ghostly white and frightened. Moving closer, Adam caressed her pale cheek reassuringly.

"You mustn't worry, Amanda. You'll be well cared for. Betty has promised that you'll always have a home with her and the captain as long as you desire. The attack should take place in two or three weeks, and I should be returning to you shortly thereafter. You needn't fear, for whatever the outcome, you won't be homeless."

For the first time tears filled the huge blue orbs looking into his, but they were not tears of sadness. Rather, they were brought on, by growing anger which also brought color flooding back into her face, as Amanda questioned in an incredulous voice, "Do you really believe my concern is for myself alone, Adam? Do you think so little of me that you could

411

believe I would have no concern at all for your welfare when you go into battle?''

Too angry to proceed, Amanda pulled herself to her feet in a huff and reached toward Jonathan so she might flee Adam's presence. But Adam, realizing her intention, curved his strong arm around her knees, catching her gently in his arms as she toppled down against his broad chest. Desperately trying to free herself, Amanda turned from him only to have his strong hand grip her chin firmly and turn her face toward his apologetic smile.

"No, I don't think so little of you, darling, but rather so much of you. My greatest concern was for your welfare and Jonathan's, should any circumstances keep me from returning; and in my anxiety, I overlooked your feelings. Please, don't be angry.''

Amanda's eyes were still averted, refusing to look into his, and Adam whispered, his lips only inches from her cheek, "Don't let our last day pass in anger, Amanda. I want this day to look back on in the many dreary ones ahead. Please, darling.''

Slowly the long, dark lashes lifted, the angry tears still clinging and sparkling on them, to reveal eyes lit with a soft azure glow that left him momentarily breathless. In his moment of hesitation, Amanda slid her arms around his neck and closed the small distance between them. The tender warmth of her kiss sent his senses reeling, and his strong arms crushed her responsively in an embrace, until a sudden tugging on his shoulder and an impatient slapping on his cheek tore Adam's attention away, to see a small, angry face close to theirs as Jonathan urgently pressed against them.

A roar of laughter escaped Adam's lips as he viewed his son's stern, disapproving countenance. With a sweep of his arm, he included the forlorn child within their embrace, closing and completing their circle of love.

Later that night, all the things that had gone unsaid that afternoon were said, and all things left undone were done. Through the long, loving night, Amanda gave kiss for kiss, caress for caress, not just accepting but returning the passion Adam offered so wildly. But still the words he so longed to hear did not come. Although in his heart Adam despaired of ever hearing Amanda declare her love for him, her spontaneous, passionate response to his lovemaking filled him simultaneously with pride and humility, and he felt an overpowering sense of awe at the depth and beauty of the emotion they shared. Clutching his tiny blond angel to him through the long night, one thought drummed over and over in his mind, I will come back. I must. I must come back to her.

Eight

The hot, humid July days slipped by with incredible speed as Adam became involved in the ever escalating activity at the camp of the attacking force. His maps, having been thoroughly scrutinized by General Amhurst, were finally given approval to be copied again and again and distributed among the officers. Adam was thankful for his assigned task of acquainting the troops with the terrain and with the problems of a virgin wilderness, for the seemingly endless task filled his mind and days with a sense of purpose. But in the dark silence of night, Adam fought most desperately the loneliness that only Amanda could assuage, when he ached in mind and body to hold her again. How had that pale young woman gained such a hold on his heart? Whatever blow life dealt, Amanda seemed to emerge herself: beautiful, spirited, gentle, loving. And at last she belonged to him alone; her son was their son; her life was his.

But nagging viciously at his peace of mind through the wakeful nights was the conversation he had overheard the second night at camp, when he

414

had been standing just out of sight of the campfire. A few men had recently encountered Robert Handley and remarked that, although he spoke constantly of moving further west, he had not yet severed the last of his ties and left the area. Not realizing Adam was within hearing, many a knowing chuckle had accompanied the remark made by a coarse, deep voice declaring, "He can't shake that little blond witch out of his blood, that's the problem. He's still hoping to wake up one day and find her willing to take him back."

The thought of Amanda in Robert's arms had been so abhorrent, that Adam's stomach had revolted violently, and he had been almost sick. The thought continued to haunt him.

July 21, 1759—The huge flotilla began to assemble. The steady influence of General Amhurst was obvious everywhere in the orderly, precise manner in which orders were issued and carried through. According to the General's own statistics, the force numbered a total of 11,756 men, all patiently waiting their turn to board the transporting fleet. First to load and sail were the grenadiers, next the light infantry, and third the rangers; behind them the Invincible, then the remaining army, with the sloop Halifax bringing up the rear.

In the eerie darkness before dawn, Adam stood in the press of thousands of men preparing to board the fleet. He watched the scene unfolding before him with an odd sense of unreality, so marked was its resemblance to the events of the year before. Warily

415

he scanned the rugged faces of the rangers around him, and with a deep sense of relief, he saw not the buoyant overconfidence of the year before, but the grim resolution they all shared—the silent, unspoken determination that this time they would not fail.

A wisp of silver-blond hair escaped the casual knot atop her head, falling to lie against the slender perspiring neck of the young woman who worked so vigorously washing her clothes in the yard at Fort Edward. Feeling strangely uneasy, she glanced around casually before resuming her work, methodically scrubbing and wringing out each item of clothing, and laying it aside to be rinsed later. Her mind was far from the sunny fort yard and her task at hand, and she mused silently how flat and joyless life had become since Adam's departure. It appeared the only joy remaining to her was the hours spent with Jonathan, and even then she sorely missed Adam's presence and his obvious delight in their bright, young son. Their son! A sharp pang of guilt cut her conscience at that thought. Was Jonathan not Chingue's son? When had that subconscious change come about in her mind? A memory of clear, copper-toned skin and black, glittering eyes filled with love returned to her, only to blur and be replaced by Adam's warm green eyes as they had appeared at their farewell. Once again Amanda felt a flush of guilt as the vision of Adam remained to replace the other in her mind.

Chingue! her mind cried in silent desperation. Forgive my weakness. I love you still and will never forget you. But to her despair, his was not the image that remained to haunt her thoughts.

Amanda was still uneasy and restless. The heat of the long day had seemed to settle oppressively in the small sitting room that had become her home, and now, in the night, not even the slightest breeze stirred the hot, moist air that lay so heavily against her skin. She glanced casually at the couch where Jonathan lay, his shining, inquisitive eyes closed in sleep, his fat, little cheek pressed against the cushion, his small lips slightly parted. She stretched impatiently and moved in an effort to find a cooler spot on the pallet on which she lay. How long had she lain there? One hour? Two? And still sleep would not come. She lifted the long, silky tresses sticking to the back of her neck and flipped them over the pillow in an effort to free herself from their warmth, but nothing seemed to help. How was it that before, with two lying so close together on this same pallet, the heat had not been a problem? Slowly the memory of Adam's long, powerful body lying next to hers returned. She could almost feel his strong arms curved around her, holding her in a loose embrace as was his custom as they slept, his lips against her hair, his hand stroking her tenderly.

What's the matter with me? Amanda suddenly raged at herself. Two weeks had passed since Adam's departure, and from the reports filtering back to Fort Edward, she knew if the attack had not already been launched, it was now only a matter of days, hours perhaps. A vision of the scar that was just beginning to fade on Adam's broad chest came to her mind and Amanda felt fear creep slowly along her spine. He

417

had been lucky last time. Many others had not survived so grave a wound. How would he fare this time?

He will come back, her worried mind insisted. But suddenly Amanda's face was wet with tears and a low sob tore from her throat. He must come back, he must. I've lost one man that I loved, I can't lose another.

Slowly, her face registering the shock she felt, Amanda raised her hand to cover her mouth, her eyes wide with realization of the fact she had subconsciously suppressed for so long: I love him. I love Adam! She could no longer with full honesty ignore the emotion he had brought back to life within her: I love him!

For a moment her newfound happiness dimmed as she remembered Chingue's sober, handsome face. "But I loved you, too, Chingue," she said to the vision that hovered within her mind's eye. "Had you lived, I would have lived my life loving you, and the bond that existed between Adam and me would never have matured into love, not for me; of that I'm certain, for while you lived, you made me complete."

Tears were coursing down her cheeks as she bared her heart to Chingue's image, so vivid in her mind. "But you were gone, and no amount of dreaming and hoping could bring you back to me. I was alone, confused, unhappy, when Adam returned into my life, bringing understanding, security, offering me love. I accepted it all, but returned little, only the physical comforts I was able to offer him. But still he loved me! Now he, too, is gone, and I know for the first time, without Adam I am again incomplete, as I was without you. Oh, my dear Chingue," Amanda implored the dark-eyed image, "I'll always love you, but now your place in my heart must be shared with another, for as I loved you, I also love him."

With Amanda's acknowledgement of her love for Adam, Chingue's last words suddenly assumed a blaring clarity. "Truly I am blessed among men, for I have had that which many men seek, never to find in a lifetime of many more summers."

"I have had. . . ." With those words, Chingue, in ultimate understanding, had released her to go on to love again. Now Amanda cried in earnest, but this time in sadness at the simplicity and beauty of heart and mind that had been Chingue, and was no more.

It was in the long hours of the night, sanctified by her tears, that Chingue's memory was buried forever within her heart.

Amanda arose the next morning and began to dress with the haste of anxiety. The same tears that had laid Chingue's memory to rest the night before had baptized a new Amanda, renewed in the determination born in the dark of the sleepless night. She could not afford to be complacent and patient now. She must see Adam immediately, before the force left for Fort Carillon, and tell him the truth she had realized the night before. She paled visibly as the thought that had tortured her through the night returned again to chill her blood: if she waited, it might be too late.

She ran a comb quickly through the length of her hair and tied it back hastily with a piece of ribbon, not bothering to examine her appearance as she moved to the Mitchells' bedroom door and knocked lightly. To Betty's answering query, she whispered softly, "Betty, will you listen for Jonathan for a few minutes? He's still sleeping and I have an errand to run."

Betty's assent sent her quietly out the door, her pace quickening as she spied the familiar military figure crossing the yard toward the dining hall. Running quickly down the steps, she called after him, her heart beating wildly as he turned in her direction.

"Colonel Webb, I must speak to you." She was breathless from running, and her heart pounded wildly as she formed the words of her plea in her mind.

"Mrs. Carstairs, is something wrong?"

"Yes, I must speak to my husband today. It's a private matter of the utmost importance. I would like your permission to accompany the morning courier to the camp at Fort William Henry."

"I'm sorry, I must refuse your request, Mrs. Carstairs. It would do you no good to go. It is too late to speak to Adam now. The attacking force left for Fort Carillon this morning, and if all is going according to plan, they should be accomplishing their landing at this very moment."

Amanda felt a breathless moment of panic, and seeing it reflected on her beautiful face, the colonel's hard shell softened briefly and he said in a kindly tone, "I'm afraid you will have to wait, but the stay should be brief. If all goes well, their objective should be accomplished and our men returned within a week."

"A week!"

"I'm sorry."

Unwilling to surrender to her disappointment and

420

fears, Amanda blurted out bluntly, "What accommodations are being made for the wounded, Colonel Webb?"

Unaccustomed to accounting to a woman, the colonel's expression hardened slightly, but finally relenting in the face of her obvious determination and anxiety, he answered stiffly, "Dr. Cartwright is leaving this morning to travel to the site of Fort William Henry and prepare the hospital rooms to accept wounded."

"Then I'll travel with him."

"My dear young woman." The colonel was beginning to become annoyed with her persistence.

"But I have experience in nursing. I helped tend the wounded when Fort William Henry was besieged. I can be of help, truly I can." She gulped guiltily as she recalled her pitiful reaction to her one and only exposure to the wounded in the casement rooms at Fort William Henry.

"Dr. Cartwright's staff is quite adequate."

"You can't be sure of that unless you know the extent of the casualties, Colonel. There could be dire need of my assistance."

"Madam." The colonel's face was beginning to redden in anger, and Amanda saw a need to change her tactics if she was to succeed.

"Then, may I have your permission, Colonel, to approach Dr. Cartwright with my request and leave it to the wisdom of his judgment whether I can accompany the column this morning? He will surely tell me to remain behind if I'm not needed."

Amanda's gamble that the impatient colonel would take advantage of an opportunity to dump a pleading and determined woman on the doctor's experienced shoulders paid off, as he responded rather haughtily, but with a degree of relief, "You have my permission, madam."

She did not spare him another look as she threw a satisfied and confident "Thank you, Colonel," over her shoulder and ran directly to Dr. Cartwright's quarters.

Within the hour, Amanda had assembled a few necessities, and stood with the soldiers assigned to Dr. Cartwright's supervision, ready to leave for camp. Jonathan had been consigned to Betty's care, and Amanda's face reflected her happiness as her mind whispered jubilantly, I'm coming, Adam. I'll be there to greet you when you return!

From a distance, unseen eyes kept the small golden figure within his intense, solemn gaze. His unknown surveillance had begun the time of Adam's departure and he had since followed her actions with dedicated, unflagging interest, the sight of her restoring his purpose for existence.

July 22, 1759—Daybreak. The attacking fleet had reached Sabbath Point, and between the hours of nine and eleven, the landing was accomplished without opposition. Immediately the light infantry, grenadiers and rangers marched on the old sawmill, which had based General Abercrombie the year before. The enemy, posted in three advantageous positions, returned only running fire at the first sign of the advancing parties, and fled their positions, abandoning the territory to the British force. Leaving

422

only the necessary guards for the landing place, vessels and stores, General Amhurst ordered his army forward.

Amanda sat back on her heels for a few moments to catch her breath. Her arms ached and beads of perspiration framed her upper lip and forehead and trickled down her spine and between her breasts. Her hair, pinned lightly to the top of her head, fell in filmy wisps, teasing her neck annoyingly, and her dress seemed to adhere to her body like a soggy second skin. She was hot and tired, but determination drove her on. She had been scrubbing floors in the hospital rooms for three hours and, looking around, realized she would probably be scrubbing for another three. The debris left behind when the wounded had finally been cleared from the hospital rooms the year before had putrified and in many spots stuck fast, proving a challenge to her well-developed cleaning skills. But her own conscience, in addition to Dr. Cartwright's personal suspicion that dirt in wounds had more often been the cause of deaths than the wounds themselves, would not allow her to leave the rooms in the condition they were in, although others saw fit to ignore the accumulation of a year's neglect. Also, in her particular case, she found hard work good therapy, which kept her anxious mind as well as her nervous hands occupied during the time of waiting.

So far they had been at the camp a full day, and no news had come from the attacking force. Was that an encouraging or discouraging sign? She was not sure, and was unwilling to risk the speculation of those around her. Glancing into the bucket beside her, she realized it was again time to change the water. Getting wearily to her feet, she brushed a flying strand of hair from her eyes and, picking up the bucket, walked outside. She had thrown the waste water into the bushes and started toward the lake when again she felt a prickling sensation at the back of her neck and glanced around suspiciously. She could see no one other than orderlies in the area. No one was paying any particular attention to her, but still the annoying sensation of eyes following her persisted.

"I mustn't allow my nerves to get the best of me," she muttered under her breath as she reached the lake and drew fresh water. Still, she again scanned the woods bordering the clearing as she started back. Seeing nothing unusual, she shrugged her uneasiness aside, reentered the hospital, and resumed her work.

Robert watched as the small, weary figure disappeared through the hospital door. He had spent so many months without so much as a glimpse of Amanda that his eyes could not seem to get their fill. If it was possible, she was even more beautiful than the day Adam had taken her away. It appeared nothing could mar her beauty, not her worried frown or harried scowl. In the infrequent intervals when she smiled, the radiance in that smile tore at his very heart. She was Adam's wife. She was happy with him. She had come all this way and volunteered for the back-breaking work she was now doing just to be a little closer to him. Oh, God, why couldn't he be the one she awaited so anxiously, whose love filled her

424

with that glow? He had surrendered her to Adam too easily that day, too easily. He would be able to handle his jealousy now. He would never make the same mistake again.

Absentmindedly he rubbed the full, reddish brown beard that covered his face, his eyes still on the doorway through which she had disappeared. The passing months had altered Robert's appearance drastically. Filled with self-hatred and anxiety after losing Amanda, he had all but lost his desire to live and had neglected and abused himself almost beyond the point of redemption. He did not shave, his hair grew long and unkempt, and his ragged buckskins became as neglected as he was himself. He lost his appetite and became increasingly thinner, until his clothes hung limply on his emaciated frame and his cheekbones jutted out sharply atop his matted beard. The dark circles beneath his eyes attested to his dangerous state of health. He had only recently glimpsed his reflection in a placid pool and, shocked at his own appearance, had sat back and finally lapsed into loud, uncontrollable laughter that had left him spent and shaken. If Amanda had despised him before, was his hopeless thought, she would now be filled with disgust and loathing at what he had become. But he loved her. He loved her still.

Another day and still no news of the attack. Amanda stood alone in the pregnant silence of the hospital room and surveyed the room critically. It was meticulously clean. Each narrow cot lining the walls had a fresh, if somewhat ragged cover. Ready, waiting, everything and everyone within the camp seemed in a state of suspended animation, and as she gazed at the cots, she prayed with every fiber in her being that most of them would go unneeded.

Shaking off her dour thoughts, she mumbled under her breath, "There's nothing more to be done in here," and walked slowly outside into the brilliant July sunshine. She looked around slowly and shook her head, a small, wry smile appearing on her lips. The warm summer sun and the lush forest foliage bordering the compound conspired to create an aura of tranquility and peace in an area that had, just days before, housed thousands of men preparing for battle. Casually she followed the undulating flight of an amber butterfly as it glided on the warm air currents and lightly touched on the array of wild-flowers growing on the forest edge. She marveled that while men engaged in a life-and-death struggle just a few miles' distance, life continued on, its easy pattern uninterrupted by the grim machinations of man.

Lulled by the deceptive tranquility, her gaze drifted leisurely out to the vast expanse of Lake George, its placid surface glittering hypnotically in the rays of the midmorning sun. Disappointingly it was still clear of craft of any kind, and she wondered with growing impatience how long it would be before this sparkling highway of the frontier brought them news of the battle.

But what was that? Amanda tensed as small dots appeared on the horizon of the lake. Floating debris? Birds? She couldn't yet tell. She strained her eyes toward the small specks that appeared to be moving toward the shore with agonizing slowness, her heartbeat accelerating, her palms becoming moist with anxiety.

"Are they? Are they? They are!" She shouted wildly, elation surging through her veins as she recognized the indistinct shapes as boats.

"They're coming! Hurry everyone, the boats are returning!" Running frantically, she was almost to the beach when her steps began to slow, her elation dimming, as she realized there were only three boats. The battle wasn't over. These boats were merely transporting dead and wounded as had been pre-arranged.

"Oh, God," she prayed, a deep sense of dread settling inside her as the boats edged ever closer, "don't let Adam be among them, please."

The three boats scraped against the shore almost simultaneously. The waiting men hoisted them firmer aground and began to unload the walking wounded. Frantically her eyes searched for Adam's face, to no avail. Noticing two covered mounds in the rear of one of the boats, she grimly walked over and in a quick, jerking movement uncovered the first and then the second. No, thank God, not Adam. But they were so young to be so irreversibly dead. Turning quickly, she shook off her pointless grief, and saw one of the wounded who walked unaided stumble. Running to his side, she pulled the weary ranger's arm around her shoulder in support and said brightly, as the blood dripping from his wound ran warmly down her arm, "Come on, soldier, I'm a pretty small crutch, but you only needed a little help anyway."

The next few hours were filled with a frenzy of activity that increased as each new day following brought more wounded to the hospital rooms.

Amanda, laboring silently through the busy days was indeed greatly needed, and no longer found the time to greet each returning boat. Still, her eyes strayed constantly toward the door and her heart leaped as each additional cot was filled, seeking that one familiar tawny head.

News of the progressing battle was sparse. The advance had been orderly. The roads and water courses from the mill had been cleared, and they had managed to take possession of the most advantageous ground near the fort.

One young colonial, basking in the light of Amanda's intense interest, related his story with theatrical zeal.

"Before daybreak on the twenty-third, we began to entrench ourselves in the very lines Montcalm used the year before. We were protected there, and the cannonade from the fort was ineffective against us, but still General Amhurst ordered that we continue to entrench as we advanced. My back still aches. I never knew the ground to be so hard." Rolling his eyes expressively, he continued, "But we all would've followed General Amhurst into hell if he had asked. We dug for three full days, and a little after midnight on the twenty-sixth, the work was done. Then we opened all batteries at once, unleashing our full firepower. Shortly afterwards there was a deafening explosion that lit the entire sky. And then I was hit." Realizing the inadequacy of the abrupt ending to his narration, he mumbled ashamedly, "I don't know what happened after that."

With a short smile, Amanda rose and said wearily, "Thank you, Edwin," before walking slowly to the door. Pausing briefly in the doorway, she gave herself a few seconds in the sun to blink away the tears and pull herself together. Then, taking a deep breath, she squared her shoulders and turned back into the room.

Robert, standing concealed on the edge of the woods, waiting most of the day, was rewarded with one brief glance of Amanda as she stood momentarily in the doorway. But it was enough to lift his love-starved spirits, and he smiled briefly, rubbing his newly clean-shaven chin, looking much like the Robert of old.

"He hasn't returned yet, has he Amanda?" He mumbled softly as he stared at the doorway through which she had disappeared. "He won't, darling. I can feel it. I know he won't return. We were meant to be together, you and I."

July 27, 1759, six o'clock—*Dirt stained and battle weary, General Amhurst and his soldiers stood at solemn attention as, with great pride and deliberation, the French flag over Fort Carillon was struck, and the flag of Great Britain was hoisted on the very same staff.*

Amanda walked silently toward the final boat, the answer to her query ringing in her ears like a solemn death knell.

"All the boats have returned from Fort Carillon, ma'am. That's the last one." Pointing to the remaining boat as it scraped ashore, he had continued in a lowered voice, "Them's the last of the dead, Ma'am."

With a quick intake of breath, her eyes flew to the covered shapes lining the bateau's hull. She moved forward again, only to be jerked to an abrupt halt by a stab of pure horror as the craft jolted in landing, causing one of the blankets to slip and reveal a thick thatch of tawny hair beneath!

"Oh, God, no! No!" she cried. The pain and shock of grief tore her courage to shreds and she ran away, sobbing blindly through the throngs of soldiers moving wearily toward the barracks. Their curious glances turned her way, and unable to bear their questioning stares, she began to run wildly toward the forest edge as tears streamed down her face and her breath caught in deep, heaving sobs. She did not stop her headlong flight until she reached the cover of trees and, weak from anguish and exhaustion, threw herself down to the ground to give full vent to her sorrow.

"No, it can't be," she sobbed over and over again, her mind refusing to accept what her eyes had seen only minutes before.

So overcome with grief was she that she failed to hear the footsteps approaching, or sense a presence beside her until, crouching down, it extended a buckskin-clad arm to close a large, calloused hand on her shoulder.

At the unexpected touch, Amanda's eyes jerked upward and she gasped aloud before crying in sudden exhilaration, "Adam! You're alive!"

Scrambling to her knees, she threw her arms around his neck in a fierce embrace as she covered his face with exuberant, salty kisses, exclaiming almost incoherently as she did, "Oh, Adam, I was so afraid it was too late to tell you I love you. I love you. I love you."

The familiar strength of his embrace tightened, almost stealing her breath, as Adam's impassioned voice whispered against her mouth moments before it closed over hers, "My darling, my only love."

A few feet away, unseen in the denseness of the summer foliage, another buckskin-clad figure turned away from the scene of joyous reunion, the dampness of tears on his face silent testimony to his own bitter grief.

Epilogue

Although the French and Indian War continued for
four more years after the battle of Fort Carillon—
renamed Fort Ticonderoga by the British—the battle
had a significant and far-reaching effect. It was with
that battle that the French lost their foothold on the
American continent and were driven into Canada,
never again to regain their former position of power.
At the conclusion of the war in 1763, the long rival-
ry between England and France was over, and
England gained supremacy, however temporarily, in
the New World.